Y029242

D1345627

THE PORTRAIT

THE PORTRAIT

ILARIA BERNARDINI

ALLEN&UNWIN

First published in Great Britain in 2020 by Allen & Unwin

Allen & Unwin
c/o Atlantic Books
Ormond House
26–27 Boswell Street
London WC1N 3JZ
Phone: 020 7269 1610
Fax: 020 7430 0916
Email: UK@allenandunwin.com
Web: www.allenandunwin.com/uk

A CIP catalogue record for this book is available from the British Library.

Internal design by Ben Cracknell Studios

Hardback ISBN: 978 1 91163 040 1
Trade paperback ISBN: 978 1 91163 042 5
E-Book ISBN: 978 1 76087 659 3

Printed in Great Britain by Bell and Bain Ltd, Glasgow

10 9 8 7 6 5 4 3 2 1

To Leo

I never did know where I was,
even when I was home.

Rebecca Solnit,
A Field Guide to Getting Lost

All human knowledge takes the
form of interpretation.

Walter Benjamin

There is a crack in everything
That's how the light gets in

Leonard Cohen

ONE

Martìn and Valeria were lovers. They had been for the better part of their lives. But six days after his stroke, Valeria still had no access to him. She was in Paris, climbing into her car and attempting a smile at her driver. She indicated that she was on the phone and whispered, 'Home, please.'

Dimitri nodded and Valeria unbuttoned her coat. It felt good to be in the warmth again.

'No more photos, Joe,' she said. Valeria pictured her agent rolling his eyes. 'I'm getting too old for this.'

Perhaps she had a fever. Her eyes were watering. She wanted tea. An aspirin. Pamela would be at home waiting for the daily debrief. Good. Or not? Debrief – awful. Not being alone – good. And that pile of letters, when was she going to read them? She could burn them all. Or chew them. She could ask Pamela to chew them for her.

'It's not going to go down well with the publishers,' Joe said.

'I know. So here's my plan: I'm going to have my portrait painted and we can use that for the book instead.'

Valeria wanted to cry. But she didn't want to cry lousy flu tears. She wanted to sob and she wanted to scream. Now? No, poor Dimitri.

'Are you aware of how pompous this will appear? No need to answer. Any painter in particular?'

'Isla Lawndale. I admire her work.' Valeria felt guilty as she uttered the name. Her fingers passed across her mouth to erase it. Entering Martìn's house through the lie of a portrait? The idea was idiotic.

'Should I have heard of her?'

'She lives in London. She was a performance artist, then became a painter. I don't know her personally but I can provide you with more details if needed.'

'And would you like to sit for this portrait in London or Paris?

'Can we stop with the "this portrait" attitude, Joe? London. Please make sure you express my admiration to her.'

'It's in the diary: admiration. Oh, and they keep calling about that jury. Toronto. Will you accept?'

'Not now, sorry.'

'It's a very important prize,' Joe pressed.

'Listen, it's just bad timing. Something is not—' What was she doing? Another lie?

'Something is not what?'

'I really can't, Joe. Speak later.'

'Any title yet?'

'Speak later, Joe.'

Valeria ended the call and closed her eyes. The car moved slowly through the traffic. It was in that same car that she had learned about Martin's stroke and about his coma. Why wasn't she in London? She tried to calm herself down by breathing more steadily. It was a grey day and Paris was packed with cars, umbrellas and livid Parisians. Was she the reason why that man with the long coat looked so disgusted? She was disgusting. Valeria's heart rate began to increase. She went back to her controlled breathing. She opened her eyes and saw Dimitri picking his nose. She coughed and he stopped. How old was Dimitri? Her age? Fifty-five? She never spoke Greek with him and hopefully she never would. Greek was forbidden.

In Greece, when she was twelve, her nearly fourteen-year-old sister Sybilla had died.

'We are leaving Rhodes and never coming back,' her mother Theodora told Valeria after Sybilla was gone. Valeria cried. They had already moved back to Greece from England because Valeria's father had disappeared on them. Now Rhodes was home, happiness, friends. It was her connection to Sybilla.

'I can't be here ever again,' Theodora said.

'But it's our home, it's where you come from, where we all come from! That's what you said when we left England and our father,' Valeria shouted.

'Well, Greece is not home any more.'

'How is my dad going to find us?' Valeria said.

'You have to be looking for someone to be able to find them.'

Valeria's father, Julian, had been a mediocre British writer. He had met Theodora at university in London and their fling had led to having Sybilla. Julian had disappeared a first time when their daughter was a month old and had returned at some point for just enough time to get Theodora pregnant again. When, twelve years later, Sybilla got sick, her mother would exclaim to the world that she wasn't going to tell him. He was the one who shouldn't have left. Valeria thought it was stupidly vengeful of her mother to not let him know about Sybilla's sickness. Even though he was a pathetic father, Julian would have definitely come to see his dying daughter. He wasn't a monster.

Valeria downloaded her emails without opening any of them. The screen made her nauseous. The name she wanted to see wasn't there.

'Are you going to go to Rhodes this year, madam?' Dimitri asked.

'Not anytime soon, no. You?' she heard herself asking back.

'I hope so. And not in August, when the *meltemi* wind is too strong.'

Had Martìn chosen Dimitri on purpose? Not sure. She didn't even know if some sort of event had led to Martìn's stroke and to his coma six days earlier. And if the fact that they had moved him back to his family home meant that he was going to recover or to die. Where would her devotion go if he died? Devotion was all of her life. Martìn was all of her life.

'I'm devoted to you,' she'd told Martìn in New York. They were in a restaurant, a private dining room, he was holding her thigh under the table. When was it, ten years ago?

'You are devoted to yourself,' he'd replied, 'Sometimes you kiss me, but this is just because you like to kiss.'

B ack home, a flat in the Latin Quarter that she had decorated thinking about Martìn's tastes more than hers, Valeria sat on the sofa, her coat still on, rain still on the coat. This would have been the perfect moment to call him. The morning about to end, the rain gushing outside, Martìn's voice as a mellow soundtrack. He was generally in a good mood and he was always available, even if he was in Shanghai, London or New York. Or if Valeria was the one in Shanghai, London or New York. He was there even though he had a wife and three kids, and he had been for most of Valeria's adult life. How had they done it?

'How are you?' her assistant Pamela asked from the sofa beside her. Valeria hadn't noticed her come into the room. She was beautiful. Young. She was wearing a tight turtleneck and the shape of her body, even with a sweater and jeans over it, seemed obscene. The red lipstick made her even more inviting. Did Pamela know Valeria's secret?

'I was feeling faint during the interview. I might have caught the flu,' Valeria said.

'I'll get you an aspirin and make you some tea.'

5

'Thank you, Pam.' Pam? When had she ever called her Pam? Never. She imagined Pam— Pamela's perfect body naked, her skin so white. She pictured her in that same kitchen, doing the same things she was probably doing right now, but without her clothes on. Imagining her from the back, fresh and gently open, was superb.

When Valeria interviewed her three years earlier, Pamela's beauty had put her off. Why would she want to see such a gorgeous girl every day, a constant reminder of her own vanishing beauty? But Pamela turned out to be funny, sweet, committed. Oxford, with a masters from Columbia. She was a fan of Valeria's work, worldly, with a strong mind. She completed the test on Valeria's sample paragraph perfectly. Fact check, no pointless comments, one suggestion on a single sentence. Her intervention was always minimal and gently attuned to Valeria's voice. She was British, which was helpful given the fact that Valeria wrote in English, and she would always give Valeria's stories one last proofread. Plus, Valeria couldn't bring herself to be the kind of woman who would turn down another woman because of her looks. That would have been completely antifeminist. So Pamela became her personal assistant. Sometimes, but not very often, they went out for a drink and she was now closer to being a friend. Even if in Valeria's world it meant that Pamela wasn't a friend at all. Looking at Pamela's body and lips came to be Valeria's daily struggle, to enquire about her promiscuous life just another one of her addictions.

Valeria woke up to the sound of the teacup being placed on the crystal table before her. Opening her eyes was sad. With a glorious woman to stare at, and sad.

'Sorry,' Pamela said.

'It's all right.'

Pamela scrutinized her list. The short story for *Balloon Magazine* – second draft. Radio 4. They had to choose the songs. Oh, and then the Aix-Marseille Université contract. Also, she needed to draw up a book list in two weeks' time for the course she would be teaching there.

'It's in two years!' Valeria sighed. Would she even be alive in two years? If she was alive in two years, would she be more or less desperate than now? And what about Martìn in two years? Would he still exist? And the world? What with climate change, jellyfish becoming every second more and more poisonous, the disappearance of the bees, terrorism, the old and the new cancer, the old and the new fascism, melancholy?

'Oh, wait wait wait!' Pamela said. She stood up and ran into the studio. She was back in seconds. 'Ta-dah! Japanese!'

The Japanese translations of her books were always Valeria's favourite. Bodasha had the best covers and the most refined paper. Valeria caressed the book. She smelled it.

'It's so beautiful,' Valeria murmured and tried a smile. 'This must be . . . *The Hawk?* Let me see. So the last word of *The Hawk* was "fear". There it is, "fear", in Japanese.' In her hands the book appeared less beautiful, so she put it on the table. The word 'fear' in Japanese looked like a sweating house. It was becoming more enormous by the second.

When Pamela left, Valeria attempted to write. She typed. Deleted. It wasn't working. It wasn't real. Nevertheless, she remained at her desk for two hours. When two hours had passed, she spent another one on her monthly column. Then, she sent it over to Pamela for fact-checking, thanking her for the hot tea and care.

It was dark when Valeria changed into her tracksuit and went for a run, music in her ears, a woollen hat on her head. The air was crisp. She switched to a fast walk. She wanted to sweat. She wanted her heart to beat faster. She wanted a title for the new book. She wanted to be hugged. She wanted Martìn. And, fuck, she needed Isla Lawndale to accept her request. The park was misty. Dogs and runners looking melancholic in the same way. She started to run. Her breath began to shorten. She found herself on her knees. With the wet stones under her and the rain pounding over her, Valeria started to scream.

TWO

Valeria woke up in the middle of the night. She took a pill and woke up again in the middle of the morning. The darkness of the sky was pretty much the same. When the phone rang she was having a second cup of coffee. The pill-induced cloudiness had to leave her. And Martìn had to survive.

'Isla Lawndale has declined,' said Joe.

'Fuck! Did she say why?' Valeria asked. She was holding a coffee in one hand and flicking through a bunch of envelopes with the other. She cradled the phone between her head and shoulder. She was, as always, looking for handwritten letters, their promise that they could be more interesting. Those from Julian, her father, she wouldn't open anyway.

'She said she hasn't painted in years,' Joe said. The line was cracking. Or was it her heart? Valeria imagined Martìn in his bed, his face paralysed.

The first time she saw Martìn Aclà he was wearing sunglasses and wouldn't take them off. She had seen herself reflected in his mirrored lenses. Her curls, her green eyes. She had also discovered that she was smiling.

'That's it?' Valeria asked Joe.

'She thanks you. Loves your work. First thing she said when she heard your name was "Wow." I think she felt guilty about saying no, so she told me that it's a really tough time for her right now – her husband is going through something, a sickness, I think. From what she was saying it sounded like he had a stroke. It was an intense call. A long one, too.'

'What did she sound like?'

'Sweet. And a mess. She said she was looking for dope in her daughter's bedroom. She swears quite a lot. I looked her up online. Did you know that her last painting, an unfinished portrait of her husband, sold for thirty-five thousand pounds ten years ago at Christie's?'

She did. More precisely, the portrait had been sold for £34,500. Flipping the envelopes, Valeria realized that the letter she was holding was an invitation to Pamela's wedding. She dressed Pamela's body in a bridal dress. Synthetic silk. Sweat. She imagined the false flu she'd come up with not to attend. She hid the invitation under a table book.

'I didn't,' Valeria said, and felt her voice breaking again. Yes, it wasn't the bad phone line, it was definitely her.

'Anyway, I know you're disappointed. I'll find you someone better,' said Joe.

There was no one better and it had to be her. Valeria hung up and tried to picture Isla Lawndale in her daughter's room. She wasn't just looking for dope. A diary would have been perfect, with all the clues on how to deal with all the problems. Isla was probably terrified that her daughter, Antonia, might commit suicide. As Valeria knew from Martìn, Antonia self-harmed, but would suicide be something she would ever really think about? Antonia would often tell Martìn she detested her body for being bulky and hated her family's lifestyle. Did the Aclàs have a 'lifestyle'? Antonia often repeated that they did, and that it was a pathetic one. Knowing all of this, knowing Antonia and the exact words she had shouted, without ever having met her, reminded Valeria of all her responsibilities.

Valeria went to her studio. She opened a Word document and drafted her apology for not going to the Toronto festival. In between the lines, the apology was to Joe, too. She then revised the first page of her piece for *Balloon*. The idea had been sitting in her memos, jotted here and there, for years. It was a true story that Martìn had once told her, about four sisters drowning in a river in France. One after another, trying to save each other from the current, they had been dragged away by the water. Martìn and Valeria had spent dinner wondering why there wasn't a name for losing a child if losing a husband made you a widow and losing a parent made you an orphan. Valeria had pointed out that some say there is no such word because the death of a child is too awful to put into words. Martìn had said that it was much more painful not to have a word because this would force parents to use more words: I did have a child but he died.

Writing wasn't working, she couldn't concentrate on the story. All Valeria wanted to do was figure out a new plan for the portrait and for being allowed into Martìn's house. Figuring out a plan always felt like being with Sybilla again. Like that day in the woods, when they were nine and seven, and had burned a pillow and a blanket. The pyre had been epic but what justification could they come up with for such a random act? After a long debate the random fire became the 'fire to celebrate the life of a little dead bird' and only out of laziness did they decide not to kill one really.

'You've been brave,' Theodora told her daughters.

'I'm way braver than you,' Sybilla whispered to Valeria.

'The fuck you are,' Valeria replied, even though it was true.

Valeria sat on the bed in her Paris apartment, tried mindful meditation. Those who say they manage not to engage with their thoughts lie, she thought. The new book was going to be out in months and there was still no title. Isla Lawndale didn't want to paint her. The love of her life, the man who had been her man for the last twenty-five years, might be dying, and she couldn't reach him. What was a lover, and a lover of her specific kind, supposed to do in a situation like this one? She'd had to learn about it from the radio!

She was used to hearing Martìn mentioned in the news and not always for good reasons. He was powerful, wealthy, and by virtue of the fact that his businesses were so diverse, was often exposed to media scrutiny. When they attacked him for the China scandal, she was terrified. And another time, when a kid lost his arm and an eye in one of his factories, she was devastated. But that morning six days ago, she'd realized abruptly what the radio was saying: 'During a speech to investors at the Baumont Hotel, the Argentine business magnate, entrepreneur and philanthropist, Martìn Aclà, aged sixty-four, collapsed. His condition worsened on the way to the hospital where he was diagnosed with a stroke.' Martìn's life was then condensed into what sounded like an obituary. Actually, it sounded concerningly similar to the Wikipedia page that Valeria had looked up so many times. They didn't forget to mention his long-lasting, unbreakable marriage that had given him three children and the fact that his twin brother Rami had died from a food allergy when they were twenty-three. This time too the details were repeated, while Valeria was vomiting in Paris.

Incapable of letting the meditation work, Valeria opened her computer and wrote an email to Isla Lawndale. She told her that she imagined the portraiture process to be intimate and exposing. Discovering her face in a sort of confession was what she was looking for, but it was also what she feared the most. She was ready to sit, but only for

Isla. She told her about a portrait of her own mother she had in front of her right now. It had been painted in Italy, and Valeria explained why as a young girl she had hated her life there. She remembered the sittings for the portrait, the chalk on the floor. The painter would sketch every day and she would sit in the same patch of sunlight. Valeria wrote that only by staring at the picture could she feel the same boredom and the same pain she'd felt back then. Those were sad days. She was heartbroken and treated her mother terribly. She still felt guilty, but she was well aware of why she'd been so angry. Valeria chose words and created arguments that she imagined would sound similar to those Isla and her daughter Antonia might have.

She wrote for hours, editing, moving sections, unable to let this letter – and her last chance – go. She added the story of her mother being an orphan, the fact that you could see it, or maybe *she* could see it, in this portrait. Theodora had lost her parents when she was seventeen. She had lost her only love when she was twenty. In her thirties, she had lost her first daughter, Sybilla. All of it, and all days and nights in between, lived in that face, in that one picture. Valeria signed off – with all her wishes and hopes. She stood up, incapable of pressing the send button. She looked around her room and wondered if she should pray to some invented god just to give the whole scene a better ending. She drank some water while looking at the empty space where supposedly she'd been staring at the portrait of her mother. It was, in fact, pure invention. There was no portrait. The painter in Rome was invented too. Some parts of his habits were stolen from a

Lucien Freud essay Valeria had once read. Apparently, her memory was better than she thought.

Valeria left the house in her tracksuit. When she entered the park it was dark. A man was lying on his stomach, his filthy coat leaving his back uncovered. Valeria could see his arse. She moved closer to him to see if he was still alive. He reeked of alcohol. His hands were twitching on the ground, as if he were attempting to swim. Was he dreaming of drowning?

'Are you OK?' Valeria asked.

The man didn't answer. He continued to swim, or drown.

She stood there for a while before deciding to look for help. But what if he was a refugee, escaped from somewhere? Oh God, maybe he was finally out of Aleppo! She didn't want to put him in danger with a policeman so called for an ambulance instead. She explained in French and very slowly to the woman at the end of the line where she had found the man.

'I have to go. I don't feel safe,' then added, 'And I'm very cold.' The sentence would have been a good summary of her current existence. So she repeated it in English, just to give it another go.

As soon as Valeria reached the street, she felt calmer. Spotting the lights of a café, she went in and ordered a glass of wine. Paris outside the windows was about to liquefy. Thank God she couldn't see any angry Parisians from there: too late, too cold, too wet. Just how horribly had the poor man from Aleppo been treated by other human beings? She hoped his swimming would keep him on the surface of life.

While sipping her wine, the sirens of an ambulance broke her heart. She wasn't responsible for the swimmer any more. Now all she wanted was to enter the Japanese character for the word 'fear' and sweat in there. She would sweat it all out. Fear, happiness, love, pain. The Greek, the Italian, the French, the bloody English too. There would be nothing left apart from a shiny puddle of her sweat.

'May I steal a cigarette?' Valeria asked the bartender.

Smoking under the awning, under the rain, under the entire universe, felt apocalyptic. The moon, the stars, her loneliness, were squeezing her. When was she going to see Martìn? She stepped back out into the rain and walked into the apocalypse. At home, she sent the email to Isla Lawndale Aclà.

THREE

Valeria married young. She was finally out of Theodora's grip and about to graduate from Columbia. She had just received a scholarship, two of her short stories had been published, another one had been shortlisted for the Young Writers' Award. Patrick Toyle was her non-fiction teacher, she was his second student wife. He was fifty-two, she was twenty-two.

'Cliché, but not with you, Valeria. I was waiting for you,' he would tell her. Valeria knew this too was a cliché, but she liked very much being this specific one.

The two of them went to lectures, concerts, book launches. At dinners he would hold onto her under the table and Valeria was always excited to have his hands on her skin. Once he brought her to orgasm, stroking her through her stockings, during a faculty dinner. At the same time he was keeping up an entire conversation about meta-something literature and pop-something, post-something culture. Back then, all this felt amazing. Even the boring post-, pop-, meta- discussion – something, it turned out, he would like to repeat quite often. He would also tell her about his childhood in Nebraska, and to Valeria it always sounded like a soothing song she was learning better with each play, imagining his past becoming hers too. He would use fascinating new words, *agnition, heuristic, weltanschauung,* and she felt lucky to be married to the smartest man she had ever met. Patrick taught graduate and undergraduate classes and was a contributor to various magazines. He had travelled around the world, he spoke Spanish and French. He also had a large jolly family that Valeria worshipped. Whenever they spent time with them in Nebraska, Valeria would say, 'Let's move here. I'll work somewhere, you'll work somewhere. We'll be fine.' He was very jealous. She wasn't jealous at all. 'Your body is mine,' he would tell her. She would always smile and say, 'Yes, it is.'

The wedding had been small, just the two of them and a couple of friends as witnesses. Valeria called her mother that afternoon to announce she had married Patrick. Theodora told her that the previous night she had dreamt about Sybilla giving birth to twins.

'She had the face of a ten-year-old but her body was that of a woman,' Theodora said.

Valeria hadn't expected Theodora to bring Sybilla up, because she never did. So they both went silent, then said goodbye. Valeria added, 'I love you.' She didn't get an 'I love you too' back, but she whispered it to herself, in Theodora's voice.

That evening she and Patrick hosted a small party at home. There were speeches about how their love was unique. They kissed and danced. Dawn arrived with one more cigarette, one more song, one more kiss. Their song was 'My Baby Just Cares for Me'. Other clichés, which she loved, 'I was waiting for you,' Patrick would repeat every day, and was never embarrassed to sound tacky. 'Come home,' he would tell her with the sexiest voice. 'Come home to me.' She always did, because for the first time since Sybilla's death she liked what it meant to have a home.

The marriage lasted less than three years, which was enough time for Patrick to feel the urge to write an essay about Valeria once she became famous. Ironically, the essay was dedicated to Valeria with his much-used phrase, 'I was waiting for you'. But during the marriage there was very soon another non-fiction student, Sophie. And yet another, Monica. There were many other women and girls. In truth, there was so much fucking around that it wasn't as painful as if there had only been one lover. Too many eyes, ears, mouths, names: it was like one single monster woman.

'Don't leave me,' Patrick had implored.

The divorce was dealt with by lawyers from afar, while Valeria went on a six-month pilgrimage around Europe before settling in Holland for another six months. It was hard to stop loving Patrick and to stop loving the word 'home', but in a tiny bed-and-breakfast facing the North Sea, she completed the first draft of her first collection of short stories, *Black Bread*.

Back in New York, Valeria wasn't married any more and she was the literary talk of the town. Her collection of stories was represented by the powerful agent Marion Latsey. Valeria had met her through Patrick years before and, even in the depths of her anger towards him, she still felt grateful for the introduction. She had even thought of thanking him and as Theodora had taught her, she rehearsed a sentence that she never actually said.

'I'm very grateful for having met you, Patrick. As I tell everyone, maybe love or sex wasn't the best with you, but I was very lucky to find you.'

The buzz was that *Black Bread* was going to be a very special debut and that there was going to be a competitive auction among potential publishers. Before the auction deadline, Valeria found out that Marion Latsey had been sleeping with her ex-husband. So she fired her swiftly and ended up with the virtually unknown Joe Riddle. She had met him at a book launch and overheard a conversation he was having with a senior agent about a French author, famous for being bizarre. Joe seemed kind. No gossip or nasty words, only compassion and a clear respect for the author's work. She sensed his sweetness and thought it would be easy to trust him. Also, he looked so goofy in that oversized yellow jacket.

Valeria was trying to write when her phone lit up. Outside still rain. And pain, everywhere. The word 'Mum' on the screen was shiny. What time was it in India? Her mother knew so little of her life. She knew so little of hers. When Sybilla was still alive they used to share breakfasts, beds, days. They used to walk around naked in the same house and to know each other's intimate habits; how Sybilla would always leave half of her toast in the morning or how Theodora brushed both her daughters' hair every other night, the recurrent nightmares they would have. Now, many years later, Valeria and Theodora were two ageing women living very far away from one another. There were only the phone calls and once a year they would meet up for a short holiday together some-where in the world.

Valeria didn't pick up and tried to go back to writing. She reread bits and moved a few things around, but the focus had gone and she was back to the thought of Isla and the portrait. When she bought the Isla Lawndale years ago, she didn't tell anyone. Not even Martìn. It was expensive. But the way in which the artist depicted her husband was very powerful. Part of the picture was still charcoal, half of the left eye never coloured. The rest of the face and the shoulders were delicately painted in earthy, vivid colours, making the whole portrait warm. It was winter in the painting. And it was night. The artist created day paintings and night paintings, something Valeria knew because she had found an article about Isla Lawndale in a niche indie paper called *ArtGeist*. The piece had been written by a friend of Isla's. Her name was Sasha Liebski. It was an intimate piece, very revealing about Isla's art and life. The title was 'The Making of Eyes'.

Sasha Liebski described the artist's journey as a 'pioneer's vision', with compulsion and repetition as the main tools of her process. Valeria, reading the article, and annoyed by the bad, pretentious writing, had focused on the artist's self-portraits, based on photos taken in a photo booth. There were twenty of them in the magazine, but it was noted that the artist had done more than a thousand such works, 'impersonating more than a thousand different women'. These performative journeys clashed with Sasha's description of Isla as a well-to-do Londoner, who had been brought up in a wealthy, conservative American family and was now married to a billionaire. 'What is it that you are looking for?' Sasha Liebski asked. The question, the author wrote, had been asked at dawn, after an endless dinner in a skyscraper. 'I'm looking for the most persistent performance ever,' Isla Lawndale answered.

When Valeria decided to buy the painting by Isla Lawndale, she knew that financially it made no sense. Isla never became more famous than she was that day. No other reviews appeared. She never had another solo show or important auction. Valeria didn't expect to pay as much as a five-figure sum, the highest estimate at Christie's had been £9,000. But there had been another bidder on the phone who wouldn't let go, so the price became ridiculous. Valeria didn't care about the bad investment. There was something secret in the portrait, and she wanted to be part of that secret. She also wanted to be able to look at Martin, and study his face over and over again. Had he and Isla kissed during the sittings? Had sex? Anytime Valeria looked at the portrait, it was evident that this wasn't just a man or a woman dealing with the process. It was a husband looking at his wife. Isla looking at Martin. Martin at Isla. It was about closeness. And distance, of course.

FOUR

Without Patrick Toyle in her life, Valeria could write day and night. She didn't have to eat with anyone, she wasn't supposed to wait for anyone. She was diligent, obsessive, disciplined. Her first collection of short stories was a success. Her second, *To the Light*, even more so. Fame wasn't expected but it didn't really surprise her either.

With things turning out well, her father's unsuccessful career would sometimes come into her mind. Despite the shame for feeling such sentiments, she enjoyed making the comparison. Was she a better writer than him or was she just luckier? Valeria quickly understood that her career would also require plenty of travelling and she relished the semesters she spent teaching at universities around the world. She was invited to teach at NYU, then at the Sorbonne, and had said yes within minutes on each occasion. She'd also accepted a few residencies that helped her become even more prolific. For one, she spent a year in Berlin. For another, six months in Tuscany. She spent three months in the north of Iceland. The mornings there were dark and writing came easy in the void. Towards the end of the third month, she ended up having boring sex with another author, but more importantly she ended up finishing an entire collection of short stories. The collection was titled *Between*. With *Between* she toured the world and she had no need to ask permission to take up any of these opportunities: she had no kids, no husband, no family. Very often this felt great and, since he had appeared in her life, Martìn was always glad to cross the globe to meet her if it was doable, or to call her every night and morning if they were apart.

Her short stories from around the world appeared in magazines and travel guides – being from nowhere became one of her distinctions, her independence one of her strongest qualities. She was once asked to speak on a feminist panel about choosing such an autonomous life, and found herself crying at the end of it. By then she believed she was special too. She won prestigious awards for her writing and the news had always arrived when she was in countries unknown to her, surrounded by unfamiliar people. When she finally moved to Paris to have a place to call home, she published a collection of poems on the theme of roots. All the interviews she gave around the book focused on this theme and the reason behind her decision. The decision was, in fact, made mostly for Martìn. She wanted to give him a home to come back to and a place where he could imagine her being. Even if he had another home, a wife, a growing family.

By then, several of Valeria's works aroused controversy and received mixed reviews because of their subject matter and her increasingly objectionable protagonists. She published the first story of her fifth collection, 'Secret', as a single piece for *The Serpentine*. It featured a suburban couple that deliberately kill a woman. A reviewer for the *Literary Journal* described it as 'a dirty and foolishly grotesque collection'. Writing in *The Mono*, on publication of the collection, a revered writer described it as 'A masterpiece. Her short stories have a profound, obscure, *secret* brilliance'. The *Revolution* review said: '"Secret" is the total theorization of love and the horror that comes with it. Valeria Costas can't be compared to any other writer. No one else is quite as comfortless and amusing and delicate all at the same time'.

By then, her work had been translated into twenty-six languages.

Valeria knew that going for a run today would be impossible. She had no strength to do so. But still, after the writing and with Martìn occupying her every thought, she had to get out of the studio. Could she succeed in being out of her body too? It was becoming an older body and living in it became less appealing with every day. If Martìn wasn't going to touch or see that body any more, was she still going to want to live, walk, write? Martìn could see her as she had been in her thirties and forties, this was one of the gifts that came from loving each other for almost three decades. She was not her age for him, she was for him all ages she had been and all ages she was going to be, in an indistinct blur of love and compassion.

She dressed in jeans and a turtleneck. She picked the jumper because of Pamela but it didn't look as good on her. She chose warm boots, her warmest coat and a big woollen hat.

Outside the wind was strong. The radio had said a storm was going to hit Paris during the night. Valeria went to the Rive Gauche and kept walking along Rue de l'Université. She took her phone out of her pocket. Last time she heard from Martìn it was just before the conference at which he had collapsed.

'Can't wait to see you. I love you,' Martìn had said. 'I miss you.'

'Can't hear you very well, but I love you too,' were Valeria's last words to Martìn.

They weren't the best words ever but they weren't too bad either. Was his wife in charge of his phone now? Valeria's name on Martìn's phone was Charlie Brown. Martìn had told her that they, like Charlie Brown and Lucy, were the protagonists of one of the longest-running comic strips in history. Valeria clicked on Martìn's contact information. His phone was off but the attempt to call him excited her. She saw Charlie Brown walking beside her. She smiled at him.

'Martìn, can you hear me?' she murmured. She held onto the phone, her fingers tight around it. 'I don't know how to do this and I don't know how to reach you. But I am writing every day just like I promised. Do you remember the wind on Broadway? We were laughing, bent over

27

trying to beat the weather.' Suddenly, Valeria was crying again. 'Are you dying, Martìn? There are so many things I must tell you. . . I lied so much. About big and tiny things. You know that time in Berlin when I joined you? I told you that I'd gone to the museum and had lunch with my publishers? Well, I was in our room all day, pretending it was our home. Didn't see anyone, didn't go anywhere. Why are all these memories coming back like this now? I'm struggling with the language too. I'm mixing them up, I'm all mixed up. I'm sure that if you die I'll die with you. Pamela will find me dead in my studio.'

Valeria's phone started to ring.

'You're telepathic,' Valeria said, looking at the name on the screen.

'Dinner tonight?' Pamela asked.

Before Valeria hired her, Pamela had been temping at a favourite restaurant of Valeria's. It was there that they first met and Valeria was never sure it hadn't all been planned. People did things like that: spy, lie. She did, for sure. Just look at the portrait plan.

'Maybe she wanted to be my friend, so she chose the restaurant I love, and then ten days after we meet, she applies for the assistant's job with the perfect CV for me to make it impossible to say no,' she'd told Martìn.

'Great one,' Martìn had said. 'Write it down.'

She did. It was a short story about a girl working on and off in restaurants. In her story, Pamela was slightly older, but otherwise it illustrated her assistant's life exactly as she had told her: in the kitchens, with the clients, her usual siesta in one of the five-star hotel rooms upstairs when they were empty. There was some mention of her relationship with Benoit – François in the story – and of her many lovers. Valeria included her ways of speaking and her bouncy ponytail. She then published the story in *Balloon Magazine* and when, months later, she finally got round to hiring Pamela, she didn't tell her about it. She could never anticipate whether those kinds of things angered the real protagonist and didn't want to risk not being able to publish a story.

'I'm in Rue de Rennes. Is Zazou OK for you?' Valeria asked.

'Give me twenty minutes,' Pamela said.

Valeria kept walking, the air biting. Seeing herself in the display window of a lingerie shop was shocking. She was decrepit. Her curly hair that used to be brown and beautiful wasn't even curly any more. Her lips were losing tone like all the rest of her body. The sight of bras and sexy underwear mixed with her reflection was disturbing. Valeria particularly hated a pair of purple silk panties before her. She wanted to destroy them. She remembered what her mother used to say about ageing women. 'There is a specific day – it could be a Tuesday – when men stop looking at you. You are, from then on, officially invisible. It happens in one second and it lasts for ever.' In some lights Valeria could still pull it off. But it wasn't real. She probably looked older not younger. Cigarettes. Wine. All the frowning while writing. How would Sybilla have aged? Valeria entered the boutique and bought the panties.

'They're for tonight,' she told the salesgirl.

The tiny smile she received back was devastating.

Sybilla would wake her up in the middle of the night not wanting to sleep alone. She would sneak into Valeria's bed, get under the covers, squeeze her.

'Idiot,' Valeria would say. Sybilla didn't mind being called an idiot. She'd laugh.

Walking together to school would often include a secret swim. The salt on their bodies would make them itch for the rest of the day. They made bets for the first dive of the season and the last one. They made bets if the weather was horrible and the currents were dangerous. They'd hidden a towel in a cave, but most of the time the towel was damp and stank.

'I'd rather die of pneumonia than dry myself with that thing. It smells like puke,' Sybilla would say.

After the swim they would try to warm up by jumping on the spot and rubbing their skin. Often they were late for school and had to run the rest of the way there. On free afternoons, they'd sometimes look for spring waters in the valleys and on weekends they'd try to drag Theodora to their most recent discovery. Theodora would moan. But when Valeria and Sybilla won her over, they would walk with her through forests of Cyprus pine. They would cross citrus orchards, vineyards and olive groves, sure of themselves, proud, incredibly happy. Theodora carried a bag with everything they could possibly need. Once in, she was properly in.

'How did you find this place?' Theodora would ask. It was as if there were infinite numbers of 'this place' on the island and her daughters could find them all.

The three of them would splash in the water for the entire day. Theodora would scrub them with sea salt, put egg yolks in their hair, brush it through with vinegar. She would rinse them and rub their skin with olive oil. They would soak endlessly, their skin becoming red.

'I love you girls,' she'd repeat over and over on the way back.

'We love you too,' they'd say. But they always changed the subject as fast as they could because they were afraid she would start talking about their father: the world *love* was always associated with him and complaints like, 'Your father should be here too.' Saying these things would mean that all their efforts had been useless and Theodora would sink into her melancholia again. For this same reason, when Valeria met her father on Hampstead Heath many years later, she didn't tell Theodora. Nor that with him she went into great detail about Sybilla's pain: it took more than twenty minutes – it took all of her life lived so far – to map her sister's suffering and let her father know the way in which Sybilla had died.

Valeria dedicated her collection, *You*, to the memory of Sybilla. As soon as she saw it in book form, she wanted all the copies back, to erase Sybilla's name. Instead, journalists started digging up her past and asking about her dead sister.

'You probably need to talk about her,' Martin suggested.

They were in a secret place. He had called it secret so it was secret for Valeria too. Martin would often come up with proposals like, 'Lausanne in three days?' Or 'Tonight I'm in Bruxelles, can you eat with me?' So that night they went to the countryside, a hideaway close to the commune Villepinte in the Paris suburbs. Valeria drove herself there. Martìn came with a driver, who he dismissed.

'You'll have to drive me back,' he told Valeria as they smoked a cigarette together while watching the driver leave. 'I'm half blind at night.'

Heading back to their table, Valeria noticed that Martìn was limping.

'You limp,' she said.

'I don't,' he smiled. 'What makes you think I do?'

At that time Valeria was enjoying substantial press attention and Martìn had read one of the reviews that alluded to Valeria's childhood.

'It must be hard to live it over and over again,' he said, 'But maybe you want it to be this way.'

'I don't,' she said. 'I hate it.'

They then had a confused argument. Or at least, Valeria had one with him and told him that she lived it over and over again because of a shitty collection of shitty short stories. But what could he possibly know about it? And it was at that point that Martìn told her he had lost his twin brother Rami and that Valeria was very beautiful with all the tears on her face. But she had some snot blowing out of her nostril.

'Well, I might have snot coming out of my nostril but you limp,' she said to Martìn.

She cleaned her nose and looked at him provocatively. She thought, *Very beautiful?* What with his face, and this closeness?

'It's too easy to only want to know about other people's limps. What about your limp?' he said.

'You always do this, repeat a part of my question in the form of a question to me. It might sound super smart but it's just annoying.'

'I think you really do limp,' Martin said. And he smiled more.

V aleria was playing with the idiotically expensive purple panties on the table when Pamela arrived at Zazou. She was wearing a gigantic coat and black boots with heels. People turned their heads to look at her. It was clear that Pamela enjoyed her entrances. Valeria and Pamela shook hands and when Valeria smelled her perfume, she felt more together. They chose red wine and binged on that, eating only bread with butter.

'If it's OK, you do the talking and I'll just look at you,' Valeria said. 'I may also close my eyes to listen more carefully.'

'Story of my life,' Pamela laughed. 'Will you also keep playing with those panties? Just so I know.'

Valeria nodded and Pamela started with her latest chronicles. If Pamela was inventing, she was good at it. She never mentioned her wedding, and for this too, Valeria was grateful. And if Pamela was just feeding Valeria's hunger, she knew her tastes very well. She was a cheater, a flirt. But also, she was hilarious. Just to balance such fun raunchiness, a few times Valeria had come up with invented tales of her own. In reality, they were always about Martìn. She just picked a new name for him and backstories to play along. But because she had changed four or five names, Pamela thought that Valeria was similar to her. Free and curious. Sex came in such ways with such life and such soul. But in truth, Valeria couldn't have been less curious. She was also nearly thirty years older than Pamela, another difference Pamela never seemed to notice. It was flattering, in a way, but completely blind in another. Men still wanted Pamela a lot.

'I'm in a sentimental coma,' Valeria said. The word *coma* arrived unasked and so strong, it made her hate herself. She saw Martìn in his coma. She saw herself in a coma. She had to run to London. 'Can we leave?' she asked Pamela.

'What about the storm?'

'Let's face it,' she said.

The following morning the storm over Paris was still raging when Valeria woke to the sound of Joe calling her from downstairs. The housekeeper must have let him in. While dressing, she tried Martìn's phone again. Still off. She had to get rid of this new addiction. Along with the sleeping pills. The cigarettes. The red wine. She brushed her teeth and rinsed her face. How did the night end? You didn't say anything too personal, right? she asked herself before joining her agent in the living room.

'You look rough,' Joe said. 'Is it the flu?'

'It's the wine from last night.' Valeria broke an aspirin with her teeth.

'One of your songs for the radio show could be "Perfect Day", by Lou Reed,' Joe said. 'You used to listen to it a lot when we first met.'

Valeria heard the song as if Lou Reed was there performing it in the room for them.

'I was using it to write a short story. The one about the divers from the national team that highjack a plane.'

'"Forever Yours". That story should be a movie.'

'Did you really just say that?'

'I didn't.'

While looking at the usual pile of letters, Valeria noticed there was a new one from Julian. Fuck.

'I underlined a sentence as something that could be interesting for the title: "when looking up to the stars",' Joe said.

'It doesn't sound like me,' Valeria said, slipping the letter in the drawer with all the others. 'Too gooey.'

'Well, it's you. It's in your story "Mr and Mrs".'

'Used alone it sounds romantic. The sentence in my story has the opposite intention,' Valeria raised her voice.

'But—'

'I'll erase it from the book too.'

'Jesus, wow,' Joe said after a pause and they both started laughing.

Joe had to take a call and Valeria found herself a comfortable position on the sofa to enjoy the presence of Joe and closed her eyes. When she opened them again, Joe was holding his phone in front of her.

'I haven't got my glasses on,' Valeria said. 'Are you showing me a boyfriend, a text, a sunset, what?'

'It's an email from Isla Lawndale. She is saying yes.'

Valeria looked at Joe and saw the boy he had been. She saw him being seven years old and she saw his bruises. She heard him saying, 'I'm sorry', and she heard all the helpless kids of the world saying, 'I'm sorry.' When he had told Valeria his story on a flight to Mexico, she had cried, then immediately thought about how to use it. But as soon as the flight was over, Joe made her promise that she would never write it down. Valeria promised and while promising, she thought that if for any reason Joe were to die before her, she would write it. In the hotel room she jotted down the few details she didn't want to forget, and when she returned from the literary festival, the memo, scribbled on the hotel's letter paper, was archived with all the others.

'What does the email say?' Valeria asked. It was nine days since Martin had collapsed. Seven days in which all the things that had happened to her hadn't been narrated to him. After twenty-five years she didn't know how to handle the silence. What if Isla was saying yes but not for three weeks?

'Ready?' Joe asked.

'Ready,' Valeria whispered.

Dear Ms Costas and dear Mr Riddle,
Thank you for your messages. I've had a change of heart and I'm willing to work on Ms Costas' portrait. I would be available to begin work immediately. I would like us to work every day, at my home, until we are finished. I'm afraid I have no idea how long the process will take.

Should you still like to have the portrait done by me,
then it only remains for us to find our way.
With best wishes,
Isla Lawndale

PS: Ms Costas will you please bring along a picture of
your mother's portrait? I'm very curious.

'Why are you crying?' Joe said.

'I'm just tired, sorry,' Valeria said. She sat motionless, the sun outside shining brightly, as if to celebrate the moment.

'Staying in London is going to be expensive,' Joe said.

'I've got a friend whose house is free. It's near them.'

'Near *them*?' Joe asked.

'Near Isla and her family.' Why can't I just keep my mouth shut? Why do I even speak?

'How do you know where she lives?' Joe asked.

'Someone that knows someone who knows... Listen, I can't remember everything that happens to me. I just know it,' Valeria replied. 'She lives near Holland Park. I guess that was easy information to keep.'

Holland Park was true. The friend's free house was a lie. Valeria was going to find something tonight online. She didn't want to stay any further than ten metres from Isla's house in Ilchester Place. She knew the address by heart. She knew the street by heart too, from Google and from reality.

'The Moscow conference is a two-thousand-dollar gig, Valeria,' Joe said.

'I'll fly in and out,' Valeria answered, 'Same thing with Stockholm. Please, now reply to Mrs Aclà that it is a yes. For Monday.'

'What do you mean you will fly in and out from Moscow? And Mrs who?'

'Sorry, I meant Ms Lawndale,' Valeria said. Fuck!

That night, after writing and after running, Valeria lay on her bed with the computer on her lap and searched online for Martìn Aclà. Nothing new came up. The same articles and pictures appeared on the screen. The ambulance outside the hotel. Martìn collapsing at the conference. Again, Valeria watched the footage. She watched it and rewatched it until she noticed that he had peed his pants. She paused the video and ran her fingers over the dark pixels.

FIVE

While Valeria was packing her things for London, she received a call from her mother but didn't pick up. She laid the clothes on the bed before starting to fit them into the suitcase, stopping halfway through to jot down the outline of a short story she wanted to go back to, once the one about the drowning sisters was finished.

> Ex-husband decides not to go to a party with the new girlfriend he loves. Eats alone in a restaurant. By coincidence meets ex-wife. She joins him. They order too much food. NEVER mention their children. They spend the night together – walk the city, eat again at a diner at 4am – and at dawn they decide NOT to have sex.

Valeria filed the piece of paper before returning to her packing.

Many of her ideas, bits of stories, fragments of dialogues, were jotted down on napkins, the backs of receipts - anything that happened to be lying around when plots or characters arrived in her head. She didn't want the ideas to be transcribed on fresh pieces of paper, but they were always filed in order, chronologically. When possible and if already titled, alphabetically, too.

Once, Valeria had agreed to publish pictures of her workspace in a literary magazine. One of them was a close-up of her archives and when Valeria saw it in print she hated how they looked. Were any of her secrets revealed? There was a pen Martìn had given her visible on her desk. It was a pen from a hotel in Shanghai. Might Martìn's wife pick up on something from it?

'I'm your lover,' Valeria had told him many times. 'You have a wife, a family and then there is me, the mistress.' Every time she said *mistress* she would also smile to make sure it wouldn't come across as nagging or her asking him to leave his wife.

'You are my love,' Martìn would tell her. 'I adore you.'

'You love only me?' she would sometimes ask. But it wasn't very often, for Valeria didn't care about being the other one. Nor did she wish to be the only one. She didn't want a husband. She didn't want a family. She loved Martìn but she wanted to be alone. And to keep the empty space, for Sybilla and for all the stories.

They both travelled so much that they would plan encounters months in advance. Valeria was pretty sure that with all those planes and trains she saw Martìn more than his wife did. Not that there was a competition, Valeria would tell herself. Of course there isn't, she would remind herself, whenever Martìn and his wife appeared in magazines holding hands.

'Will you write our story?' Martìn would ask Valeria.

'I always do,' Valeria would say. 'We are in all my stories.'

It was true. Many of their conversations, just like many of the rooms they had slept in, ended up in her stories. A version of the time they thought they were going to die in a storm during a transatlantic flight to New York appeared on the front page of the *Sunday Meta*.

That day, even though they had different bookings for the flight, everything had been orchestrated for them to end up seated side by side. During the turbulence, despite the possibility of them being recognized, he had kissed her and with the storm at its peak, the other passengers screaming and praying, Valeria said to Martìn, 'I want to be your wife. I want your kids.' It was the first and last time she ever said it. It was true only for that second but it was so true it was painful. In the short story Valeria didn't even change his name. The title was 'Martìn'.

When they landed in New York it was 6pm. They went through Customs separately and there were two different cars waiting for them. Once in hers, Valeria cried upon seeing the bright lights of the city. At the hotel they both showered in their separate rooms before making their way in separate cars to a private club on the Upper East Side, where they ordered Bloody Marys and French fries and listened to the most incredible jazz singer. Her name was Lola Bazaan.

'She's sexy isn't she, this Miss Bazaan,' Valeria said.

Martìn kissed Valeria and squeezed her leg.

'What?' she asked.

'We're lucky,' Martìn said.

After three days together, they boarded two different planes back to Europe. Before disappearing in the hazy cloud induced by her sleeping pills, she had scribbled on a napkin: *Lola Bazaan, name to use.* Bazaan soon appeared in one of Valeria's stories. It was about two women in their sixties who abandon their families and go live in remote Canada. They never come back home to visit. They never get to meet their grandchildren. They never use their real names again. As a surname, Lady Smith chooses Bazaan. Lady Fletcher, Pascal. The small community accepts Bazaan and Pascal with time, suspicions giving way because of their kindness, and when they both die from the explosion of a gas cylinder in their modest home, their few neighbours set up a bonfire in the forest to wave them goodbye.

Valeria went back to choosing the clothes she wanted to take to London. What was she going to wear for the portrait? She picked up another two pairs of shoes, some silk shirts, gym shoes and boots. She added her beauty case, pill pouch and a kimono.

Valeria's mobile rang.

'What's missing?' Pamela asked her.

'Nothing,' Valeria replied. Everything was missing.

'Tonight I have to cancel the dinner with the guy from the Bordeaux library – the one I met after your speech,' Pamela muttered.

Yes, Valeria thought, maybe Pamela just hoped that Valeria would write her stories and they both lied in the same way.

Valeria didn't recall any guy Pamela had met at the Bordeaux library. She didn't even recall the Bordeaux library.

'Benoit found out about some flirtations of mine. He's not happy.' Saying it aloud made Pamela cry. 'That was a nice end for our night out.'

'What happened?'

'The usual. A friend of a friend said something. Another one confirmed the story. . . Truth is, he went through my phone. He was so precise about hours and stuff. Anyway, the point is I thought Benoit always kind of knew. I thought he actually embraced it. Well, turns out he didn't.'

'You said the other night that the fear of losing him sometimes does get in the way'

'I was lying?' Pamela's voice broke. 'Sorry.'

'You were lying now or back then?'

'I'm sorry,' Pamela said.

'Stop saying you're sorry,' Valeria said. How much more of this call? She wanted an assistant, not a crying semi-friend right now.

Pamela took a deep breath and cleared her voice.

Valeria pictured Pamela redoing her ponytail to feel calmer. A bird crashed into Valeria's guestroom window.

'Don't worry,' said Valeria. She moved towards the window. The remains of a bird slid down the pane. Blood. Something else slimy, transparent. 'And you two are getting married. I just saw your invitation.'

'Maybe it's not even what I want,' Pamela said. Then, 'Shall I come help you?'

'No need,' Valeria replied. 'Everything is going to be OK, Pam.'

'Maybe I don't want that either.'

Valeria placed a few bras on the pillow. She should write a story about two brothers, a dead bird and a natural disaster. Tsunami or earthquake? Title, 'The Bird'. No. Title, 'Bird'. She counted the T-shirts. Seven should do. Where were the new purple panties? Did the bird need her help to die or was it already dead? Sybilla had once killed a lizard, Valeria had once killed a snail. They had also planned to kill an eel, a rat and maybe one day a shark, but they hadn't had the time to make all their killer dreams come true.

'You there?' Valeria asked.

'I'm going through your agenda one more time,' Pamela said. 'Give me a sec.'

Two jumpers slid off the bed. Valeria kneeled on the floor, put the jumpers back.

'Sorry,' Pamela said, crying again. 'Before I forget, the purple panties are in the drawer of your bedside table. Gotta go now. Safe travels.'

Always good telepathy. Valeria opened the bedside table drawer and grabbed the purple panties. She looked closer at the shape, the silk, and ended up rubbing the panties over her face. Then she made her way downstairs and outside. She walked barefoot on the freezing paving. No tsunamis in sight, but she found the bird and it was dead. I wish the two brothers from the short story were here to help me. She buried the bird in a pot in her courtyard, her hands covered in soil. Where are you, Sybilla?

'I need a bra,' Sybilla had announced while they were taking a shower. 'See?'

Valeria couldn't see anything. She returned to shampooing her hair.

'Come closer,' Sybilla insisted.

Valeria looked closer and yes, maybe there was something happening under the skin. Just maybe.

'Why do you need one?' Valeria asked, as shampoo foam dripped into her eyes.

'They hurt when I run,' Sybilla said after a pause.

It sounded like a made-up excuse she might have overheard during PE. Probably Sybilla was just being competitive with some other girl at school who really did have tits.

'I want a bra too,' Valeria said. If there were going to be bras around, she would be part of the deal. If there was going to be a 'let's pretend we have tits' game, so be it.

'Of course you can have one,' Sybilla answered. She helped Valeria with her conditioner, brushing it through her sister's hair beneath the stream of water. Then, 'You are all set.'

Valeria and Sybilla took the bus from Lindos to the Rodini Park. The town was bleached white, the heat insufferable. The sisters made their way to the water, where some fishermen who had just returned to port showed the girls how to cut up a swordfish.

'We already know how to do it,' Sybilla told them in Greek.

Minutes later she was cutting fish with a bunch of fishermen and smoking cigarettes. She made a bet on how long it would take her to clean one, and she won.

When Valeria and Sybilla left the harbour they had a free fish to take back home. They'd also won a cigarette each.

'Mum will be happy about the fish,' the sisters said to each other. Even though Theodora never quite was.

At the lingerie shop on their way home the sisters still smelled like fish and the manager was clearly annoyed when they dropped the bag with their win by the entrance.

'Her face looks like it's melting,' Sybilla whispered. 'She must be a hundred years old.'

The hundred-year-old lady made it very clear that she wanted the whole ordeal to be over as quickly as possible. She detested the girls with their fishy smell and their fishy fish. She probably detested children and bras and anything young that crossed paths with her, all human beings, life, afternoons and mornings.

'Wash your hands,' she ordered, pointing towards a back room. Sybilla and Valeria washed their hands, using the moment to steal a bar of soap from under the sink. Valeria hid it in her pants and for the whole trying-on session she was nervous it would fall out. And that it would make it look like she had a penis.

'Touch my penis,' she told Sybilla in the changing room.

After a few tries and numerous laughs, they went for a pink cotton bra for Sybilla and a light blue one for Valeria. Valeria's came with a matching slip but they didn't buy it. They didn't want to give the melting hag all their money.

'I can tell,' whispered Sybilla, 'that she'll be dead soon.'

Valeria and Sybilla left the shop with flushed cheeks and high hopes now that they were girls with bras. That night they slept wearing them. It was exciting. But it was also itchy and uncomfortable. They sensed it was kind of sexy too but Valeria couldn't really say why. In the morning they had breakfast with their bras beneath their shirts, their oblivious mother in front of them. They both felt something radical had happened.

'We bought you this soap,' they told Theodora.

'I love you girls,' Theodora said. 'It smells like heaven.' After sniffing the soap and breaking into the smallest smile ever, she went back to being black.

The word for heaven in Greek is *paredeisos.*

SIX

Dimitri placed the two suitcases in the back of the car. Valeria knew his payments came from Martìn's New York office. Possibly Dimitri didn't even know who Martìn was and had been hired by a secretary from one of Martìn's many companies.

Valeria had a driver organized for her in every city she visited and she always felt very ashamed of it. A woman with a driver paid for by a man? A writer with a driver? She was invited at panels to give talks about independence, freedom, emancipation: she was a liar, a bluff.

'It would make me feel controlled by you,' she had told Martìn. 'And that's the opposite of who we are.'

'You're right,' he had admitted. 'Completely. But I'm not always close enough and I'm terrified something bad could happen to you when I'm not there.'

Eventually, after saying no for months, she gave in. The main reason for her change of mind was that the sentence he'd constantly use to win his argument was identical to the one he'd use for the night of Rami's tragedy.

Her first driver was Romeo, then there had been Frederic. Three years ago, Dimitri arrived.

'Why is Dimitri from Rhodes?' she asked him.

'He was born there,' Martìn said.

'Oh fuck, come on,' Valeria smiled.

They laughed, had sex and Valeria had welcomed Dimitri from Rhodes too.

Valeria pressed her forehead against the glass and the chill on her skin felt like a cloth for high fever. Maybe her wrinkles would disappear. Maybe she could disappear too. Valeria's breath shortened again. In the absence of air, gripped by the fear of everything, she saw the Gare du Nord.

'Will you help me find the train?' Valeria asked Dimitri. She was shaking.

Valeria and Dimitri took the lift to the station. It was so packed Valeria could smell Dimitri's cologne. His beard was growing. Was he kind to his family? Had he ever punched someone? The carpet on the floor said *Direction Angleterre*.

'*Kali tichi* for the trip,' Dimitri said, wishing her luck.

'I would prefer it if you didn't speak Greek with me,' Valeria said.

There was a queue and Valeria tried to focus on how everyone was dressed and how many people there were. She wanted to return to this memory in two hours. Then in a week. But would she remember at those times that she wanted to remember this moment? All this blur could be a reaction from the sleeping pills, she thought. They do fuck with your short-term memory.

'Why don't you go there now, on holiday?' Valeria asked Dimitri. She wanted to leave him in a good mood. 'I'm away anyway.'

'I'd like that, thank you,' he said. 'I'll talk with my wife about it.'

They shook hands and she went through security. There were nine other people queuing with her at check-in. A couple in their forties; three businessmen, one with a grey suit, two in blue suits; a chubby man dressed in leather who looked like a bad fashion designer; a decrepit man with a very old brown leather briefcase; a young girl; a woman in a green hostess-style uniform tight enough to show her panties cutting her arse into four.

Ten minutes later, when she stowed her luggage in the overhead compartment, she could still remember them all.

Valeria sat on the train, the air stifling. The outskirts of Paris were covered in mist. Her phone rang. It was Theodora. She swiped her finger across the screen to answer.

'Vale, how are you?' her mother asked.

Valeria imagined the effort a voice had to put in to make it from India to Paris. Even more so that of an eighty-three-year-old woman.

'I'm fine, Mum. You?' Valeria closed her eyes. She saw Theodora's plaited, silver hair.

'I'm well. The two monks that take care of me want to talk to you,' Theodora said. 'I'll put you on speaker.'

Valeria didn't even attempt to stop her. When Theodora moved to Sunville, Valeria had tried to convince her to change her mind. Her mother had been travelling around the world for a decade, looking for a place in which to spend her old age. There had been Mexico. There had been Kenya. Then she had discovered Sunville. It was the 'ideal city', where there was no money and everything had to be shared, according to the print-out Theodora had sent her:

Sunville is an experimental utopia and was designed to be a town where men and women are able to live in peace and with progressive cooperation. The purpose of Sunville is to achieve human unity.

On that printed page, during a phone call with Martìn, Valeria wrote, *fuuuuuuuuck.*

'We are Kateshi and Gibi,' one of the monks said.

'Very nice to meet you, Kateshi and Gibi.'

'Don't use names,' they said. 'Everyone is everyone.'

'You just used them,' Valeria said. 'Or what did you mean?'

'No shout. We just wanted to tell you that Moma Theodora is very strong.'

'That's true.' She agreed. She wasn't shouting, she was whispering, 'It's good to know she's in loving hands.'

'Soon you two will see each other. In Rhodes.'

'Wait, *what?* Rhodes? Can you put my mother back on?' Valeria said.

She could hear all three of them now, breathing at different paces. Even if everyone was everyone, they still had different lungs. The sound of something smashing deafened her. She hated the monks.

'Mum!' she shouted. Valeria imagined Theodora being kidnapped, then killed. With her mother she always spoke in English, because Greek was too painful and their Italian wasn't as good. Maybe now Valeria could switch to a language the monks wouldn't understand, so they would be able to talk freely? But talking in Greek would make Theodora desperate. It was in Greek that the worst had happened and it was in Greek that the worst had been said.

'*Vale*, I've been trying to call you for days,' Theodora said. 'I'm going to Rhodes tomorrow, can you come?'

Valeria's heart opened up. She let Theodora in.

'What do you mean you are going to Rhodes *tomorrow*?' Valeria said.

'The day after today. We've found good tickets. We are going.'

'I thought we were never going back?' Valeria said. She saw the plane taking off from Rhodes when she was twelve. It was empty. She was empty. 'I thought *you* could never go back.'

'Is this too sudden?' Theodora said.

Was she being sarcastic? It had taken her over forty years! 'Sudden' was not even remotely the right word.

'Is it also sudden in a nice way? Like a surprise?'

'I'm not sure, Mum. No. And right now it's impossible for me to come.' Would she go as soon as Martin was well again? Or as soon as Martìn was dead? Were they really talking Rhodes? Her fist clenched.

'I'll be waiting for you there,' Theodora said. 'Come when you can.'

'Rhodes,' the monks repeated. 'ASAP!'

Valeria started crying.

'Don't cry, you make me worry,' Theodora said.

Valeria tried to stop crying even if making Theodora worry was the whole point of being a daughter, crying with a mother.

'I wasn't really crying,' Valeria said. 'I was pretending.'

'Hey, you know that I run every day?' Theodora said. 'Up to the forest and back.'

'Do you really?' Valeria asked. She pictured Theodora running up to the forest and back.

'I was just pretending,' Theodora said, a smile in her voice. 'OK, gotta go, my love.'

Valeria hung on to *my love* and remained there, lying on the phrase, looking for peace while resting on the word *love*. It was the first time since Sybilla's death that Theodora had called her this, and that Rhodes was back in their lives.

Maybe they were all about to die.

At St Pancras Valeria ordered an Uber to the Portobello Club. She was going to stay at the hotel for a couple of nights, while she waited for her rental flat to be available. It seemed like the quickest way of leaving Paris and settling

53

in to London. The roads around the station were blocked with buses, black cabs, motorbikes flashing their lights. Further out, the city turned quiet, the neighbourhoods almost ghostly.

'Good evening,' Valeria told the young man at the hotel reception when she arrived. Was he Indian? Aged about twenty-eight? Possibly named Ari. Sisters and brothers, six or maybe ten. Still looking for love. Believes in a god. Which one? She wasn't able to recall all religions in India. But this man prayed, she was sure. And he believed in the good things. What were the good things? Purity. Love. Bread when you are hungry. Water when you are thirsty. OK, stop now.

'Good evening, madam,' the young man said.

Valeria handed over her passport to Ari.

'This is your key,' he said. 'Your room number is twenty-three. It's a beautiful room. My favourite. I hope you will find it as charming as I do. Should you need any help please don't hesitate to call me.'

Valeria hoped for a new guest to arrive soon enough for her to be able to overhear his speech about room 22.

Room 23 was covered in green-leaved wallpaper. Valeria sat on the bed and started counting the leaves from left to right. Then she ran a hot bath and once in the water, she recounted and remembered all the people queuing with her in Paris. Nine. She still had them all with her.

'I am here,' she whispered to Martin. And she submerged herself in the water.

L ondon was the city in which Valeria and Martin had spent least time together. He lived there with his wife, so it was neither wise nor desirable to share the city. And on those occasions when they had met there - for a quick lunch or to spend an afternoon together - they always avoided Holland Park. Only once in all those years had Valeria travelled to London without letting Martin know. She had gone precisely not to avoid Holland Park. She had taken a long walk in the park and drank coffee on a wet bench.

'You wanted me in Paris because you can commute easily between your two lives,' she had told Martin.

'Firstly, I only have one life. Secondly, this plan seems to work for both of us. Thirdly, you chose Paris!' he had said, smiling.

T he following morning, breakfast at the Portobello Club was served in a room with flowers cascading down the wallpaper, blooming on the cushions and carpets. The waitress showed Valeria to a table near the window, where she was soon joined by Ari. Ari and the waitress stared at her.

'Did you sleep well, Ms Costas?' asked Ari.

'I did, Ari, thank you for asking.'

'My name is Leo,' Ari said.

'Sorry, Leo. Are you burning cinnamon in the fireplace?'

'It's one of our secrets,' Ari-Leo smiled. 'You will never guess them all.'

'Are there many?'

'Are there many?' Ari-Leo repeated with another smile.

Were they all, *all*, doing it – repeating things – in her life? And was it possible that for all her life she had been speaking to only one person, who had the superpower of changing shape and gender and age? Was Ari-Leo Martìn, Sybilla and her own self? Is all that I'm told an echo of what I say? The monks did say that everyone is everyone.

To cheer herself and the waitress up, Valeria ordered everything. Sandwiches. Croissants. Eggs. Green tea but also coffee. Hot water with lemon. Yoghurt and granola. Salmon. Scribbling it all down gave the waitress the boost she needed and when the food arrived Valeria nodded in appreciation.

She ate for a good fifteen minutes and washed it all down with several cups of hot water. When she stood up she was so full she could barely move. But she closed her coat, wrapped her scarf around her neck and left the hotel.

She walked out into the crisp wind up to Bayswater until she reached Hyde Park.

In the park the ground was covered with leaves. Valeria crossed paths with kids. Nannies. Dogs. Joggers. She definitely didn't want to be a kid. She didn't want to be a nanny either. A jogger, definitely not now. A dog, maybe. Martìn and his family always had dogs. The last one, the one that was still alive, was called Rock.

'Because you love rock 'n' roll?' Valeria had asked.

'We found it under a rock,' Martìn had said.

We is all that Valeria heard. *We.* Isla and Martìn.

Valeria checked the map on her phone to see if the directions to the National Portrait Gallery were correct. It said 2.8 miles, one hour. She kept walking south-east and was going to try to be there in 45 minutes. If she arrived at the gallery in less than 45 minutes, Martìn would wake up from his coma. They would be back together. Maybe, as he had told her two weeks ago, they would go and live together.

'I'm not sure I want to,' Valeria said. But she had smiled. 'And what about your wife?'

'I need more time with you.'

'Because you feel you've been unfair to me?'

'Have I?'

'Not at all.'

'So let's try?'

'I don't like the "try" thing.'

'Do you want to do it or not?'

He wasn't smiling but he was fine. She loved him.

'Is it up to me?'

'Valeria?'

'We could "try", I guess.'

She had smiled because neither of them were sad nor angry at the end of the conversation. It wasn't straightforward.

Without her noticing, Martìn had recorded the exchange on his phone and sent it to her via instant messenger an hour later. It was sweet of him, and it was unexpected, but she got scared from not recognizing her own voice. She replied with the audio clip of a jazz song being broadcast at that moment on Radio 2. He replied with a text that said, 'Well played.'

To stay within her given time, Valeria walked as fast as she could. She reached Oxford Circus, Piccadilly, and, looking the wrong way, nearly walked into the path of an oncoming bus, but she arrived at the museum within 40 minutes so started her tour feeling very proud. Thanks to her strength she had it all sorted out. She had beaten time and Martìn was going to wake up. There wasn't going to be a death, a funeral and the end of it all. In fact, there could soon be a new beginning.

SEVEN

By the end of the summer in which Valeria turned ten, Sybilla had started getting bruises – first on her legs, then on her hands. Often her gums would bleed. She was always tired.

'Eat something,' Theodora would tell her.

'I'm not hungry,' Sybilla would always reply.

In early September, Theodora told her, 'Don't go to school if you don't want to.'

She would squeeze oranges, grate carrots, prepare anything that she remembered might be healthy. Cook chicken broth. Add ginger.

'Stay home another day,' Theodora pleaded.

Walking to school without Sybilla was boring. One step after the other Valeria acknowledged the passing of minutes. Another one. And wow, yet another one. She found herself inventing stories.

'Where is your sister?' kids asked her at school.

'Swimming at the Northern Cove,' she replied. Or, 'In London with our father' or, 'She's been cast in a movie.'

In the afternoons, back home from school, Valeria would lie on the bed with Sybilla.

'What's with the breathing?' she asked. Sybilla was gasping for air.

'Oh, it's nothing,' Sybilla said. She didn't look as terrified as Valeria felt.

'You are not fucking underwater. Breathe normally,' Valeria told her.

They would spend the rest of the day lying on the bed or, if it was not too windy, on the sofa outside. From the sofa outside they contemplated their tiny piece of land, its olive trees, cats, starving dogs. Sometimes a porcupine would pass by.

'I miss school,' Sybilla said after a couple of weeks at home.

'School was shut down,' Valeria replied.

'Really?' Sybilla didn't even open her eyes. She was too tired or maybe the sun was just too bright.

'Do you keep your eyes closed because of the sun?' Valeria asked.

'Exactly because of that. I love our telepathy. So what about the school?'

'They think it's pointless keeping them open given the fact that everybody is learning the same things.'

'It does make sense,' Sybilla said. 'Is this a decision for the entire planet?'

'Yeah,' Valeria said. 'They've now realized that they've bred way too many people reading the same books and learning maths or history in the same exact way. Not only is it boring given that people kind of talk about things they all already know, it doesn't do anything to help the human race evolve either. '

Soon, Theodora couldn't pretend any more. Doctors became involved. There were daily visits to specialists and constant blood tests and scans. There was a trip to Athens. After Athens and the diagnosis of acute myelogenous leukaemia, going to the Rhodes hospital became routine. It was day visits at first but soon Sybilla was admitted full time. Only Theodora could stay with her and Valeria was asked if she wanted to go stay with a family from school.

'I don't want to sleep anywhere but with Sybilla,' she said.

'That's not allowed,' Theodora repeated.

'Then I will be at home. Our home,' Valeria said.

In the mornings, Valeria would have breakfast with the babysitter, the nineteen-year-old daughter of the farmer living next door. Her name was Calypso and she was hairy. She was also sweet and placid. Valeria didn't mind having her around, especially as she prepared yoghurt, nuts and fruit for her every day. And despite her timid personality, Calypso would sometimes share random sex-related anecdotes.

'I'm a virgin but I like sex,' she once told Valeria. 'I masturbate before sleeping. Makes me rest better.'

Valeria always struggled with the association of that hairy body and sex and in her thoughts Calypso's vagina was very, very dark.

At school, everybody soon knew about Sybilla. The teachers and kids started treating Valeria differently. They stared at her. They would use awkward, honeyed voices to talk to her. They would send letters to Sybilla. All the letters had hearts or stars on them.

'I don't want to go to school,' Valeria told Theodora. 'I want to be with Sybilla.'

Theodora said no but Valeria ignored her. She'd leave for school in the morning but go back to the hospital as soon as she knew Theodora would be out running errands.

'School still closed?' Sybilla would say.

'It's a gym now,' Valeria would answer. Or she'd say, 'Now it's a porn cinema.' A church. A space shuttle. It's been bombed.

Valeria caressed Sybilla's skin and prayed. She would ask the sky or anyone on the planet to save her soulmate. She made sacrifices, promises to the unknown. If Sybilla survives I will never do this again. If Sybilla survives I will do this other thing always. Valeria gave up chocolate, swimming, reading. She donated all her coins to the church. She compulsively lit candles. If I clean the bathroom floor for one hour she will survive. If I plant a tree she will survive. If I drink this whole bottle of water she will survive. If I walk in less than one hour from hospital to home she will survive. If I do it in 40 minutes, by spring we'll be swimming together.

'I still feel like I'm falling,' Sybilla told her.

'Hold me,' Valeria said. 'Grab me and don't let go.'

'I don't like you when you're nice.'

'Fuck you,' Valeria said, 'Shut the fuck up, shithead. '

'That's better.'

'Who fucking cares what's fucking better for you?'

'Don't overdo it. Otherwise it doesn't work.'

A t the Portrait Gallery Valeria lost herself in the bookshop. She opened *500 Portraits,* the book on the past 25 years of the British Portrait Award. In the introduction, the director of the museum announced, *'Whether they are true to the sitter's looks or expressively convey their character, painted portraits have a wider significance that relates to our common interest in learning about other people.'* This was a good sentence to use with the publishers, and with Joe. Would she be able to learn it by heart and pretend it was her own? She opened the book *The Face of Britain,* by Simon Schama. Valeria read: *'You spend a little time in front of a portrait and then you move on. But you have the odd feeling that the eyes of that painted face are tracking you round the gallery. It's a cliché, a joke, a fable, the kind of thing that has the guards rolling their eyes. But you are not altogether deluded. From somewhere deep in the temporal cortex of your brain has come, unbidden, the act which made you human in the first place: the locking of eyes.'*

She flipped through the pages of *Reality and Self: Of Identity and Creation,* and she found a portrait by Isla Lawndale with an accompanying caption: *'Born in America, Isla Lawndale studied at the Royal College* of Art in London and at Sarah Lawrence, Bronxville, New York. Lawndale's commissions as a portrait artist include politicians, artists and common people. Lawndale currently lives in London, with her husband and their three children. The portrait is of her daughter Antonia, aged 1, with her pet cat.'

Valeria bought the book and wandered through the galleries. The gazes, secrets and stories were overwhelming. Famous faces appeared alongside obscure ones, all of them making eye contact with her. The locking of eyes became frantic. Valeria stared at the Queen's portrait. Sitting near the Queen there was a dog. The aim of the artist, according to the label, was 'to create a rather informal picture that would tend to play down the remoteness of Her Majesty'.

'I need a hug,' Valeria said out loud to the Queen. 'And maybe a dog, too.'

On the ground floor Valeria walked into an exhibition of Alberto Giacometti. On the walls, the synopsis of Alberto's life occupied two large rectangles. Leaving the first room, Valeria felt that she was already starting to know the artist. By tomorrow, she would have forgotten most details. Maybe the fact that Giacometti was born in Switzerland, or that he concentrated on the human head and preferred models he was close to, like his sister Ottilia and his mother, would stay with her? Walking through the rooms, she suddenly remembered having been to

Giacometti's birthplace, Stampa, on the way to meet Martìn in Sils Maria many years ago.

Valeria read the label on the wall: '*The comfortable, cheerful homes Annetta created for her family were a vital part of Alberto's childhood "paradise", the opposite to the ramshackle studio he later occupied in Paris.*'

She would never be able to create 'a cheerful childhood paradise'. Maybe Isla Lawndale had been? Giacometti had married Annetta, a woman with the same name as his mother, and she soon became another one of his favourite sitters. How had it felt to be looked at by her husband through all those years? Valeria would now have to be studied too. Isla Lawndale would stare at her wrinkles, her ageing features, everything that in Valeria's face was now sagging and revealing of time and pain. Was she ready for her stare?

Valeria reached the last room of the Giacometti exhibition, which was dedicated entirely to Caroline, his last lover. So he had watched his mother ageing. He had watched his wife ageing. Then the artist had chosen youth again. He was sixty, Caroline just twenty. He spent his final years drawing only her. And it was her hands that Alberto wanted to hold when he died.

What was he holding on to? Youth? The past?

Valeria called Pamela. 'What should I wear for the portrait?'

'I like you in that silk shirt,' Pamela said. 'That colour's good on you. The shape's perfect.'

'What silk shirt?'

'The amber one. Did you take it with you to London? You look stunning in that.'

Pam—Pamela knew her shirts. She also had her preferences.

'The brown pencil skirt would work perfectly with that shirt,' she added.

Valeria imagined herself according to Pamela's description. The silk shirt, that pencil skirt, snug and well fitted. She was more beautiful in her assistant's mind than in reality. It was the same with Sybilla. She'd tell her something like, 'You look pretty with a ponytail,' and Valeria would not only feel better, she'd actually look better. Like with her ponytail, life was wonderful when Sybilla said it was. Abracadabra.

EIGHT

In the morning, Valeria left the Portobello Club and waved Ari goodbye from the taxi. If things didn't work out with Isla, with Martìn and the portrait, if the world was coming to an end, it would be to him that she would cling on to for survival.

As soon as the car approached the Aclàs' road, Valeria's heart began to race. It was happening. She was fifty metres away from the house in Holland Park, fifty metres away from her lover's bedroom. From the portrait, from his wife. In one hour the women would have their first encounter. In two hours she would be seated in front of her.

The taxi stopped in front of her rental flat and new home-to-be.

She pushed both her bags inside, closing the door behind her. The flat was on the ground floor. From the front door to the end of the room was three metres at the most. The living-room window was dirty, the tiny garden barely visible through the glass. Valeria had chosen the flat precisely because of that view. It was disappointing. This apartment was costing thousands of pounds per month and it had only a bedroom, a kitchenette, the tiniest living room. Without spring, the garden didn't make much sense. Valeria recalled some pink flowers in the rental pictures. Those too had disappeared.

In front of the mirror, Valeria attempted a bit of make-up and, after trying all other options, ended up wearing the exact outfit Pamela had suggested. She left the flat and walked down her new road. Somehow the whole idea of being so close to Ilchester Place didn't feel quite right now, and too soon she found herself in front of the Aclà house. There were just eight elegant steps dividing her life from Isla Lawndale's. She stared at the windows and lost her balance. Am I really doing this?

'Legs, move,' Valeria whispered. The wind gusted, as if to push her up the steps, while the gigantic magnolia tree branches overhead swayed, as if to brush her off. She closed her eyes. 'It's OK,' she muttered.

And then Valeria heard Isla Lawndale's voice. She was calling her. From an upstairs window. Was that their marital bedroom? The one in which they had sex? Maybe constantly, for the two decades they had lived there?

'Ms Costas!' Isla was yelling.

'Open your eyes,' Valeria told herself. 'Isla Lawndale is calling you.' Come on. Valeria opened her eyes just as Isla whistled down to her. She looked up, the sun almost blinding her and she saw a blond head, a smile, panic, love, fear. The sun disappeared and Valeria's last bit of calm disappeared with it. And it was overcast.

'I'll be down in one second!' Isla shouted. 'Mirela is coming to open the door.'

Valeria nodded, her heart about to leap out of her chest.

'Keep it together,' she told herself. 'Just get in this house, sit for her. And stop talking to yourself.' She walked up the steps, charged with adrenalin. She reached for the doorbell with *Aclà* inscribed beside it.

'Martìn,' Valeria whispered. 'I am here.' As soon as she was close enough to be taken by surprise, the entrance door opened. And the rain started gushing down.

'Good morning,' said a statuesque woman, inviting Valeria inside and taking her coat. It felt like being tended to by a gigantic, stunning polar bear. Valeria kept hold of her jacket, though the beautiful creature wanted to take that from her too.

'Wait here, please. Would you like some coffee?' asked the polar bear. Her English had an Argentine inflection.

'No coffee, thank you,' said Valeria.

'If you need me, just say "Mirela",' she mumbled before disappearing from the room.

Valeria was inside. She was in her lover's house and she had spoken to Mirela, his housekeeper. On her right, hanging on the hallway wall, a picture of Isla with Martìn and their three children had her sweating within seconds. Their daughter Antonia looked happy in the picture, her long hair shining in the sun. Cosmo and Nico were still little, seated on a child-size motorbike. Over the years, Martìn had shown her many photos of his children. This one, he hadn't.

In front of her was the open doorway to a large living room, furnished with colourful sofas, armchairs, coffee tables, books and beautiful *objets d'art* from far-flung places.

There must be something among all the relics and figurines from their trip to Madagascar, right? A pair of eyes was staring at her. They belonged to a giant wooden head.

'Stop looking at me,' Valeria whispered to the wooden head.

She was finally here, she was near Martìn, the love of her life, but now she couldn't escape the fact that she had to be with Isla too. Isla the wife. The painter. Isla the other one.

No, wait, I'm the other one, she reasoned. Isla is the one.

Now she really would have to sit for her and spend the coming hours, days, maybe weeks with her. In an intimate set-up. Or would Valeria ruin something very soon and be kicked out before the day was over? Is the wooden mask going to reveal the truth? she wondered. If she didn't run away, or wasn't going to be thrown out, how could she possibly reach Martìn's room? The house was vast. Her plan had seemed feasible until now. Before having to actually walk upstairs, open doors, fight a polar bear. Would Martìn hate her for being in his house? Or would he expect her to do exactly this? For twenty-five years they had kept their secret. What now?

'I won't tell anyone,' Martìn had said. 'Not even one single friend. Not even Luc.'

'Men can't do that,' Valeria had smiled. 'Plus, you tell Luc everything.'

'I'll prove you wrong.'

'I won't tell anyone, ever,' Valeria said. It was true, she never did. Or so she thought.

'Don't look around,' Valeria whispered to herself, 'and stop speaking to yourself.'

She turned her back to the living room and faced the front door. It would probably appear strange to be looking out, rather than in, but it certainly felt better. Inside: Martìn. Inside: Martìn and Isla. Inside: Martìn, Isla and the voodoo face and all the Aclà family memories displayed. Outside: the world, herself, Martìn and her together. Shanghai. Paris. No polar bears.

'Welcome,' Isla said out loud.

And just like that, Isla Lawndale-Aclà was standing behind her. Here she was. There they were. Valeria turned around in slow motion. She smiled. Is this woman beautiful? she wondered. Does she know? Who's the better artist, woman, fuck, person? All questions mixed up, without leaving any space for possible answers.

'Thank you,' Valeria said standing in front of the wife of the man of her life. She beamed at her. 'And thank you for saying yes.' Her upper lip was tingling, her mouth dry, her heart a husk.

'The truth is Antonia, my daughter, bullied me into it,' Isla laughed, 'but I'm glad she did. She said I was a hopeless human being if I didn't paint the amazing writer Valeria Costas. Apparently, one of your stories changed her life.'

'Really? Which one?' Valeria asked. So it wasn't her letter that made Isla decide. Antonia the daughter wanted Valeria the mistress to pose for Isla the mother because she knew about her lifelong affair with Martìn the father?

'She wouldn't say,' Isla said. 'Maybe she'll tell you.'

Isla was standing so close to Valeria she could study her mouth, her nose, her eyes. Did the two of them look at all like each other? Valeria could see Isla's faint wrinkles, her full lips, the yellow lightning cut into her blue eyes. So this is what Martìn looks at. This is the perfume he breathes.

Isla was wearing an oversized jumper with shapeless jeans and biker boots. From what Valeria had seen in pictures, Isla weighed at least five kilos more now than she used to. Seven, even. And she probably looked younger than Valeria. It wasn't just her softened form, it was the eyes. Childlike. Fresh.

'My outfit's a mess,' Isla laughed. 'I thought I'd dress up a little for you, but then I was overwhelmed by other things. Sorry.'

'You look perfect,' Valeria said. Calm down, don't overdo it: 'perfect' is way too much.

Isla smiled and took a deep breath. What was that on her jumper? A food stain? Isla was tired. Of course she was. How terrible was it upstairs, in Martìn's room? In *their* room.

'I don't know if we will end up with something good,' Isla said. She seemed to be scrutinizing Valeria.

Was she working out whether she found Valeria beautiful? Did Isla know?

'But let's give it a go, shall we? I have made space for us in the studio. I would have found us a place elsewhere but I have to be around. My husband is very sick.'

Valeria nodded. She counted. She told her legs to move again. And her heart to keep on beating. Both her eyes and Isla's filled with tears that neither let out. The sky rained for them.

'I'm sorry to hear that,' Valeria managed to say.

'It's horrible. But at least he's not in any pain,' Isla said. 'Or so they assure me.'

NINE

Valeria followed Isla. They took the wooden stairs down to the basement, a single open-plan space with another living area displaying more family pictures. Martìn, Martìn and Isla, their friends, everywhere. Smiles. Teeth. Ears. Memories. An enormous silvery kitchen at one end led out towards a huge garden. In the garden there was a slide and a sledge. There was also an apple tree. There were no children in this family now, so the slide and the sledge appeared locked in the past. Like Giacometti's mother Annetta, it seemed that Isla had made this floor cheerful for her family.

'Would you like something to drink?' Isla said.

'No, thank you,' Valeria said. 'My stomach is kind of closed right now. I'm a bit nervous.'

'Don't be,' Isla smiled. She opened the door to the studio. 'It's going to be good.'

It's going to be good. Another good title? Not really.

Martìn had told Valeria that he was married the first time they talked, in their first half hour together. Not that at that point it was a problem. She didn't love him yet. Plus, his daughter Antonia didn't exist. Neither, of course, did Cosmo or Nico.

'I'm not a cheater,' Martìn said a few months after they started seeing each other.

'What are you then?' Valeria smiled.

'I'm a fan of yours and felt I had to meet you,' he said.

Valeria couldn't help enjoying the idea that Martìn 'had' to meet her.

'So I'm here. But now I also love you. Which makes it strange.'

That was the first time Martìn had ever told Valeria that he loved her.

'I have to admit I wanted to meet you because I knew I would then love you. So now it feels, at the same time, strange and not strange at all.'

'It feels "strange and not strange"?' Valeria repeated. Her sarcasm filled her mouth. It was like an oversized orange. A bitter one too.

'I can't make myself say I feel bad or guilty. I don't.'

'Is your marriage broken?' Valeria asked him.

'No,' Martìn said. 'We're in love.'

That was also the first time Martìn said I love you and I love my wife too.

'Would your wife be sad if she knew? Or is it one of those open marriages?'

'She'd be devastated.'

'Oh, OK. All this makes it really easy.'

'Well, at least we don't have kids.'

And then the kids arrived, one after the other. Here was a thought Valeria had actually had: with kids they might start fighting. Maybe their family will break up over duties and nagging?

'We are having a child,' Martìn had said when Isla was pregnant with Antonia. That too was a time during which they thought of not seeing each other any more. That too was a time in which Valeria had to picture Martìn having sex with his wife. Martìn telling Isla luminous words about them becoming parents.

'Let's stop this,' Valeria told Martìn.

'I can't,' Martìn said. 'I don't want to.'

But they had taken a pause. And Valeria didn't back down, even though she missed him terribly. She was used to not seeing him, but not seeing him indefinitely was different. What if Martìn would never be hers again?

'What shall I do?' Valeria said. Isla was preparing the paint. She drew the curtains to balance the light.

'Don't go away,' Isla said with a smile. 'About everything else, I'm not sure.'

Don't go away. What's with the titles today?

As Isla set about moving evidence of Cosmo and Nico's music rehearsals – drumsticks, a towel, a trumpet – into a corner, Valeria pulled her sleeves up, adjusted her bra. She found herself staring at Isla's body. Generous, healthy, very feminine. Her cheeks were pink, as if she had just returned from a run.

'I'm definitely not sure about the chair,' Isla murmured, kicking off her boots. She was now barefoot.

Do I want to look at her feet? Shall I? She did.

'Can you sit there instead?' Isla asked Valeria.

Valeria sat down on an armchair.

'Can you try to stand up and then sit down again?' Isla asked her. Valeria stood up and took her jacket off. She did it slowly, while taking a deep breath.

'Was it better with the jacket?' Valeria asked, sitting down.

'No, it's better this way,'

They were really doing it. She was there for a portrait. She was a writer, with a painter. A woman in front of another woman. She was in front of the wife of her lifelong lover. She could even study her feet.

Am I ever going to use the portrait anyway?

Isla observed Valeria. She was looking at her but also through her, as though Valeria were a shape not a person. Something in the panorama that she needed to record.

'It's just—' Isla said. And didn't add more.

Valeria remained seated while Isla moved around the room. When Isla got very close Valeria tried not to change the pace of her breathing. Isla was looking at the light on her skin, the shape of her nose. Her position in the world.

'When you stand up I can see you more,' Isla said. 'Can you stand up again?'

Her words were coming out slowly, they sounded distant, like when people speak under hypnosis.

Valeria stood and remained standing there, in the centre of the room, the shadow from the half-drawn curtain cutting her body in two. I am split, she thought. I'm divided.

'See what I mean?' said Isla. 'Not that we were planning the whole body, but I like your face when you stand.'

'I don't mind standing,' Valeria said, even though she was already tired. She did mind standing. And she had no idea if this process was going to last just a week or go on for months. Asking felt rude, but imagining what the future may hold felt wrong too. I just need to be here, now, she thought. Be in the present, will you? It's written on every T-shirt and on every mug.

'In ten minutes you will. And in two hours you will be back to using photos on your covers.'

Valeria blushed. How embarrassing was the lie of not wanting ever to be photographed again?

There was a knock on the door. Martìn? Of course not. But the very idea made Valeria's heart thump in her chest.

The beautiful polar bear entered the room with the juice. She was at least ten centimetres taller than she was half an hour ago. Did she know Martìn and Rami when they were teenagers? Mirela gave Isla the glass and waited for her to finish it. Isla cleaned the beetroot moustache off her skin. She was suddenly six again and she had all the vitamins she needed.

'Thank you,' Isla said. 'We'll start working now. So please, no phone calls. Interrupt me only if Martìn needs me.'

Martìn needs me, Valeria repeated in her head while Isla left the room. She was back in seconds with a stool from the kitchen and put it in the middle of the room. She returned to her position by the wall.

'Sit?' she asked Valeria.

Valeria sat and gave her a three-quarter stare, locking her eyes with Isla's.

Over the next hour together, they remained silent. Isla muttered words, such as *maybe* or *yes*. She was studying Valeria while sketching her in charcoal. She moved fast, partially hidden, so close was she standing to the canvas, her feet sometimes stopping in odd positions. As Isla examined Valeria's face, Valeria studied Isla. She could look at her in a way that wouldn't have been acceptable in any other situation: staring, ceaselessly and shamelessly.

'If you could go as far as smelling or tasting people you would,' Martìn had told Valeria once. Isla seemed just like her.

Valeria knew how Isla and Martìn had met. Or at least she knew what Martìn had told her. It was in New York, when Isla was already engaged to an American tennis player. Isla had left the champion after a six months 'negotiation-courtship' with Martìn. Quite recently, Valeria had seen the ex-tennis champion on a magazine cover. He was now an overweight man with the swollen face of an alcoholic. *Rehab vs. Tom*

Tallick, 6–0 Game, Set and Match, the headline read.

Isla had probably chosen Martìn from the start, just as Valeria had done, but she wanted to test him. She came from a traditional American family and had always been the different one. Her siblings were all lawyers, she was the only artist. They were Catholic, she was a Buddhist. Her sisters were slender, she was curvaceous, loved to drink and enjoyed her food. She was also an activist and a feminist, who often ended up naked for her art.

How badly had she disappointed them, cutting off her engagement to a tennis world champion for this enigmatic Argentine? How embarrassed had they been by that video installation, where Isla had interpreted her own mother and took her same antidepressants? Couldn't she just *drink* the milk in a nightgown for that bloody performance? And where and how did this Martìn make all that money? Surely no one could buy into his story of starting a business selling pinball machines to barber shops!

'You went for two women who look at the world and reinterpret it. Your wife stares at the world, decides on her angle and colour, then draws it. I look at the world, decide my rhythm, a voice, and write it,' Valeria had told Martìn at the beginning.

'I think it is very generous, living like you both do,' Martìn said. 'To really look at others, constantly. It seems to me very much about devotion. And love.'

'I'm more obsessive than devoted,' Valeria said. 'And nosy.'

But these conversations were rare. Speaking about Isla made Valeria nervous. Isla and Martìn for sure didn't speak about her at all, so for Valeria and Martìn to do so would have been unbalanced.

Isla was looking around the room, trying to choose her angle and light.

Why had Isla neglected her art for all those years? Valeria wondered. Could Valeria stop writing one day? Her head would fill up with stories, adjectives, faces. Sybilla. Rhodes.

'Do you mind if I put some music on?' Isla asked, still looking at the canvas.

'Not at all,' Valeria said.

Isla walked over to an old-fashioned stereo in the corner and pressed *play*.

Valeria took advantage of the pause to stand up and stretch her legs. She went near the window, looked at the garden and made a bet in her head: if it's classical music I'll be able to see Martìn today. If it's rock 'n' roll, it will be tomorrow.

It was Bach.

Valeria was happy. She was here, in his home. And Bach had just told her she was going to be with Martìn very soon.

'My husband loves Bach,' Isla said.

Martìn had never spoken about Bach with Valeria. She didn't know Martìn loved Bach more than people in general love Bach.

'Can I ask you,' Valeria attempted, 'why is he sick?'

'He had a stroke. Now he's in a coma,' said Isla.

'I'm so sorry,' murmured Valeria.

Isla approached her. They both looked out of the window. Rain.

'What will happen?' Valeria asked.

'I hope he wakes up,' Isla said, 'but he may never do so.'

The door creaked and Antonia walked into the room. Valeria's heart opened so widely at the sight of her that it was painful. Antonia was dressed in black from head to toe and the black eyeliner made her green eyes shinier. Valeria knew those eyes, they were Martìn's eyes. With Bach as a soundtrack her entrance was glorious.

'Hi, Anty,' Isla said. 'What're you doing home?'

'Don't call me that,' Antonia said, then, in a whisper, 'Hello,' acknowledging Valeria without looking at her. She appeared nervous, pale. 'I was feeling sick.' Her hair was wet from the rain. Or was it just unwashed? She had Martìn's athletic build, with the shapely legs of her mother.

'Articulate, please?' Isla said.

'Oh, all right,' Antonia said, 'let me *articulate*, Mum. So my period arrived, and it was, I dunno, like a tsunami. Follow me? A bloody river of menstruation. It stained everything. Or at least my jeans. I pretended to faint out of shame. Professor Lane brought me home. For the record: he's not a paedo. Didn't touch me or anything. I called on the way but Mirela said you weren't taking any calls.'

'Oh, I'm so sorry, darling,' Isla said. She was trying not to look concerned or laugh. 'How are you feeling now?' She went up to her daughter and understood there was no way she was going to let Isla hug her. 'I'm glad you're home now.' Then, 'Antonia, this is Valeria Costas, your favourite writer.'

'"Your favourite writer" – what is she, an ice-cream flavour? Don't talk like this, Mum.' This was mumbled, but her face lit up. She walked over to Valeria and smiled a beautiful smile. She was full of light and Valeria absorbed it all.

'It's an honour to meet you, Ms Costas. Of course it's you. Sorry for the tsunami fun. You are a great and true inspiration. I know one of your stories by heart.'

'Thank you,' Valeria said. 'I'm so glad you took the time to read my stories, Antonia. And thank you for making it possible for me to be here.'

'Why would you thank me?'

'For convincing your mother.'

'She wanted this badly,' Antonia smiled, looking between the two adults. 'Get your stories straight, girls.'

'Well, thank you anyway,' Valeria said. So Isla was a liar too?

'We're lucky to have you here,' Antonia said. 'Thank *you.*'

Both Isla and Valeria were impressed with Antonia's performance. In a matter of seconds though, Antonia was back to being a teenager and to her own darkness.

'Oh, and Mum? You should be aware that your son Cosmo is an absolute prick. Today he was tormenting one of the older kids at school. He is a pain in the arse. Kill him.' And with that, she left the room.

'She's beautiful,' Valeria said. 'Does she write?'

'I've no idea,' Isla said. 'She used to tell me everything, but now she doesn't tell me a thing. Anyway, shall we?' She darted her eyes in the direction of the stool.

Valeria resumed her position. She adjusted her shoulder, put her right foot slightly in front of her. Isla looked at her, her head tilted to one side. She came closer.

'May I?' Isla said, and with her hands she gently moved Valeria's body.

Her touch was electric. From the remote lands of coma, Martin was unable to touch them.

TEN

'Antonia can't sleep, we don't understand why,' Martìn had told Valeria, six or seven years before. 'She used to be so easy as a little girl, always cuddling, sleeping well, treating people kindly. Now she's nervous and unhappy.'

Valeria imagined Antonia being angry because of some mistake her parents were making. Childhood for her and Sybilla had been shaped that way. England. Greece. Anger.

When Antonia came back from school with bite marks on her arm, Martìn and Isla decided that she should start seeing a psychologist.

'Who did it?' Isla had asked Antonia. 'Let me call the parents of this beast.'

Antonia wouldn't answer. She wouldn't say a name. After hours of cuddling and talking, bursting into tears, her mouth trembling, Antonia had finally said, 'I did it to myself.'

The biting went on for a while. She had bites on her

legs. On her shoulders. She would bite her tongue so hard it bled.

The only thing that would sometimes stop her was food.

It took another six months of anxiety and therapy to put some of the pieces together. Antonia had fallen in love with a girl, a redhead named Julia, who was the daughter of a model and a footballer. Antonia and Julia were in class together. They were best friends, the two of them, with a third girl in their group, Lara. Antonia had sleepovers at their house and Julia used to come visit them often. Antonia, Julia and Lara were seen as the cool girls.

When Antonia realized that she loved Julia, she also realized that she might become unpopular. Still, given the fact that there might be a chance for Julia to love her back, she was tempted by the idea of telling her everything. She'd dream that they could love each other. She'd dream of that love being part of their coolness too.

'She is only nine,' Valeria said to Martìn, when she heard the whole story.

'You mean love can't hurt you when you are nine?'

'I mean it's a lot to hold in a tiny heart.'

Antonia had decided to tell Julia. She did it while they were watching a cartoon in Julia's bed, holding hands.

'I love you,' Antonia said, just as the mice were being attacked by the cat, which turned out to be a mouse in a cat costume. The lousy, lying mouse.

'I love you too,' Julia answered looking at the screen.

'I love you like a girlfriend,' Antonia said. 'Do you love me like a girlfriend? Can I kiss you?' She was smiling.

Julia didn't look at Antonia. She released her hand. She switched off the cartoon and all the mice disappeared. With them, all the lousy liars of the world disappeared too. Julia moved from the bed and turned on the bedroom light. She stood near the door.

'Go away,' she told her. 'Go away, gay.'

Antonia begged. She told Julia that she was sorry. That actually it was a joke! Like the mouse with the cat. Was she such a good actress?

'You are disgusting and you are gay,' Julia said. 'Get out.'

From that day on Julia didn't speak to Antonia. Neither did Lara. Had Julia told Lara that Antonia was disgusting and gay? Antonia didn't even know what gay meant. She had to look it up in the dictionary: *Of a person (especially a man) homosexual.* The definition didn't make it any clearer. Especially a man? The only thing she knew for sure was that Julia's parents never spoke to Antonia or her parents again. That's when the biting started. Antonia was restless, until finally there came the summer, when the Aclàs spent their time together as a family in Sicily. During that Sicilian summer, Antonia learned that pain does ease with time and decided that Julia was a bitch.

'I want to live like this always,' she had told her father. They were lying on a rock, drying in the sunshine after a swim. The twins were playing in the water. 'Always, all of us, together. No one going anywhere. Well, you might want to get rid of the twins, and that's fine, you can. But for the rest, this is all very good for me.'

That summer Martìn didn't fly back to Valeria.

'Antonia is well for the first time in two years,' he told her.

He didn't add he couldn't leave Isla either. That she too was a mess that summer. He didn't know how to help his wife and he couldn't share that with Valeria, even though it was obvious to her. His secrecy from her about his marriage difficulties was a first, but Valeria knew she only had to say, 'I understand. It's the right thing to do.'

So Valeria fled Paris and ended up in a house on Shelter Island, owned by one of Joe's friends. Singles, and people without families, would gather there each August. During her time there, she partied hard, smoked a lot and didn't take Martìn's phone calls. The house was full of random dogs too, so she would walk on the beach with them.

'Deal with your thing,' she had told Martìn after he had called ten times in one morning. 'I understand that you must be there. But be there and don't call me.'

When they finally met up again in September, it was clear that out of the two of them, Martìn had missed Valeria more. They were in her house in Paris, it was a warm night. They were lying in bed. The lights were off, the only brightness coming from the fading blue of the late summer sky.

'I might teach that seminar in Bilbao. I won't be able to see you for a while,' Valeria had said.

'Is it a good university?' Martìn had asked.

Valeria ignored his question. 'The real plus for me is that I could eat *pinchos* every night. For three months,' she had said instead.

She had already declined Bilbao. She also thought *pinchos* were disgusting. She only wanted to make Martìn feel worse, to scare him and let him know that he could lose her. She wanted to show him a possible story in which their relationship would fall apart.

Martìn was in a delicate mood throughout the rest of that evening. Then he became inquisitive. Who had been with her in that house in Shelter Island? What had Valeria done? Who had she talked to most of the time?

'How is Antonia doing?' Valeria asked him the morning after.

They were having coffee in bed. They had cancelled everything that was in their diaries until eleven. Then they cancelled everything until 2pm. Eventually, they decided to take the whole day off and stay in bed.

'She looks happy again, most of the time,' Martìn said.

Antonia's happiness lasted for about two years. It became more about the twins turning eleven – apparently an intense phase for boys – and all the difficulties that came with it. Cosmo was constantly answering back, while Nico was completely dependent upon Cosmo.

'Is it hard for you?' Valeria asked Martìn. 'With the twins, I mean.'

'Because there are two of them?'

'Because you and Rami were twins.'

'Yeah, got that one the first time around.'

'Well, is it?'

'It's healing, actually,' Martìn said. 'Rami and I are back with many of our memories.'

'Doesn't it also make you miss him more?'

'Everything does.'

Then Antonia became a teenager and her happiness dried up, while the twins adjusted once more. Cosmo and Nico discovered music. Nico was good at mathematics, Cosmo at drama. So Antonia was again the protagonist of many of Martìn's conversations.

'She ran away from home. We had to call the police,' Martìn had told Valeria. 'We found her with a group of women in this sort of anti-establishment commune. She told her mother she hates us and all we represent. She called her a spoilt hopeless bitch. Me, I'm just a dirty selfish capitalist.'

There were countless stories about Antonia of this sort. Valeria's favourite was very recent, just six months ago. It involved pole dancers and strippers.

'What do you mean she has her dinner at a strip joint?' Valeria had asked Martìn at the time.

'She's dating one of them,' Martìn said. 'Her name is Oksana, she's eighteen.'

'How did they even meet? Antonia is what, fifteen?' Valeria said.

'Antonia says it's none of our business how they met. And the twins also said that Oksana models bikinis for money. On social media.'

'How old are you?' Isla asked Valeria.

They had been in silence for the last half hour. The rain hadn't stopped. Valeria's back twinged.

This felt like how a friendship starts at a playground: what's your name? How old are you? Your husband always liked Bach?

'Fifty-five. You?'

Valeria knew they were the same age. She also knew that Isla was a Libra, wanted to visit Zimbabwe and still played tennis. She knew that she had broken her leg ten years ago, skiing in Switzerland, and that she did Ashtanga yoga on Sundays and Tuesdays at eleven. Valeria and Martìn's phone calls were longer when Isla was at yoga. She also knew that when Isla and Martìn found out they were going to have twins, Isla had laughed so hard she peed in her trousers.

Valeria had asked for a break then. The pee anecdote hadn't helped and the whole concept of another pregnancy was this time too close to that of Martìn holding Isla, caressing her belly, kissing her, choosing her over and over again.

'I will always come back,' Martìn said. 'Unless you tell me otherwise.'

'That's a shitty thing to say. I'll just imagine you're dead,' Valeria said with the saddest of smiles. 'Does a plane crash sound good to you?'

'Have you seen the Giacometti exhibition?' Valeria asked Isla.

What was it, small-talk? Theodora's monks would have hated it. 'I haven't, no,' Isla said, her eyes darting away from the canvas only briefly towards Valeria. 'I'm scared to leave the house. I'm scared that my husband will die while I'm out. I can't even make myself go get groceries.'

'What do the doctors say?' Valeria asked.

'They say that groceries are not important,' Isla said. 'That I can do online shopping or someone else can go.'

The joke was so sweet they both smiled.

'They say he has locked-in syndrome now,' continued Isla. For a moment she stopped drawing. She looked at Valeria. Was she checking her reaction? Did Isla know about them?

'It's a condition in which the patient is aware but cannot move or communicate verbally, due to complete paralysis. Even his eyes are paralysed.'

'How do they know he is aware?' Valeria's voice broke halfway through *aware*. The 'a' was like climbing a Himalayan-high capital A.

'They know because it's characteristic of the syndrome.'

Valeria tried to remain calm. But her stomach clenched into a ball. Then a black hole. Isla went on, her voice flat and robotic, her words coming one after the other without respite, like a chant, a mantra, a curse.

Valeria imagined building a space shuttle to be able to float in the black hole of her fear.

'Locked-in syndrome usually results in quadriplegia and the inability to speak in otherwise cognitively intact individuals. Those with locked-in syndrome can communicate with others through coded messages by blinking or moving their eyes.' Isla sounded as though she were reading from a medical textbook. 'But Martin's eyes, as I was telling you, are paralysed, so, too bad: no coded messages in this house. Patients with locked-in syndrome can sometimes retain sensation throughout their bodies. Which is frightening. And claustrophobic.'

Isla had not stopped drawing. She stepped back from the easel and observed the sketch on the canvas.

Valeria counted. To twenty. Then thirty. Sixteen billion.

'I'll try a bit more but we might have to start again,' Isla said, looking at what she had just done. 'If I can't get the head right... I'm sorry, it's going to take a while.'

Hold it together, Valeria. Her palms were sweating, all the air in the room had disappeared. She tried counting some more. Then thinking about how the sketch might look. She imagined a weirdly shaped head. A pear? Breathe.

'That's verbatim, from Wikipedia,' Isla said. 'Locked-in. What a horrifying end.'

Did Isla just say end?

'Sorry,' Valeria said and quickly left the room. In the cloakroom beyond the kitchen, she fell to her knees and threw up.

'Is he even a boyfriend?' Valeria has asked her mother in Rome.

'Yes,' Theodora had said. 'Matteo is my boyfriend.'

Valeria had vomited on the floor, just like any time Valeria's claustrophobia became unbearable. Of course it always made the situation much worse.

'I hate you,' she had told Theodora.

And as if the word *hate* was an abracadabra, the lift jolted and began moving again. Valeria could not remember Theodora being with a man since her father. It was absurd to have met this Italian at the airport after flying in from Rhodes, then to have gone for a coffee with him in Rome and, after only a handful more dinners, to have moved to his neighbourhood. Two months later they were living together and by the summer they were getting married. Clearly it was fucked up.

'Who is this man we are living with?' Valeria had protested. 'Why are you doing this to us?'

Theodora couldn't say Sybilla. Theodora couldn't say Rhodes. Theodora couldn't mention Valeria's father unless in the form of her rehearsed sentence. She couldn't listen to her daughter or be the person she had been before. She had become a character in a play, and she was performing her lines with effort. She wanted to be real like actresses want to be real and just like most actresses, she wasn't. Theodora didn't know how to walk, or eat, or smile without faking it. From that broken smile a monster would one day emerge, screaming all its agony.

'You are inadequate,' Valeria had told her, 'you are a terrible mother.'

Valeria would constantly try to make Theodora cry. Making her cry felt real. After all it was common knowledge that actresses who can cry are generally better. She wanted her words to be able to hurt, to reach her mother's heart and allow the sadness to sink in. After many failed attempts, one morning she succeeded.

'Sybilla got cancer because you raised us in your pain. You never let us be happy. Our life is your fault. Her death is your fault.'

The sentence seemed to do the trick and Theodora had given in to tears, but after half an hour, she emerged from her bedroom as if nothing had happened. She was wearing a blue dress and sunglasses. Theodora asked Valeria if she wanted to go with her to see the Modern Art Museum near Villa Borghese, so they went to the museum and walked through the rooms in silence. She studied her mother's shoes as they glided over the wooden floors, the rhythm of her steps in sync with the beat of Valeria's heart.

'I'm not going to learn Italian,' Valeria had told her mother.

'Me neither,' Theodora had said.

They both did. Valeria, now fifteen years old, also managed to get a scholarship for the American High School in Rome where she hung out with privileged kids who spoke English and Italian. They talked about smoking, snorting, snogging and having sex. None of them had the vaguest idea of what growing up barefoot on a tiny island was like. None knew of the space left by the loss of Sybilla and that there was a crater between Valeria and the rest of the world.

A couple of times Valeria attended parties thrown by the spoilt, druggie kids. Once she was asked to the countryside by one of them and only accepted the invite because it was a chance to get away from Theodora and her flaky new husband.

'What do you do in your life?' Valeria would ask Matteo.

'I have that land, outside Rome. We make wine.'

'You mean your family has that land,' Valeria would clarify. '*They* make wine.'

'We do it together,' Matteo would answer.

Valeria never smiled at him. Sometimes, in her twenties, and even in her thirties, Valeria had thought of tracking him down just to go and give him a smile. 'Here are the two hundred smiles I never gave you,' she would tell Matteo. Then she would attempt two hundred different smiles in sequence.

Still in the cloakroom Valeria rinsed her face and her mouth. There was a knock on the door. She breathed deeply. Another knock. I want to disappear, she thought. She snapped her fingers, but didn't disappear. Why am I not able to use my superpowers yet?

'Are you OK?' Isla asked from outside the door.

'I am. Just give me two minutes.'

The minutes became five. Ten. When Valeria came out she still wasn't OK at all. 'Sorry, it's been a rough week,' she said.

'Are you crying?' Isla asked.

'I might have a cold,' Valeria said. 'Having a cold makes me very sad, that's it.'

They both tried to smile at the silly joke, somehow pretending that nothing major had happened, and agreed to meet again the following morning.

'I'm sorry, Martìn,' Valeria murmured when descending the eight elegant steps outside. 'Maybe I won't be able to come to you after all. See? I'm leaving your home. You are locked-in up there, I'm locked-in down here.'

ELEVEN

Ten years before, Martìn had been arrested. Everything, in a day like any other, for Valeria collapsed. The minutes and hours that passed from when she heard the news, until Martìn's phone call, felt eternal. She was in prison too.

'I have a cold,' she said to Martìn when he finally rang. Back then too, she had been crying. How she could think of herself as strong and independent, yet cry so much, was a mystery to her.

'It's nothing terrible, Valeria,' Martìn was telling her. 'I can't be on top of everything. I can't control what the people I work with do. If a CFO in China is a thief, or if engineers sell our ideas under the counter, I might very well be the last one to know. That's the whole point of stealing.'

'You are the one going to jail,' Valeria said.

'They need a few days where nobody can have access to anything,' Martìn told her.

Valeria imagined herself being the wife of some mafia guy. She was wearing a lace dress that would have been perfect in a black-and-white film. Even if her husband was a murderer she would still love him. Who fucking cared about the victims, right? She loved him and he loved her, their five children and the enormous farm in the countryside where they grew truckloads of oranges. Oranges were just a cover-up for their criminal life, but nevertheless they were juicy ones. When Valeria cut them, the juice of the oranges was so red it reminded her of all the blood on which their farm was built. But then again, it was also full of vitamin C, for all her criminal children and all her criminal relatives, to cure the flu.

Valeria wrote a story while Martin was in jail. It was called 'The Light Line'. The story started with a ten-page-long telephone conversation between a nun and a man named Nick who was now in jail for armed robbery and kidnapping. The man had asked to speak to his mother, who had declined. Then, to his second wife, who had also declined. Speaking to the nun had been a policeman's idea. The previous Wednesday, during the weekly meeting, and still drunk from the night before, the policeman, Steven, had in fact been talked through one of the new services available to inmates: a suicide-prevention line they could use when in need, called the Light Line. Listening to the presentation, Steven the policeman had sipped his black coffee, nodding excessively. He was sure he was about to lose his job. His drinking was out of control and he had ended too many nights sleeping in the car, hoping that nobody would find out. In a way, being fired was going to be a relief.

'Mitch, I know nothing about you,' the nun said to Nick. 'How can I get to know you better?'

'You could start by remembering my name,' the convicted man smiled. 'It's Nick.'

The nun had a very young voice. It was difficult for Nick not to think about her sexually. He imagined her bent over a table, her buttocks fresh and gently open, just for him to stare at. He felt guilty.

'And you, at what age did you became a nun?'

'I was sixteen.'

Nick did what he could not to picture the nun at sixteen, on her knees, praying. He got an erection, which he disliked, and turned to face the wall so the alcoholic policeman would not see it. Why was he sitting there anyway? Did he really have to listen to all Nick's conversations or was he just lazy?

'What's your name?' Nick asked the nun.

'Eugenie.'

'Are you a talker or a listener, Sister Eugenie?'

'It depends on the situation,' Eugenie answered.

'What are you now?'

'You called me, Nick, so I guess I'm more of a listener tonight.'

Nick was already in love. And he remained so for ever. He spent another twenty-two years in jail, never thinking about killing himself again. Only when a policeman named Steven committed suicide in the showers, and because Nick remembered him as one of the kind ones, did he realize how close he had been to taking his own life.

He would call Eugenie every Friday and most times the call would last one hour. After a few of these calls, Eugenie started to visit him. The first time Nick saw her he could barely open his mouth. Eugenie was tiny, pale.

'Shall I be a talker today?' Eugenie asked him.

That morning she spoke non-stop for the entire meeting. She told him about the school where she was teaching French.

'I'm very lucky to have you in my life,' she also told Nick.

Years later, he was moved to a new prison, a modern, progressive place, without cells. The prisoners were called the *inhabitants* and on Friday nights they could have guests. Nick was one of the cooks and he often invited Eugenie. If he didn't invite her, he wouldn't invite anyone. He had written tens of letters to his wives and said his sorrys to all his ex-business partners. *I'm sorry for all your pain and all my mistakes,* he told everybody. *I wish I could do it all differently. I pray for having the chance. I pray for there to be a next life, very similar to this one but simpler, in which I will be honest and kind. As for now, and from this one life, I am asking you to forgive me and, if in any way possible, to let go of the anger.*

After another ten years, Nick left prison.

'Do you want to come and live with me?' Eugenie asked him that day. And Nick had immediately answered yes.

After leaving the Aclàs' home, Valeria headed for Holland Park Avenue. There, she entered an organic deli. The lighting was perfect, cheerful. The shelves were made of a wood that begged to be caressed. So be it. And what was with the over-joyous sentences written everywhere? *Keep calm* and then? *Your coffee* is my what? Over the fridge she read, *Follow Your Dreams.* The sentence was right above the soy-based products. To the right side of the products was written, *What if soy milk was Spanish for regular milk?*

Valeria sat down at the counter by the window. Overhead hung a giant blackboard with *Inhale Love, Exhale Gratitude* handwritten on it in chalk. Valeria accepted the advice and inhaled love and exhaled gratitude. Some sadness was inhaled too. Bits of angst were also exhaled. She grabbed an overpriced apple juice labelled *Life, Like Apples* and went to pay.

The cashier was a red-headed girl with rainbow braces on her teeth and what looked like a hundred glittery earrings in one ear. Her name must have been something like Polly or Sally. Sally/Polly hated Holland Park. She hated everything about her life and all the reasons that led her to being here now. Her earrings were a sarcastic weapon with which to blind the rich, making fun of their idiotic love for idiotically expensive things that idiotically shine.

That afternoon, Valeria wrote for a couple of hours and was out for her run by seven. She jogged to Holland Park, zipped up in a rain jacket. She turned up her music. At least let's make the darkness portentous, she thought. At least let's make it epic. She ran for forty minutes and it was so wet it felt like she was swimming. Back at home she undressed and stretched, naked. Her body was changing at such a pace it made her think about how soon she would lose her teeth and eventually die. She took a long, warm shower, washed her sitter clothes, the purple panties and her stockings. She hung them near the heater and and called an Indian take-away.

'Do you have red wine?' Valeria asked after ordering too much food.

'Yes, we have a Shianti,' answered the woman at the other end of the call.

'Sorry? Shanti?'

'Toscanna wine, Sh-i-anti.'

'Oh, Chianti. Toscana. Yes, perfect.'

When the food arrived the wine bottle said Shianti, Toscanna. It was probably a fake Chianti, grown in this invented place called Toscanna. Valeria googled the wine. On the website there was a customer care number. What time was it where the call centre was? Valeria clicked on the phone symbol.

'I'm Milo, how can I help you?'

'Oh, hello Milo,' Valeria said. 'Where is Toscanna?'

'Our farm is called Toscanna. So the vineyards around here are called Toscanna too. It's where we do the wine.'

'What is Shianti?' she asked.

'A grape.'

'Is this to try and make people think they are drinking Chianti from Tuscany?'

'What is Chianti?' Milo said.

Valeria poured herself some wine. She tried it. Could she toast to Milo?

'How is the weather there?' she asked him. What was the weather like in Rhodes? What was Theodora looking at this second?

'No windows. I don't know,' Milo said. 'And there?'

'It's raining in London. And it's night-time.'

'Have you been helped by my answers?'

'A great deal.'

'So, good night and enjoy Shianti, the wine from the hills of Toscanna,' Milo said, sounding like a voiceover for a TV commercial. The commercial would have a sunset, a big, large glass of wine on a wooden table on a fake hill in fake Toscanna.

'Are there hills there?' Valeria asked.

'I didn't say hills. I said the wine from the mills of Toscanna,' Milo muttered.

Valeria ended the call and the hills disappeared from her mind's eye. She found the corkscrew and opened the Shianti. She drank while eating the vegetarian curry, the samosas and the dhal, while watching a documentary about Alberto Giacometti on YouTube. The Wi-Fi connection was bad, probably because of the rain, or maybe because of her sins, some kind of divine retribution. The documentary kept freezing. The best unwanted pause was a shot of the hand of Giacometti drawing. On the canvas, the eyes of the sitter were starting to appear. Valeria paused together with the video's pause, and so she stopped everything, all actions, all thoughts. Only when the video started again did she breathe again and finish her second glass of wine.

She then went to brush her teeth. The wrinkles cutting across her mouth were sad. Poor mouth, she thought. Poor me. With a fingertip she tried to erase the wrinkles around her lips. Going back and forth with the tip of it was like caressing the void. She was the void. The wrinkles disappeared. The mouth disappeared.

Maybe if I go back and forth with my finger over my entire body, over all these words, I will disappear too.

TWELVE

Good morning, Ms Costas,' Mirela said, walking Valeria to the living room. 'Mrs Aclà is upstairs with the doctor. She apologizes for making you wait. Last night wasn't so good.'

'Oh, not to worry,' Valeria said.

Last night wasn't so good? Are you dying, Martìn, because I am not near you? Or was last night not so good because I'm *too* near you and you feel me as a threat?

'Something to drink?' Mirela asked. Valeria hesitated, during which time Mirela probably felt homesick thinking about the North Pole, the icebergs and all those beautiful seals.

'A juice would be great, thanks. It looked very healthy yesterday,' Valeria said.

'Red, green or blue?' Mirela asked.

'Red?'

As soon as Mirela had disappeared, Valeria made her way upstairs. She took every step as quietly as possible, but her heart was beating so fast it was unthinkable that no one else could hear it. Besides, the stairs were wooden, complete silence was impossible.

Is their bedroom on the first floor? she wondered. I bet they chose the top floor for them – privacy from the kids and all that crap. Why have kids if you don't want to be close to them?

Valeria couldn't hear any voices or movement. She stopped at the first landing, in front of a painting. It was of Antonia, seated, her head turned to face the painter, her tongue sticking out in happiness. Had Antonia sat with her tongue out at her mother for days?

'Let me get it for you,' Isla was saying.

Valeria stopped breathing. She heard Isla walking, opening a door and walking back again. They were on the same floor. Martìn and Isla had chosen the first floor, not the privacy of the third one. Shit, Mirela was going to come back with the red juice any minute now. Valeria walked up one last step and found herself in the corridor. She could hear where the voices were coming from, so she followed them. Her back was covered in sweat. Her mouth was dry. She heard the sound of an oxygen machine. Other random beeps and medical noises made their way to her brain. Behind that door was Martìn! They were divided by ten or fifteen steps maximum.

She remembered when she and Martìn had that discussion about how women are more able to be near sickness than men. Martìn argued that it wasn't true. The two of them were in bed in Spain, lights off, the window open with the sounds of Madrid filling the room.

'Would you be near me, during a long sickness?' Valeria asked.

Martìn lit a cigarette. Valeria smiled, even though he couldn't see her. She didn't want the night to be a sad one.

'What's with the suspense?'

'I will be the one to die first,' Martìn said.

'No way. This time I want to die first,' Valeria replied.

The bleeps were getting closer. It was the sound of anxiety. Of losing control, identity, the future. It was a countdown. Valeria took another step, tried another breath, then another one. Through the slightly open door she suddenly saw Martìn. Oh. Oh my. Her heart was about to explode. There you are, my love.

With his face just visible to Valeria, the beeps and bleeps started getting easier. Now they were the sound of life, the rhythm of when things are calm and ready to heal. No alarms were sounding, because nothing was alarming. Life is still here. We are still here, too.

Martìn's eyes were closed, his face looked serene. Even though he had a cannula coming out of his neck, which looked painful, he seemed fine. His face wasn't any different.

Open your eyes, Martìn, now you can – now I'm here for you to look at me.

Perhaps he was slightly different – chunkier? Valeria tilted her head to mirror his.

I love you. Not seeing Shibuya Tokyo together is totally fine. Who needs Shibuya anyway. We have us.

'I think it's still worth trying, Isly,' a man was saying. 'It's definitely what I'd do.'

'He was blue, Lenny,' Isla was saying. 'This morning, at breakfast, Antonia couldn't even speak. Still, I know Martìn wants to stay home. It's something we discussed. We want to be together.'

Blue? What the fuck. What did she mean they'd 'discussed' it? Had he already known he was sick and never mentioned it to Valeria? She imagined Martìn's face in blue like a character in a kids' movie. She couldn't bring herself to think of him medically blue, choking. About to die. And why did the man call Isla 'Isly'?

'Ms Costas?' Valeria heard from downstairs.

Mirela was already back. From Martìn's room there was a silence. Valeria moved as quickly and as soundlessly as she could. She tried to surf down the wooden stairs but her panic didn't help. Some steps were creaking and squeaking. It could be Rock the dog, right? Or Mirela, or someone else. Why would Isla have to think it was her? Valeria made it back to the ground floor before Isla appeared, looking down from the first floor.

'Oh, good morning, Valeria. It *is* you. Everything all right?' she said.

'Yes, sorry, good morning. I was just, um, looking for the loo?' It came out like a question, as if to say, *Is this lie that I'm offering you believable?*

Isla paused.

No, the lie wasn't going to work.

A man appeared beside her. He was handsome, in his late fifties.

'Good morning,' he said to Valeria. He was looking down, she was looking up. 'I'm Doctor Hayes.'

'Nice to meet you, Doctor Hayes. I'm Writer Costas. These days I'm also Sitter Costas.' The little joke didn't come out as funny as Valeria had hoped. It wasn't even a joke, she realized. 'I didn't want to disturb you. Sorry.'

'We were just finishing,' Isla said. 'Two minutes and I'll be all yours. '

Valeria walked to the living room. Two minutes and Isla was going to be all hers. That was a very short time, two minutes, and a very big commitment. When and how did Martìn ask Isla to marry her? Valeria wondered during those two minutes. Oh yes, after the tennis champion had been beaten, Martìn proposed at the cinema, before a movie. An elastic band as the ring.

'After Isla said yes, I heard some crying from the seat behind us. I turned around and it was two elderly ladies. We went for dinner with them afterwards,' Martìn had told Valeria.

Were they at that point in New York or in London? Valeria couldn't remember. She imagined them with both Big Ben and the Empire State Building behind them. In her mind she made two postcards of the scene. On the back she wrote 'the beginning of us'. Then she erased 'the beginning' and just left 'us'. She imagined sending the postcards to Antonia.

'Ms Costas, your juice is on the table,' Mirela said, joining her near the fireplace. The stunning polar bear seemed annoyed. 'You have to drink it now for the vitamins. They die soon.'

Valeria picked up the glass. Her legs were shaking and her stomach had shrunk to the size of a marble. She sipped the juice.

'You're pale, Ms Costas,' Mirela said. 'I will make you a juice every day: I will make all colours.' And she went back downstairs to the basement. Or maybe to an igloo.

Valeria sat next to the fireplace. The excitement of seeing Martìn - his marvellous, calm, beautiful face - and the juice in her stomach was comforting. Strangely right. But it left her without strength. She closed her eyes. Antonia in the painting, with her tongue out, was graceful. She was beautiful, like her father.

'Ms Costas?' Dr Hayes was saying.

Valeria pulled herself together and attempted a smile. Dr Hayes walked towards her and she stood. They shook hands. He smelled of pepper, lemon, something sweet. Another fruit? Was he an old friend of Martìn? What was his first name? Lenny. Nope, didn't ring a bell.

'I have to go,' he said, pointing at the door. 'I'm running late for the hospital. But I wanted to tell you that I'm a huge fan, Ms Costas. I'm glad you and Isla are working on a portrait. It's very good for her right now. She needs distraction, she deserves beauty. I can't wait to see what you two come up with.'

'I'm very glad too,' Valeria said. 'Thank you for reading my work.'

Did he mean that Valeria was beautiful or that the process of drawing was beautiful?

Dr Hayes smiled again, and there was an awkward pause in which neither of them said anything. Valeria imagined a short film of all the awkward pauses in one's life, the truth revealed in the seconds before social skills kicked in, between silence and wanting to speak, raw epiphanies of humankind. In today's pause Len Hayes smiled again. And Valeria did the same. When he had gone, Valeria turned around and caught a glimpse of herself in the mirror. She wore a gigantic beetroot moustache.

When Isla and Valeria entered the studio, it was much colder than in the other rooms. Valeria shivered.

'Something must be wrong with the radiator. Let's light the fire,' Isla said.

She disappeared into the kitchen and returned with more wood.

Valeria saw herself having sex with Martìn in front of a lit fireplace in Bruxelles.

Isla looked ten years older than the previous day. All her movements were nervous, unsettled. What had she seen last night? Valeria knew Isla hadn't been lucky these last few years. Martìn had told her that she had nursed her mother for a long time. Her mother was still living in New York, which made it worse: Isla felt guilty when she wasn't there with her, but whenever she went to New York to visit, she felt guilty about not being with her children. What was Isla's mother's name? Valeria had pinned it down somewhere. Leona! Yes. Leona had dementia and had deteriorated rapidly.

'Mirela, sorry, can I please have a coffee?' Isla called out. 'Would you like one?' she asked Valeria.

'No, thank you. I had juice.'

'I need it. I haven't slept a wink. My husband had a breathing crisis last night. I still feel like I'm choking. I can't get rid of this sense of emergency.'

Valeria's throat tightened and she felt like choking too.

'What happened?' she asked.

'Can you believe it? Fucking saliva. Went down the wrong fucking way.'

I love Martìn's saliva, Valeria thought. I will for ever. How can I go upstairs and see him? If I touch him I will understand if he is going to be OK. Or if he's going to die. Why can Isla be near him and I can't? I should tell everyone. Now.

Isla drank her coffee. She went to the stereo and switched on Bach. Then she turned it off.

'Are you sure you want to do this now? I can come back tomorrow,' Valeria said. 'I'm not writing nearly enough. I could use the morning.'

'Please, stay,' Isla said. 'We have to do this.'

THIRTEEN

When Valeria bought Isla's painting of Martìn, she was prepared to spend up to ten thousand pounds. As soon as she learnt from Martìn that four of Isla's works were going to go on sale, she registered for the auction. Filling in the Christie's form felt like a declaration of guilt. She now existed officially in Isla's life and she existed with a surname, a phone number, a date of birth, a bank account. From this day on the two women were linked. Even if there was a privacy protection clause in the contract, still, somewhere, somehow, in a folder inside some random office drawer, Valeria's name was now connected to Isla's. But the decision was made and Valeria was going to bid over the phone.

The month before the auction, Valeria compulsively studied the portrait of Martìn. The unfinished section, or the part that appeared unfinished, was elusive, leaving space for interpretation. How long had it taken to paint? A single month? Longer? Why was Isla selling it? It was magnificent, moving. How could Valeria buy it and be sure that Martìn would never know? Even if she bought it, she would never be able to hang it. Hiding it and having just another secret was more like her. And them.

'How is it possible to sell a portrait of your husband or daughter?' Valeria had asked Martìn. She immediately regretted the question. She didn't want to reveal how much she knew about the auction. Martìn looked surprised.

'How is it possible to sell a story of your mother?' he asked.

'There is only one copy of a portrait. Maybe the painting will never be on display again. How can a painter accept that? How can you let it go?'

There was something missing in the equation. But she was afraid of appearing too involved, of being caught saying something too Isla-related that would make Martìn suspicious. She could have spent the rest of the day speaking about the portrait. Perhaps even the rest of her life. But she didn't, and when the auction took place Valeria made a point of not asking Martìn anything about it afterwards. She was in Paris, he was in London. That evening she cut the phone call short.

'I'm sorry, it's been such a busy day. Tomorrow we'll have more time,' Valeria said.

'I'm happy I heard your voice,' Martìn said.

After winning the auction, Valeria made sure she hid all letters from Christie's, and the catalogue. Just to be safe, she made sure the portrait was delivered on a day when Martìn was in China.

The stool was in its place from the day before, its exact position drawn out in white chalk on the floor. Valeria walked towards it. It felt both like having to sit in a session with a therapist, and going onstage. It was intimate and completely public. The process of finding yesterday's position, before looking at Isla, had already become a rehearsed performance. Valeria walking to the stool, Valeria slowly taking off her jacket – with exactly the same movements as the previous day – and sitting in the same way. Occupying that same space, physically and emotionally.

Isla was looking at Valeria. Just as it had the previous day, her gaze changed as she assessed her subject. Valeria's face felt like it was changing too, as she looked inside herself to become what she had been yesterday. Or what she intended to be from now on. Was that even possible? There was going to be a layer of time on that portrait and every day her face was different – not only her face but everything about her, and the world, and Isla.

'How will you paint me?' Valeria said. She didn't say 'fuck you'. Or 'Martìn has always loved me too, you know?'

'That depends entirely on what you show me, sir,' Isla smiled.

'Sir?' Valeria asked.

'It's what Graham Sutherland said to Winston Churchill. He was asked the same question.'

Isla walked towards Valeria and lifted her chin up. She went back a few steps and again she was near Valeria, adjusting her blouse. Valeria could smell Martìn on Isla. Her heart opened.

Come here, Isla. Closer.

'Here we are,' Isla said and she went back to her painting. When Isla drew Martìn what did she see? What did he show her?

'Have you ever been a sitter?' Valeria asked.

'Sitting is for the brave,' Isla smiled.

I'm braver, Valeria thought. The fuck you are, Sybilla answered.

'So you have.'

'It wasn't my choice, but I did,' Isla said. 'I'd always rather be on this side.'

'We both would, I'm afraid.'

'We don't want to fade. On either side,' Isla said. Or maybe it was Valeria who said it. But the sentence was voiced, in the Aclà home, by someone, that day, in that studio.

The rest of the morning was spent in silence. Stopping herself from running upstairs to Martìn's room was Valeria's sole mission. *Don't die. Wait for me. Don't disappear.* It was probably the same for Isla too. The rain outside was incessant, the grey and darkness worsening with each passing minute. Their work went uninterrupted, apart from when Valeria stood up to shake off the tingling in her legs. Bach remained on stand-by.

'I think I need to go take a nap,' Isla said at around noon. 'I'm sorry.'

Valeria produced a tiny smile. Already?

She left the stool, put on her jacket and was escorted upstairs by Isla.

I am about to leave your house again, Martìn. But what can I do? Shall I scream, shall I come up?

'For the first time last night I thought that he was going to die,' Isla said when Valeria had her coat back on. 'I want to be in bed. Near him.'

Valeria bent her head and managed to nod again. She saw Isla spooning Martìn, the breathing machine as the soundtrack. She was never going to be able to do the same. Her lips tightened.

Martìn had just told me he wanted to live with me. I should be able to be in that bed too. Maybe it would help him, Valeria thought of telling her now. But instead she said, 'I hope you rest and feel better tomorrow. I hope your husband will be healthy again soon. I'm sure he is strong and tenacious.'

'He is, I'm not,' Isla said.

She handed Valeria her scarf and Valeria wrapped it around her neck with the door already open. It was so windy outside the curtains in the living room blew outwards. Valeria glanced over at the enormous voodoo face.

'Do you want to text me later to let me know if tomorrow is still on?' Valeria said.

'Tomorrow is on. We can have lunch here, then maybe work a while more in the afternoon.'

Lunch? Valeria panicked. She had to come up with something. But she was already out of the house.

Valeria didn't want to go back to the flat. Walking as fast as she could, she left Ilchester Place and after crossing Abbotsbury Road, she found herself in front of a bookshop and stood under its green awning. One of the windows displayed children's books. Adventures. Elephants. Space shuttles. The wind was getting stronger and it felt like a sign. She entered the shop because she believed the wind meant that, by pushing harder towards her.

'Welcome,' said a middle-aged woman. She was opening a box.

'Thank you,' Valeria said. Could she go out for lunch with the woman? Could they become fast friends so that she could receive a hug? 'What's in that box?' Valeria asked.

'Copies of a book on the best restaurants chosen by socially aware celebrities,' the woman said.

'Doesn't seem an easy sell,' Valeria said.

'Last year the yoga retreats picked by the same celebrities sold more than half a million copies here. Two in America.'

'May I?' Valeria picked up a copy. It weighed at least ten kilos. Before giving it back to the bookseller, she noticed her name badge. Rebecca. The badge looked home-made, shaped like a tiny mushroom. How old was Rebecca? Fifty? Three boys? Intelligent, cultivated. Secretly, she wishes she was more beautiful. But she has been loved and she loves in return. Maybe Valeria should tell Rebecca she is Valeria Costas the writer, so it would be easier to win her over for lunch?

'Rebecca, excuse me,' Valeria said, 'I don't want to

bother you. I'm a writer and I—'

'I know who you are,' Rebecca said. 'Valeria Costas. I love your work.'

'Oh, thank you,' Valeria mumbled, 'and thank you for reading me.'

'"Millennium" is one of the most important stories I've read in my life.'

'Wow. Thank you.'

'For what?' Rebecca asked.

'Oh. Right. Would you have any books on portraits?' Valeria tried.

'We do. Over there.' She gestured towards the back of the store. 'Let me know if you can't find them,' Rebecca said, and moved away from Valeria.

The hug wasn't going to come from her.

'Millennium' was a dark and raw story. Simple, without hope or warmth. It had been written over a couple of weeks, during Valeria's stay in the bed-and-breakfast where she was still trying to forget Patrick Toyle. It was about a woman living with her dogs on the outskirts of a small town outside Denver. It was one of the snowiest places in America. The woman liked living in a place that held a record. A record that had to do with snow, even more so. Sometimes the woman, whose name was possibly Anita, but Valeria by now couldn't remember any more, would drive for miles all the way back to Alamosa, to visit her brother whose name was possibly Sean. To do so, she would have to pay some random kid from her village to feed her dogs. Once in Alamosa, she would help out her brother for a few days with the kitchen, the house, the shopping. They'd always prepare a very rich dinner and they'd drink beer. Maybe-Anita and Maybe-Sean had lived this way all their lives. Her brother, just like Anita, didn't have a family of his own. She was a nurse, he was a mechanic. But one day, when Maybe-Anita was sixty and she was driving to see Maybe-Sean, her car broke down. Although her brother would have been able to fix it in minutes, she had no idea what to do, so she froze to death, trapped in the snow, near the Zapata Falls. Her last thought was how beautiful the Monte Vista looked that Monday, just before the white cancelled all things.

Valeria was looking at the poetry section without being grabbed by any of the books. Nothing directly about portraits around here. Or about how to deal with the pain of having a lover in a coma.

'Ms Costas?' someone said from the back.

Turning around she saw Antonia. She was holding a book in her hand, her finger in between the pages so as not to lose her place. Her hoodie was pulled over her head, black eyeliner smudged around her eyes and down her cheeks.

'Why aren't you at home with Mum?' Antonia said.

'She was tired so we called it a day. I'm sorry about last night,' Valeria told Antonia. 'I'm sorry for your father.'

'Yeah. It sucks,' Antonia said. 'Couldn't bring myself to go to school today. But I didn't want to be at home either. Please don't tell her.'

Oh right, school. Antonia was hiding. In a bookshop. Isla would love knowing that when Antonia skips school she hides in a bookshop round the corner from home. Had Martìn ever bought Valeria a book in this shop?

'Your secret is safe,' Valeria said. 'At your age I skipped school for months. Will you help me choose a few books? I want to read about portraits.'

Antonia nodded and together they explored the bookshop, picking up essays about artists, novels about paintings, a book on the colour red, a couple of painters' memoirs, a study about personal identity in the philosophy of science.

'Are you looking at this stuff because of Mum?' Antonia asked Valeria.

'Yes?' Valeria said. But as usual she wasn't sure, so as usual she added the question mark. Then, 'Lunch?'

'I will disappear,' Valeria had told Martìn. She sometimes wanted to scare him just to see what he would do. They were walking in the West Village, the air cold but the sun trying to make its way into their bodies. People with dogs had passed by, models, kids on skateboards. Valeria believed her own lie, because she could sometimes pretend she was a character from one of her stories. This particular character was strong, didn't need anybody, walked looking flawless around lower Manhattan. This character thought that if the world was such a striking place, like it was right here, on this corner, she was never going to be alone. There were so many roads to walk, so many people to get to know. She wanted to try all mouths, all tongues. She wanted to try the taste of all coffees in all of New York. Then, the world.

'You will disappear from me too?' Martin asked.

They were drinking green tea. Valeria hated green tea, but she was pretending that she liked it, being a woman who walks with green tea and is ready for life to surprise her. The only problem was that reaching Bank Street, Valeria realized she wanted to tell Martin the exact opposite. She wanted to tell him I love walking with you. How can it be so many years already, us walking the cities of this world? She wanted the romance, and to hear all of their words for love.

In New York they had to be careful, they knew people there, so they couldn't kiss, or hold hands. But walk closely to each other, that they could do. And sometimes touch each other's arms pretending it was casual, that they could do too.

'What would you do?' Valeria asked him.

'I would let you go,' Martin told her.

Valeria was so sad her expression changed. She tried her best not to show her pain and was thankful for the scarf that hid half of her face. She wanted to hear that he would never survive Valeria disappearing from his life. But instead, he would 'let her go'?

They walked to the Whitney Museum and through the *Collective Shiny Works* exhibition. Valeria lay down under a screening projected onto the ceiling, all bubbles and lines. She felt like she was going to sink into the floor, into the darkness of this day, of their story.

'You shouldn't let me go,' Valeria said to Martìn when he joined her under the projection. 'When I disappear you always come and look for me. And always bring me back.'

'Can you wear a colour I will see?' Martìn asked her. 'Purple? It would help me find you. I will come and get you but can you make it easier for me?'

'Purple will do,' Valeria said.

She moved her back closer to his, her body against his body. On the ceiling, bubbles and shapes that looked like little fish appeared. It was like being underwater without ever gasping for air.

FOURTEEN

Antonia and Valeria went to the pub around the corner. They asked for the menu and ordered drinks. Lemonade for Antonia, a beer for Valeria. All around them, chalkboards and papers on the tables let them know that the burger-and-drinks combo was ten pounds.

'Apple juice at the organic shop up the road costs the same,' Valeria said.

'But this makes you die. So what's more expensive?' Antonia said. 'I will have the three-cheese beef burger.'

'I'll have the three-cheese beef burger too.'

The rain outside the pub window fell horizontally, blown by wind gusts travelling at a thousand miles an hour. Was Martin still breathing all right? Can one gasp for air throughout an entire life?

'Aren't you writing today?' Antonia asked.

'I write every day for three or four hours, always and only in the afternoon,' Valeria replied, with more or less the same wording she had always used. She had been asked about her writing routine hundreds of times. And about where her ideas or her inspiration came from. She didn't mind such questions. Or those about writing in a second language. What she disliked were 'Is it autobiographical?' or 'Why did you not have kids?'

'Mum had a routine too. When she switched from performative art to painting, I mean.'

'When did she stop?'

'Too long ago to even remember.'

'What about the portrait of you with your tongue out?' Valeria said.

'Where did you see that?'

'I got lost at your place, looking for the loo.'

'Did you find it?' Antonia asked.

'Thanks, yes. So, did Isla stop painting because she had to take care of you kids?'

'Not quite sure of the real reasons. But thank you for blaming us,' Antonia smiled. 'Dad calls it "the performance". And he says it's a mystery.'

The mega burgers arrived, the three cheeses melting down the sides. Lettuce, bacon and what looked like half a kilo of meat were screaming to be eaten. Grabbing her bun Valeria was thrilled. The performance?

They attacked the bread and the meat, and halfway through the meal, Valeria attempted to ask Antonia about school, but Antonia refused to be distracted from the pleasure of eating.

Instead, she asked Valeria, 'So what's new? As a writer, I mean.'

'I've just finished a book, it'll be out in a few months. I still haven't got a title for it,' Valeria said. Some lettuce fell on the plate. She put it back in the bun, squeezing the bread around the burger.

'Isn't it late for the title?' Antonia asked.

'I guess so. The portrait your mother is painting is for that one.'

'Why did you choose Mum?'

'I find her work beautiful?' Question mark.

'She pretended she'd never heard of you. Not that I bought it. I'm sure you didn't either.'

Antonia said this with a rage that hadn't been there beforehand. Why did she say 'pretended'? Did Antonia know about Valeria and her father?

'I think she doesn't care about her work anyway. She's all about us, now,' Antonia said.

She said it as if the word 'us' had a smell and the smell wasn't too good.

'Usually kids complain about how much their parents work. Not about how much they devote their life to their family,' Valeria said.

'I didn't say she devoted herself to her family,' Antonia said. And she began to talk about how 'random' Isla was. Isla and her idiotic American family of lawyers and tennis whites, who had wanted their Isla to be pretty. To speak French. Spanish. To play the piano and be able to style her hair. The same boring basic things they wanted for their granddaughter. This, of course, until Grandma Leona developed dementia, which in a way came as a blessing because she became a nicer person and forgetting things meant forgetting Antonia's 'strange nose' too. Once she had even asked Antonia if

127

she wanted a new one for Christmas. Antonia was ten or eleven at the time. She hadn't even thought about her nose until that day.

'Well, after the call, I hated my nose. I still do,' Antonia said rubbing her nose. 'Of course, when Mum stopped being a radical artist and became a reassuring portrait artist, it cheered them all up. When she stopped being that too, she become exactly what they had hoped for: a mother who does school runs and yoga in edgy Ladbroke Grove. But the new Isla needed new ways to keep her mind occupied in the void.'

'What ways?' Valeria asked her.

'What do you think?' Antonia said. 'Banoffee?'

'Sure,' Valeria said, though she didn't really want the banoffee. She just wanted her voice to sound light and for Antonia not to stop talking. What new ways had Isla found to occupy the void? Lovers?

'My only hope is that she was faking that character too,' Antonia said.

'Was?' Valeria said. *Too?*

'Before Dad's stroke. And before you made her a painter again.'

Martin had told her many times that Antonia hated their set-up and their *lifestyle*. When Valeria was Antonia's age she had hated her family's *lifestyle* too, if their life had any style whatsoever. All she could see in Theodora was a selfish mother who had separated her from her father first, then from Sybilla. And from Rhodes. She was a mother who had coerced her daughter to live an absurd life, with a very odd Italian man. Theodora too was becoming a cliché, acting out a character for a performance. One that involved another man to call husband. 'What shall we have for dinner?' that character could say. 'And do you prefer to fuck with me on top tonight?'

'What is it that you like doing?' Valeria asked Antonia.

'What do you mean?'

'What makes you happy?'

'Do you have your own answer for that same question?'

'Right. Let me rephrase. What's your plan for this afternoon?'

'I wish I could just go to bed and sleep,' Antonia said. 'But usually I'm not back till three, so I'll have to stay out for quite a while. Can you lend me this one?' She touched the book about portraits in British history that Valeria had bought.

'Sure, keep it for as long as you want.'

Was Antonia also going to lie near her father later today? If nobody knows the truth, nobody will know my pain. And nobody will ever help me.

'My father loves your writing,' Antonia said.

The perfect timing caused Valeria's stomach to clench.

'He introduced me to your stories. The one I learned by heart, I chose for him.'

'Which one is it?' Valeria asked.

Antonia smiled. She wasn't going to tell.

'Does your father know that you know it by heart?'

Antonia shook her head. A tear came out of her eye and her eyeliner smudged. It was a Rorschach test and Valeria saw a bird in it. Antonia grabbed a tissue and wiped her nose.

'You are seeing my first tear since this whole fucking tragedy happened,' said Antonia. 'Also, I think we should be vegan. Why did we just eat an animal?'

'Thank you for your first tear and thank you for being with me today,' Valeria said. 'I think we should soon be vegan too. But this lunch with you was perfect.' What Valeria really wanted to say was, you are perfect, Antonia.

Before Valeria left the pub, they managed a shy hug, Valeria being the shyer one of the two. Surrounded by drawings of hamburgers, nothing seemed as horrible as it had a couple of hours earlier.

'So, do you reckon life is doable?' Antonia asked Valeria.

'Oh wow,' Valeria replied. 'Yes?'

'You have to answer without a question mark at the end.'

'I do,' Valeria said. 'But it's a mood-related belief.'

Antonia pulled her hood up and accepted that mood-related beliefs were understandable. Valeria wrapped her scarf around her neck and turned to leave.

'What do you think about monogamy?' Antonia asked.

Valeria turned back. She looked at Antonia and faked a smile. Did Antonia know? Or was she creating her own theories asking about all that mattered, life or love, to her favourite writer?

'Another mood-related belief,' Valeria said in response.

Writing that day wasn't too bad. After starting a story and deleting it, Valeria began another – with Isla in it. She named it *I/P*. The *P* was there for portrait. Valeria wrote Isla's story from all that she knew so far. America. Tennis whites. Martìn. Anty-Antonia. Descriptions of Isla's posture. She then made a list of all Isla's paintings she knew about, then searched online for Sasha Liebski, Isla's friend who had written the article about her in *ArtGeist*. Sasha was now a curator at a gallery that had a golden entrance in St Petersburg, Russia. Valeria wrote about Sasha and the bright entrance, her clothes in the picture, the fact that she was probably anorexic. Did Isla and Sasha still have at least one dinner a year together? During those dinners, did Sasha pretend to eat but just did vodka shots? Valeria added a description of Isla's body, the rooms of her house she had seen, Isla's movements while painting. She also wrote a paragraph focusing on the portrait that she owned: was Martìn, with his unfinished face, his untraceable life, the point of it all? The unfinished had to be the untold.

She wrote about how sitting for a portrait must, in some cases, feel like being desired and how being watched and mapped feels like being touched. In Isla's portrait of Martìn, desire was fed by total devotion. Painting your love, searching for their soul, was what lovers tried to achieve by caressing, and holding. Isla drawing Martìn was Isla caressing Martìn. She was holding him. Or she was holding onto him? *Don't disappear. Don't leave me. Stay.* Was Martìn, the husband, the sitter, answering his wife, 'I'm not going anywhere'? Were his eyes saying, 'I'm sorry'? Was the white of the canvas, the representation of Martìn, disappearing from her? Maybe Isla, the painter

131

and the wife, had him all, before, but he had now started to fade, just like we all do. His eyes could be saying none of us is going to stay, no matter how good this portrait is. No matter how good we are. The picture was going to be finished when completely white, not when completely coloured. Was that why Isla sold it?

She texted Isla to confirm the next visit, realizing too late her mistake: what if Isla recognized that number as the one that had been calling her husband? Perhaps there was a time when Isla had wondered who that Charlie Brown that sometimes appeared on her husband's screen was. Maybe they had argued about it. 'Who the fuck is this Charlie Brown?' What would Martìn's answer have been to such an accusation? 'Isly, my love, Charlie Brown is Valeria Costas. I have loved her for almost as long as I have loved you.'

It was raining so heavily it was impossible to go for a run. Valeria changed into her tracksuit, went onto YouTube and chose a cardio workout. The trainer had fake tits, blond hair, and a shiny outfit. She was jumping in a sleek studio, maybe in Miami, or Los Angeles or even in Detroit. But Detroit pretending to be Miami.

'Let's start with some warm-up? OK?' the trainer said.

'OK,' Valeria answered. She told her body to start with some warm-up. Could she warm it up only by thinking it? Warm-up, legs. Warm-up, heart.

'Ready? You were born ready, ladies,' the trainer said.

She smiled with a smile so white Valeria was reminded of a pearl necklace her mother had sent her when she married Patrick. 'Congratulations,' the card had said. Valeria had lost the necklace within a couple of weeks. Did she have to go back to the same places to look for it, thirty years later?

'Jump, ladies!' the trainer screamed.

And in the middle of the emptiest living room and what seemed the emptiest life, Valeria started to jump in tandem with the blond trainer, doing all she could to avoid her own reflection in the dark window. She followed the instructions, adding the arms, the squats, and all the upper- and lower-body exercises. I will be the best, my white-toothed trainer, I will be your favourite.

'Good! Well done!' the trainer shouted. 'You're doing good!'

Valeria believed her. She was doing good. She was fucking amazing. She was working those abs. Shaping those arms. Could Valeria feel the burn? Could Valeria feel the change? She could! She was changing.

FIFTEEN

The next morning Valeria woke up to the sound of her mobile. She was still in her tracksuit. Why did I take the sleeping pill before showering? I said I was changing and I lied. When the phone started ringing again, Valeria managed to pick it up without opening her eyes.

'I'm at yours, in front of what looks like a tiny grave,' Pamela said.

Valeria's ear was filled with the sound of Paris wind. Her mind filled with at least four or five different memories of death, birds, feathers and graves.

'Your writing on the cross says "Bird",' Pamela said.

'Shall we pray?' Valeria asked. 'For the bird and for our souls?'

'Got a specific prayer in mind?'

'Just make one up, please?' Valeria replied.

While Pamela was making her prayer up, something sweet about flying, stars and wings, Valeria tried to get back to sleep.

'Are you still there?' Pamela asked. 'The prayer's finished. Did you like it?'

'Absolutely,' Valeria said, 'I loved it. How's my house doing?'

'She misses you.'

'She's lying.'

'We both miss you.'

'I'll see you in two days. How is it going with Benoit?'

'I'm not sure,' Pamela said. 'I'm not sure I'm still there. Or here.'

'I thought it was him who was angry.'

'I thought so too.'

After the phone call, Valeria realized she had received a text from Theodora: *Waiting for you x.* She took a shower, put on some light make-up, dried and brushed her hair. When she was ready to go, she sat on the bed, incapable of standing up again and walking out the door. Sitting? Why? And *waiting for you* from Rhodes? Why? Valeria ran to the bathroom and threw up.

During spring, Sybilla had been declared free from cancer. The whole island was blossoming, not because of spring but because it was celebrating Sybilla's victory. They were all healed. Soon enough, Sybilla became stronger and her hair grew back. It was short, new. Valeria would stroke Sybilla's hair while lying down in bed.

'It's like touching an apricot. Or the fur of a cat.'

By May the sisters were swimming again. Not every day, because Sybilla was still too skinny for the chilly water, but at least once a week. They would choose a spot and make it their own. Sybilla would always say, 'I transformed from a fish to a lizard.' Now she loved getting all the warmth she could from the rocks.

With each day the water become warmer, and every day Sybilla would look and feel better. Theodora was so happy she decided to host a dinner for their few friends, the doctors and a handful of nurses. Theodora, Sybilla and Valeria had never hosted a party. They spent the day before the dinner looking for flowers in the fields.

'A hippie party?' Sybilla said.

'A rock 'n' roll party,' Valeria suggested.

'A Greek summer party,' Theodora said. 'Nothing beats Rhodes.'

It was the first time the girls heard Theodora being positive about Rhodes. Or in general.

They cooked meat, roasted vegetables and baked a cake, together with Calypso, the girl who had slept so many nights in their house with Valeria. They then went to town in the car for a last-minute errand – the wind fresh in their eyes and the island so solid in its new grace. Theodora, Sybilla and Valeria didn't speak, everything was warm, easy, and Calypso sang along to the radio. She knew all the words by heart even if her English was poor. The words she didn't know she would invent. They sounded even better, just like abracadabra sounds better than any real word.

'I want to wear my hair like yours,' Valeria said to Sybilla at sunset. They had a quick shower in the garden, wetting each other with the hose. They lay naked on their towels, their bodies drying in the last rays of light.

'From fish to lizard,' Sybilla repeated. 'So what next? Maybe bird?'

They wore their linen dresses while waiting for their guests to arrive. The music was on and the food ready. Sybilla plaited Valeria's hair, every now and then adding a flower into her sister's dark curls.

'You'd look like shit with short hair,' Sybilla said. 'Your face is not as symmetrical as mine. Trust me, you wouldn't pull it off.'

Valeria wondered if it was true or just a smart way for Sybilla to stop her from doing something drastic. But she did suddenly feel that her face was asymmetrical. That was another abracadabra: what Sybilla said became true. Valeria grew her hair long and kept it long for years to come.

The party was fun. Theodora was wearing a new green dress. She laughed. She danced. Sybilla and Valeria observed their mother from a distance, not only the physical one, but the one between who they thought their mother was, and who she could actually be.

Guests would approach Sybilla, tell her how pleased they were that she was well, better, strong. Each time Sybilla would hug them. 'Thank you,' she'd say. And she would smile at them before going back to dancing with Valeria.

After a while, the sisters sat down in the darkness, on the top of an old table.

'Maybe she will have sex with one of the doctors,' said

Calypso staring at Theodora. She had joined the sisters in the darkest corner of the garden, smoking a hand-rolled cigarette and drinking wine. The three girls were now sitting on the table, their six legs going back and forth to the rhythm of the music. Calypso pushed her glass over for Sybilla to taste. After a few sips Sybilla passed it to Valeria. The sisters agreed that wine was not so good and gave it back to Calypso. They also agreed that there were two almost handsome men out of eleven, while there were six or seven pretty ladies out of ten.

'The universe is just unfair, right?' Valeria said. 'Fuck off, universe.'

'Theodora is so hot,' Calypso said.

'She's way too strange to be hot,' Valeria replied.

Calypso shrugged her shoulders and puffed on her cigarette. 'She's as hot as hell,' she said. Valeria saw her mother on fire, hot as hell. She saw her burning like Calypso's tobacco in the cigarette. She saw hell.

Over the next few days and weeks, everything in Theodora's household seemed possible. Happiness was the easiest thing, celebrating life and love all they were going to do from now on. They were going to believe that laughing was compulsory and healing possible, opening their house and hearts to other people.

In June, when the school results were issued, Theodora received a letter stating that both Sybilla and Valeria would have to repeat the year.

'It's the least of our problems,' Theodora said. They had so many years ahead of them, for school and for everything else. But what they had right now was the best summer of their lives so far. They were not going to waste a minute worrying over the letter or other pointless things like school, jobs or anger.

'Let's just be,' Theodora said.

'What do you mean?' Valeria asked.

'Like cats, like cherries,' Theodora replied.

Then it was the end of summer. The cancer had been back probably since late July, but Sybilla hadn't told anyone how weak she was feeling. Or that there was blood in her mouth every day. Sybilla didn't want to go through all the fear and pain again. She didn't want to lose her hair or for her mother to cry. She just wanted to be. Like cats, like cherries.

'I have kissed with tongue,' Sybilla said, when they were back at the hospital.

She had contracted pneumonia. She was lighter than she had ever been. Valeria was holding her, Sybilla was shaking. Or they both were, and the outcome was a shared shake.

'How is it?' Valeria asked her.

'Warm,' she replied, 'and not scary at all.'

Valeria didn't know if Sybilla was referring only to the kiss or to death also. Maybe they both were, warm and not scary at all.

SIXTEEN

The Aclàs' door was open and Mirela was staring at her. The juice looked gigantic on top of the hallway cabinet. The more Valeria's guilt grew, the bigger the glass became.

'Sorry I'm late,' she said to the marvellous polar bear. 'It won't happen again.'

Mirela nodded, showing that she was a beautiful polar bear able to forgive. Look at what they are doing to my land and to the eternal ice! She took Valeria's coat, and gave her the glass. Valeria drank it as fast as she could, the enormous voodoo face veering towards her from the living room. Isla came up from downstairs.

She shouldn't be downstairs! Valeria thought, she should be upstairs with Martin.

'Sorry I'm late,' Valeria said, 'I was very tired.'

'It's only half an hour,' Isla said. 'We'll learn our routine soon.'

They went down to the studio. The fire had been on for a while. Bach was already playing. It was a completely different atmosphere to the day before. Easy. Almost desirable. Valeria walked to her stool, removed her jacket, and sat, looking for her sitter-self, for her position and her meaning in this room. Isla smiled at her, watching her movements. 'I couldn't wait to start today,' she said. 'I kept thinking about your face.'

Just an hour ago the sitting felt like torture, now Valeria couldn't find any unpleasant sensations in her. Mirela, the juice, the warmth. Isla's enthusiasm. She was flattered that Isla couldn't stop thinking about her face. Or did Isla just say it as if it were a nightmare: I couldn't stop thinking about your face, you are an obsession, a bad one?

'My husband used to ask me why I'd turn down so many requests. But I can't paint if I'm not curious about the person. Sometimes I'm drawn by a shape. A look. A mystery. It must be the same for you, with your stories.'

'I usually know why I've chosen to write a story,' Valeria said. 'But I have to start it to understand if I want to really finish it.'

'Last night I went into Antonia's room and looked for your book. I wanted to know which story she'd learned by heart. Thought it might reveal something to me about her. Or maybe about you,' Isla said with a smile. 'Didn't find it.'

Should I tell her that Antonia and I had lunch yesterday? No, I will keep Antonia's secrets. Just like I have kept Martìn's. This is me, in this house, the one that knows things Isla doesn't. If Martìn was the one to give Antonia the book, did he write something on the first page? I bet it's *To the Light*.

'I've still not read anything by you,' Isla said. Had Joe lied or was Isla lying? 'Looks like I'm the only one.'

'It's OK,' Valeria said.

'It's not,' Isla answered. Her hand was moving faster, frantic.

Was the witchcraft underway? Did her swift hand movements mean she was happy with what she was doing, or the opposite?

'We can get to know each other without other stories between us,' Valeria said. 'They'd just get in the way.'

The music elevated the moment to an epic one. Just like the rain outside. Isla and Valeria were both more heroic with the rain, Bach, the fire.

'Restless. Asking yourself who to be?' Isla smiled.

'More like trying to stay still,' Valeria said.

'Just stay. Still.'

'It's never been my main talent,' Valeria said.

'Would it help knowing that I get to choose who you are? At least in this one house?'

'Only if I get to choose who you are outside this one house,' Valeria smiled.

'Not to self-cite myself, but everyone is everyone,' Isla said. 'But you know that too.'

Without budging, using only her imagination, Valeria pretended to be a queen. Then she pretended to be a little girl. She pretended to be light. Very sad again. All of this without moving her face, or mouth, or hands. Could Isla perceive that Valeria had just been a queen and a little girl?

'Do people around you, people you love, always read you?' Isla asked her.

'My mother doesn't,' Valeria said. Saying it felt as shameful as a bad review. Also, it was her secret.

'Maybe she pretends she doesn't,' Isla said without pausing.

Valeria nodded. She too had never believed her mother. Weren't the books a key to her daughter's soul? Even if Theodora had always said she didn't read her, and that she was not going to read her again after *Black Bread*, Valeria thought it couldn't possibly be true. She had also said she was never going to go back to Rhodes and look now.

'You could have told me,' Theodora had said. 'It was painful.'

'The short story is me telling you,' Valeria had replied. 'That's the whole point. And a lot is pure fiction.'

'If you felt that way, you could have told me so yourself – in your own voice, not with a book. In a proper conversation. And sharing our story, our intimacy, with everybody? Why would you do that?'

'If I were a singer I would have sung it. Writing is my voice.'

'Stop being so self-centred. You should've asked me if I wanted to be involved.'

'That is never going to happen, Mum,' Valeria said. 'We all have to find a way to survive, just like you did. I'm sorry you don't like my work. But I will keep on writing the things I think I should be writing.'

'I will not read you any more,' Theodora said.

And even though Valeria's heart was broken at her mother choosing blindness instead of peering inside her daughter's soul, she accepted it.

'Fine, don't read me. You should only do what makes you happy, Mum,' she said.

After that call, Valeria had gone back to her book to read the short story that had led her mother to be so angry. It was called 'The Sleeping Child'.

The story was set on an imaginary Greek island that went by the name of Peristèra, where a mother raises her three boys. She calls them A, B and C, even though their names are Theo, Georgios and Alexis. The mother is sad, the father has abandoned them, so she is left with the bitterness, and hasn't got the energy to make life warmer. Even pronouncing her kids' names has become a torture. Their full names, and their joy, remind her of their father. The boys are left to live within a dark household, forever conjuring up ideas to cheer their mother up. They take her to swim in the hot springs, hidden in the centre of the island. They cook her food. They try to kiss her even if very rarely does she kiss them back. A, B and C manage to make the challenge bearable: it's a competition, so it's also fun. But then B dies in a bike accident, at the age of thirteen. The mother spends one last night beside B, and B looks like the sleeping child he had been when he was born. She had felt so lonely and desperate back then. Maybe even more than now. Yes, she had never been as sad as when he was first born. After B is buried, the mother never speaks again. A and C have to move on, with no other choice than to leave the island. Sometimes they visit her, for Christmas or for a week during summer, but they always feel lonely in Peristèra, even when they bring their wives and their children along with them. They call each other by their real names now, Theo and Alexis, but the hole remains, and the hole has the shape of Peristèra. When they are called back to attend their mother's funeral, it is the shape of that island that they draw in the sand and it is in the name of Peristèra that they toast to letting go of A, B and C, during an endless night of crazy *meltemi* winds.

SEVENTEEN

L et's go have lunch,' Isla said.

Valeria left her sitting-self and put her jacket back on. She put her usual self back on too. Let's choose a more confident and cheerful one if possible, she thought.

'I'm very hungry,' Valeria said. Try to be authentic too, please?

The two women left the studio to find lunch waiting for them on the long, wooden table. The place mats were light blue, all the plates white, the glasses thick and blue. Did Isla and Martìn buy them on one of their trips? The food was still perfectly warm, as though it had just been placed there, but Mirela was nowhere in sight. She had also placed a vase with flowers in the centre of the table.

'I'll wash my hands,' Isla said. She rubbed her hands, one against the other, maybe to show what 'washing hands' meant.

'I'll rush upstairs and wash mine too?' Valeria said. Freedom. Why did she always put a question mark? She didn't have to ask permission, of course Isla was going to say no if given the chance.

'I'll just be a minute,' Isla said. And that was the expected no. So Valeria obeyed, and remained in the room, alone with the chicken, the flowers and a million pictures of the Aclà family. Was she going to meet Cosmo and Nico? She walked to the window that faced the garden and watched the rain shower the conservatory, drops trickling everywhere. Valeria turned around to look again at the kitchen, all those hanging tea cups. Which one was Martìn's favourite?

'Your turn,' Isla said behind her.

Valeria smiled, went in the cloakroom and washed her hands. What will we talk about during lunch? Why don't I concentrate on listening and make her talk? Valeria walked back to the table and sat in front of Isla. She was texting someone but stopped as soon as Valeria was in front of her.

'Just updating Dr Len,' Isla said.

Valeria noticed Mirela had added colourful petals to the chicken. When exactly was she going to become vegan?

She sat down.

'Has Mirela been living here with you for a long time?' Valeria said. She started serving herself. Please tell me there is some wine.

'She has known Martìn for ever. They are both from Buenos Aires. Have you ever been to Buenos Aires?'

'I have, yes,' Valeria said.

Valeria had been there with Martìn. They had been chasing his memories, his streets, they had gone for lunch where he used to have lunch with his family and to the park where he and Rami used to play baseball. They were there for three days and three nights, in the middle of a very busy February. He had planned to meet with someone for business but it was an excuse. She had planned to see her publishers but it was an excuse. They had wanted that trip and come up with the excuses to make it happen.

'I love Buenos Aires,' Isla said. 'Mirela is the daughter of someone from Martìn's past.'

Why hadn't Martìn ever told Valeria about Mirela? Isla stood up, went towards the kitchen and came back with the red wine. Thank God. She poured some into Valeria's glass and some into her own.

'Her mother used to work for Martìn's father,' Isla said. 'She's been here for something like thirteen years now.'

'She lives with you?' Valeria asked.

'Not any more, she has a family now. Her daughter is called Helena, in memory of Martìn's mother. Lena.'

Helena. *Lena*. The poet-mother. There was no name for a mother that loses a child, so there was no name for Lena's pain. Or for Theodora's. Did Mirela know about Valeria and Martìn? If she had lived in this house that long, she must've come to know many of Martìn's secrets. 'I'm glad we are doing this,' Isla said.

'Lunch? Me too,' Valeria said.

'And the portrait.' She was eating so quickly Valeria couldn't stop staring at her mouth.

'Why did you stop painting?' The rain was getting heavier, turning into a storm. It could be one last good day on planet Earth. If it is, I should kiss my love goodbye.

'I had to survive my pain,' Isla said. 'So I did a couple of things to try and help me out.'

'Not painting and?'

'And a few other adjustments.' Isla smiled. 'I've changed art projects, let's put it that way.'

'Why were you sad?' Valeria asked, unable to get the mouthful of chicken down her throat.

'I'm not sure we want to make this lunch so blue,' Isla said, 'or about me.'

'But then you got better,' Valeria said, and tried to be sweet. 'Clearly.'

'I did,' Isla replied. 'Look at me! But to get better I had to let go of many things. And so did my husband. My last painting was of him.'

Valeria couldn't bring herself to say anything. She couldn't ask Isla if she regretted selling it, because Isla hadn't mentioned it being sold. Valeria hoped that she would just keep on talking about it without needing any further questioning. There wasn't going to be the bottom of anything, anywhere. It was the deepest sea she'd swum.

'Martìn would be very happy knowing I'm drawing you,' Isla said.

'Have you told him?' Valeria asked.

'I have, but I'm not sure he hears me,' Isla said. 'Both pieces of news, the fact that I'm painting, and you, one of his beloved authors, being in our house, would fill him with joy. I set myself a challenge: if I keep on drawing you and I finish the portrait, he'll come back to us.'

Oh no. She does these things too? And now what? If Valeria were to stop sitting, Martìn would die? The three of them were locked in now. Martìn and Isla must have spoken about her. What if Martìn had told Isla everything, and Isla was the real 'other woman', the one who knew all the secrets, and not Valeria? He hadn't told Valeria about Mirela, so was this a pattern?

'I'm sure you feel the pressure now,' Isla laughed. 'Should you stop coming here, you would have the responsibility of me and my family. I'm sorry!'

She didn't look sorry.

'Well,' Valeria smiled, 'sitting on that stool isn't going to get any easier now that I know what's at stake!'

'I'm sure you'd have kept on coming anyway,' Isla said. 'So what is your new book about?'

Maybe Isla was just being sadistic. Maybe it was all an evil plan and eventually she was going to poison Valeria. Maybe she had poisoned Martìn too and all of this was her revenge.

'I only write short stories, so the new book is a collection of different stories,' Valeria said. 'I have been obsessing over its title. I can't seem to find it. It's the first time it's ever been like this.'

Lunch went on, the two women marking their territories and getting to know each other better. Isla's children were mentioned, the absence of children in Valeria's life was mentioned too. Rock the dog came and sat near Isla, making Valeria feel unchosen again. These thoughts of mine now include dogs? Really? She was a fraud in every area of her life. A liar. A daughter unable to join her mother in Greece. A writer who only delivered short stories and not a novel. Who had run out of titles. She had been a life-long invisible lover and she was going to end in an invisible way. She listened to the woman before her. Isla was the soul of the house. And of life. Someone made Isla juices. Martìn made Isla happy. Isla could touch Martìn. Valeria had a minuscule rental flat with an empty bottle of Shianti on a shelf. She didn't even have a dog.

'Hmm, a hot flush,' said Isla. Then she closed her eyes. She became red. And opened her eyes again. 'Don't you hate it?' Isla asked Valeria.

Holy fuck. Valeria detested even pronouncing the actual word out loud. Why was Isla asking about her oestrogen levels? Could Isla see the sweat on Valeria's forehead?

'I'm not sure,' Valeria said. She checked her pockets, searching for nothing.

'What do you mean?' Isla asked.

'I'm trying not to think about it,' Valeria said, looking around for something in the room to distract them both. Bears? Elephants? Their faces looked older here than in the studio. The light was raw, milky, with nowhere to hide the softening musculature under their skin or the lines around their mouths, their eyes, their necks. Maybe that was why Isla asked.

'I should go,' Valeria said. 'I write in the afternoons.'

'Can I have another thirty minutes of your time?' Isla said. 'Please?'

Valeria nodded. Of course Isla could have another thirty minutes of her time. Especially to add all the wrinkles she had just seen, and the saggy bits under Valeria's chin.

Valeria followed Isla back into the studio, took her jacket off, sat on her stool and became Valeria the sitter again.

Here I am. Dissect me and prepare your curse.

Isla drew. Valeria counted. To a thousand. Then to another thousand. She made it to five thousand before Isla said thank you and finally dismissed her.

'Thank you. Also for the lovely lunch,' Valeria said. 'Please give my compliments to Mirela. I loved the petals.'

'What petals?' Isla asked.

'The ones on the dish?' Valeria said. 'Right on the chicken?' Stop. Fucking. Using. Question marks.

'I hadn't noticed,' Isla said.

Valeria wondered which of them had a brain problem. Probably she herself. Was this to do with her oestrogen levels too?

They walked up the stairs. Isla gave Valeria her coat and her scarf.

'Tomorrow my assistant will be in town. Can she come to the sitting?'

'Sure,' Isla said, 'I like to have people around. The more, the better.'

And that day too, Valeria was out of Martin's house without having even touched him.

EIGHTEEN

Valeria walked in the pouring rain for more than an hour, wandering in the darkness of that day. The warmly lit houses she passed were a constant reminder of her loneliness. She kept walking, through Bayswater and on towards Hyde Park. Her walking was so fast it became a slow run. But the slow run wasn't working, so she switched to proper running, which, dressed in a pencil skirt, silk shirt, tailored jacket and coat, felt very uncomfortable. But it also felt like something she would have liked to witness: a quite sophisticated if dishevelled woman running fast in the rain, pounding the pavements in the middle of the carriage drive and clearly in the middle of her own disaster.

Valeria kept on running until she reached Marble Arch and its buses, black fumes and noise. Crossing the vastest road she had possibly ever crossed, she made it to Hill Street. It was quieter there. Rich. Maybe there was a gigantic invisible umbrella protecting the wealthy residents, because here the rain felt gentler.

She entered Brown's Café and chose a table near the heater. Even the heater was splendid.

'May I have some tea, please?' Valeria asked the waiter. Valeria's hair was sopping wet.

I'm a mermaid, she thought. I can't have kids. Or dogs. And I can't take pictures with Ulysses in Shibuya, Tokyo, because I die on planet Earth. I'm a secret.

At the other end of the café, a group of people were entering through a wooden door. Old people, young people. Beside the door hung a description of what was behind it, but it was so far away Valeria couldn't read it. Was it a business convention? The end of the world?

'What's behind that door?' Valeria asked the waiter. He was an incredible tea pourer. The tea was dropping from at least a metre above her head.

'Thursday Mass,' he said, 'by the Society of Life.'

'What's that?'

'You may want to see it for yourself,' the waiter said. He was waiting for Valeria to drink her first cup of tea, just to be able to pour a second one. 'They always start with singing. Could be David Bowie, could be Soko the Cat. The organizer loves Lou Reed so one song is always his.'

Because Valeria had taken three sips and left the cup on the table, the waiter topped her up.

'I think I will drink it slowly,' Valeria said.

He made an effort to smile and left the teapot on the table. With a tiny bow, he departed.

The queue at the door became longer. The people were all moving gently, no pushing, only smiling faces. Within a few minutes they were all inside the room beyond. Valeria couldn't resist any more. She stood up and walked over to the door, reading the sign beside it: *The Society of Life – Thursday Mass. TODAY: On Beauty. A sermon led by the philosopher Omar Pinè and the Buddhist Monk Shishtan. Songs by: Lou Reed, Nine Inch Nails, Adele.*

Valeria stepped into the room, thinking about her tea getting cold and that her bag and coat were probably going to be stolen. The room was enormous and set like a theatre. Wood everywhere, cushioned seats, the stage set with two chairs waiting for the philosopher and piano. Valeria found a place to sit and as soon as she did so, everyone stood. A girl appeared on the stage. So Valeria stood up too.

'It's great to see you all here!' the girl was saying.

She was wearing a denim shirt buttoned up to the neck, flat black shoes. Her hair was held back with wax, Elvis Presley style.

'Welcome, all of you. Welcome and welcome to me too! We are now going to sing together. We are now going to wake up to this day, for this day, and celebrate life, strength and vulnerability!' She smiled. She was in the best mood in the world.

Drugs? Which ones? I want them, Valeria thought. She turned around and all she could see were cheery faces and nodding heads.

On the wall behind the Presley girl, a projector screen was switched on, lights were turned up and the jolliest girl on Earth approached the piano. The lyrics of 'Perfect Day' appeared on the screen and, as soon as the girl started to play, the room started to sing along. Valeria wondered which was the best way out but because she didn't know how to escape, and because she thought it was rude to stand up and remain mute, she shyly started singing along with them. By the time she got to the second refrain she sang a bit louder and when the song reached its crescendo she was ready to shout, now singing so loudly that the woman beside her smiled. Possibly with worry.

When they finished singing, Valeria was out of breath. Then, because everyone in the room sat, she sat too.

'That was great, thank you,' the girl said. She was smiling so much her whole body seemed to state that life was beautiful. 'I will be back with some more music later. Now let's welcome our pastors for today's mass.'

With a warm applause the science-philosopher, who was very, very old, and the monk, who was very, very fat, were welcomed onto the stage of the Society of Life.

During the hour that followed, Valeria didn't listen to the philosopher or the monk. Their voices were white noise from the very beginning. Their first statements about the here and now, the purity of intent, the honesty of wisdom, pissed her off. But every time the girl returned, Valeria stood up, fully engaged. She committed herself to filling her lungs, to being a good scholar, a devoted singer. Then, with the rest of the enthusiastic audience, she left the room.

'Your table's gone,' the waiter told Valeria, seeing her panic. 'But I've got all your stuff.'

'I'm so sorry,' Valeria said. 'My tea must be cold by now.'

'Oh, it happens all the time,' the waiter said. 'That's why we are here.'

Valeria followed him. At the counter she was served another cup of tea. Maybe the singer would soon be seated on a stool close by and it was from her that a hug would finally come?

I did give Martìn the full role of embracing me through-out life, she reasoned. Those embraces held me together when I was thirty, thirty-six, fifty. He is everything that happened and the thread that binds it all together.

She grabbed her phone and called him. The voicemail response played.

'Martìn,' Valeria said. 'I come to your house every day. I sit with your wife, I use your dishes. But I cannot touch you,' she whispered, a tear trickling down her cheek. 'Even if I'll be able to touch you soon, you'll probably never be able to touch me again. What is it that I should be doing? Walk away? Learn how to let go? If I tell them everything, just to be near you, Antonia will suffer. She's so familiar but unknown at the same time. Even if she is broken, I think she will be fine. I'm desperate to know which one of my stories she learned by heart for you.' A smile appeared on Valeria's face at this thought. 'If I could, I would scan her body in my search for bits of you.'

The waiter was looking at her. Were the other customers looking at her too?

'These days, when I look at myself in the mirror I see all of the years that have passed. It's as though being my age just sort of happened. Today. In this past hour. Isla looking at me, you not being able to look at me any more, makes it all more confusing.' She sipped her tea. 'I love you,' she said into the phone. 'I miss you.'

When Valeria left the café it was late evening and it was raining. She caught a taxi back to the flat but was immediately stuck in traffic. For every centimetre the car progressed in the jam, her sense of anonymity grew increasingly overwhelming. Nobody on planet Earth knows I am here, she thought. Valeria zoomed out from the car, and out of Mayfair, London, Europe, the planet. Her loneliness became too much to bear. She texted her address in London to Pamela, to her mother in Rhodes, to Joe. At least someone out there now knew where she was, and where she was headed. To her mother she also wrote, *Have you been back to our farm?*

NINETEEN

The following morning, Valeria was putting on her almost-dry sitter shirt and skirt when the doorbell rang. Pamela stood in front of her, looking as fresh as someone who had just enjoyed a massage, rather than someone who had arrived on the 5.45am Eurostar from Paris. She was wearing a wet coat, a hat and a smile. Removing her hat, Pamela freed her jolly ponytail. Her mouth was a darker red than usual, probably because of the wind, of winter, of England. Valeria kissed her on both cheeks.

'It's good to have you here, Pam,' she said. Yes, two kisses were a bit much, but she was desperate for some affection.

'This neighbourhood is fabulous,' Pamela said.

Pamela appeared at ease as she followed Valeria through the living room. She looked around without seeming nosy, there while not being too much there, a clear sign of her knowing Valeria. Pamela's newly liberated ponytail bobbed with her every glance, her every step.

'Nice energy in here,' Pamela said.

There was no such thing as 'an energy', was there? And even if there was – like aliens, like Sybilla still by her side – in this house it couldn't be a good one.

'Your friends have a nice place,' Pamela added.

Friends? Oh, right, her 'friends'. She must have had strange friends that owned nothing at all. Come up with a name for the *friends*? George and Anna.

'It's a house they usually rent out,' Valeria said. 'Anna and George have another one in Islington. With more furniture.' Then, 'Do you need to wash your face, use the loo, anything at all? Because we have to go very soon. Sitting starts at ten thirty.'

'I'm good to go,' Pamela said.

Of course she was. When would she ever not be good to go?

'Shall I bring the mail and all the other stuff along or shall I just leave it all here?' she asked, pointing at her backpack.

It was the leathery, very used backpack that she always wore. Did she once take it to Greece when she was sixteen, island-hopping in the Dodecanese with her classmates, drinking ouzo, playing cards in village squares, swimming in the bluest of seas? Maybe that summer she had also lost her virginity in Patmos, or Leros, or Kalymnos. Maybe it had been in Rhodes.

'Bring it with you,' Valeria said. 'If you get bored you can work at the kitchen table. The house is very comfortable. There's a great energy there too.' She couldn't help it. Anyway, it was at least truer there than here.

'Perfect,' Pamela said, 'and I adore your outfit. I knew you would be stunning in it.' She scanned Valeria's body, confirming her opinion with a smile. 'You are beautiful.'

For five seconds Valeria felt stunning. It was a great feeling. Quite unbeatable. But a fake one, like good energy or aliens. Like Sybilla still by her side. So it disappeared. 'Let's go,' she said.

She opened the door and Pamela trotted near her. Was Pamela proud to be Ms Costas' assistant? Ms Costas, the independent woman, Ms Costas, the accomplished and the free, the feminist, who had exquisitely cut clothes in which she looked stunning? Possibly. But if Pamela came close enough to know who she was actually walking around with, she would have been desperate.

I n the living room at the Aclàs' townhouse, three glasses of juice were waiting for Valeria and Pamela. The third one was probably for Isla, whose new routine now included sharing vitamin drinks with her sitter. One juice was blue, one was green and one was red.

'What a gorgeous house,' Pamela murmured to Valeria.

Valeria focused on the voodoo face, and realized she had forgotten to tell Pamela not to reveal how close by she was living.

'Do you like the scary voodoo face?' Valeria asked Pamela.

But Pamela didn't answer because both Mirela the elegant polar bear and Isla the wife had appeared, so instead of locking eyes with the voodoo face she locked them with Isla.

'It's a pleasure to meet you, Mrs Aclà,' Pamela said. 'My name is Pamela Williams. I'm a huge fan.'

Why did she use Martìn's surname? Was Isla annoyed by Pamela? Let her just mention the energy and she'll be screwed for good.

'It's a pleasure to meet you too,' Isla smiled.

Her smile wasn't very gentle. Was it the Aclà bit or the 'huge fan' that had ruined the atmosphere? Maybe Isla was put off by Pamela's beauty just like Valeria had been.

'Please, ladies.' Isla pointed at the glasses of juice.

Ladies? Oh come on, you too, Isla.

'Thank you, Mirela,' Valeria and Pamela said, like two schoolgirls. She sensed her white gym socks.

'Which one's mine?' Valeria asked Mirela. And just like that she was a middle-aged woman again. With tight purple panties, a serious memory problem and a dying lover. No good schoolgirl with shiny black shoes had a dying lover.

'You choose your own colour,' Mirela said. Valeria went for the red.

'Please, now you,' Isla said to Pamela.

Pamela went for the blue. Was blue better for being beautiful? Damn. Valeria did vaguely recall something about blueberries and antioxidants. Isla got the green one, the three of them raised their glasses and drank their vitamins. The living room flashed with lightning and echoed with thunder, while the women's bodies were flashed with health bombs. Maybe they would soon discover their super powers and finally learn all abracadabras and save the world, the three of them together, each one with a specific magic.

They went down to the basement. Pamela was glancing at everything with desire. Maybe she was going to abandon Valeria and go and work for Isla. Maybe with this portrait Isla was going to become incredibly famous, while Valeria, without any more titles for her books, would be forgotten. It was right for Pamela to want to be in this house. Both Pamela and Isla believed in marriage, wanted to have a family, a home. Isla had offered Pamela juice, not red wine. Isla did have a warmer, bigger house than Valeria and probably a warmer and bigger soul. Isla said things like, 'Mirela is part of our family.' Valeria would never say the same about Pamela or Joe. She didn't even have a family to be able to make such comparisons and surely Isla didn't lie as much as Valeria did? Isla wasn't a fraud.

'You might want to get one of those chairs,' Isla said to Pamela.

In the studio, Bach was playing, the fireplace was crackling and the portrait was hidden from view, turned to face the wall. Valeria sensed the wall in front of her future. She hated it like she hated the one between Mexico and the USA, the one between China and Korea, Egypt and Gaza, and all sixty-five of them in the world.

'You can sit there,' Isla said. She wanted Pamela to sit away from the drawing, strategically between Valeria and Isla. 'I'm also going to ask you not to look at it, sorry,' she said. 'I don't like to show my work before it's done.'

'Of course,' Pamela said. 'That's completely under-standable.'

Was she or wasn't she the perfect assistant to any artist? She completely understood.

Valeria took her jacket off in her usual sitter manner, went through her usual sitter ritual. She walked over to the stool and sat down. It felt faker this morning. She needed to try harder to become the sitter, give her face to Isla and to the world. She had to be seductive and at the same time, distant. With humility and flair. She was so conscious of Pamela looking at her that she had to count to a hundred to try and become at least half as true as she had been the day before. Not that she had been very true the day before. Or the one before that. But she had been better at faking it.

Pamela walked to her spot, holding the chair. She sat down. Valeria imagined the three of them in a movie, seen from outside the window, through the rain. She herself, seated. Isla in her dungarees, Pamela with that good-girl posture and her breasts pointing towards the moon. Were they all sad? Or were they all much stronger than they thought? 'Ladies' would be the title of the feature.

TWENTY

'Last night I dreamt about you,' Isla said to Valeria. 'You were seated, I was drawing, we were both naked.'

She went on drawing and there was a pause during which Valeria imagined it all. Isla just like she was right now but naked, herself as she was seated right now, but naked too. The first thing Valeria thought was that her tits wouldn't look too good. And her flesh would be much flabbier than expected. Expected by whom? Herself or the painter, the wife, the watcher? And Isla? How big was her stomach? Did she have pink nipples or brown nipples? Had Martìn ever seen them both naked in the same day? And had sex? Quite likely.

'It wasn't just me studying you or your face, we were both doing it, sort of scanning our bodies, mirroring one another. We were checking each other's flesh, where we were beautiful, where things were letting us down. We confronted our chins, how they felt, with some parts beginning to loosen up and we sort of weighed our breasts, mirroring each other. All in silence. You had tiny, minuscule breasts. It wasn't erotic or embarrassing at all. It was delicate. In some way, melancholic.'

'Were you drawing me naked in the dream? I mean, the portrait, was it of a naked me?' Valeria asked. She asked it only because she didn't want the silence to follow the dream download. It was a stupid question. 'I don't know,' Isla said. 'The door was open. There was this sensation of not wanting to get caught. Nobody else was to know we were doing it. It was a secret.'

Pamela, the perfect assistant, received a text. She said sorry and turned her phone to silent. Valeria and Isla didn't say anything else. The text had stalled the confession but it lingered in Valeria's mind. Was Isla still thinking about the dream?

Later, when Valeria was trying not to fall asleep, the door banged open. It was Antonia. She was dressed in black and she was angry. Staring first at her mother then at Valeria, she breathed her nervousness.

'Who are you?' Antonia said, glaring at Pamela.

'Oh come on, really? Don't be so rude, Antonia,' Isla said. 'And what are you doing home again?' Her body tensed. Her cheeks reddened. She had a dying husband. A raging teenage daughter. A damn portrait of a woman who changed her face every day to deliver. The hormones and the weird dreams. How much more pressure could she handle?

'You're right, Mum. Where did all my graciousness go? Good morning, Mother, good morning, Ms Costas. And sorry to you too,' Antonia approached Pamela.

Pamela stood up, they shook hands. Then Antonia walked towards the door and looked at her mother again.

'Can I talk to you alone?' Antonia said. 'Now?'

'I'm sorry,' Isla said. She put down the paint, wiped her hands on a rag and stepped outside the room with her daughter.

'What's the fucking point of going there right now?' Antonia said as soon as they left the room. 'Why is it a duty of mine to be learning all that pointless shit now, when I should be here? Listen to me: I can't.'

Their voices became more distant, but the words could still be heard from the studio. Mean. Alone. Love. School. Dad.

'Valeria, sorry, that was Joe earlier. I have to call him back,' Pamela said.

Valeria managed to divert her attention from the conversation Antonia and Isla were having.

'He needs to go through a couple of things on the Aix-Marseille Université contract, shall I do it now?'

'Sure,' Valeria said. 'Why don't you do it from here and I'll go freshen up one sec?'

Pamela nodded. There was a lot of nodding in this life of hers.

Valeria didn't go and freshen up one sec. She left the room and sneaked up the stairs as fast as she could. She reached the landing on the ground floor, giving the finger to the voodoo face. Then she started climbing the stairs to the first floor. No breath. No time. No idea of what was going to happen now. Was Mirela tidying the bedrooms? Was there a nurse up there? Valeria carried on up, past Antonia's painting, and, with her heart about to explode, entered Martìn's room.

'Martìn,' Valeria murmured. She grabbed his hand. Oh, his hand. That exact weight. That exact texture. I am here.

Martìn was immobilized but it wasn't as scary as she had expected, and yes, her heart was broken, all of her was broken, she was already crying, and his body was sick and motionless, but they were still here. They were close again. Don't disappear. Don't fade. Don't let me fade.

Valeria knelt on the floor – her legs shaky – caressing Martìn's hands, kissing them. She couldn't breathe properly, all this love – this profound, painful love – the fear of being caught and the secret hope that Martìn would wake up now because she had finally made it to his bedside. She could breathe better than Martìn who now needed a ventilator to help him out, but still, she wasn't the best of breathers either. They were at least breathing the same air.

'Martìn,' Valeria said again, more loudly, leaning forward to rest her forehead against his hands. 'Don't be scared,' she said to him, 'I'm not.'

As soon as she said it, she realized it was true.

Valeria kissed Martìn's hands again. The brown marks. The usual, familiar marks, her own constellation and theory of beauty. All still there! Valeria kissed his arm around the cannulas and she kissed his lips, next to the inhaler, and his cheeks.

'You are the love of my life,' Valeria said.

She remained there, her cheek to his, kissing his eyes, kissing his lips again.

'This is my place. I can't be anywhere else.'

But had she been there too long? Were Antonia and Isla still arguing? Antonia had a point. She didn't want to leave Martìn and the house either.

Valeria hadn't closed the door, but she couldn't close it, could she? It would be impossible to justify her being in Martìn's room with the door closed. Not that being in there with the door open made it any better, but nevertheless it looked less premeditated. It was going to be impossible to explain her being in Martìn's life too, but they had to start somewhere.

It's going to be something eventually, she thought. The answering machine, someone who knows, me holding your hand. So let it be from me being in your room, from me kissing you.

'I thought you knew who I was,' Martìn had told Valeria the first time they met.

'Is that why you're wearing your sunglasses in the dark?' Valeria asked him.

He took them off, grinning. Earlier, at the charity event, they had been sitting together, observing each other for hours. During the never-ending auction, Valeria had gone up onstage to sell a first-edition Virginia Woolf book that she had donated and it was Martìn who bought it. He had also bought a dinner with some anti-everything philosopher, a set of travel bags and two tickets to a movie premiere.

'I asked to be seated next to you,' Martìn told her. Valeria smiled. Then he recalled an interview Valeria had given after her recent collection. 'You spoke about loneliness in a very delicate way. I could hear you very clearly.' He also told her that he knew the last sentence of 'Red Hair' by heart, quoting her, and Valeria thought he had a deep voice, a gentle smile. It all felt warm and caring. Maybe he'll do this for ever and maybe I'll feel this way for ever.

'I wish I was able to say it like you write it.'

'Say what?' Valeria asked. Was she using her sexy voice?

'Look at me, even when I don't want you to look at me. Don't let me disappear.'

They spent every free moment of that night together, even if in the official auction photo they were standing apart, separated by two actors, a writer and a Michelin-star chef. That picture was the only picture ever taken of the two of them together.

When Valeria returned home that evening, she called Joe.

'Who is that actor?' she asked Joe, faking interest. 'Where is the chef's restaurant?' Finally, she managed to fit in the real question, 'Who is Martìn Aclà?'

Soon, through Joe, the papers, and asking here and there, she knew enough about Martìn in Argentina and Martìn in America, about his wife and his family. She reconstructed his past and figured out his present, filling in the blanks with her own imagination to create his backstory.

Valeria gave Martìn one last kiss on the mouth, then stood up and moved closer to the corridor. She remained there, trying not to breathe, to listen carefully for any noise. Hadn't she been doing this all her life? Standing still, trying not to breathe, to listen carefully for any noise?

She turned around, ran back to Martìn and tried to lie on top of him, stretching her body over his, trying not to weigh too much and trying to be felt. She closed her eyes, inhaled and exhaled deeply, imitating his pace. She held him tight, wanting to keep him with her. For ever. Whatever the for ever. She said, 'I will not go anywhere.'

She kissed him again and left the room.

Just don't disappear, she thought. Stay.

Valeria walked down the stairs to the basement with a steady rhythm. She needed to get to the kitchen fast but at the same time to look calm. What had she been doing upstairs? A phone call. Yes, perfect. Not that she had her phone with her but still, what were they, spies? She descended another flight of stairs, then she got down the last steps. Reaching the kitchen, Valeria tried to breathe a bit of her exaltation away. She had made it! Martìn and her, together again. Here they were. Here was their story, with the best plot they could write for it.

TWENTY-ONE

When Rami died, Martìn had been close by, but, as he always said, 'not close enough'. The brothers were together at a party upstate New York in a lakeside villa they had squatted in months before. They had tents, bonfires, they had music. Beer was kept in ice buckets, joints were rolled, pills were popped. Mattresses were scattered around the garden and people would crash on them. All afternoon had been spent swimming, sunbathing. Martìn was dating a girl called Mary.

'Her hair was long to her butt. When she was naked, looking at her from the back was mystical,' he told Valeria. 'In Kanawauke, Mary was often naked. So in Kanawauke I liked her a lot. Sometimes her long hair would remain trapped in her buttocks.' He smiled.

At that time Rami was in love with two girls.

There was Ady, an American, preppy blonde who was going through a rebel phase that was clearly going to end in a couple of months. And there was Lila, a petite Argentinian activist who had moved to New York to study cinema. That weekend, Lila was back in Buenos Aires for a funeral, so Ady was the one in Kanawauke with him.

'I'm so happy I want to scream,' Ady told Rami when they were all sitting together.

'Give me some,' Rami told her.

Ady thought he meant the joint she had in her hand. So she passed it to him. Rami had meant happiness, give me some happiness, but the joint was OK too.

Because Lila wasn't with him, Rami had been obsessing only about her. He was always like this, the fear of missing out, the pain of the abandonment, would rule him. So would his mania.

Poor Ady was invisible despite the show she was putting on by the bonfire. No matter the transparent white dress, her smiles, the joints and her happiness, she was a ghost to him.

'I love Lila. I will marry her,' he told Martìn. 'I want to go to Buenos Aires tomorrow. Actually, I want to go, now.'

'Lila is fantastic, Rami, she really is. But right now Ady is here, five metres from us. I can see her nipples through the linen. She's been dancing for you for about ten hours non-stop,' Martìn told him. 'Don't be an idiot and enjoy the weekend.'

When he was a little boy, Martìn would find Rami crying in the strangest places. Once he found him hiding inside the fireplace at their home in the Argentinian countryside. He came out covered in black dust. Martìn ran him a bath and Rami continued crying in the bathtub. Back then, Martin still had to understand his extreme excitements, his extreme sadness.

'Why are you crying?' Martin would ask him from time to time. Other times he would just accept the tears. Rami's answer was always the same.

'Sadness,' he'd say.

During high school Rami was often so sad that he would skip school. The only teacher who understood him would often call their mother to have a chat about the boy for whom she cared so much. Rami's love for his teacher was so intense that he would pray for her husband to die. That's another way love was for Rami, exclusive of all other people, with fear and anger all built in.

'If he dies then what?' Martin asked him.

'She will be mine,' Rami smiled.

Rami wrote his teacher letters that he wouldn't send. He kept them in a large, wooden box he had bought at a flea market. He had taken it home only to discover that the box contained a double layer inside. In the double layer he found a collection of pictures of naked women to which he very often masturbated. Behind all the pictures the women had names. Bella. Anna. Lola. Sam. Mina was by far his favourite because she was very hot and busty. Rami would sometimes talk to Mina's picture and he would ask her, do you like it if I do this? Do you like it if I suck your nipple? Martin happened to overhear, even if he tried not to. Once he heard Rami say, would you like me to kill myself?

'The crying happened when Rami was sad,' Martin told Valeria. 'It may seem obvious. But his sadness was like a season. When he was happy he was so happy you couldn't imagine him being any other way. He was so excited his body was restless. He was always running. Jumping, even. But the sadness would always come back. Anyway, both the sadness and the happiness were so extreme I feared them equally.'

Rami loved and trusted Martìn more than anyone. So when, that weekend, in Kanuwauke Martìn had told him 'stay', Rami had stayed. Beers, pot, another swim at sunset and sex with Ady brought Rami back to making the most of the choice that had been made for him. Martìn, in the meantime, could enjoy his own girlfriend, Mary, who loved being naked.

'We have our whole lives,' Rami told Martìn.

Lying near the bonfire, Rami was again in a chipper mood. He was explaining to the gang his plans for the farm that he and Martìn had bought. The two brothers often felt guilty for now being richer than most of their friends. But they would always make it very clear that they wanted to share their luck. And – in the meantime – they wanted to change the world. Martìn had noticed that Rami was becoming nervous. He sensed danger but pushed the sensation away with more pot. He felt the disaster coming closer and asked himself, will harm come from the fire, from the drugs or from our bodies?

'We could buy some other land and start a self-sustainable community. Perhaps, Ady, you will be my queen. We'll have many kids,' Rami said. His voice was loud. He was drunk, couldn't stop talking. And drunk or not drunk, Martìn didn't like his brother to share their plans. What about all the love for his Argentinian wife-to-be? Ady was 'the queen' now. Sometimes, even if he knew him so well, he couldn't help being irritated by Rami's behaviour. Why couldn't he just keep it together?

'And Lila?' Martìn asked. But no one heard him except Rami. Martìn stood up, whispered, 'Rami, shut the fuck up, will you?' and went to the beach with Mary. Mary was naked once again and Martìn looked at her again from the back. Then she blew him with dedication and care, before he went down on her, wanting to own her, but knowing that the wish would disappear once he came. When he was pushing himself inside her, he felt so good he wanted to say, 'I love you.' But he didn't love her and was careful enough not to spoil it.

Then he heard the screams.

In the kitchen, Antonia and Isla were still arguing. Valeria walked past them. She could hear Pamela on the phone. Valeria was so excited she felt hysterical. Martìn was in a coma, how could she feel so good? What was wrong with her? But she had kissed him. If Martìn could hear or feel anything at all, then he had most definitely felt her now. His smell lingered on her. She could be near him, under the same roof, and that was what mattered. They were going to live and fight the sickness together. So she was good. She was so good she suddenly felt at ease about being in this house. What had she been so paranoid about? She wanted a glass of water. She was so at ease that pouring herself a glass of water from the kitchen was the least she could do.

'Well, you didn't have to cheat on him!' Antonia shouted.

There was a pause. As if the entire world had stopped, Valeria saw people freezing at their computers. Ships halting in the middle of oceans. Martìn's breathing machine stopping. All toddlers in the world dropping their games. She also saw Isla cheating and in her imagination Isla was in a dark alleyway, being taken from behind, the filthy street stinking of urine and alcohol. Cigarette butts on the ground, tourists walking past. The rain, in the sex scene and in the present moment, also stopped.

'What are you talking about?' Isla said.

The rain started again. And because it had stopped, it came down more violently. In Valeria's imagination, Isla was now dressed in white, praying in a church. She wasn't cheating and she was a Madonna. She was pure, honest. An honourable mother, a decent wife.

'You know exactly what I'm talking about,' Antonia said.

Valeria was already visible to them both and she couldn't use any invisible powers. Or could she?

'I don't. I need to get back to the painting. Just like you wanted me to. So this is the first and the last time that you skive school and come in here, shouting cryptic nonsense and ruining everyone's day. We'll take this up later, now I suggest you disappear upstairs.'

Don't really disappear, Antonia, Valeria thought, just go upstairs. Chill. Listen to music.

'I'd say calling you a cheater is pretty non-cryptic but I'm so sorry for ruining your day,' Antonia continued. 'You're ruining my life but I guess that's just fine!'

Antonia stormed upstairs, after throwing a quick glance at Valeria. What was that glance? Embarrassment? Anger? Did Antonia know everything about everybody?

Valeria poured herself a glass of water then one for Isla. She tried to re-enact the tea-pouring from Brown's Café. It didn't work as well.

'Oh, thank you,' Isla said and she drank the entire glass of water in one gulp. 'Shall we?'

They returned to the studio. The painter and the sitter. The wife and the lover. The mother and the non-mother.

The sitting was tense. Had Isla really cheated on Martìn? Pamela didn't budge. Maybe she wanted to be chosen as the sitter? Valeria, on the other hand, couldn't sit still. She was claustrophobic, restless. The purple panties were killing her. She wanted to rip them off and chuck them. Or better yet, to take them off and hide them somewhere near Martìn. Somewhere that was just his, not for a nurse or a wife to find, but still close enough for him to know. Was she going to be able to do it today?

'As promised, because your assistant is here, we'll stop now,' Isla said, 'though I'd gladly keep on working for another ten hours today.'

'Thanks,' Valeria said, 'Pamela needs to catch the train back to Paris tonight, so yeah, we'd better get cracking.'

Valeria rose and put her jacket on while Isla rinsed her paintbrushes. She stopped the music. Had Isla been cheating on Martìn out of passion or revenge?

In the kitchen there was Mirela. Had she been there all morning?

'Antonia is here,' Isla said to Mirela on the way up. 'We'll be having lunch upstairs with Martìn.'

'Good,' Mirela said and she went back to rinsing whatever she was rinsing. A seal pup? Valeria and Pamela waved goodbye Isla, the voodoo face and the Aclà house. Then they were outside, under the rain and back into their real lives. Because this other one wasn't real, right?

'Lunch?' Valeria asked Pamela. But before Pamela could answer, Valeria turned back to the Aclàs' door and banged it. With way too much strength. What if nobody was ever to open that door again?

'Valeria?' Pamela asked. 'Is everything all right?'

Isla opened the door.

Could this woman standing before her even begin to imagine that Valeria feared her whole life would disappear if a door closed?

'What about the weekend? Are we seeing each other?' Valeria said.

'Oh, I hadn't thought about it,' Isla said. 'What do you reckon?'

'I'm happy to come, but of course it's up to you.' Every drop of the happiness she had felt an hour ago had disappeared. She was in the desert. She was thirsty and she was hungry. They were guilty, all of them.

'Let me check with the kids and their weekend plans and I'll get back to you,' Isla said.

'Absolutely,' Valeria answered. I need to be with you, she thought. You have to say yes. We have to save Martìn.

They both tried to smile, then separated again.

Valeria and Pamela walked to Holland Park Road. If Wednesday was burger day at the pub, then what was Friday?

'Is the pub OK?' Valeria asked Pamela.

'Sure,' Pamela answered.

Valeria made herself a secret promise to come up with something horrible for lunch with Pamela soon, like eating raw brains or a grasshopper, just to hear her say 'sure' with that enthusiastic tone of voice.

'Isla seems nice,' Pamela said. 'I didn't expect her to be.'

'You had expectations?' Valeria said. She sounded bitter. Probably because she was. Pamela shouldn't use the word 'nice' anyway.

'From the things I've read about her, her performances and paintings, I did, yes,' Pamela said. 'I expected her to be darker, if you know what I mean.'

Valeria's phone rang. It was Theodora. She could not bear a conversation in which Rhodes might appear. Or one where it might disappear again, after being back.

'You know what?' Valeria said to Pamela. 'Let's go home instead of eating. Work. No pub.'

And Pamela, who must have been very hungry, said 'sure' to that too.

TWENTY-TWO

Valeria had met her father in a park because any location with walls, or a roof, would have felt too intimate. She was twenty-nine years old, divorced, with a successful first book and a second one just sold to a publisher. Tracking Julian Spander down had been easy. She had called his editor before leaving New York saying she wanted to write a piece about their author, and that was that. As soon as Julian Spander heard her name, he would know that he was going to meet his daughter. The daughter who went by her mother's surname. Valeria had also thought of approaching the editor under a pseudonym, but the surprise effect didn't seem as appealing to her as the panic he'd surely feel leading up to their meeting. She hoped that would be another penance for him. Was he going to develop an ulcer? Panic attacks? Did he have a therapist to whom he spoke about all his mistakes, and would the two of them talk about the possibility of Julian taking benzodiazepines to assist him throughout the wait?

When Valeria landed in London the whole plan seemed less appealing. She hadn't told Theodora, and it felt more wrong than she had anticipated.

She had slept fitfully that night, waking intermittently through dreadful nightmares. Why didn't she travel with sleeping pills for nights like these?

In the morning, walking to Hampstead Heath, her mood perked up. It was a sunny day, spring was in full bloom, the wind was strong, fresh, and it helped. She had survived Rhodes. She had survived Sybilla's death. She had survived Italy. Julian's absence. She had survived Theodora's pain. Patrick Toyle's betrayal. None of that had destroyed her and all of it had led her here.

Valeria was ready to appear her most confident self. She was wearing a polo neck, a pair of jeans and sunglasses. Her leather jacket was too warm, but it made her feel safe while walking to the top of Parliament Hill.

She sat down on the bench, opposite two old men. It occurred to her that she could just leave. Let the pointless Julian down. But she would have let down herself too. And it would have been too easy for him not to have to face the shame and the pain. Not to have to face her.

'I wish you were here,' she said to Sybilla as she saw Julian-not-father-not-even-man climbing the hill.

I can look at him with the disgust that I feel, and then leave, she thought. This man, heading towards me, wasn't there when it could have been beautiful to be with us. And when it would have been right. He knows nothing about me and about those days. He doesn't know me or Sybilla or Theodora. He doesn't know the Northern Cove.

'Hello, Valeria,' Julian said.

Valeria didn't stand up. But she looked at him. He was more handsome than she had expected. His eyes were Sybilla's eyes. Valeria saw a monster and she saw herself beating the shit out of the monster.

Julian sat down on the bench next to her, looking at Valeria and then at the panorama. London, basking in the brightest light, had fast clouds dashing across its sky.

'I'm glad you called,' Julian said.

Valeria was pretty sure she wasn't going to shed a single tear on the lamest of men, but there was a remote possibility. So she counted. She breathed. Then she related all the details of Sybilla's sickness to not-father-not-man Julian. She told him about every medicine his daughter had taken, all the words she had screamed – and the nights when she wasn't able to scream any more, when she had fainted, vomited, struggled to breathe. Valeria told Julian about Theodora and herself, the time they stopped speaking to each other, having nothing more to say and no one there to help them. She told him about the days in which Sybilla and Valeria tried to make Theodora feel better. How they would walk with her through the empty valleys, afraid to speak, afraid to revive thoughts in Theodora of the most horrible of men, that would make her feel the most horrible of pain. Valeria told Julian about Sybilla asking for her father just before dying – a lie, made up in that moment, to destroy him.

'She repeated it over and over, in the last forty-eight hours before her death. Will Dad come? Will Dad come?' Valeria said. 'You never did.'

She didn't look at Julian. She stood up. 'Sybilla was the

most incredible person, she had the sweetest of souls,' she said. 'She was my sister and she had your eyes, but you will never fucking know because you will never fucking know.'

Valeria closed her jacket and walked down the hill. She walked away without looking back and crossed the park only to start crying when she was out of it. She didn't stop walking or crying for another hour until she reached a high street, where she found herself standing in front of a hairdresser. She entered the salon and had her hair cut very short. Like the doll she had when she was twelve. A few months later, she started receiving Julian's letters.

Pamela and Valeria were still re-reading the four drowned sisters story, when the phone rang. At the other end, Isla was crying. Valeria's heart changed beat, from already too fast to unbearably fast. Valeria's entire world changed aspect, her body morphed. Let me hold something before I drown, she thought. She held on to Pamela's thigh. Don't disappear, Martìn. Don't go.

'I need your help,' Isla said at the other end of the line.

Valeria was now standing up, already walking towards her coat. Pamela looked at her.

'What happened?' her eyes were asking.

'I need you to come back here. Now,' Isla repeated. 'Please?'

'Of course,' Valeria said, mouth dry, legs shaking. 'I'm on my way.'

Martìn, I would feel something if you were going, right? Does life exist if you don't? Valeria closed her computer, wrapped herself in her coat and scarf. Pamela gathered her things together.

'You should stay here,' Valeria told Pamela.

She repeated her usual prayer: I survived Rhodes. I can survive this too.

'I'll come along,' Pamela said.

'You have a train in an hour. I suggest you call a car in twenty minutes.'

'What? No!' Pamela said. She left her things on the table, put on her coat and scarf. 'I want to be here. With you.'

It is almost eight o'clock, Valeria thought. At seven minutes past eight, eight minutes past eight maximum, I will know everything there is to know. Are you ready for this to be the Friday that changed your life, Valeria? Are you going to collapse in front of them all?

She received a text from Theodora: it was a picture of her and Sybilla's school. Her jaw clenched.

As Valeria and Pamela reached the stairs leading to the Aclàs' front door, Valeria looked at the sky above the house and saw the word *paradeisos* written in the clouds, like a neon light at a Greek village party. How could she ever leave now to go to Rhodes? She had to be here. She raised one hand towards the sky to erase the writing, hoping that Pamela wouldn't notice.

'What's going on?' Pamela asked.

'Mosquito,' Valeria said.

She rang the bell, imagining a mosquito buzzing around in zero degrees. The door opened and the look on Mirela's face spelled disaster. Nico and Cosmo appeared. Here they are.

Cosmo, an exact copy of Martìn. Nico, more Isla. Was this like getting to know Martìn when he was thirteen? Is it this that I have missed in not having kids? Seeing you again from the beginning? Seeing me, or seeing Sybilla and Theodora as we were?

Come here, little Cosmo-Martìn, come here, little Nico-Isla.

The twins introduced themselves.

'It's a pleasure to meet you, I'm Nico,' Nico said.

'It's a pleasure to meet you, I'm Cosmo,' Cosmo said.

Valeria was ready for a handshake, but they both hugged her. Closeness. Warmth. Martìn's skin.

'Mum said to tell you to join her upstairs,' Nico said.

'Yes, she said to tell you to join her upstairs,' Cosmo repeated.

Nico glanced at him. 'Cut the shit, Cosmo,' he murmured.

'I'll now cut the shit,' Cosmo confirmed.

'When we first meet someone, he does this totally idiotic thing of pretending we speak the same!'

'When he first. . .' Cosmo murmured. 'Whatever,' he finished.

The boys looked stressed but not as if their father had just died. Or were they just horrible human beings? Was it like this too – having kids? Generating possible horrible human beings who don't care if you die? Her own father,

Julian, a horrible human being, had been the son of someone. He had written her all those letters after that day on Parliament Hill but Valeria hadn't opened a single one. How many were there? Seventy? Two hundred? Was Theodora receiving Julian's letters too? Valeria couldn't ask, because she couldn't mention Julian to her ever again.

TWENTY-THREE

Valeria went upstairs to Isla, leaving Pamela in the front room with the boys. She walked up the steps and they felt different because she had been invited to go up. She was needed. She took a glimpse at Antonia sticking her tongue out in the portrait: I'm allowed to be this close to Martìn and to you all today.

'Isla?' she murmured. The machines from Martìn's room were still making noise. 'Isla?' Valeria repeated, louder.

The door opened. Isla appeared in tears, her face swollen, her eyes red.

'Valeria, thank you,' Isla said. 'Come with me.'

She walked out of the room and closed the door slowly. Did this mean he was still alive? Because I'm sure I would feel it if you were gone, Martìn. Valeria had no other choice but to follow Isla. They entered another room.

'This is Antonia's room,' Isla said, shutting the door. 'Have a seat.' But Isla didn't sit down and Valeria didn't sit either.

Antonia's room was a mess. Posters, clothes, books, notebooks, a guitar, papers. Valeria noticed a pack of cigarettes too.

'We had a terrible fight,' Isla said.

Who? Not Martìn and her. Well, wait, in one of her stories a fight with someone in a coma could turn out to be a good one. Title? 'Listen to Me'. But what was important now was that Isla would have already said that Martìn had died. She wouldn't have invited Valeria over to be there with them during the disaster, right?

'Antonia was beside herself. She started screaming that if Martìn died, she was going to die too,' Isla croaked. 'She cut herself. She made a whole scene, it was horrible. Martìn too, from wherever he is, must have heard everything.'

'How is your husband doing?' Valeria slipped in.

'The same,' Isla said. 'But Antonia is falling apart. She admires you so much, she might want to speak to you. I'm sorry. I don't even know. . .'

'I'm glad you called me.' It was so true it shocked her. Hadn't she wanted to be in this house just to be close to Martìn? To eventually be able to tell Isla that she herself had loved Martìn all her life and that Martìn had told her he wanted to spend his future with Valeria?

'She hates everything and she hates me because I cheated on her father,' Isla said, whispering. 'Now that her father might be dying, she blames me for that too. Like his body broke down because I broke his heart.'

So what Antonia said this morning was true. And Isla was a liar as well. In almost thirty years, Valeria had never imagined it. Not even remotely. Martìn knew?

'It was more than a year ago,' Isla said, as if answering Valeria's unuttered questions. 'It didn't mean anything.

And it didn't break his heart. It was a deal between us. But I don't want to share all of this with Antonia. It's our relationship, our love, our choice. Not all that happens to us has to be about the kids or anyone else either.'

'Right.' Right?

'I told her everything would work out somehow. I hate having to be the one that says that. I wish I could collapse, too.' She paused, then, 'Antonia told me you two had lunch together, as if it were a secret between you because there are things I'm just not capable of understanding. I'm hopeless, always. I'm a cheater, a loser, an enemy.'

'I should have told you,' Valeria said. 'I don't know why I didn't, sorry.'

'I would have done the same,' Isla said. 'Actually, I think you two are a good match.'

Was she angry or not? She should be angry with me anyway, for ever, Valeria thought.

'Martìn wanted to have more kids after the twins,' Isla said. 'And even at the beginning, he was the one to really want a family. As soon as Antonia arrived I was grateful, but getting pregnant was something I would have postponed as long as possible.'

Had he wanted more kids?

When she was forty, Valeria became pregnant. She had been pregnant once before: he was one of the organizers of a literary festival, and Valeria had an abortion as soon as she found out. When she found out the second time, her first thought was whether to abort again. But then, she knew she couldn't.

Martin was away. In Africa, then in London. She wanted to tell him face-to-face, when they were together.

Even as a mother, she wouldn't want a husband or a shared house, Martin himself was present enough. Being independent had made her free, she wasn't going to give it all up. Perhaps if it's a girl we could call her Sybilla, Valeria had thought. She was sure that Martin would not want things to be secret. If they could approach everything in a rational manner, perhaps they would all be spared the guilt, and the pain? For he loved them all. And he was a good man. They would find their way. But she had to wait until their next meeting. After all, Sybilla wasn't going to be the right name.

They were the longest two weeks Valeria had ever experienced. During those days, she wrote a short story in which a mother and a daughter live in the wilderness, waiting for an apocalypse that never arrives.

'Where will the end come from? Will it come from the sky?' the daughter would ask the mother.

'It might not,' the mother would reply. 'It might come from us.'

Valeria had used the same phrasing Martin had used to tell her about the night when Rami died. Will the disaster come from the fire, the drugs, our bodies?

Four days before Martin returned, Valeria printed out the story, which she had entitled 'Deer'. As she watched the pages come out of the printer, she began to bleed. At the hospital, the blood was everywhere and she had to cover her trousers with a blanket. When she woke up in a bedroom, the doctor told her that it was a miracle she was still alive. He also told her that the baby was gone and that she could return home in three days.

'I have to cancel Thursday,' Valeria told Martìn on the phone that evening. 'I'm so sorry. I love you.'

Martìn thought she was in her own bed. In reality, she was in the hospital. She stared at the label on her bed linen, hoping for something to happen. Just like the girl in her short story, Valeria wondered, will the apocalypse come from the sky? She looked out the window and something did happen in the sky: a cloud shaped like a snail distracted her from the pain. And that's how she knew that the next day she would be OK for an entire minute. By the end of the month for a stretch of two hours. And so on.

'After lunch, Antonia kissed her father and disappeared into the bathroom,' Isla said. 'She was in there for half an hour, perhaps longer.'

Valeria saw Antonia on all fours, sobbing. She saw herself being able to caress her back, calm her.

'I got scared so I forced her to open the door,' Isla continued. 'I hugged her and for a few seconds she let me. But then I saw that she had cut herself. I couldn't help it and I screamed, "What the fuck have you done?" She ran off and left me there, still screaming.'

'I'm sure she doesn't think you were screaming at her.'

'She does. I also told her it was selfish putting herself at the centre of attention at times like these. I just lost it.' Isla cried, but it was like a quick breath, a blink, then she stopped.

'Where d'you think she might've gone?' Valeria asked her.

'She has no real friends at school. I have called the only two she sometimes mentions,' Isla said. 'She could be anywhere.'

'Is her phone off?'

'It rings, but she doesn't pick up,' Isla answered, her voice trembling. 'I know I'm asking you to enter into a mess with me. But, would you join me in the shit storm?'

TWENTY-FOUR

Isla, Valeria and Pamela left the house and climbed into Isla's car. Valeria could smell Martìn. They had very rarely shared a car: too dangerous. While Isla and Martìn had driven the world together. So he hadn't convinced his wife too to go around with a driver? Had Isla been a better feminist, artist, woman, fuck, person?

'To where?' Valeria asked Isla.

Pamela was sitting in the back seat. Why was she even coming?

'Are you sure you want to come?' Isla asked Pamela. 'I can drop you off at the tube station.'

Maybe Isla didn't want her around either.

'What about Benoit?' Valeria said. 'He might be waiting for you.'

'I'd rather be here with you,' Pamela said. She typed something on her mobile. To him? Or was she typing ideas for a book that would include all that she knew so far about Isla, Valeria, Martìn – all the cheating, all the lies? It would be a good repayment for all the stories Valeria had stolen throughout her life.

'I think we should split up,' Isla suggested.

Pamela nodded. Valeria herself wasn't going to nod because she wasn't sure splitting up was such a good idea. Ever.

'Sounds perfect,' Pamela said. She opened the tiny notebook she kept in her pocket, took out a pen. She was playing the squad game properly.

'Do you want to give us some addresses of places you want us to check?'

'Two places I know she usually hangs out at are a squat and a strip joint she manages to sneak in to. Then where else?' Isla was thinking out loud, frantic. 'Should we call the police and tell them she's missing? I don't want to be out doing this, away from home, far from Martin. Fuck!'

'Is this the first time you've left the house since the stroke?' Valeria asked. Isla's panic became Valeria's panic.

'But what else am I supposed to do?' Isla said.

Valeria put a hand on Isla's shoulder. Still robotic, so she removed it.

'Why don't Pamela and I continue to look for her, and you go back home?' Valeria said.

Luckily, Pamela hadn't left. If Isla being away from Martin meant that Martin might die, Valeria had to ensure that Isla returned home. Antonia was her duty now. This she knew even before tonight.

'No,' Isla said wiping the tears off her cheeks. 'Not for now, but thank you. I couldn't stand being there either.

Let's not split up. I'm too scared to be on my own. Always have been.'

They drove to all of the places Isla could think of. A church Antonia liked when she was ten. The entrance to Antonia's school. Bridges they used to cross when the family would go on outings together to the Southbank or the Tate, and Antonia had said, 'I like it here.' A diner Antonia loved. They went to a pub where Antonia often wanted to eat fish and chips. Oksana had told her about it and Antonia had told Isla.

'This was before Antonia started saying no to me,' Isla said, 'or stopped speaking about things we might want to try together.'

They made their way to the girls' Squat for Riot Grrrls and it was not like Valeria had expected from Martin's stories. The squat was pretty, spartan and from the outside it looked like a family home. Inside there were flowers, cute drawings on the walls, lamps dotted around the place, jazz playing in the background. The odours of soup and bath foam filled the air.

Isla approached one of the girls in the living room. She was sitting on the sofa rolling a spliff. The search party sat down too and were soon offered herbal tea, while a girl with blue hair and an enormous skirt stoked the fire with more logs.

'We haven't seen Antonia for a while,' the blue-haired girl said. 'Do you want to have a look at what she left for us? We all love it.'

The three women nodded. They left their cups on the low table and followed the girl to the top floor. Each stair had a word written on it. *Free. Red. Alone. Power. Sex. Eyes.* The escalation was like a trippy meditation. *Pussy. Nirvana. Run. Eat. Wet.*

How did they choose the words? Was it a collective stream of consciousness? Or did every girl get one stair on which to write her own word for happiness?

When they reached the top floor they stood beneath a large skylight. The rain beat down incessantly on the glass, drumming away like Morse code. SOS? What word do you want for your step, Valeria? *Title? Martín? Rhodes?*

Below the window there was a drawing on the wooden floor that looked like an enormous mandala. It also looked like those circles doodled when on the phone. Only larger. Perhaps a metre wide. A doodle made during the longest phone call ever. The lines were drawn in different colours. Antonia had done it when?

Antonia drew. Antonia was cutting herself again. Antonia was angry and knew secrets.

Valeria's and Isla's eyes welled up. Pamela moved closer.

'In the middle,' Pamela read aloud.

'What in the middle?' Isla asked, while getting closer too.

'Antonia wrote *in the middle* in the middle.'

The three women knelt down to inspect the writing.

198

When they walked back downstairs, leaving all the steps and the words for ascension behind, Isla and Valeria returned to their herbal teas while Pamela stared at the blue-haired girl.

Why were they still hanging around? Did Isla think the girls would confess something? *In the Middle* was a good title. It could be a title for so many different stories: *in the middle* of a conflict, a life, a stroke, a speech, meeting someone in the middle of nowhere, writing *in the middle* in the middle of a giant coloured round doodle. In the middle of my life, in the middle of this family. In the middle of the storm where everything is calm. Here, everything is calm.

'It's a good title,' Valeria said to Pamela as they were climbing back into the car. '*In the Middle*, I mean.'

Pamela jotted the words down in her notebook but she didn't smile or say 'perfect'. Maybe she was judging Valeria for stealing something from Antonia. Or was she judging her because it was inappropriate for Valeria to be thinking of titles while *in the middle* of such a scary evening? The absence of her smile meant that Valeria was selfish and that she grabbed whatever she needed? Titles, husbands, stories: Pamela was just beginning to realize the extent of Valeria's thievery. The sooner, the better.

'It reminds me of a night Antonia and I looked everywhere for Milou,' Isla said. 'You know, that cat in the portrait on the first floor, the one with the kid sticking her tongue out? That's Antonia and Milou.'

'Oh yes, I noticed that today,' Valeria said. 'So where was Milou?'

'We never found her. Antonia didn't give up for months. She went round the neighbourhood putting up photocopies with Milou's picture on it. She wasn't even seven at the time,' Isla said. 'She's like that with everything.'

'She doesn't give up?' Valeria asked.

'She can't let go. Maybe we're all like that, she just doesn't pretend.'

There was silence in the car. The elephant in the room was the cheating. The other was Martìn dying.

'Is this coming up now because of her dad and wanting to defend him? So she has someone to blame for her anger. How does she even know?' Isla said.

Valeria and Pamela didn't answer. They had no way of knowing why or how Antonia knew. Isla kept driving, turned left, slowed down and stopped at a petrol station with a convenience store.

'I cannot tell her that Martìn had been cheating on me too. It would kill her and it wouldn't be fair. Even if it could save me from her rage, I won't.'

Valeria's stomach lurched. It was like having a crater in the middle – in the middle – of her chest and of her body.

'I need to fill the car. Want something from inside?' Isla asked. 'A coffee?'

Maybe the cheating was an invention to punish Valeria and slowly, bit by bit, Isla was going to destroy all that Valeria thought she was, all of what Martìn had been.

'Yes, please,' Valeria said. 'A coffee.'

She was nine. She was twelve. She was Antonia, Sybilla, she was Valeria. She was the cheater, and she had been cheated on. She was the one and she was the other.

Martìn was alive, or was Martìn already dead? They had fucked, they would never fuck again. They knew each other and would never really know each other. Everyone is everyone.

'A coffee,' Isla repeated, as if it was something complicated to memorize.

Valeria sympathized. It was complicated to memorize. The bits, the whole.

'Just water, thank you,' Pamela said.

Valeria wished she had given the same answer. That's all she needed, water.

Isla got out. She took a few steps and locked the car behind her.

'Has she just fucking locked the car?' Valeria said. She tried to open the door and the door didn't open. She tried to click the buttons for the windows and the buttons didn't work. 'Fuck!' Valeria banged her fist against the window. The air in her lungs disappeared. The back of her neck tensed. She was freezing. And she was boiling.

'She'll be back in no time,' Pamela said.

'I will fucking die in no time! Open!' Valeria shouted.

'Come here,' Pamela said. 'Pretend we're not in this car.'

'How can I do that? There's no air. We *are* in this car.'

'Hug me,' Pamela said.

Valeria hated Pamela and everything in life, but she crawled into the seat behind and because she wasn't able to hug her, she let Pamela hug her.

'Can I hug you tighter?' Pamela said.

Valeria was now squeezing her nose next to Pamela's breasts. It wasn't a hug, it was more like choking. Why did

Pamela want to hug her tighter? She breathed in Pamela's perfume, the lingering smell of laundry. She breathed in the smells from the squat, from her own house, from the paint in Isla's studio.

'I don't know,' Valeria said. 'I can't breathe.'

She hated the shaking of her body for a fucking stupid thing like being stuck in a fucking stupid car. She had survived much more. How could she lose it this way? Had Martìn lied to her? The word 'fear' in Japanese morphed from the shape of a sweating house to that of a locked car.

'Stay with me,' Pamela said.

Valeria hated the *stay with me* too and Pamela's solid young body. At the same time, there was no other place for Valeria to want to be if not there, near a solid young body, where Pamela was inviting her to stay. Was she freaking out like this just because of the lack of air, or because once the air and Isla were back she might discover whether Martìn had been lying to her too all these years and had other lovers? She was trapped, she was being held hostage. What if Isla were to make this whole car explode?

'Here she comes,' Pamela said.

Valeria moved up again and crawled back to her seat. Letting go of Pamela wasn't as easy as she thought.

'Here's the coffee and the water,' Isla said. 'Let's go to the strip joint, shall we? Maybe Antonia would turn to Oksana on a night like this. I'm not sure I like Oksana, she was the one to let her in that place even though Antonia is underage. But she did welcome her, so I guess I also like Oksana for having opened a door to my daughter.'

'*Stay With Me* is a good title too,' Valeria said to

Pamela as they drove. Her voice was that of someone else. Someone fragile. Who's been cheated on.

'Giving titles is a curious thing,' Isla said. 'As if we were trying to sum it up, give a thesis to what happens. And to life.'

'Don't you give titles to your paintings?' Pamela asked.

'I just write down who's in the painting. Kid. Cat. Husband. Writer,' said Isla.

Isla's titles too were trying to sum up only one part of the story, pick one name out of the thousands we carry, Valeria thought.

'Will you call my portrait *Writer*?' Valeria asked. Or was she going to call it 'lover'? Or 'other woman'?

Isla's phone rang. The loudspeaker went on.

'Everything is all right,' Mirela said. 'Mr Aclà is fine. The boys are in bed. I'll try to sleep a little, in Antonia's room, so I can hear everything.'

'Thank you, Mirela. If I've got any news I'll call you,' Isla said, parking in front of the Scheherazade Bliss.

TWENTY-FIVE

The club was all pink. Pink carpets, pink walls, even the counter was pink. The girl standing behind it was wearing a pink bra with an open pink shirt as a dressing gown. She had shiny pink lips.

'Good evening, ladies, it's lovely to see you again,' the shiny girl smiled.

Isla, Pamela and Valeria smiled back. Which of them had been here before?

'Let me take your coats. For those of you who don't know me, my name is Lucy. Don't hesitate to ask if you need anything. I want you to enjoy your night. You are very special to us.'

Lucy took their coats, one after the other, giving the coat-taking a sexy new meaning.

The three women were escorted downstairs. Lucy kept smiling and with every step that she took she would smile and sometimes she stopped for no other reason than that of smiling. Following Lucy and her smile, they crossed a dark room, with mirrors on the walls, candles on the tables and into a curtained-off area with low lighting and a small stage.

No other guests were in there.

'It's like your own private party,' Lucy said. 'I'm glad you can experience this exclusivity tonight. It's very rare, you're very lucky.'

'Can I ask you something, Lucy?' Isla said.

Valeria could see her impatience. Her fear too. A bottle of champagne appeared, some music started playing in the background and lasers lit up the stage.

Lucy opened up her gown. One nipple was covered with a star sticker like those given to children for being good.

'Ask me anything,' Lucy smiled. 'I was hoping for a question and, not to disappoint you ladies, I was hoping it was going to come from you. I guess this is my lucky night, too.'

Isla was blushing. Lucy was flirting. Valeria was jealous. Pamela was nervous but still acting worldly. When the laser light hit her ponytail, it turned red.

'I'm here for my daughter,' Isla said.

Lucy's face changed. Her whole body moved back. The star disappeared, so did her happiness. She closed her nightgown but not completely, because it was too small and maybe because she didn't want to give the impression that mothers made her close nightgowns.

The show on the stage had started, a girl in her twenties appeared, naked but for a golden necklace.

Lucy looked sad. This wasn't her lucky night any more. She remained seated with Pamela, Isla and Valeria, opened the bottle of champagne and poured glasses for them all. They drank while watching the mellow dance.

'Her name is Naji,' Lucy said when Naji was about to finish her dance.

The music ended, Naji smiled at the three women and Lucy raised her glass to her.

'My daughter's name is Antonia,' Isla said. 'She's a friend of Oksana. Antonia ran away from home today.'

Lucy poured them each another glass of champagne. At least there was going to be a payment from the ladies. Could Lucy possibly make them buy two bottles of champagne? Maybe she could make them buy another bottle by talking very slowly about Antonia. It would pay some bills and buy new stars for the nipples.

'Oksana is back in Russia,' Lucy said. 'She had to hand in her thesis.'

Lucy had heard this story before. A runaway daughter. A chasing, worried mother. It was the story of her life, and daughters were usually right in doing whatever they wished, especially when running away from home.

'Oh, Russia,' Isla said. She finished her second glass of champagne.

Was this still part of the drink-to-get-information plan? Valeria imagined Isla having a drinking problem. The pain it had brought in her life. Fights with Martìn, meltdowns with the kids, crying alone in bars, varicose veins in her legs.

'Oksana is studying to be an architect,' Lucy added, then, looking at Isla's empty glass, 'Another bottle?'

'Do you know Antonia?' Pamela asked.

With some effort Lucy decided to look at Pamela too.

'I do,' Lucy said.

Isla nodded but her nod was rigid. Lucy probably carried a secret microphone somewhere because Naji appeared with the champagne. Then she disappeared as if she already knew that no other money would come from the ladies tonight.

'Antonia is very funny,' Lucy said.

Isla's eyes lit up. She looked like she was attending a parent-teacher meeting.

'She is funny, full of life. Once she made me laugh so hard I ended up having to lock myself in the loo to stop.'

'Her father is very sick. He might die,' Isla said.

'We all have a dying father, right?' Lucy said. 'I mean, metaphorically. It's important to leave them the space to die.'

'Well, her father is really dying. It's not a metaphor,' Pamela said. She poured herself a glass of champagne. She drank it.

'Still, he needs the space to do so. That's my two cents,' Lucy replied.

Isla put a hundred pounds on the table. Lucy didn't flinch. Her eyes didn't even look at the money.

'It's three hundred,' she said and Isla handed her a credit card. Lucy slipped out a machine from the tiny pocket of her tiny nightgown. She swiped the card, gave the receipt to Isla.

'Antonia's going to be OK,' Lucy said to Isla while Isla was signing the receipt. 'She just needs to stop wearing black. It doesn't do anything for her,' she said.

'Another metaphor?' Pamela asked her.

Lucy walked ahead of them, the three ladies following her, three hundred pounds lighter. She wasn't smiling any more on the way back upstairs, but probably to go back upstairs no smile was needed.

As soon as they were outdoors Isla's phone started to beep with one text after another. Isla grabbed her chest. Valeria, without moving and without actually using her hands, grabbed her chest too. Too many texts. What were they saying? Come back home immediately, Martin is dead? He needed the space to end his life and now that they were all out he had done it?

'Antonia is back home!' Isla told Valeria and Pamela.

She hugged Valeria. And because Isla knew how to hug, she hugged Pamela too. She then walked back to the Scheherazade Bliss, opening its doors widely, the neon lights inside revealing the new atmosphere. Lucy had a pair of jeans round her ankles.

'Antonia's back,' Isla told Lucy.

Lucy smiled. She pulled up the jeans, unglued the star sticker. Her nipple reddened. She slipped into a Mickey Mouse sweater.

'Buy her some clothes!' Lucy shouted at Isla while she walked back to the car. 'Avoid black.'

Isla drove back to Holland Park. Asking her if she was sober enough to do so wasn't an option. Approaching Westbourne Grove, Valeria asked if Isla could drop them off.

'Here?' Isla said.

'Yes, thank you,' Valeria answered.

The rain hadn't stopped, but was no longer a downpour.

Pamela followed Valeria out of the car without questioning her decision.

'I guess tomorrow morning we'll be too tired for the sitting,' Isla said before they closed the door.

'You wake up and let me know,' Valeria answered. She wanted to be in the Aclàs' house no matter how tired she was. She wanted to see Martìn. And Antonia too.

'Thank you for tonight. Without you two it would have been a nightmare,' Isla said.

'Don't worry,' they both answered. 'It's the least we could do. Goodnight.'

Valeria and Pamela faced the streets to the flat. It was so cold they couldn't even speak. They just walked, quickly, Pamela probably wondering why they hadn't been dropped off at their precise address.

'I think the couch is a sofa bed,' Valeria said when they arrived.

'The couch is fine anyway,' Pamela said, 'I'm able to sleep on the floor.'

Of course she was.

Valeria boiled some water for tea to warm them up. They washed one after the other, Pamela using toothpaste on her finger. The couch was just a couch. Valeria gave Pamela a cushion and a blanket.

'Goodnight,' Valeria said, before closing her door. 'I hope you manage to rest.'

'I'll probably be gone by the time you wake up.'

'I'm sorry you didn't make it to Paris tonight.'

'I'm glad I was with you. I would have hated being in Paris.'

Pamela turned her back to Valeria, showing her how comfortable she was on the couch. Was she going to pretend she was snoring too? Valeria closed the door, then looked at her phone and saw there had been calls from Theodora. She listened to the answering machine. There was a message from the monks: 'Valeria, Moma Saint really needs you to book your trip to Rhodes. She would love for it to be very soon. Please come back to the secretary monks.'

Moma Saint? Very soon? What the fuck?

Valeria switched off the lights and lay down on the bed. Feeling around in the darkness she found the sleeping pills and took one. Then she waited for Sybilla, Rami, for Theodora forbidding Rhodes forever and now wanting Rhodes immediately, the four drowned sisters and for Martìn to be near her. One by one they all made it to her room, and into her heart.

'Hello everyone,' Valeria whispered. 'Welcome back.'

TWENTY-SIX

At the crack of dawn, London was awakened by a wind so strong it felt like houses would fly away. One of the shutters was banging and Valeria had to peel herself off the bed and close it. She lay down again. When she woke up it was late morning. She rinsed her face, opened the shutters. Still no flowers in the garden. She opened the door to the living room and Pamela was nowhere to be seen. Not having to share a breakfast with her was a relief. Valeria undressed and prepared coffee, naked. She was too hot to wear clothes. Hormones? Flu? Seeing her reflection in the windows was an experience about decay, depression and death. Was this what Isla was portraying?

'You are the change,' Valeria said, trying to remember the YouTube trainer's exact words. 'Embrace the burn.'

She took a shower and put on some trousers, a jumper, thick socks and boots. She wore a woollen hat and scarf, grabbed the keys and left the house.

The woollen hat isn't a good idea, she told herself once under the rain – not that anything else in her life seemed to be. Her phone rang.

'I love the title,' Joe said.

'Which title?' A double-decker bus nearly hit her, blasting air so close to her face it made her mouth tighten. I could have been dead before you, Martìn. See? Especially if I keep on crossing the streets of London.

'*In the Middle* is great,' Joe answered. 'Pamela texted it to me this morning.'

'I just told her to jot it down. It's nothing official.'

'I love it,' Joe repeated. *I love it*? Less Joe, less. 'I keep on saying it out loud and it sounds very good. Anyway, by next week you need to give them the final one.'

'How's life?' Valeria asked. She didn't want Joe talking about the title. If he kept on repeating that he loved it she wouldn't like it any more.

'Life is good,' Joe said. 'Tiu, my ex, has been back in New York and we had a lovely evening out last night. But my mum died.'

There was a pause. Thousands of insects crawled around Valeria's feet, gathering there to cry for Joe and his mother. She turned left and found herself on Ladbroke Grove. She managed to leave behind the insects but in all the houses the crying was there. And in the whole solar system too.

'I'm very sorry, Joe,' Valeria said. 'When did she die?'

'Apparently, it's been months. No one told me.'

'How are you feeling?' Valeria said.

'Numb,' Joe said, 'which is scary. I'm scared by my coldness.'

'What do you want to do?'

'In general I intend to live,' Joe said.

Joe had told Valeria his story only once, when on a flight together they had been talking about childhoods. He had started by saying that he had been raised in a radical Christian family. Their church was called Word of Spirit. His mother had been home-schooled until the age of ten and had never read a book since, so the Bible was pretty much all she knew. Joe's house was in the middle of nowhere in Montana and was run like a dictatorship under the laws of God and Joe's father.

Joe grew up with ten siblings who were all involved in ecumenical work within the community: the kids went around reading from the Bible door-to-door and none attended school.

Since he could remember, Joe always knew he liked men. Through prayers and self-punishment he tried not to like them. When he was twelve he confessed to his mother and asked her if she could help him. He told her he was sorry and not to tell his father. Melissa had him beaten by his older brothers Jeremiah and Paul on a day when his father wasn't at home. Joe was hospitalized for two weeks. The testimony he gave the police had been about some unknown gang that beat him while shouting things against Jesus Christ.

Still not cured of his curse, Melissa decided with Joe's father – who by now had become involved – to send him to a 'Christian camp'. Joe went there still hoping to be cured. He didn't fight back when his parents explained it would be for the best. He loved them. On his return from the camp, Joe tried to hang himself but didn't manage to do it properly. Still going door-to-door, he one day met

Charles Lee, a gay man in his thirties. They started talking about the Bible and Charles Lee ended up saving Joe. Charles Lee slowly educated him and gave him books that Joe kept in a shack. With a loan from his only friend and as soon as he was old enough, Joe escaped from his family and went to New York. When he turned seventeen, he stayed with one of Charles Lee's university friends.

Lawrence was a well-known poet. He would often rehearse his readings at home, with Joe as his audience. To earn money, Joe worked in the secretarial office of a small law firm, then did the same work for the Actor's Studio. He studied night and day, English and French literature being his passion. With Lawrence, he would go to the movies and the theatre. He discovered he had a gift for editing, and very quickly became a junior agent at a small literary agency. He now shared a flat with a Frenchman and an American-Chinese dancer called Tiu, who was on a scholarship at Juilliard. Joe had sex for the first time in his life with Tiu, two months after he moved into the shared house, and they were a couple until Tiu received another scholarship at La Scala in Milan. At the beginning they wrote each other letters, then lost touch for a very long time.

Many years later, Joe and Tiu met again in Los Angeles. Tiu was there for a show that Joe had gone to see with a client. They slept together for three nights and on the third evening they ended up having sex on some grass near Mulholland Drive. Pictures of the two were taken by a random crack addict. By now, Tiu was famous and Joe represented authors who wouldn't necessarily want their names to be slurred by having their agent exposed in a sex scandal. Tiu and Joe had to secretly pay the blackmailer off with $35,000 so as not to have the pictures sold. After a year, they had to pay him another $20,000. Finally, they signed a binding deal and all the pictures were destroyed.

Joe and Tiu would sometimes catch up, and send occasional congratulatory emails and texts. One of the first exchanges of this nature that Joe had ever received from Tiu said something like *I hear you're the It agent of the It writer, my Joe. You are a fantastic human being. You deserve all beauty.*

Joe's career and life had changed when Valeria Costas, the new literary and indeed *It* writer at the time, whom he had only met once, decided to sign with him. It was completely unexpected: 'I like you' was all she had said. He didn't even have the courage to ask why. He blushed and accepted the good karma. Until that day, he'd always had low hopes about luck and karma, but now he let go of some of his cynicism – and it was a revelation. Joe could still remember the physical sensation of his first book auction. His legs were paralysed, his squeal was heard by the entire office. God exists! he said. Even if by then he was sure He didn't. Joe then drove two days and two nights, all the way back to Charles Lee's house, and on the doorstep, when Charles greeted him, Joe was holding a magnum of champagne and the money he owed him. A few weeks later, Charles Lee died in a car crash. At the funeral Lawrence read one of his poems. It was called, 'Peace in Your Hands'.

' I've heard all sorts of rumours about Isla Lawndale's husband, Martìn Aclà,' Joe said. Didn't he want to talk more about his mother?

'Like what?' Valeria asked.

'For example, they say that with his immense fortune he finances eco-warrior groups and tens of radical pacifist collectives. I also read that he owns a house in the middle of the Amazon Forest.'

'Joe, please,' she stopped him. 'What are you on about?'

'I also heard his twins have a channel on YouTube where they try marijuana oils. So, I've watched a couple.'

'Shall I tell their mother?'

'Maybe?' Joe said. 'I'm really not sure.'

Valeria was passing a small park, empty because of the rain. The Amazon Forest? She kept on walking and she thought maybe where this road ends the world ends. I will fall down and it will be the longest dive. She pictured Nico and Cosmo inhaling clouds of cannabis. She saw them laughing. Joe's mother was staring at them beside a cross. Theodora was staring at Valeria judging her for not going to her or to Rhodes.

'Keeps on being interesting, this whole business of having a family,' Joe said.

'Whatever that means,' Valeria replied. 'Joe, I'm so sorry for your loss.'

'She was my mother,' Joe said. 'And now she is dead.'

Valeria managed to hold a pause in which she breathed audibly, so as not to make Joe feel abandoned, and to let the word *dead* float in silence. She was inhaling and exhaling, a little louder than usual, to make herself heard, as though she were caressing her friend. Was he her friend? He was still Joe even after his mother had died. He hadn't disappeared. He wasn't invisible.

As they ended their call, she looked at the dark screen, covered in raindrops. Just like the screen, reality was blurry.

She texted Pamela. *In the Middle: not so sure. Please send over Julian's box of letters. And please check if Dimitri is in Rhodes. Thank you for helping me and for making my life and my work easier. Valeria.*

Writing *In the Middle: not so sure* was only there to worry Pamela.

Valeria found herself near a cemetery and walked past some railway tracks and a road where all the houses were brown. She reached All Souls Avenue, where the houses were identical but white. It was like being a loop. She was feeling so lost that she called an Uber. Muhammad was going to pick her up in four minutes. She had already rated Muhammad five stars, the app was telling her, so Muhammad was a person she knew and she had already shared kilometres with him. She had already told him, 'I want to go there.' Through a postcode, but still, they had shared something. The last time she was in London or this one? The last time she had been in London she had met Martìn in Richmond, in the park. It must have been more than a year ago. It was spring, but it was freezing.

'Hello,' Muhammad said when he arrived. 'Don't cancel the app, I'll lose my job.'

'Sure,' she answered. 'I wasn't going to.'

'Not a lie?' Muhammad said.

'I never lie,' Valeria said, lying.

'Not even to yourself?' Muhammad started the car.

That spring in Richmond Park, Valeria and Martìn only had a couple of hours together. London was always a mistake. It was not only the possibility of someone seeing them, it was home, for him. She had to put herself through seeing Martìn as less hers than ever. But Valeria was there for a TV show, she had walked in the footsteps of Virginia Woolf, someone in front of her showing where to turn, when to pause, while she was speaking. After the shoot, they had met up.

'Would your brother have liked me?' Valeria had asked Martìn at the park.

'I think that you would have understood each other,' he said. 'Probably even better than we do.'

Another thing that would happen when they met in London, is that they both became impatient, jumpy.

'Anyhow, you would have never introduced me to him,' she said.

She knew she was being harsh, and that her tone of voice was sharp, but it was the truth. She had never met Martìn's friends, she had never met his mother or his father Bernardo.

Bernardo had died years before Helena, in his sleep, at home in Argentina and Helena had organized a small funeral on their land. Martìn flew there with Isla and the kids. He called Valeria only once while there and told her that the days were somehow pleasant – warm and full of love. He wished he'd seen his father one last time, he had told her. He was still learning things about him on this same visit home. His father had kept a diary, who would have guessed?

'Should I read it?' Martìn asked Valeria.

'I only know that if I left a diary behind me, you reading it would be my worst nightmare,' Valeria said. 'Mine, you would have to burn.'

When Martìn returned from Argentina, he told Valeria he hadn't burned his father's diary, but he hadn't read it either. He had found a secret place, under an oak tree, and buried it there in a metal box, which he had covered with a plastic bag. And the plastic bag with another plastic bag.

'What for?' Valeria asked.

'For a stranger to find it and read it from the right distance.'

'That stranger might be me,' she smiled.

TWENTY-SEVEN

Back home Valeria dried her hair with a towel and played some music. She flipped through the books she had bought with Antonia and grabbed one about Alighiero Boetti. She looked at some of Alighiero Boetti's works made with stamps and postcards. She turned to his paintings where the letters of his first and second name were reassembled, in alphabetical order. They were self-portraits. Other self-portraits, by other artists, were displayed. *My last name exaggerated fourteen times vertically,* by Bruce Nauman, read the description. Then there was Mel Bochner's *Self/Portrait,* where on every line of a piece of notebook paper the sequence of words was *ego/portrayal, oneself/head,* and so on, until the last line read *being/lifestudy. Being/Lifestudy.* Nice way of putting it. Valeria kept reading and found Alighiero Boetti's works *I vedenti,* 'those who see', which was his name for artists.

The doorbell rang. Nobody knew she lived there, right? Finally, a killer? Gun or knife? She opened the door.

'Hey,' Antonia said. 'I wanted to say I'm sorry.'

'How are you feeling today?' How could Antonia be here?

'Better,' she said, 'until the next thunderstorm.'

'Tell me about thunderstorms! Where were you last night?'

'On the stairs of this building but on the first floor. I followed you the other day. Took me two minutes.'

So Valeria wasn't the only one spying on people.

'I haven't told Mum,' Antonia said, as though she could hear Valeria's thoughts.

If I think 'I love Martìn', can you hear me?

'I was about to ring your bell but you left the apartment with that Pamela of yours. Hey, what's the deal there?'

'There's no deal, what do you mean?'

The rain turned to hail and the noise on the roof was the usual Morse code message. Was it saying L.O.V.E.? Antonia sat on the couch, scanning the room.

'I liked the place for the riot girls,' Valeria said. 'Your drawing upstairs is stunning.'

'I only draw those circles,' Antonia explained keeping her eyes down. Then she looked at Valeria. 'I started in the squat, to thank the girls for a few meals.'

'Meals there must be good. I'd love to go with you one day.'

'Sure. Listen, Mum sent me to buy groceries because she's back to not wanting to leave the house. What are you doing today?' Antonia started flicking through the same pages Valeria had just been reading.

'Have you two made peace?' Valeria asked.

'It's not about making peace,' Antonia said, her head nodding as if she was saying yes to a question that she was the only one to know. 'If he dies, what will we do?'

Valeria's heart shrank. It was like a cherry stone now. Please, not so small, I cannot breathe, it cannot beat. So she breathed and her heart remained small but became slightly bigger, like an apricot stone.

'If he dies,' Antonia continued, 'Mum will die too.'

'She will not,' Valeria said. She said it so quickly it came out more like a burp than a sentence. 'And you won't either.'

'Let's go,' Antonia said standing up again, clearly wanting to avoid the topic. 'Come with me.'

They left the flat and Valeria followed Antonia to buy the biscuits that the twins liked, the milk, and all the shopping for the Aclà household. They stopped at the dry cleaner's, they went to the delicatessen and bought two pieces of goat's cheese. They ended up at the organic deli. Valeria wanted to follow this kid for ever.

'Hey, bitch,' the Sally-Poppy girl with blinding earrings said to Antonia.

'Hey, Bea,' Antonia said. She kissed her.

During the kiss, Valeria saw Bea slipping something in Antonia's pocket. Antonia smiled, slipping something in Bea's pocket too. Valeria looked over the counter. *You will never have this day again so make it count* was written up there. Did Valeria have to tell Antonia she'd seen? But she was never going to have this day again, so she had to make it count.

Walking back home, the shopping bags hanging from her forearms, Antonia took out something from her pocket, another something from her other pocket. Valeria looked at her. Antonia had a joint in her mouth. She lit it, they smoked it. They walked on and Valeria imagined Antonia diving at the Northern Cove.

'I'm sorry last night was so terrible for you,' Valeria said.

'I'm not sorry for me,' Antonia said. 'I'm disgusting.'

'Not one little bit.'

'I feel sorry for them, for having me as a daughter. What's wrong with me?'

'Nothing. They love you very much,' Valeria said. Then, 'You look like your father.'

Antonia stared at Valeria. Eyeliner now stained her cheeks. She was studying Valeria, trying to solve a puzzle. But what image was on the cover of this box?

'How d'you know?' Antonia asked.

'I've seen him.'

Was she now going to say when, where and how? Or would Antonia just let it go, imagining that Valeria had seen Martìn in some picture, or thought she had searched him online or seen him in a magazine or perhaps upstairs just yesterday, with her mother, in their house?

'You'll be fine, Antonia,' Valeria whispered. 'I know it and Lucy from the Scheherazade Bliss knows it too.'

Perhaps whispering that the future would be fine would make Antonia fine.

Valeria remembered what Martìn had told her about Antonia banging her body against walls. She had asked him what one could possibly say to someone so desperate.

Martìn had replied that the only words he could utter were that she was going to be fine, and that he loved her. Should Valeria fake his voice now, too?

'You are smart. Funny. You are very kind. At least, with me you are,' Valeria smiled. 'That's all I care about.'

'Yourself? You mean you only care if I am kind to you?' She smiled too.

'I like you very much,' Valeria told her. 'I like the way you speak, I like what you say. I like your drawings and your face and I like bumping into you. In London, you're my favourite person.' She didn't say in the world so as not to scare her, but she could have said that too. Because it was true. Antonia was currently her favourite person in the world.

'That's because I'm good literary material,' Antonia smiled. 'You're just here to steal.'

'I only steal good stuff. You should be flattered.'

'Why don't you have kids?' Antonia asked.

'I'm not sure,' Valeria had always answered that she didn't want them, but she wasn't sure any more. 'I got pregnant once, but it didn't happen.' Valeria considered that if that child had been born, it would have been Antonia's half-brother or sister. Could she say that now? *I got pregnant once, it would have been your brother or sister.* That way Antonia would have something very specific to worry about. 'I have never told anyone before,' she told Antonia, 'so please, keep my secret.'

'Story of our lives,' Antonia said.

When they separated, Valeria played it cool until she reached her flat's front door. Once inside, she had an epic panic attack and remembered why she didn't smoke grass. At the same time, she really, really wanted to eat curry. Before managing to order an Indian delivery, and trying to figure out if the magnolia tree outside the Aclàs' house could be climbable and a way to Martìn's room, she fell asleep.

The following morning Valeria woke up to the sound of the phone. Saliva had dribbled down the side of her mouth. She wiped it with the back of her hand. Her phone rang again.

'Sorry for calling so early,' Isla said.

'Is it early?'

'There've been people coming and going since yesterday. Some of our friends keep on bringing me food and then they stay here and eat for hours. Luc, this friend of Martìn's, always stays too long. Anyway, sorry.'

I could ask whether you remember that time you, Martìn and Luc were in Spain and he drank so much you all ended up at the police station for stealing three bikes. I could ask if you think Luc still wants to see if he will ever have you. He did love you back then. Does he now? Is he the one you had an affair with?

'I just wanted to ask you,' Isla said, 'if we could do lunch too. We have to find a way to finish all this food.'

'Lunch is perfect. What shall I bring?'

'Bring yourself and please be very hungry,' Isla said. Then she paused.

'Yes?' Valeria asked. She pictured Isla as though in a cartoon when someone has an idea and a light bulb lights up over their head. Valeria saw the light. The flash. With an imaginary device and imaginary electricity-related abilities, she dimmed the bulb.

'Yes, there's a catch.' Valeria could hear Isla's smile in her voice. 'My call was mainly to ask you if you could bring one of your new stories.'

'Do you mean *Ruby*, my last published collection?'

'No, we have *Ruby*. Or at least if it's out I'm sure we do. I mean *new* new. Unpublished,' Isla said. 'I would like to have Antonia read one or two stories to Martìn. He was, he is, a big fan of yours. They both are. It would be a great gift.'

Valeria went to the sink. Filled a glass of water. Of course, Martìn had already read nearly all of them. But she could choose those that he had liked the most. She could definitely give him 'Rain'. Or she could give him 'The Actress', about Theodora's wedding with Matteo. It ended with her mother's sentence on beauty.

'Beauty is simple,' Theodora had told Valeria. The wedding was held on Matteo's family land, just outside Rome. 'It works the other way around too. Simple is very beautiful.'

Valeria shrugged her shoulders. She was made to wear a gown cut with the same fabric Theodora used for her bridal dress and, despite the irritation, Valeria had done all that she was told by her new family of strangers. Matteo's mother, a devout Christian, did her best to make Valeria feel welcome and Matteo's sister, a petite girl who was deaf, welcomed Valeria with all her smiles. The words that Matteo's mother used for her acquired new granddaughter were words probably overheard somewhere. *You are part of the family now. You are the granddaughter I never had.* Valeria didn't believe in marriage or in these words. She didn't believe in Theodora's new smile. But in the meantime, she tried to behave well in front of Matteo's family. She helped around the house, she brushed her hair, she was tidy and never complained. She was obedient, with no needs or desires of her own. She created a docile alternative persona for when Matteo's family were around. For this alternative persona, she also invented a past and a future – a short story that would last for this specific chapter of their life.

On the day of the wedding, following her new invented character's identity, Valeria was well behaved. She brushed her long hair, she even put on some of Theodora's mascara. She let her eyes look engaged and pretended to find everything charming. She listened to her new grandmother – grandmother, grandmother, repeat: grandmother – uttering sentimental lines about how today would complete her family. She listened to them all, not liking herself for being so cold but still so damn good an actress.

Less than an hour before the celebration, Theodora told Valeria that Matteo wanted them both to take up his surname. Valeria felt her stomach clench. She tried to put her name together with that of Matteo's. It sounded fake even to her alternative persona and even without having to pronounce it. Theodora was rubbing sun cream on her legs and arms, because this way they would look shinier. Valeria adored the smell. And that smell wouldn't change, even if her mother were to change her surname, even if she were to pretend that she was this other woman who didn't have a past or a present and was getting married in the vineyard of some random family, the roses and the honey in that Greek lotion would always reveal the truth. The body cream had made it through escape and through pain, until today. Theodora was still Theodora Costas. She would always be the mother of Sybilla Costas and Valeria Costas. Good actresses wouldn't let themselves fall in such an easy trap, they would choose a different lotion, not a different surname.

'I want to keep my surname,' Valeria said. She put the lotion in her hands, rubbed some into her arms.

'If you keep that one, then you and I will end up having different surnames,' Theodora said.

That one is Costas. It's *the* one.

'It would be better if we all had the same surname.'

'Yes, Mum, I get the *better* concept. But I'll keep my surname, because if I keep our surname, the one we have been carrying all our lives, Sybilla and I will still have the same one. She can't change it, right? So I'll stick to us, and I'll stick to her.'

When Valeria saw Theodora again, she was waiting in the aisle of the church. She immediately knew that her mother didn't believe the script any more. And by the time Theodora said, 'Yes, I do' in English and Italian, the credibility of the character had disintegrated. Valeria's abracadabra had brought Sybilla back.

'I'm sorry,' Valeria told her mother that night.

Theodora was closing the shutters. Valeria could hear her crying. Why did she want her mother to feel desperate? She had to be simple, just like beauty was. Hadn't it been a promise between Sybilla and her to do all they could to make Theodora happy?

'I'm sorry,' Valeria repeated, louder.

Theodora sat on Valeria's bed and held her shoulder. She didn't say don't be sorry. She didn't say you should be sorry. She held her shoulder and let it go.

For years Valeria was torn with doubt that if it hadn't been for her, Theodora could have been happy. If not for ever then perhaps for a long sunny season.

When, a few months later, Theodora and Valeria left Matteo's house for good, without a fight or an argument, they closed their boxes, said their thank yous and their sorrys, and never mentioned that chapter of their lives again. Valeria also managed to hug her fake grandmother, listening to the bitter comments about Theodora. Once again, Valeria wasn't able to smile at Matteo and it made her feel bad. He had believed in them when he shouldn't have.

'I hope you two will be all right, Valeria,' Matteo told her.

Valeria nodded as though she had just been ordered to finish her homework. She nodded because nodding usually worked – but she felt absolutely nothing. And she was pretty sure Theodora was feeling nothing too. They checked in to a flight bound for New York. Together with

England that represented Julian, Greece that was Sybilla, Italy that was Matteo, Theodora and Valeria's previous year was locked away into the unspeakable section, the incomprehensible, the erased. The past that didn't have to contaminate the future.

Why New York as a future? Valeria didn't even ask. She kind of knew the answer. It was a rational, cold one. It was far away. It didn't mean anything to them. It was easy. It was America, which sounded new and unknown but at the same time possible, just as America does. A big plus was probably that it was night-time there when in Europe it was daytime. With the help of that night-and-day trick, they could pretend that their life until now had been a dream.

TWENTY-EIGHT

The Aclàs' door opened and Isla was standing in front of her. She was wearing a red dress. It fell to her knees, it wrapped around her chest. She had a bit of lipstick on.

'I dressed up for you,' Isla smiled. 'Thought you might have had enough of seeing me in a jumpsuit.'

Valeria smiled back, took her coat off and in her mind cursed the voodoo face and told her, This is my house too for these days, just swallow the pill. Even if it's Sunday, I'm invited in. I have brought a cake suggested by Bea from the deli, three stories, and Isla is wearing a red dress for me.

'It's been another long night,' Isla said. 'Hope yours was easier.'

'Everything is better now?'

'Yes, it is,' Isla said.

Valeria smiled again. Could she stop smiling?

Isla and Valeria sat in the living room. Valeria chose the low seat and moved it closer to the fireplace.

'Are those the stories?' Isla asked, pointing at the printed pages.

Valeria nodded.

'Last night I finally read one of your old ones,' Isla continued. 'I was doing my usual search for secrets in Antonia's room, which by the way never gives me any satisfaction. I feel like I am betraying her, but at the same time she is always winning the game of hide and seek.' Then, 'In Antonia's mess I found *The End of All.*'

The End of All. Just like now, the end of all. Valeria very rarely read her stories once they had been published. She would only go through bits of them at launches or readings, mostly the same sections each time. She would choose which parts to recite at the beginning of each tour, and return to them night after night. If she improvised, or someone read other parts for her, she would feel embarrassed. She didn't read dialogue out loud either, because she wasn't good at it. She didn't read parts where there was sex or swearing, because she didn't like the sound of sex scenes or swearing at readings. What she mostly read aloud were thoughts, monologues or descriptions of places, the weather, objects.

The End of All had toured quite extensively. Her own copy, with the parts selected for readings, was on the second shelf at the right end of her studio in Paris, with all of her other books for readings.

How much information had Isla acquired from the book? In that collection there were at least three stories that were connected to Martìn. And there was

'Limp' too. Limp! Was Isla looking at her in a different way today?

'I read almost all of it,' Isla said.

Was it the copy that she had dedicated to Martìn? She always wrote only one word to him: *for ever*. Even if it was tacky. Even if it was too romantic. But repeating it had made it less basic and it had been *for ever* from the beginning and it had been *for ever* since. That *for ever* seemed too much from here, right now, on this low chair in front of his attractive wife dressed in red.

'Do you think the story Antonia knows by heart is in there?' Valeria asked.

'I can't tell her I found the book,' Isla said. 'There are a couple of stories that have been underlined. I think the copy is Martìn's, not Antonia's.'

'Why?' Valeria said.

'Because of what is underlined,' Isla said. 'One of the sentences is something he always says. And there is a bookmark from a bookshop in Istanbul. Antonia has never been to Istanbul.'

Valeria knew which bookshop Isla was talking about. She'd been to Istanbul with Martìn, he had a board meeting, she had walked around the city, in the district of Bebek. In a bookshop, she had bought two handmade postcards, one for Theodora and one for herself. She had written to her – *I'm well, I write every day, you would love pomegranate juice, they sell it everywhere here.* Then she had bought the handmade bookmark for Martìn. On it there was a crayon drawing of a naked woman with short hair – very simple, delicate. She thought the women looked a bit like her. She had checked out the Turkish editions of her books and she had found two copies in the English section too. She didn't buy one of her own books, it was bad luck. Probably the bookmark had had the desired effect though, making Martìn think of Valeria, and once back from Istanbul he had positioned it – her – between her own pages.

What had Martìn underlined in those pages? Could she ask Isla to see? No, she had to steal the book.

'How do you think the portrait is going?' Valeria asked. She couldn't stay in the danger zone. She wanted them to move elsewhere.

'I'm thinking that you are completely different from what I see right now,' Isla said. 'So I'm not sure if I'm going in the right direction. If this is your face or if it's the one I see in the studio. That one is harder.' There was a pause. 'That one seems more intellectual. Scripted?'

'I feel the same,' Valeria said. 'I can feel my face change, when in there. Sitting in front of you made me realize how completely unaware I am of what I look like. And, as you say, I also feel like I could change, morph into another me, to look how I think you might want me to look. Then there is me, how I want to be, and then I guess there should be who I am, which most of the time is only a concept, it hasn't got anything to do with reality.'

Isla smiled. She pulled her chair closer to the fire and stretched out her hands towards the warmth. Maybe they would start dancing to the fire and to the voodoo face and their next scene was going to be a musical. Antonia, the twins, the gigantic Mirela, and Martìn in his coma would join the dance too.

'Portraits are a lot about this. Who we are, how we perceive others. And the relationship between, which is that of narration,' Isla said. 'The feelings both for the painter and the sitter are contradictory. It's an intangible search for who knows what. Mostly it's a movement that goes from fascination to repulsion, and those two forces keep fighting to win. Maybe the winner is the one who gets to tell the story. But again, you are both the painter and the sitter, all the time. The painting – the portrait – really happens *in the middle* of the shared space and time.'

'Was it like this with your performances too? Being both the sitter and the painter?'

'I don't know,' Isla said. 'But painting portraits does feel a natural outcome of impersonating other people.' The rain outside confirmed that too, positioning its drops in the shape of a big mouth, with no teeth and a great laugh. 'I've been doing self-portraits too,' she continued. 'There's this adjustment we make, like when we're in front of a mirror, or before taking a picture, when posing, that immediately changes our faces. On myself, I'm trying to capture the face we have before adjusting. Before the others. Before our own judgement. It's less flattering, I guess, has less to do with vanity, and what we want the other to see in us. But still, it is more like how people really see us. It has to do with hope, desire. Fear.'

'Can I look at them?' Valeria asked.

Isla paused, the rain laughed more.

'They are secret,' Isla said. 'I can't really show them. But come with me.'

Valeria followed Isla, looking at her body in that red dress. She looked at it, knowing that Martìn had loved it very much. Both the body and the dress. And the woman. The dress was similar to one Valeria had, even if hers was a bit tighter, more austere. Like her soul, probably. Following Isla up the stairs she noticed the door to Martìn's room was slightly open. The sound of the breathing machine caressed her ears.

May you never break.

'The nurse is still here,' Isla said. 'Last night was rough. Nights are always the rougher part of the day when you're sick, have you noticed?'

They walked past Antonia's room. The door was shut, music playing inside.

'Maybe we're all still just scared of the dark,' Isla smiled.

'I'm still scared of the dark for sure.'

'I'm scared of everything. That's maybe why I try to not always be me. I need a holiday from my brain!'

They walked to the end of the corridor. The cheater inside Valeria felt at the same time proud and guilty. From the window she saw the crown of the magnolia tree. She thought that yes, she could very probably use it as a ladder to reach Martìn. She would just need to learn how to climb a tree and jump from the last branch to his window. And the window had to be open.

'No one knows me like Martìn,' Isla said. 'It's terrifying letting all of this knowledge go. Where will all our secrets end up? What will they become if just mine?'

Valeria grabbed the handrail and tried to hold herself up. The window and the first floor had gone. So had the magnolia tree.

'I could start writing them down,' Isla continued. 'Or I could tell our story to you, for it to become a novel. Believe me, if I told you it would be an entertaining one.'

TWENTY-NINE

On their way upstairs, Valeria noted the postcards and framed letters alongside family portraits and pictures hanging from the walls. There was a framed poem in Spanish. Was it by Martìn's mother Helena? Beside it hung a picture of two kids playing tug of war. Were they Rami and Martìn? The two women arrived on the second floor, passing another room with a gigantic screen, a sofa and a window that faced the garden. Nico and Cosmo were in there, headphones on, playing a football match.

'They are allowed one hour, usually,' Isla said. 'But I now let them play for longer. Last Sunday I reckon they were in here for seven.'

They walked up more flights of steps, past more pictures of a distant past. The photos were all black and white and, now she was sure, the two boys that kept on appearing were Rami and Martìn. She had always thought of them looking more similar, but Martìn was shorter and Rami's hair was curlier. The pictures of that blond girl must have been Isla's. It was a rewind with every step.

If we were to walk ten floors, would we make it to the beginning of it all? To the first man on Earth?

Martìn had told her only once of when Rami had died. After hearing the screams coming from the bonfire, Martìn had run from the beach where he was with Mary. When he arrived near the pyre, he found himself in front of the terrible scene, the worst of his life, and that would haunt him for ever.

Rami was lying on the floor, unconscious, surrounded by people screaming and crying. Beside him stood Ady, mute, her eyes terrified, her hands pressed on her mouth.

Martìn had felt his heart breaking. His entire life, breaking.

He ran towards Rami, knelt down and pulled his brother's head up. His brother was cyanotic, his body rigid even if his feet were shaking. Then, the feet too had stopped shaking and the whole body suddenly lost all its tension. Martìn had tried to revive him, breathing in his mouth, then trying to give him a cardiac massage.

'I didn't even know what I was doing. I pressed my palms on his chest with the rhythm I'd seen in the movies. I kept repeating, please, Rami, please, stay here.'

While talking, Martìn cried. Valeria cried too and felt on her chest that same cardiac massage. Martìn's hands. His breath in her mouth.

'If only I had let him go to Lila,' Martìn told Valeria. 'Or if, at least, I had been close enough to help him.'

'It's not your fault. You cannot really think it is.'

'If I'd let him go to Lila, he wouldn't have been there, drunk like shit, dying for a fucking allergic reaction.'

'Didn't he know?'

'Of course he knew. Rami was allergic to many things and had an anaphylactic shock when we were kids. From that day, not to risk it, he would never eat if not at home. But that night he wasn't thinking. Or he was thinking that eating a couple of nuts was just another possible way to go. Maybe he even found it exhilarating. It doesn't matter, right? He died.'

'If it was what he wanted it would have happened anyway,' Valeria said. 'He would have waited another moment, when you weren't around, and found another way.'

Valeria remembered when Sybilla asked her if she could jump off that roof in Rhodes. She imagined sitting her sister near Rami. She saw them jumping.

'I could have saved him. Possibly for ever,' Martìn said. 'And what awful last words are "'shut the fuck up"?'

Reaching the third floor, Valeria had new wishes and new afflictions. One of her wishes was to sit in this studio alone, be up here by herself. Not have to pretend or lie or leave when she was supposed to. 'Can you just let me stay here with you guys?' she would ask. And maybe they would say, 'You know what, yes, stay.'

At the far end of the corridor was another room, which Isla used a key to open. Once they were both inside, she locked it again. They were standing in a space much larger than the others, and with no furniture – as if a gallery had been squeezed into this grand house. Possibly, there was a different climate in there too. At least a dozen wooden boxes were on the floor, all with the keyholes, all labelled.

'The self-portraits are in there. They are in order, starting with that one.' Isla pointed to the far-right corner, the darkest place in the room. 'So you can experience the ageing too.'

Valeria walked over to the corner, near the box. Then she walked around the entire room reading the different labels as Isla watched her.

'You never stopped drawing,' Valeria said.

She continued to look around the room, overwhelmed by it all. Isla in here was everywhere, and she was also everything.

Isla moved closer to Valeria, to see what she was looking at.

'I know, it's creepy,' Isla smiled.

Valeria didn't know what to say. Boxes and boxes with Isla inside, recording the passing of time, the flashes of unflattering moments, the seconds before adjustments. Valeria moved in closer, and for every box there was written other dates, hours, places. London. America. Sicily. Madrid. Madrid? Was Isla going to open one now? Would she let Valeria pick a city and a year?

'It's an egomaniac's room,' Isla said. 'That's why I don't let anyone in here.'

'It doesn't feel like that,' Valeria said. 'It feels like a scientific study of life, using yourself as a tool. And it being a secret is part of the deal.'

'Funny you use the word "deal",' Isla said. 'That's Martin's favourite word.' Was it? Then, pointing at one of the boxes, 'Many of the recent ones are invented. I imagine what I will end up looking like. In case I don't make it to a hundred. Or to be immortal.'

'Is no one allowed?'

'To be immortal?'

'That – and to be in here?' Valeria asked. 'Not even your husband?'

'No,' Isla said. 'Not even Martin.'

Was this even true? Did it matter?

'How did you get them all to accept a locked door?'

'I told them I needed a secret,' Isla said. 'But they're very curious. I probably want you to be curious too.'

Valeria was in fact now very curious. Was she going to be able, one of these days, to steal the keys, run up there and spy inside the boxes?

'Does Antonia know?' Valeria asked her. 'At least that you still draw?'

'I don't think so,' Isla said. 'No.'

They left the room, locking the door behind them. 'What other secrets have you got hidden on the fourth floor?' Valeria asked on their way down.

'Can't tell you. He who sees the fourth floor must die,' Isla said. She laughed.

'Is that what happened to your husband?' No. Had she really said it? 'Sorry. Sorry. I didn't mean to.'

Valeria asked herself if she should fall from the steps to divert attention and erase her last sentence from Isla's mind. She started counting.

'Don't worry,' Isla said. 'It's funny.'

'It's not. I can't believe I really said it,' Valeria murmured. 'I'm so sorry.'

But Isla smiled again.

'Luc says that in your stories many characters count. I hadn't noticed. I knew it, but hadn't spotted it,' Martìn had said once.

'You and Luc have been talking about me?' Valeria asked. The idea that Martìn may want to share this incredible, possibly wrong love of theirs, was sweet but terrifying.

'About your stories. I gave him *Black Bread* for Christmas. At another dinner I gave him *The End of All*.'

'What's he like, Luc?'

'Funny, smart. Lonely. He was the one to introduce me to Isla. He was going out with one of her roommates, Matilda or Melissa, can't remember. We never saw her again. At least, I haven't. With Luc you never know.'

'Was it a double date?' Valeria asked. Her voice cracked. She didn't have to know all the stories on planet Earth. She could let this specific one go too.

'It was a dinner with a few other people in Brooklyn and she was there.'

And she was there sounded to Valeria like the way Martìn and Isla began narrating their love to others. Could she put her smile back on?

'Luc was in love with her,' Martìn said.

'Matilda – Melissa?'

'Isla. His plan for that night was to hook me up with the girl he was dating to free him for Isla.'

Valeria nodded. So Martìn had persuaded Isla out of a wedding with a tennis player, and he had taken her away from Luc too. What was this Isla like? Gorgeous? A genius? Hilarious? Why did Martìn love her?

B ack in the kitchen with the boys and Antonia, the table was set and lunch was ready. Mirela had clearly just left.

Valeria sat with Cosmo, Nico and Antonia, while Isla took the roast meat and the potatoes out of the oven. Rock the dog was there too, licking the window.

'The windows and his balls,' Nico said.

'And his arsehole,' Antonia said.

'And his own shit,' Cosmo said.

'And then you all kiss him anyway,' Isla said. She poured the red wine, and topped up Valeria's glass.

'How long will the nurse be with Dad?' Nico asked.

'Probably another hour,' Isla said.

Valeria felt jealous of another woman touching and moving Martìn's body. Couldn't it be her?

Cosmo said, 'I miss him.' And the others started saying it too, so Valeria repeated it with them, hiding her words in a whisper.

They ate everything. It was the best roast Valeria had ever had. She had never had one on a Sunday, with a family, so maybe it was tastier because all the ingredients were there: the chatting, the window-licking dog, the mother with secrets, the kids that talked shit, the troubled-but-soon-to-be-OK girl.

The boys were now talking about a schoolmate who had a sauna at home, saying how they were going around naked at some party last week. The mother was famous from a reality TV show and had left Nathan's father for an old Russian billionaire.

Suddenly, Antonia started yelling at them about how stupid they were, asking how they could care about saunas. 'When will you get it, life is not about that? Also, Mum, why are we not vegan yet?' Then she started talking for at least five minutes, maybe ten, seemingly without taking a breath, about a friend of hers, Selina, who was a refugee from Afghanistan.

'Who's Selina?' Isla asked, and 'Who's Selina?' the boys asked too, adding, 'You have no friends, Anty, you just invented this Selina.'

'Shut up, you fuckers! And don't call me Anty!'

'You're all red,' Nico told Antonia, bored now.

'I'm fucking not.'

'You are,' Cosmo said, bored too. 'Chill.'

'Whatever,' Antonia said. 'Your eyes are red.'

'Yes, they are, why?' Isla asked.

Isla knew the truth or maybe not, Valeria couldn't tell, but she seemed far away.

Antonia rinsed the strawberries, dabbing them with a cloth to dry them, while the boys brought to the table the cake from the deli and the goat's cheese from the delicatessen. Isla poured more wine for herself and for Valeria.

'Martìn loves strawberries and loves red wine, shall I give some to him?' she asked, but the kids shook their heads *no*. They then turned to something that happened a few years back, when the whole family was in Sicily and Isla and Martìn had drank too much and ended up dancing near the church with three elderly men.

'It was a nice summer,' Antonia said.

'You cried all the time,' said Cosmo.

'She didn't,' Isla said. 'She was just doing what she had to.'

Antonia looked at her mother and was thankful but unable to say it. She cleared up the remaining plates with the boys.

Valeria knew that they were talking about the summer in which she was left waiting for Martìn in Shelter Island. She felt an anger that shamed her.

The boys hugged her and left the room.

'Coffee?' Isla asked.

'Yes, please,' Valeria replied. 'The food was delicious, thank you.'

Isla stood up to make coffee and Rock the dog barked at something, maybe the rain, maybe Valeria. Was he hoping that she knew how to transform him into a man? Maybe she could, she just had to remember the right words to do so. Antonia moved to sit near her and despite the fact that her shirt was buttoned to the wrists, Valeria saw everything – her new cuts, the older scars – without having to see it.

'Are you feeling better?' Valeria asked her.

Antonia nodded. 'Rock likes you,' she said and patted the dog's head.

'I wonder why.'

'Either you stink or you are kind. Those are his two favourite things in life.'

Valeria showed Antonia the print-out of the stories she had brought for Martìn, and Antonia started flicking through the pages, then reading from them out loud.

'Dad told us about these sisters,' Antonia said. When she said it she looked surprised but at the same time as if it was normal for Valeria, Antonia and Martìn to be choosing the same stories, looking at the same things.

'Can I keep them and go upstairs to him?' Antonia asked.

'They are for you and for him,' Valeria said. 'So yes, sure.'

Isla watched her daughter leave the room and Valeria saw the light in Isla's eyes disappear.

THIRTY

Isla and Valeria were left with the duty of the portrait. Now that she knew about Isla's work upstairs, Valeria had a new idea for herself and for her face, of what to do. She was going to try to let go of her struggle for a purpose, her vanity. She was going to try to not play a character.

When they entered the studio, the fire was already lit. Isla pressed play on Bach, Valeria took off her jumper, wearing just her silk shirt and pencil skirt. She sat down on her stool. Isla prepared her palette and stood up, looking at Valeria, then staring at her, moving her eyes slowly. She frowned.

Was she the one trying too much? Maybe her being a painter truly was a performance, a re-enactment of this one job, of this one life.

'Thank you,' Isla said. 'Much better.'

Valeria tried not to be too pleased by the compliment, that too would be vanity. She tried to relax more, to focus on the boxes upstairs. What was in them? A younger Isla, then an older Isla, the pause before being looked at. Laughter, frowning. The passing of time. Valeria imagined the self-portraits, sometimes just scribbled, others completely coloured.

Being simple. From today this was going to be the idea. Was it this that Theodora meant when she explained what beauty was? Valeria focused on the music and the sound of the crackling fire. None of this will mean anything if Martìn dies. If I'm not able to tell him about the time I spent in his house – that it was impossible for me to be anywhere else but here – nothing will matter. But if you wake up, Martìn, I will go. I will leave you.

She couldn't pretend that she didn't know any more. She *did* know.

'I'll tell Antonia about the cheating,' Isla suddenly said. 'I'll be open about it, without giving Martìn away, explaining that those were hard times and I was wretched. I wouldn't want to talk about it, frankly, but I think Antonia needs me to. I'll tell her I have only loved her father, but I needed some relief, some sort of comfort. That, by the way, didn't arrive. I'll be honest and say I don't feel guilty about it. And that she shouldn't be angry with me because of that. She shouldn't be angry, full stop.'

'Why do you think she would need to hear any of this?' Valeria asked.

'I cannot let her build an enemy in me. I have to tell her that the idea of losing him is terrifying, but I will survive. And she will survive too. She thinks she wants to see me in more pain. But would she be ready to see her mother collapse?'

'My mother collapsed. No one is ready for that, ever.'

'Are you and your mother close now?'

'We are far, geographically. But we are all the family we've got,' Valeria said. 'She wants me to go see her soon. In Greece, where I grew up.'

'Will you go?'

'We've not been there for forty years. It's not that simple.'

'Maybe Antonia will be far from me like this one day. Maybe she'll grow so different from me, that she'll want to be far away. Her father would have made her stay close, for ever.'

'I didn't want my mother to feel better either,' Valeria said. 'When I was more or less the twins' age, I lost my sister. I wanted my mother to always be in pain.'

'And she wasn't?'

'She was. Desperately. I just couldn't see it. Any time she would try a way to ease her suffering – a new husband, life or surname – I would bring her back. To me and my sister.'

'You would have been too lonely otherwise?'

'Yes. And above all, I thought she would have been.'

'It must have been terrible,' Isla said. 'I'm sorry.'

Valeria could collapse without dragging anyone else down. One upside of her life alone. She would have to say something to Theodora if she were to collapse. But what? Goodbye. I love you. From a distance, but I do. Too bad I couldn't make it back to where you dragged me away from. It might have been nice to surrender. Living has been great. Leaving could be great too.

Valeria and Isla continued working. Valeria looked at Isla and she saw Theodora when she collapsed. But Valeria did survive even then. She wanted to free Isla from such a burden too.

'If she were to see your room she would like you more,' Valeria said. 'She would also see that you are cooler than she imagines.'

'Has this just happened to you too?' Isla said. She smiled. 'Do you like me more now?'

'Probably.'

'I still don't want her to know about it,' Isla said.

They fell into silence then, remaining so until darkness arrived. Isla put her paintbrush down and ran her paint-covered hands through her hair.

'It won't take months,' Isla said. 'It's going to be a matter of days.'

Valeria slipped off the stool, she wasn't sure if this sudden acceleration was a good or a bad thing, for herself and for Martìn. For the portrait and for life.

'Want to smoke a spliff?' Isla asked Valeria.

They walked to the window and opened it wide. Looking at the darkness outside and puffing on the pimped cigarette, Valeria saw blue marks from Isla's fingers on the cigarette paper. Like water, like drops.

'The twins pretend they try drugs for their YouTube followers,' Isla said.

'Pretend?' Valeria said puffing on the joint.

'They think it's cool. So they pretend they try joints or oils or I don't know what. But they don't even inhale. They don't have drugs either.'

'So what's with the red eyes?'

'They breathe into each other's eyes to irritate them, to try to prove they're stoned.'

'Jesus,' Valeria laughed. 'It's beyond.'

'It is,' Isla laughed. 'But you gotta do what you gotta do to keep up with your script. It's a performance like any other.'

'How d'you even know?'

'Antonia spied on them and after getting the story straight, she told me and told me not to worry.'

'Sweet,' Valeria said. 'Marijuana is really bad for me. We will never do it again.'

They both started laughing. The downpour become more violent, so they closed the window.

'Thank you,' Isla said. 'For everything.'

Guilt tightened around Valeria's throat.

Valeria walked up the stairs with Isla behind her. As soon as they reached the ground floor, the sounds of violent weather could be heard, wind howling and torrential rain hitting the windowpanes. The storm welcomed them back to life, telling them they were a part of this world, a part of this particular script where there was an endless tempest.

'Mum!' Nico shouted from upstairs.

'It's just a storm,' Isla shouted back. She looked at Valeria, still holding back her laughter. 'Don't go yet, wait for the wind to die down. I have to go upstairs, Nico freaks out when there's a storm. You can sit in the living room, by the fire, read something or make your calls.'

'I'll be fine,' Valeria said. 'I'll walk fast.'

'Please, stay. There's no reason for you to leave immediately. Do me this favour?'

Isla was already by the staircase. She was waiting for Valeria to say yes, so Valeria nodded.

She sat near the fire, saluted the voodoo face with her finger. She grabbed a book about walking in Norway from the ottoman and flicked through the pages, photos of fjords seeming magical then suddenly scary. She listened to the noises coming from upstairs and outside, turning to see the trees being ravaged by the wind. Her phone buzzed in her pocket with a text message. *Madame, I'm back home in Rhodes with my wife. Thank you for the holiday, parakalo, Dimitri*. Valeria shut her eyes and fell asleep.

THIRTY-ONE

'What are you dreaming about?' Antonia asked her, waking her up.

'I can't remember,' Valeria said, even though she did. Sex. 'What time is it?'

'Dinner time,' Antonia said. 'Help us lay the table?'

'I really should get going. I've been out all day.'

'Why is that a problem?'

She was wearing a dress Valeria vaguely recognised. Over the dress Antonia was wearing a cardigan.

'Nice dress,' Valeria said.

'Dad bought it for me,' Antonia said, 'in Turkey, I think. Or in Malta.'

Of course Valeria knew the dress. She had bought it with Martìn and had bought herself a similar one. In Turkey, not in Malta. To her knowledge, Martìn had never been to Malta. Where was Valeria's dress? She must have lost it. She'd left so many things behind her around the globe. Now she wanted the same dress back, all the lost pens, and the glasses. The pearl necklace Theodora had bought for her wedding with Patrick. And her days with Martìn.

'Is this the first time you've worn it?'

'How did you know?' Antonia looked at the dress, searching for the tag.

'It just feels new,' Valeria said. 'It's really elegant.'

'I'd never wear it outside this house,' Antonia said. 'I'm wearing it sarcastically. And for Dad. Who would appreciate both me wearing it, and the sarcasm.'

'What is your father like?' Valeria asked.

Antonia sat closer to Valeria, grabbing one of the tiny chairs by the fireplace. Valeria felt guilty because any time she talked about Martìn she hesitated on the tense to use. With Antonia, the present tense felt better. He is alive.

'I'm very close to him,' Antonia said. 'Are you close to your father?'

'I don't know him.'

Over the years Valeria had decided this was the better answer. *I have never met him* wasn't true. *He abandoned us* felt too dramatic and private. *I don't know him* had mystery, no judgement, required no pity. It was matter of fact. What would she do with Julian's letters this week? Burn them in this fireplace beside her now? Send them all back to him, unopened? Give them to Antonia as a gift?

Antonia took a piece of wood, put it on the fire. 'Would you like to know him?' she asked.

In that dress Antonia spoke differently, it was subtle but it was as though it gave Antonia a slightly altered personality. Valeria experienced the same change when she spoke other languages or chose a character for a story. A distinct persona appeared to speak French, another

Spanish. English brought out another one too. Was the one speaking Greek ever going to return? For the first time she thought, Maybe, yes. She had seen the writing *paradeisos* in the sky above this very roof.

'I'm not sure I want to,' Valeria said.

'But is he alive?' Antonia said. 'So you could, right?'

'I was the one to ask you about your father, why am I the one answering now?'

'Would you like to talk to me about my father?'

'What do you mean?'

'Whatever. Not now. Is yours alive?'

'He is alive,' Valeria said. Not now? Then she thought what if Julian is dead and I haven't been told, just like it happened with Joe's mother.

Antonia stood up and looked at her dress.

'Hideous,' she repeated, then, 'So are you staying? Come on, there's a tornado outside, it will kill you, while downstairs there's all of us and tonnes of leftovers. Wine. The fire. Rock the dog. Me.'

Maybe she can become mine, Valeria thought. Maybe she will live with me and she will know me and I will become very old and she will not leave me, ever. It won't matter to her if I become old or very ugly or I completely lose my mind. She will still have a mother in Isla, but in me she will have another certainty, throughout life. I could be the other woman for her too.

'Please,' Antonia repeated.

'OK, fine,' Valeria said, 'I'll stay, thank you.' She stood up, stretched her neck and shoulders, and followed Antonia downstairs.

'Careful,' Antonia said, 'My father has fallen down twice. But his limp never helps.'

Valeria saw Martìn walking towards her, with that limp, just a month ago. She saw him walking towards her five years ago, fifteen, twenty-five.

In the kitchen Isla had lit the candles. There were nine places ready at the table and the fireplace was crackling. Who are the other four? Valeria wondered. And didn't I have to help lay the table? Were guests appropriate at a time like this? Or was that the good way to live? Not being alone in the pain, not extracting themselves from life, keeping links with others, holding on to life?

'Good. You're staying,' Isla said. She smiled. 'We don't want you out there.'

'Yes, she is staying, Mother,' Antonia said, 'but I had to pay her to convince her. She is a famous writer and deserves to be rewarded for her time with us.'

'Thank you,' Valeria said to Isla. 'Who are we eating with?'

Isla poured her a glass of red wine. Had Isla had a nap near Martìn while Valeria was sleeping alone on the ground floor?

'Len and his wife. And Luc is coming with someone. I guess the current girlfriend.'

Valeria sipped the wine and realized Antonia had on her dress, Isla had on make-up, Luc was coming with a girlfriend and she herself looked terrible after having slept on an armchair and having lived fifty-five years already. Damn. She was going to meet Luc for the first time and she looked tired, probably even older than usual. While thinking through her options – I could go home to change, I could go home to bed – she helped chop the carrots and the fennel for the salad. She was let in, preparing food with the Aclà family. She had to at least put some lipstick on and check her hair.

'Why don't the twins ever help?' Antonia asked.

'If you want them in the kitchen just go get them,' Isla said. 'Right now I prefer being with you.'

'Dad always helped,' Antonia said.

Isla stopped chopping. She looked at her daughter.

'Why do you say that?' Isla asked. 'He never did.'

'Once he made me a sandwich,' Antonia answered without looking at her. 'The best ever.'

'What was it like?'

'It had mayonnaise.'

'I love your father very much,' Isla said. 'Just for the record.'

'I love him more than I love you,' Antonia said. 'I don't mean it in a bad way.'

'Of course,' Isla smiled. 'It's the same for me.'

'You love him more than you love me?'

'I love you more than I love anybody,' Isla said. 'That's the truth. Once you know the truth, you have to deal with it.'

Antonia's eyes brimmed.

What was Antonia doing? Rewriting Martìn already? Valeria drank more wine. She silently thanked Martìn for choosing it, because she was sure he had. If needed, she could help rewrite parts of stories for everybody too. Those on sandwiches, on love or death. But before that, she had to become presentable for Martìn's best friend, who had loved Isla when Martìn had wanted Isla too.

'I need to put a bit of make-up on,' Valeria said, laying down the knife on the counter.

'You're beautiful,' Antonia said.

'You look great,' Isla reinforced.

The chopping continued. They could feed carrots and fennel to fifty people. Isla poured herself more wine. Valeria took another sip from her own glass.

'Thank you, but I'd rather have a look at myself in the mirror. Maybe put some lipstick on. Can I borrow some?'

'You look beautiful exactly because you are not wearing make-up,' Antonia said. 'Don't do it.'

'True,' Isla echoed. 'Don't!'

Valeria thought about Sybilla telling her confusing things like this. She could never understand if they were true, if she really did look prettier without those pigtails or if Sybilla just wanted to be the pretty one, so she would say the opposite of what was true.

'Can I at least brush my hair?' Valeria said, smiling.

'You look beautiful with those knots at your nape. You look scruffy and interesting,' Antonia said. 'You should never brush your hair.'

'You should never wash it or brush it again,' Isla said. 'No matter what happens.'

'You can have one of the boys' T-shirts if you want something clean,' Antonia laughed.

'Why don't you wear Cosmo's onesie? It's great. It's a panda.' Isla laughed too.

Valeria looked at them. She started laughing. They placed the salads on the table. Isla took out the leftovers from the fridge and turned on the oven.

'OK, OK, give me a second,' Isla said.

'Don't do it, Valeria,' Antonia whispered. 'Go, panda!'

THIRTY-TWO

Valeria stood alone in Isla's bathroom. It was connected to the master bedroom. Holding the messy bag of make-up Isla had given her, she started snooping around. It wasn't Martìn's bathroom. No men's toiletries. No razors. They clearly had two bathrooms adjoining the marital bedroom. She opened the sink cabinet: hairdryer, toilet paper, brushes. Valeria took one of the soaps stored there in her hands. She smelled it. I will steal soaps for my entire life, she thought.

After lightly making up her face, she brushed her hair and smiled, thinking about the kitchen scene. She gently opened the door into the bedroom. If Isla were to be there, Valeria could have kept on brushing her hair and pretended she had something to tell her, something like, Do you also have a red lipstick? Or, May I steal some of your cream?

Opening the door, Valeria saw that Martìn was facing her. It was a shock. His head was tilted towards her and even if his eyes were closed, it gave the impression that he had moved to look at her. Valeria gave another quick glance around the room, then closed the door that led to the stairs. She dashed towards him. Anywhere in the world where she would see him, she would dash towards him. She felt warm all over – her back, her head. The heart.

'Martìn,' Valeria whispered, 'I'm here.'

She kissed him on the forehead, went down on her knees, still holding the brush in her hand. And the soap. It looked like he had just turned his face towards her. Was it the nurse or Isla who regularly moved his head so as not to be always facing the same side? This side saw the house, the other one the outside world. Isla. Valeria. Voodoo face, hotel room in Istanbul.

'I shouldn't be here, Martìn, but I can't be anywhere else,' Valeria took off her purple panties. She squeezed them into a ball, and pushed them under Martìn's mattress.

'I'm putting my panties here. So you know where they are.'

Would he like this plan? Or was he – aware of this moment but unable to choose for himself – terrified that someone would find Valeria's panties? Would he stop loving her for this? Finally? She had always known their boundaries, their lands, she cherished them, but now everything was unintelligible. The new role, the lover in his own house while he was suffering and possibly dying, wasn't her best so far. She didn't know how to write it.

'I'll push them to the very middle, don't you worry,' Valeria whispered, quickly realizing her arm was trapped. She started sweating. 'Just a little further,' she said. She felt

Martìn's head on her shoulder. In a panic she thought he was moving and she had to force herself not to scream. She stopped, her arm still stuck under the mattress, Martìn about to roll over her. What if someone were to find them like this? What if the breathing machine stopped working because of Valeria and her purple panties? Was his ventilator still in his mouth? Was she killing him? Pushing against the mattress with all her strength, Valeria finally managed to lift Martìn back onto the mattress as well. She felt like she was exploding with heat. Keeping her eyes on Martìn, with her free hand she put his breathing tube back in place. She managed to pull her arm out from under the mattress and sat on the floor, exhausted. She started crying. She reached for Martìn's hand and caressed it. Then, squeezed it.

'What are you doing?' Isla asked her.

Valeria froze.

'Why are you holding my husband's hand?' Isla said. 'Why were you touching his breather?'

Valeria let go of Martìn's hand. She slowly stood up and turned towards Isla. Her legs were barely holding her up. What could she invent to justify her presence in this room? The brush, the soap, the shoe? And then yes, of course, the fact that she was holding her husband's hand.

'I'm sorry,' Valeria muttered. She slipped her foot back into her shoe. She willed her eyes to stop tearing up. She prayed for a good lie and a good story to come to her soon. Or was it time to tell Isla? She was chopping carrots with her and using her lipstick, she was smoking joints with her and given access to the secret rooms. She spent time with her daughter, drank her home-made healthy juices. Yes, it was about time.

'I left the bathroom the wrong way,' Valeria managed to say.

Isla checked Martìn, his machine. She wasn't sure yet. She wasn't sure whether to be scared or angry. She was irritated. Worried.

'It's so sad,' Valeria said, 'I just held his hand. I had this thought that he might feel invisible. Coming out of the bathroom the wrong way, I found myself in his room and felt I should introduce myself properly. So I did.'

Without even being aware of it, Valeria stepped back, leaving Isla the space to be closer to her husband. That space was hers. The whole house was. And this life. Valeria took the soap from the floor where she'd dropped it, squeezed it in her hand. Did Isla believe her? And you, Martìn, will you ever say something again or will you leave us for good in this awkward situation, where we try our best not to fuck it all up?

'Are you crying?' Isla asked her.

'No,' Valeria said. Hadn't she told her tears not to come out?

'You've got mascara all over your face.'

Valeria saw that Isla was crying too. She was pretending to be busy now, fixing the sheets, fluffing up the cushion, tapping the breathing machine. She caressed Martìn's forehead.

'I'm sorry,' Valeria said. 'It just came naturally.'

'It's anything but natural.'

'I should go,' said Valeria. But she didn't go.

'It's OK,' Isla said. 'I cannot pretend the whole time.'

Was Isla telling her that she couldn't pretend not to know about Valeria and Martìn the whole time or was she saying she couldn't pretend not to be in terrible pain the whole time? Her husband was dying. Crying was permissible, so was surrendering to despair.

'We were deciding what to do,' Isla said. 'I wasn't sure I wanted us to be together any more. Probably he wasn't either.'

Valeria felt joy and guilt simultaneously. What happens to the brain when you feel joy and guilt at exactly the same time? And when your wife and your lover both need you? What happens when your head is moved to face inside the house one day, and to face the outside world the day after? Maybe Martìn had told Valeria that he wanted to be with her because Isla was going to leave him.

While Valeria kept holding the soap, Isla kept doing things that looked unnecessary and told her that in these last years she had felt increasingly lonely.

'It didn't even have to do with happiness, but with new, blurry wishes,' she said.

She had felt distant from him, then free. She had changed, and so had her desires, which were still unreadable, and unknown. But Antonia was right: Isla had had to walk away from him. Had she been selfish? She had been confused, mostly. They still loved each other, profoundly. And were also able to say it. But she was scared, terrified. Of life, mostly. Of disappearing. Had she cheated on him out of fear? Revenge? She wasn't sure.

'Maybe I wanted him to prove me wrong. But I had

this constant hunger, this constant wanting. From others. From him. How could the person you love save you from yourself, from the time that passes, from the confusion? Then what, from death? I can't stand not being able to let him know.'

'To let him know what?' Valeria murmured.

'That I want to be with him. And that being lost doesn't scare me any more.'

Valeria couldn't bring herself to say anything else. How had Martìn managed all of this? Isla and Valeria, all of their love and also all of their pain, for all of his life? What had he wanted? Having two women for all his life; great on paper, but it must have also been confusing, draining and difficult. The needs, the fears, the weakness. The territory.

'What did he want?' Valeria asked.

'He wanted who he loved to be happy,' Isla said. 'He could easily morph into whatever was needed by those who he cared about. Like you.'

'Like me?'

'You, with the portrait.'

'Do you think he hears you?'

'I do,' Isla said. 'He hears us.'

Isla turned around, finally facing Valeria, finally stopping pretending to straighten up the sheets. Her eyes red, her cheeks shiny with tears. She was so beautiful it was painful. Valeria desperately wanted Martìn to see them both now. To ask him, what shall we do with all of this? Of us, you, the meaning of it all?

'Why were you crying?' Isla asked.

Because Martìn is the love of my life, Valeria thought.

Because I am alone and I have no one to hold me. Because I'm getting old, and everything is falling, and fading. I am losing it, the hands I've touched, the words I've said. I'm losing my muscles, and memories, and all of those I love. I'm tired – of titles, lies and all the stories that I have to keep holding together and making sense of. The only person who could see me can't see me any more. I'm invisible.

'I should go fix this,' Valeria whispered indicating her face. She tried a smile. 'It's kind of a panda look, right?'

'Can't you fix this instead, panda?' Isla smiled too. She pointed at the room, at Martìn. She was pointing at their lives and everyone else's in this world. And in the other worlds too.

THIRTY-THREE

Valeria took a sip from her glass, looking at the couple at the door. A handsome, well-dressed bearded man in his late fifties stood beside a skinny, well-to-do girl wearing a turquoise necklace. She was also wearing a perfect little black dress. Probably she was in her late thirties. Or early forties if a non-smoker.

'There's the biggest dump a dog has ever taken outside your front door,' the man said.

'Hello, Luc,' Isla said as she approached him. She was blushing. Was it the wine or the warmth from the fireplaces? The unpronounceable oestrogen-linked word? Luc kissed Antonia on the cheeks, leaving space for Isla to take her place there, in the hug, in his bulky arms. Maybe if I'm good over dinner, I'll manage to get a hug too, Valeria thought.

'Antonia, can you go clean it?' Isla said. 'Please.'

'There's nothing I'd like to do more,' Antonia said. 'Thank you for asking me and not the twins.' She went to the kitchen drawer and took out a plastic bag.

Watching Antonia move in that dress was like watching two separate creatures in the same shot. Like a fish with wings. Or a bird underwater.

'I'd come with you but I do think it's an experience worth having alone,' Luc said.

He made a funny face, hands together clasped in prayer, like a guru.

'You look very pretty in that dress,' he added.

Antonia stuck her tongue out at Luc just as she had done in that portrait with her cat Milou. Had she done it to him back then too? She covered her head with another plastic bag and walked to the door. She shook hands with Charlotte. They smiled.

'My dear Isly,' Luc said, and he kissed Isla on the cheeks. 'You look beautiful. Let me introduce you to my friend Charlotte. Boys, you too, come and introduce yourselves.'

Nico and Cosmo nodded and followed Luc's instructions. They did it with a smile, clearly liking him.

'Wasn't the last one called Charlotte too?' Nico whispered to Cosmo, walking back a few steps. Valeria smiled. Can I be one of you guys?

'No, that was Cecilia,' Cosmo said. 'Cecilia was prettier.'

'Cecilia had a hair on her chin,' Nico whispered. 'A really long one too.'

'But she had bigger boobs.'

'Yeah, that's right, she did,' Nico confirmed. 'Cecilia wins.'

Charlotte smiled at them all and said, 'It's so nice to be here' and 'It's lovely to meet you.'

The twins took Charlotte's and Luc's coats and went

over to the wardrobe to hang them. Antonia opened the door and walked outside, under the storm. It was the wrong day to be wearing a linen dress created for Mediterranean summers. It was the wrong day to be two things together too. Inside, the house. Outside, the world.

'And finally, more importantly, Luc, Charlotte, let me introduce you to Valeria,' Isla said.

Valeria, who was now near them and had been practising her smile, smiled even more. Stop smiling, you look mad, be pretty. Be normal, she told herself. Be two people at the same time, not six hundred.

'Valeria and I are currently working on her portrait, so I invited her to join the family table,' Isla said.

'Thank you for having me with you tonight,' Valeria said. She was now so close to Luc she had to move slightly backwards. Charlotte was nodding as if repeating to herself everything is fine, everything is fine. Was it?

'I didn't know you were painting again, Isly,' Luc said.

Isla shrugged. Valeria sipped more wine because she didn't know what else to do. She caught a second glance in her direction from Luc. What was it? Interest? A man–woman interest? Was this an 'and she was there' moment? If they had all been friends and had all been healthy, with no one in a coma upstairs, no one ageing by the second downstairs and ageing everywhere, from Japan to Africa, if they all had different lives, even just slightly different from this one, maybe Luc would have told Martin that he found Valeria intriguing. At twenty, it would have been easier. But at twenty she wanted to be invisible. Now she wanted to be seen.

'What would you like to drink, Charlotte?' Isla asked. 'And you, Luc? Red?'

They opened a bottle of wine and Antonia returned, sopping wet, Len and his wife coming in with her. Melanie and Charlotte and Melanie and Valeria were introduced. Len and Luc quickly shared updates about Martìn, muttering so as not to involve everyone.

Naming two characters Len and Luc was something Valeria would never have given herself permission to do.

T he bottle of wine was placed on the table. They all sat. Antonia had now changed back into her usual baggy black clothes, much to the table's disappointment, and the boys were chewing and staring at the guests. What did they see? Gorillas? Aliens?

Valeria started speaking to Len on her left, then for a while to Melanie on her right. Someone had once taught her that you should do this, start from the left, then go to the right. Who had it been? It wasn't the type of information Theodora would know or pass on. All of the correct things that a woman or a man should do had seemed completely pointless to her mother.

'Don't be ostentatious,' Theodora would tell them or 'Don't be vain. It's stupid.'

Valeria always used the same technique, she'd listen, nod, sometimes with surprise, then, when asked, she'd drop in the writer thing, which always worked quite well and always got the same kind of response. How interesting, I wish I could write too, what are your books about? Valeria sometimes thought that one day she would really answer the question and tell the unfortunate person what her stories were about: she would not only unfold the complete series of synopses, but also get into the reviews and explain all the meanings and aims of all her stories. The cruelty of kids. Of parents. The loneliness of ageing. Fear. Happiness when unknown and sudden. The melancholy of celebrations. The freedom in one's lies. The punishment that comes from greed. The punishment that comes from nothing at all. The language of couples. Sex, lust, melancholy. Decadence. Void. And so on. There were at least, what, three hundred stories of hers out there? Let's begin and get cracking with the plots, OK? Here comes story number one. It's called 'Coriander'.

'Where are you originally from?' Melanie asked her. 'You have an accent, but I can't quite place it.'

Valeria looked at Melanie's graceful build, her gold bracelets, how well her nails were kept. What did she secretly do that no one knew about? Coke? Hate one of her sisters? Did she really love blow jobs, like she always said to men when blowing, or was she repulsed by men?

'I was born here, in London,' Valeria told her, 'but I was raised in Greece and Italy and then we moved to New York.'

'Oh, we were in Greece last year. I always say that you don't swim anywhere like you swim in Greece. Don't you think? But this last time, I couldn't stop thinking that I was swimming over all those refugee kids' bodies,' Melanie said. She then took a mouthful of lasagne.

Valeria imagined it all. Greece. The sea. The corpses of the children.

Melanie turned her face to say something to Antonia about a friend of hers – Segoléne, a former banker, whose daughter went to Antonia's school, did she know her? Melanie was chewing, waiting for an answer. No answer arrived so she added, 'She sometimes does advertising for shampoo, because of her long blond hair. Her name is that of a colour, like Pink or Violet.'

'Doesn't ring a bell, sorry,' Antonia said. She didn't even lift her eyes to meet Melanie's.

Melanie kept smiling, waiting for something that was never going to arrive. Eventually she turned to ask Len.

'Her name is Petal,' he said.

'Really?' Melanie exclaimed, 'Oh, that's a nice name, right?'

She looked so surprised it was scary.

'Oh, Petal,' Antonia said, 'I know her.'

Melanie looked at her again, and when Antonia didn't add anything, she turned her attention elsewhere. Antonia went back to Valeria and whispered, 'Petal fucks men for money. Mostly in hotel rooms. But sometimes at their offices. She lets them come inside her.'

'What?' Nico whispered. 'Who fucks who?'

They opened more bottles of red and sliced the cake that Luc had bought. The light of the candles made them all look healthy. And happier.

Every time Valeria lifted her eyes Luc was looking at her. The wine had gone down well and she was so tired that flirting came easily. She wanted Luc to like her, so any time she spoke, Valeria would glance over at him and make sure they locked eyes. Charlotte didn't seem too impressed. How long was she going to be his girl for, anyway? But then again, maybe Luc and Charlotte would love each other for the next fifty years. Luc would die before her, of course, but Charlotte would keep on loving him, till the end of time.

'And you, Charlotte? Tell us about yourself,' Isla said.

Charlotte told them about her job at a non-profit art foundation that dealt with disadvantaged neighbourhoods. She then explained that she'd just moved back from Los Angeles, where she had worked for a commercial design house, but it had all become too pointless and superficial for her. This new job was the opposite: challenging, politically engaging. She was an activist. It was time to be one.

'And you, what do you do?' Charlotte asked Valeria.

She was eating the cake with her fingers, licking every last crumb. Valeria thought of her work as more similar to that of building chairs than to changing lives.

'I am a writer,' Valeria said. She cut herself another slice of cake. She was going to eat it with her fingers too.

'What's your surname?' Charlotte asked her. She sipped the wine. 'Perhaps I've read something of yours.'

'Costas,' Valeria whispered. She liked delivering her surname. It was a famous surname of a famous writer and she couldn't help feeling good about it.

'Oh my God,' Charlotte exploded, 'I've read three or, actually, four books of yours. I am a huge, huge fan.'

And because it was surprising for Valeria that the thing hadn't been said before – not by Isla during the phone call when she invited them over, nor during that same dinner, she blushed.

'Can I involve you in our work with the kids? We always invite writers. It's one of the best things we do there,' Charlotte said.

'Yes, of course,' Valeria said, 'I'd love that.' Her work could be worthwhile too. Perhaps she was already an activist? She glanced over at Luc. Was he blushing?

They carried on with shots of vodka, the kids sloping off, and Valeria told a couple of good stories about her writing – a residency in Iceland where she had felt very lonely but had written an entire collection, then a festival in Patagonia. She managed to drop in a couple of big names, adding something poetic and something funny, because by now she was quite drunk. Isla opened the windows leading onto the garden, lit a cigarette and Valeria went over to smoke one too. She liked Isla. She was glad to know her. Was it because of the wine and the vodka? It felt good, anyway.

'Shall I make coffee?' Valeria asked her.

'Please, yes,' Isla said and went back to sit at the table.

Valeria moved into the kitchen, and with her back to the room, she thought, I hope I look pretty from the back, I hope Isla likes me, I hope we will all be fine, I hope Antonia is not upstairs smoking one of Bea's joints, because that shit is too strong. And then she heard Luc saying, 'Shall I help you?'

'Thank you,' Valeria answered.

Her heart beat faster, she blushed.

When Luc got even closer, she thought, Martìn, I miss you. But I can stay here with them, because they like me, and I don't have to give away our secret. Ever. I don't have to cause any pain. I've been good and I'm going to be good always.

Luc had turned his back to the rest of the room, just like her. He took one of the coffee cups out of her hand. She liked his hands. Did he like hers?

'You fucking disappear tonight and never come back,' Luc hissed. 'Her husband, let me repeat this, *her* husband, is dying upstairs. What are you even doing in their house? You need to leave.'

Valeria's eyes filled with tears. Luc picked up the other cups, put them on a tray. He lifted it.

'There we go,' Luc said, louder. He turned around with a smile, the tray in his hands, looking at his friends. 'Here's the coffee. Drinking it doesn't mean that anyone can drive home, OK?'

THIRTY-FOUR

Valeria was on an expedition with Sybilla - she had convinced her to go to the lake to catch tadpoles – and they had crossed paths with a bride. The bride was walking alone and was barefoot, her white train trailing behind her in the dust.

'What do you think has happened?' Valeria asked her sister.

'He didn't deserve her,' Sybilla said. 'That's for sure.'

For a few more weeks the bride did not take off her dress. She walked around with that white train and eventually went back to work in a taverna near the Mandraki harbour, still wearing the gown. Even so, the gown remained clean. Probably, the girls decided, she washed it every evening.

'Or maybe the dress of really cool brides never gets dirty,' Sybilla said.

The sisters would go sit at the café nearby, and look at her. Sipping juice through their straws, they would whisper comments, trying both to be noticed by Olympia and not to be noticed. The story of that dress became mythology, and in the mythology was its beauty. Legends could be introduced. Super powers and allegories combined.

Sybilla and Valeria were huge fans of Olympia's. She was pretty but humble. She was brave. She was different.

'Olympia has understood being free is for the brave,' Valeria would say.

'Olympia has married herself,' Sybilla would add. 'To marry oneself is a great plan. We could marry ourselves but pick the same day, so we would be free but united. We need to be special too, to always add magic to our story, and then to the story of them all.' She'd open her hands and stretch her arms, as though embracing the rest of the world in a gesture that made her look like she was onstage. Valeria was sure she'd also seen some magic powder floating away from Sybilla's hands.

Years later, when Valeria was studying at Columbia, she wrote a story about Olympia. In the story she made the bride wear the dress for years. In those years, every two days, Olympia would wash it. At the beginning, wearing the dress hadn't been a rational choice, she was just too sad to change her clothes. She was also embarrassed being the bride left at the altar, and wearing the white dress at work had been easier than imagining the gossip, overhearing the expressions of pity. The dress was somehow a clean way to deal with it and it had to be carried and exhibited to lose all the promises it held. And it did happen. One day in July, after a swim, dried by the sun, Olympia had been too hot to put the dress back on. She left it on the beach and went home in her panties and bra.

After it was published, 'The Bride's Dress' was turned into a movie, shot by an Italian director on the island of Lampedusa. When Valeria watched it at home during one humid Paris night, she resented the fact that the dress got dirty and that the protagonist was bitter.

Throughout her viewing, she thought about calling Theodora. Did anyone know if Olympia was still alive and what she'd done with her life? But when the credits began to roll, she instead called the director and said that she had very much enjoyed the picture. When the actress won a prize at the Berlinale, she called her too.

'Let's have dinner soon,' the actress had told Valeria.

They had not heard from each other since.

'I'm not sure we are ever going to do this again,' Valeria told Joe.

'They said you liked it.'

Valeria felt sorry for Joe. She felt sorry because he had been beaten when he was four, six, twelve, and because they hadn't let him go to school. She felt sorry he had tried to kill himself when he was twelve, thirteen and fourteen. She wanted to give him back a childhood which would bring him an easier present, where he could sleep better, breathe better, love more.

'I'm sorry,' Valeria told him. 'It's too painful.'

You fucking disappear tonight and never come back.
Valeria counted. She breathed. So Martìn had told someone. He had told Luc. He had broken their deal. Had he broken all the others too? Had Luc recognized her as soon as he had stepped in, and pretended until he found the right moment in which to destroy her? Or at the beginning of the evening had he wondered if the two Valerias were the same person but had only realized when he heard her surname - that famous, uncommon surname? Or had it been something about the stories she had told Len or Charlotte? Had Luc not recognized Valeria immediately because the pictures Luc had seen of her in the papers were of someone younger, happier, healthier? *Fucking disappear tonight and never come back.*

I have to leave this house and I will be out - of his life, of this house - again. No matter the story I come up with, this door for me will be closed. What will Isla think if I abandon her now that she has opened her door and her family to me, and is back to officially drawing again? And Antonia? But Luc has ordered me to fucking disappear. Tonight. And to never come back.

'Valeria, sugar?' Isla asked her.

Was Isla very soon going to put a hand on Valeria's shoulder too?

'How many?' Isla added.

'Three,' Valeria said. Wow, three. And now, Valeria, drink your overly sugared coffee and go. Disappear. How to survive? You will find out later. Where to go? That too. Back to black. To the rental apartment, the books about portraits, the empty bottle of Shianti. To your life before the Aclà house. To before Martìn too? To the Big Bang?

Valeria breathed deeply. If I breathe deeper than this, they will be able to see a hole opening in my chest. Luc wasn't looking at her. Nobody was. She walked to the table, sat down and picked up the cup of coffee, trying not to expose her shaking hands too much.

'Are you all right?' Isla asked her.

She was sitting beside her now. Everything that was on the other side was scary. Secrets. Craters. Monsters. Valeria nodded and smiled in response.

Isla whispered, 'Sure?' so Valeria nodded again and smiled badly again. She saw Sybilla nodding too and saying that everything was fine, just like that morning when she couldn't pretend any more and had fainted in the bathroom. Holding her sister's hand on the freezing tiles of that bathroom in Rhodes, Valeria had prayed to God. Please don't take her away. Please don't leave me alone.

She didn't pray again, ever.

'Last shot,' Isla told Valeria.

Valeria drank hers immediately. For another three or ten thousand minutes, Valeria remained silent, listening to the discussion around her. It was mostly about upcoming elections, and how London was becoming less liveable, more and more conservative and violent. They went on and on, while Valeria was busy trying to imagine the second, the evening, the exact place in which Martìn had chosen to tell Luc. What were his words? Had this happened twenty years ago? Or last month? Had Martìn asked for Luc's advice and did Luc disapprove of the affair, the lies, or was he the kind of friend that bonds over cheating, lovers, passions, and helps you with your secrets?

'I really have to go,' Valeria whispered to Isla. She started vaguely cleaning up the table and found herself holding a sticky spoon, not knowing what you do when in life you have sticky spoons in your hands.

'Oh, you don't need to do this. Thank you,' Isla said. 'Can you feel how the pot effect comes back with the vodka?' she murmured in her ear.

Isla looked at the sticky spoon still clasped in Valeria's hand. She was now very attached to the spoon. It couldn't hurt her. Couldn't hurt anyone. She could feel the pot big-time and she hated it. It made it impossible not to have paranoid thoughts about Luc, about death and about the end of the world.

'Valeria is leaving us,' Isla told the table.

As stoned as she was, Valeria perceived this last sentence as a death knell. She was going to leave them, she was going to die.

One by one they asked her to stay a bit longer. Even Luc said, 'Oh, I wish we'd talked more,' and Valeria was tempted to say, No you don't, and have you and Isla slept together? Did you really just tell me to *fucking* disappear, Luc? Would your best friend Martìn accept this? I was being good to this family. I was getting closer to Antonia, Isla is painting again. I was near Martìn and he loves me.

'How is the portrait coming along?' Len the doctor said.

Isla took the spoon out of Valeria's hand.

'Is it for something specific?' Charlotte asked.

'It's for Valeria's next book,' Isla said. 'For which we are still to find a title.'

'What is it about?' Len asked.

'It must be about love, like all the others,' Isla said.

Valeria looked at Luc. Were her books all about love? Did it mean Isla had read them all? Did it mean Valeria was a repetitive author?

'So is this portrait of hers,' Isla added.

The word 'love' was standing in the middle of the table. Stop following me!

'I really have to go,' Valeria said. Then, suddenly, she asked the group, 'What's your favourite song?'

The question was so random it wasn't even funny. But at least the word 'love' disappeared from the room. Isla looked at her guests, and in her stare Valeria saw that she was commanding them to answer.

'Isla's favourite song is called "Paloma". Do you know it?' Luc said. 'Martìn chose it for their wedding.'

'It's not,' Isla complained. 'My favourite song is Lou Reed's "Perfect Day".'

'I should go,' Valeria said again. 'See you all soon, I hope, and thank you for being so welcoming.' Then she left the Aclàs' house, from where she had to fucking disappear tonight, never to come back.

THIRTY-FIVE

When she heard the doorbell ring, Valeria peeled herself off the sofa and opened the door still half naked: the kimono she was wearing was too short. Not that she cared, the world had to deal with her changing flesh. Last night she had been told to fucking disappear, so not being pretty or young wasn't really a problem, if anything it was the problem of the person looking at her.

'Delivery,' the man said. He glanced at Valeria's thighs. 'You need to sign this for me.' He smelled strongly of cologne and had black circles under his eyes. Rough night? Fight? Taking heroin since forever? Or only for the past two days?

'Madam, please can you sign? I'm in a bit of a rush,' he said.

Valeria signed, her silk kimono slipping off one shoulder. The man heaved the box at his feet into the house and left. Valeria closed the door and pushed the box in front of the couch. She went to the kitchen, got a knife and cut the tape.

Is this light coming from inside me?

The calligraphy of her father was on every envelope. Her name was on every envelope. Her past, her present. Valeria sat on the couch and so she remained for a long hour, replaying her story so far, for what she wanted to remember today. Then she went back to the beginning of all things and at the beginning of all things it was blurry, like being underwater.

'So fucking be it,' she said. She opened her computer, checked the flights to Rhodes, grabbed a credit card and bought a ticket for the following morning.

'Joe, I am off to Rhodes,' she told her agent an hour later, while packing. She pushed her trolley-case out from under the bed. She opened the chest of drawers, dropped in a few panties, T-shirts, and a couple of pairs of trousers into the case. She grabbed the computer, the charger, the external disk drive. She congratulated herself for still being able to manage a few basic practicalities while having to fucking disappear.

'How long will you be gone for?' Joe asked.

'Are you on the treadmill?'

'The lack of breathing is related to you going to Rhodes. Is this a break from the break?'

Valeria grabbed some of Julian's letters, adding them to her suitcase, covering her clothes. She put the rest in her handbag. Ten. She added another ten. The flight took three and a half hours. Another twenty.

'I need to go,' Valeria told Joe. 'I'm sorry.'

'Title?' Joe managed to say, '*In the Middle* stays?'

And mostly because she felt sorry and she needed to please him, but also because she now knew it didn't matter, not any more, possibly ever, Valeria said, 'Yes, it stays. I also have a new idea – for a novel.'

'Are you already writing it?' Joe asked.

She heard joy invade her agent's voice. How could his mother have died never having seen how easy it was to make Joe happy? Why hadn't Valeria flown there to tell that woman the perfect story, using all her skills and all her writing techniques, to make her seek redemption? But what was she hoping to obtain from that trip? Revenge? Come on, love. And by going to Rhodes?

She was so bad at it all. She just had to disappear. From everywhere.

'Are you already writing it?' Joe repeated.

'I am, yes,' Valeria said.

'What is it about?' Joe said.

The words poured from Valeria. And it was a tsunami.

'It's about a woman who is a writer. She gets her portrait done by the wife, a painter, of her lover. The writer has been the other woman in her mind – maybe also in this man's mind – for twenty-five years. Because he is dying and she has no access to him, she decides to find a way into his house. So every day she sits before the wife, while the man she loves is dying upstairs. And every day something happens in this messy house, in this warm and frantic family, where there is a complicated and brilliant teenage daughter, two boys, there are the friends of the family too.

And whatever has happened the day before, lies, secrets revealed, the writer will return the morning after. Does the wife know? Will the writer tell? Will the man die? What is it to love? How do we survive our stories and our pain? It's about letting it all go, life, possession, jealousy, youth, the past. It's about surrendering and surviving. Eventually, let the surviving go too.'

Joe remained silent. Valeria was shocked too. She had to see a therapist, a neurosurgeon, someone. She sat on the bed, looking at the case of her father's letters. The rain outside, in Morse code, tapped on the window: You stupid little girl. You tiny thing. You orphan of your sister, of love. Survive? You don't even know where to begin.

'Please tell Pamela to skip our Friday in London,' Valeria said. 'But don't tell her about the new story yet.'

'Sure. And remember Russia next Tuesday?' Joe whispered. 'In case you need to rearrange.'

Did she have something to say in Russia? To Russia? To the world? About wars? Maybe she could deliver, in Russia, the best speech ever that would lead to world peace. She had to call Isla, say goodbye.

'Can you please tell Isla?' Valeria said. 'She will understand.'

'Are you sure?' Joe asked. 'I mean are you sure you want to go and are you sure I should be the one calling Isla Lawndale?'

'I'm not,' Valeria answered. Then, 'You take care.'

And because of the things that had happened over these last few weeks and over the last fifty-five years, she was scared it might be the last time they heard from each other and these were going to be their last words, so she said, 'I love you.'

'I love you too,' he answered.

'Remember to give me five stars,' the driver said before starting the engine the following morning.

It was so early it was still dark. It was so dark it might be a dream. Valeria blinked her eyes a few times just to make sure it wasn't. Had this technique ever worked?

'If you remember to give me just one,' she told him. He didn't laugh.

'Don't cancel the app, I'd lose my job.'

'And you don't cancel me, I'd disappear.'

She needed to think more thoroughly about the Greece plan. Was she ready? She only had the aeroplane ticket to Rhodes. Seat 8A, and being a speedy boarder was as far as she could get in terms of understanding who she was. She was a woman who could pay money to sit in the front row and preferred to be by the window. She was now a woman that bought last-minute tickets to fucking disappear. And to possibly meet her mother in the very place from which she had once been torn away.

Outside the window London was bleary, as though Valeria had never been here and this could never be her place. The miles between her and Martìn were clocking up, and her body ached with the growing distance. Valeria passed the petrol station where Isla had locked her in the car with Pamela, and she felt a nostalgia for Brown's Café, where the waiter would be pouring infinite lines of tea. What were they singing today at the Mass? She vaguely heard a song, only in her brain, but it did work as a good soundtrack. It was a Greek lullaby, one Theodora would always sing. It was called 'Nani Mine'. Valeria switched her phone off. She didn't want to be reached.

'Your phone is off, madam,' the driver said.

Fuck.

'Has to be on, madam,' he snapped.

In the movies this wouldn't happen. In the movies she would now be free, with the sound of the Greek lullaby growing in volume and intensity, into an explosion of emotions and significance. And maybe all of London's 9 million inhabitants would sing it for her. But in real life someone in Cupertino or Berlin had built a technology that needed her phone to be on. The soundtrack was gone.

Valeria put her phone on aeroplane mode.

'You are a one-star for sure,' the driver said, suddenly pulling over.

'I know I'm a star,' Valeria replied, stepping out of the car. In the pouring rain she dragged her case towards the station, asking for directions as she went.

'Where's the station?' she asked them all.

'Which station?' they all answered. She was far from everything.

Outside the train windows the rain was torrential. Valeria saw all the faces she had met in London: Antonia, the twins, Bea from the deli. She saw Luc, Len, Charlotte, Melanie. She saw the girls all dressed in pink at the Scheherazade Bliss, the kind girls at the Squat for Riot Grrrls, and the phenomenal singer at the Mass. Mirela and Ari-Leo from the Portobello club. She saw Martìn, his head tilted to the window, the breathing apparatus in his mouth, she heard the sound of the machines in his room. She waved her hand to all of them. A royal wave.

She said goodbye.

Walking through airport security, Valeria knew that she was a dangerous person and hoped someone would stop her for good. She sat at the departure gate, the word 'Rhodes' shining before her, leading towards her future. Or was it her past, all contained in that dark box, in those well-written letters? She was about to take off to her past. It had been more than forty years since she had been there. It was only £49 to fly back today.

She breathed deeply and closed her eyes.

'Last call for Ms Costas. Ms Costas, this is the last call for Ms Costas,' she heard suddenly. She had fallen asleep. 'Last call for Ms Costas. Ms Costas, this is the last call for Ms Costas,' the tannoy repeated. She stood up, walked over to the counter. It was a last call and last call sounded pretty inevitable. Instead of the air hostess she might find God. Seeing God she would smile and say, I knew you existed even if I always said I didn't. Forgive me? For everything?

'Forgive me,' Valeria told the air hostess as she boarded the plane. She was panting. 'For everything.'

'I hear it's sunny there,' said the air hostess in reply, and smiled. 'Sit back, relax and enjoy the flight.'

Valeria walked to her seat. She sat down, ready to do all she could to relax and enjoy the flight.

THIRTY-SIX

In the first letter, Julian approached the story from the point of view of a carpenter, who lived nearby. The man had a tiny house and often saw Theodora, Sybilla and Valeria around. He would call them mermaids. He would try to find clues about why these three creatures were living without a father, and would fantasize about a disaster that had eliminated the man from their lives. Being lonely himself, the carpenter would hope to create a new, joyful family.

The second letter took the form of a diary entry from Sybilla, and Valeria wasn't able to finish it. It was too painful. How did he even dare? It was the sacred voice of Sybilla.

The third letter was Julian's excuses for being a horrible man, a quitter, a loser. He mentioned addiction. His words were fill of self-pity – mentioning his mother, who was bipolar and abusive.

Another letter, again in Julian's voice but now as though very old, writing from his death bed, relating his life story to a bored nurse. The nurse pretended to listen, but would sometimes text and even make calls, imagining that the old man wouldn't notice. He did, in fact, notice. The last pages of this letter were dedicated to Julian's first months in London with Theodora. Apart from some nights, in which he felt alive and connected to the world through Theodora, he hadn't been able to really feel anything, ever. He recalled Sybilla arriving into the world, always crying. He related his fights with Theodora, his impatient, miserable reactions. He was afraid of himself, unsure of his mood. Then came Greece, and Rhodes. He was on a boat back to London within a few weeks. After they made peace, Theodora was back with him in London for a weekend and she became pregnant again. When Valeria was born, she too was always crying. He became impatient again. And angry. After a massive fight, Theodora took the girls back to Greece and he let them go; he and Theodora both now knew he was unable to control himself, his anger, his demons. He described how he had lost everything, then in just two lines he summarized the rest of his life. Living alone in London, sad. The imbalance between the first part of the story and the second – the first part of his life and the second – said it all. He didn't exist out of that one story to represent him, he had been a monster, an embarrassing man, a failure.

Valeria felt disgust. He should have let the silence be. She opened another letter. It was a love letter, from a man to a woman, from Julian to Theodora. He described her body, and her beauty, he was passionate, warm. He described one of her dresses and Valeria cried because she knew the dress he was describing. She opened another letter. Their family story again, but told in the third person, as a synopsis that ended with the father learning his eldest daughter had died. He finds out about it from some old acquaintance at a restaurant, one year later. Because of this, he tries to kill himself. But fails at that too. Valeria closed her eyes. She saw the dress again. She saw her mother wearing it to Sybilla's piano concert.

'Vegetarian wrap or chicken sandwich?' the hostess asked her. The girl was an angel that had come to rescue her. There was turbulence but the sky outside was clear blue.

'Chicken sandwich,' Valeria said. Not vegan, she thought.

The hostess had red curly hair and was very curvy. Maybe she ate many chicken sandwiches while in the aeroplane loos. I love you, hostess, Valeria thought.

'It'll be four euros ninety,' she said. 'Any drinks to go with it? Beer, Coke, juice, water?'

Valeria hoped that the list would never end. She didn't want anything else from life.

'What other drinks do you have?' Valeria asked, noticing the hostess had paused.

'Lemonade, iced tea, coffee, cappuccino, frappuccino, mochaccino.'

Valeria wanted water but she had been so keen on listening, she now had to want something very special.

'Frappuccino!' she requested. 'And still water, please.'

The hostess shook up a paper cup, performing her magic. The plane shook with her, to help with the coffee foam. Valeria thought of buying a round of drinks for the entire plane. But instead she opened another letter. And another one. She read twenty of them and not a single one wasn't related to Theodora and the girls.

Valeria tried to remember when the letters started to arrive. Was it in New York? How did Julian know her address? By then, Valeria was not even interested in asking. In the letter that Valeria read while landing, Julian had added a third pregnancy to the story. There was Valeria, Sybilla and there had been another visit from Julian, sex another night after a fight, Christmas, rain. Nine weeks later, Theodora had decided to have an abortion. Theodora told Julian afterwards, 'You are not a father, why should you even care?' Then, 'I'm not a good mother either.' When was that? Immediately after Valeria's birth? Many years later?

The letter didn't say.

When the plane landed in Rhodes, Valeria couldn't stand up. Seat 8A was more comfortable than stepping back into Greece. The passengers grabbed their bags and left the plane, all the children seemed happy to be here. So did everyone else. If there were cats in some of the cases, the cats were probably happy too. Valeria heard people talking in Greek. Every word was a bomb exploding. A caress. A memory. Some of the words were scary, others very cold. Some she didn't understand any more.

'Everything all right?' the hostess asked her.

'Catching my breath one second,' Valeria said. I've been trying to do so for fifty-five years, she thought.

'Can I help you?' whispered the hostess.

Maybe the girl could really help her catch her breath, and to do so Valeria could directly use her younger lungs, her different childhood. She looked outside the window and stood up. 'Your bag,' the hostess said behind her.

Valeria turned around and took hold of her bag. She could leave all her letters to the hostess.

'You are kind,' Valeria told her. 'And you are beautiful.'

Valeria walked across the baggage claim area towards the exit sign. The Greek alphabet was the beginning and the end of all things, the alpha and the omega. So when she saw the alpha and the omega, she acknowledged their way back to her heart. The welcomes were all around her, hugs, smiles, names written on boards, eyes wide open looking to lock. The automatic doors opened and Valeria walked out into the sunshine. The wind was picking up, the light was bright, her eyes full of tears. 'To the port, please?' she said, getting into one of the waiting taxis.

If the driver had other ideas she had given him an option with the question mark.

'Are you Greek?' the driver asked.

'*Pros to Limani*,' Valeria repeated in Greek. To the Port. And for every Greek word she said from then on, a tear followed. It's hot. *Kanei zesti*. The island is quiet. *To nisi enai isycho*. I haven't been here in a long time. *Ego poli kairo na ertho edo.*

'*Parakalo*,' Valeria said, stepping down out of the car. Rhodes answered with its warm breeze.

THIRTY-SEVEN

The port was frantic. Tourists, ferries, fishermen. Kids playing football.

Valeria breathed it all in and started walking and stumbling near the shore, leaving behind the shiny stones of the old city of Rhodes with their black-and-white pattern. They were a maze Valeria knew by heart.

With Sybilla, they'd thrown stones through the windows of abandoned houses near Lindos. Valeria had once cut her hand on some glass. For a few seconds the blood gushed so fast she thought, This is it.

Now, walking along the coastline from the port and to the north of the island, Valeria could see her sister in the waves, swimming back to her.

Even if the sea was big, Sybilla wasn't getting tired.

'All good?' Valeria asked her.

Sybilla kept swimming and Valeria kept walking. With every step she took, for every metre of Rhodes she covered, she thought, We are here.

The island was dreamlike. Valeria was an astronaut, touching the soil of the moon for the first time. Planet

Earth felt very, very distant and when an hour later she sat down on a rock, Sybilla rested too, floating on her back, her palms spread open towards the sun.

Valeria switched her phone on. She had lots of new texts. Joe was saying, *Please don't take a break from the break of the break.* Antonia: *I need to hide at your place, can I?* Isla: *Spoke with Joe, when are you next coming for a sitting?* Pamela: 1) *Do you have the final list of the songs?* 2) *Do I need to cancel Moscow?* 3) *The cover tests for* In the Middle *are on the go.* 4) *Shall I come to you?*

Valeria pictured Pamela's ponytail and it was as big as the tail of a shooting star. She texted her back, *Please get in contact with Antonia Aclà, would love her circular drawings for the cover, can we arrange? Speak soon. X Valeria.* She wrote to Dimitri: *I'm in Rhodes too.*

To all the others she just wrote, *I'm so sorry. Can't now.*

She turned towards the sea. Sybilla was still there. The waves crashed beside her, it was the perfect sea for a day and a journey like this one. Full-on. Epic.

A boy joined Valeria on the rocks, hiding from a girl near the road. It was a furious, bumpy hide and seek. Their mother was watching them from the road.

'*Yassas,*' Valeria told the boy. She smiled.

'*Yassas,*' he whispered but didn't smile.

Who says hi to someone hiding anyway? The children's mother called them back and Valeria, who had no mother that made her stay away from a rough sea and had no children to take away from a rough sea, stayed there, being sprayed by the waters.

In the middle of the sea, she thought. In the middle of you all.

She picked up her phone and texted Joe and Pamela: *Cancel Russia, sorry. V.* Would they, at least for one second, think they had to cancel Russia from planet Earth?

She called Martin. The call went straight to the answering machine.

'Martin, I'm sorry,' Valeria said. 'I was selfish in wanting to be near you without thinking through the consequences. Things got out of control, because I like your family very much. If not, I could have kept it tighter – only the sittings and no nights spent in strip clubs looking for Antonia. I'm glad that I managed to hold your hand but now I feel the cheating more than ever. I need to be straight with you, in telling you about my love for you, and that there are things I would do very differently. I cheated on you. I've been more jealous than I could ever admit. I was scared of asking you about your job, your life, you. I missed you all the time. I've tried to be the best that I could possibly be, creating a version of myself for you. I liked that woman, on paper.' Valeria walked back to the shore. 'What I'm not sure of, is if it was just another story I was telling myself. One that I was writing for you.' She kept walking, this road she had walked so many times when she was a girl, when they were two girls. 'I was pregnant with a child of yours and never told you.'

At that she ended the call.

Approaching the next bay, the sea became rougher, the waves higher – just like Rhodes under her feet coming back to life, everywhere around her and inside her. She imagined one of Antonia's circles, drawn on a Greek rock. She saw a taverna. She entered it.

'*Apo pou pernaei to leoforeio?*' Valeria asked.

'The bus is over there,' a woman replied. 'About to depart.'

'To Prasonisi?'

'Yes, to Prasonisi too.'

Valeria ran out into the square. She sat in the very back of the bus and Sybilla took a seat beside her. Was her sister glad that she was back in Rhodes? Valeria not returning to Greece for all these years meant that Sybilla hadn't gone back either? Or maybe for all these years Sybilla had been stuck in Rhodes and this was Valeria's first time to be close to her again.

The bus travelled through the valleys, leaving behind the houses and rows of olive trees. Upon reaching Prasonisi, Valeria saw Sybilla rising to her feet.

They stepped down from the bus together and watched it leave.

Nothing had changed. The small church, the side chapel to the monastery and the steps leading down to the sea, were all the same. Valeria began her descent along the signed path and along her past, stumbling upon the sloping trail that she and Sybilla had discovered together.

As she followed its path down to the sea, the vertigo rose through Valeria's legs. She quickened her pace, the trail becoming steeper. She squeezed herself against the cliff-face, her back exposed to the void. Had her belly been squeezed against that exact same rock more than forty years earlier?

'Be careful!' she heard Sybilla say. Now or in the past?

The wind picked up and Valeria walked along with her head down, quickening her step. As soon as the trail was wider again, Valeria started running until she arrived at the small bay with its soft sand. Now that she had seen more of the world, she knew there was no other place as beautiful. The water was crystal clear. It was always calm here, even when the waves were enormous beyond the bay, as indeed they were today. She undressed. She closed her eyes.

'It's so scary,' Valeria had said.

'What is? The water?' Sybilla had laughed.

'My thoughts in the water,' Valeria had replied.

With her eyes closed Valeria imagined Sybilla getting undressed beside her. A middle-aged woman and a tiny girl were now naked, in the middle of nowhere, in the middle of the bay, on the softest sand. Looking around it could have been any year, any era, from the dawn of humanity until the present day. In the middle of history, in the middle of their story.

'Shall we?' Sybilla smiled.

Valeria stretched her arms and spread her fingers wide, trying to feel Sybilla's fingers interlaced with hers. They walked to the water.

'It's cold!' Valeria screamed.

Sybilla was light and serene. Valeria looked at her, entering the water to her ankles, to her knees. To her belly button. Then, she couldn't follow her. She turned around and quickly went back to the beach. She walked on the sand and stood near the mountain, her back pressed against a rock, catching her breath. She called her mother.

'Mum,' Valeria said, 'I'm here.'

THIRTY-EIGHT

After walking up a mountain with Martìn, Valeria wrote 'La Promenade'. They were in Sils Maria. It was May. The mountains were in full blossom, even though it was still cold. During the walk back they crossed paths with a couple hiking with a child who was probably not more than four years old. As soon as they had passed by, 'La Promenade' took hold of Valeria's imagination.

She pictured the couple, very much in love, good people, fun and kind. They had been together for the past ten years. The same very good couple, today, on these mountains, were going to kill their little boy, making him slip on purpose. Why? Because the boy was ill, so they had chosen for the pain to be avoided, for the fear to be eliminated.

It had been the woman's idea. At the beginning her husband had refused, terrified. But then it had been him who came up with the whole plan.

'They will carry out an autopsy and they will understand it was us,' he had said. 'I know what we need to do. We have to buy him a dog and he will be sacrificed. He will jump, following a ball. We'll say the boy was trying to save his dog.'

The woman had vomited. Had her husband really invented that meticulous plan?

And then the day came, and it was rainy. She thought – let's cancel. She thought – it's a sign, we don't have to go ahead. But the boy wanted to take his puppy for a walk and her husband had been very sure about not cancelling, so while preparing the sandwiches for the picnic she crushed an anti-anxiety pill under her teeth.

The boy came in with his water bottle to be filled, he didn't notice her tears, he was so small. She wanted to fill water bottles for him for all of her life. They walked under a gentle rain, wearing their waterproof jackets. As they walked along, she stopped to point out the flowers, the butterflies, the village below.

'They are cute,' the boy said.

'The village houses?' she asked.

'I don't remember,' he said.

They travelled up to the promenade in a cable-car. The boy loved it, while she had a panic attack. They walked along the narrow path that led to the second mountain and near the final precipice reached a huge field. The husband said, 'Let's have our picnic here.'

She wanted more time with her boy.

'Please,' she murmured. It didn't have to be today. Or ever.

They sat and ate their sandwiches. She couldn't swallow.

The boy said, 'I am tired.'

She said, 'I am tired too, come here.'

She lay down with him, his tiny body keeping her warm. She squeezed her son tighter and pictured him collapsing on the floor at school. She pictured him at the hospital, in his tiny pyjamas, his wide eyes.

Her heart broke for ever. She felt the crack, the pain, and the immensity of the disaster.

She heard the first doctor saying it would be months. She heard the second one saying it could be more like weeks. She heard herself asking, 'Is it painful?' And the entire world responding: It is.

She stood up near the precipice and the dog ran over to her. So did her boy. She threw the remains of the sandwich over the edge and the dog followed. Her boy screamed, running to the edge of the cliff. And then she pushed him.

As soon as she pushed him, she screamed too, trying to pull him back. But he was gone.

'What have we done?' she asked.

But she thought, What have I done?

The sky grew darker as her husband approached the cliff. He managed to look down but couldn't see his boy.

A few weeks later the woman disappeared and her husband didn't find her for years, even though searching for her was all he did. When eventually he found her – she had moved to a different country, changed her name and language – he told her the story of how they had met, how it had been to love her. He said that all the happiness of his life came from her.

'Why are you doing this to me?' she asked him. As soon as she spoke she saw her hand pushing the boy, and trying to pull him back. But the fabric was slippery and her fingers could not grasp it. She had killed their child.

She wiped her mouth, did up her coat, walked away.

Again that night she heard the doctors telling her which parts of Damien's body, one after the other, would give up. She saw her boy having the first seizure. Then the ones that followed. She saw him crying for his headaches. Then she heard the doctor telling her there would be an option, very new, very experimental. Painful, but one that would give them something to fight for, right?

'Talk about it with your husband,' the doctor had said.

She didn't do it. For a 5 to 10 per cent possibility? Alone, she chose not to go for that option. So she lied.

'We are moving to the mountains for the next few months,' she had told the doctor. 'We are not willing to spend the time we have left with our child in hospitals.'

So they had moved to the mountains.

After having written the story chronologically, Valeria reordered the paragraphs, so it began with a woman who is constantly being followed by a man and speaks a language which is not her own. Slowly, and going backwards, the reader would discover her past.

'I can't finish it. It's too painful,' Martin told her.

'Can't you finish painful things?' she smiled. 'How do you cope with life?'

'I suffer,' Martin said with a tiny smile.

'You can invent stories for that pain too. I do it all the time. I change narrator, name, all meanings of all things.'

'You often think that you are the only one who can invent stories for others,' he said. 'But many of us do it just as often.'

'What do you mean?'

'I sometimes find it difficult to be a character in your story. Because you don't realize you are one in mine too. This should come as a relief for you: you are not the only one in charge of the plot. Or that can write the ending.'

Valeria arrived at the Calliope Hotel when the sun was setting. The entrance had both an olive tree and an almond tree, and the windows were painted in blue. Valeria was about to talk to the woman behind the counter when she saw a smaller, weaker version of Theodora. Her mother's hair was coiffed in a grey plait, she was wearing a very long red shirt over red trousers. Sandals.

Theodora had shrunk and not only in stature, even her eyes and mouth seemed smaller. Turning around to see her daughter, she smiled. Valeria smiled too and for the first time in decades, they hugged. During the hug Valeria saw, standing behind her mother, two monks. They were dressed simply and each had a star drawn in the middle of their foreheads, that looked more like an indie rock band statement than a third-eye symbol. They were nodding. To what?

'Monk One, or Gibi,' the first monk said. He shook hands with Valeria.

'Monk Two, or Kateshi,' said the second monk.

Monk One was chubbier. As for the rest, they could have been twins: their brown eyes, the shape of their mouths and their noses slightly curved to the right, made them identical. If her life were one of her stories, Valeria would have made them twins. Or maybe they were, and would soon reveal it to her.

'Mum,' Valeria said again, tightening her arms around her mother. She closed her eyes and inhaled deeply to take all of her in. She smelled her cream. That one. Rose, honey.

'Mum,' she repeated. And while she was looking again into her mother's eyes, Theodora fainted.

Valeria slowly sank to the floor with her.

'It's the cancer,' the monks said to her ear.

Valeria stood up. The 'M' of Mum pulverized. How much more pain could she bear?

The monks went to get Theodora some water, and carried her over to a chair, where she slowly came back to them, her face very white, the circles under her eyes very dark. Valeria tried to adjust to this new version of her mother. Skinny. Aged. A general sense of fragility.

'Hey,' Valeria said.

'Sorry,' Theodora whispered.

The whole island was in shock. The boats went still and so did the waves, the wind, the cars, the birds and the clouds.

'It's been seven years,' Theodora added. 'At least. How long has it been?' she asked the monks.

'Nine years,' they said. 'But you had no cancer for three years during the nine. So how long is it?'

'What are you even talking about?' Valeria whispered. 'Why haven't you told me?'

They'd seen each other every year, how had she never guessed it?

'I don't like to say the word,' Theodora smiled. 'Especially to you.'

'I'm so sorry, Mum,' Valeria said. 'Is this why we are back?'

THIRTY-NINE

As Valeria and Sybilla had known since they were small, Theodora's parents had died when their mother was seventeen. They had a car crash and it was all so sudden that nothing had been planned for Theodora. She received the money her father had left behind, which was enough to make her life comfortable, and inherited a tiny derelict farmhouse in Lindos. She lived with her auntie Vasiliki until she turned eighteen, then moved to London. Years later, Theodora moved back to Lindos with the girls, and Vasiliki came to visit twice. She was a doctor and was very busy, but would always reply to the girls' postcards. When Sybilla was already very sick, it was one of Vasiliki's colleagues – Tilla – who gave Theodora the incurable sentence.

'It's way more aggressive than the first time. You are basically asking me if you can hope for a miracle,' the doctor had said.

Theodora had despised Tilla, her voice, and the entire world in which no miracles were expected. Where Sybilla was going to die and everything Theodora loved got pulverized.

'Fuck off,' Theodora had told Tilla. 'Fuck the fuck off you fucker,' she screamed and hung up the phone.

In her room, lying on the bed pretending to be asleep, Valeria had been listening. Her eyes wide open, her heart so closed.

The following morning Valeria woke up to a black coffee and bread with olive oil. Eating on the front porch felt like summer. Could Theodora get better and heal? Or was she here because it was impossible? Opening her work in progress document on her laptop, Valeria started adding things about Isla, recording Isla's questions to her about ageing and loneliness.

'I feel lonely,' Isla had said. 'I feel lonely and I feel death. Even with you, now, here with me.'

We have to let him go, Valeria had thought but not said. But maybe it was time to call her now, and say, It's time to let him go, Isla, to let it all go. She saved the Word document with a new name. *P/The Portrait.* Then, to avoid focusing on her heart beating too fast or on the word cancer, she called Pamela.

'I don't know if I should come and get you,' Pamela said.

'You should definitely not come and get me,' Valeria answered. Or should she? 'My mother is very sick. I will be back when I can.'

'I'm sorry for your mother,' Pamela said.

'Thank you. How's it going with Benoit?'

'Not going,' Pamela said. 'And it's not coming together either.'

'Still up for the wedding?'

'I was up for going to Moscow with my boss, the famous writer.'

'Sorry about that,' Valeria said. But she wasn't sorry. And she knew she shouldn't lie any more. Lies then needed other lies and she didn't have the necessary memory or strength to keep up with them all. 'We will make up for it.' Another lie. Then, 'Has Antonia sent the drawings for the cover?'

'She said she will send them today and also she said – I'm quoting – you should "fuck off" for abandoning her. And she wants to sleep at your flat.'

Valeria smiled. 'Fair enough.'

'Can she?'

'Nah. She needs to be near her father,' Valeria said. 'I have to go now, my mum is here.'

Valeria hung up the call and walked towards the weaker and smaller version of Theodora and again, she hugged her. Again, it felt like hugging dust. Still, better than hugging nothing.

O n the side of the Hotel Calliope that faced the sea a gigantic bougainvillea climbed up to the roof. At midday, the monks went for a walk and Theodora and Valeria had lunch under the pink flowers.

Valeria ordered fish, salad, followed by coffee. She also ordered yoghurt and nuts for dessert. Theodora was eating so little that Valeria thought that ordering everything available on the menu would be a good plan. She didn't want to see Theodora faint again.

'So, what's the deal with the monks?' Valeria asked. 'Do you pay them?'

'We don't have money in Sunville, you know that.'

'I forgot,' Valeria lied. When exactly was she going to give up lies? And eating animals? She ate more bread. Maybe some of the bread she was swallowing would nourish Theodora. Maybe some of the bread would push down the pain. From her chest to her feet. Pain in the feet she could do. In the chest, too scary.

'They are here to be with me, I'm willing to die in Rhodes,' Theodora answered. 'Please pass the coffee?'

Valeria forced herself not to say, 'Don't die, please.' Here or ever.

'What kind of cancer is it?' she asked her. 'Can you explain this to me?'

'Valeria, no,' Theodora stopped her. 'There's no need.'

Valeria picked up the coffee pot and poured it for her mother. She saw herself pouring coffee for Theodora when she was six. She looked down at her skin for a burn: the coffee had scalded her hand and she had cracked a tile on the floor dropping the percolator. Theodora had slapped her. Valeria remembered another time she had been slapped by Theodora. She had called her mother a whore in relation to the fucking Italian husband. The burn on the skin had gone. But then again, so much else had happened in the meantime. All of it had made the scars vanish.

'Can you help us find a small flat in Lindos?' Theodora said, and she looked around as if she might be able to find a flat by scrutinizing the land from under there. 'We are terrible at organizing this kind of thing.'

'Yes, Mum,' Valeria said. 'I will also ask my assistant to help us look online.'

'Thank you, Vale. This is such a perfect day,' Theodora said.

The soundtrack of the Society of Life's Mass started playing in Valeria's synapses and in her heart. Lou Reed was there too. She searched for the song on her phone. She pressed play.

'If you had to pick a song for your life, which one would it be?' Valeria asked her mother.

'It would be a Greek lullaby,' Theodora said.

'Do you know it by heart?'

'I do, yes. But now I can't sing it, Vale,' Theodora said. 'Now I'll rest.'

Their lunch plates cleared, Valeria put two chairs under the olive tree. She prepared a blanket and lay down in the shade of the leaves, the warm wind blowing from the south.

'This was quick,' Theodora said. 'Coming back, I mean.'

And they both smiled because it had taken so long. Valeria saw a young Theodora walking alone to a clinic, having the abortion and walking back to the girls. She chose winter as a season, fish stew for their dinner. Wishful thinking. She added few candles. She even bought her mum a new car.

'I miss Sybilla every day,' Valeria said.

Theodora had always said, no matter how sad she felt, *I love you girls*. But from the day Sybilla died she hadn't been able to come up with anything for Valeria alone.

'Do you remember how to speak Greek?' Theodora asked her.

'A little, yes.' Valeria closed her eyes and saw the timetables of the ferries to the islands. Lipsi, Symi, Pserimos. Every island was a memory. The cheap meat in Pserimos. The clear sea in Symi. The fabric shop of the old lady in Lipsi. Every place was Sybilla.

'Sometimes,' Theodora said, 'when you were a child, I looked at you and knew that you were going to be the lucky one.'

'I'm not so sure it happened,' Valeria smiled. 'I'm not even sure I know what that means.'

The two sisters used to go to Symi any time they could. It took one hour if the weather was good. One and a half if the sea was rough. There had been one day in Symi that she had elected for ever as her favourite. With Sybilla, they had walked to the beach, the pebbles so tiny they didn't hurt under their feet. The shade of blue was the exact colour of happiness. They swam in that happiness for hours, a tomato and a peach for lunch. At sunset, they jumped on the boat back to Rhodes, arriving too late for dinner. Theodora was angry but surrendered, Sybilla and Valeria so happy their chests hurt.

'In some way, perhaps?' Theodora asked her.

'What?'

Theodora was asking her if she had been happy, not

only if she had survived. 'Yes, I have been happy, Mum.' The 'M's of Mum were as big as mountains, the highest ones in the whole world. 'And you?' she asked her. But Theodora had fallen asleep.

Valeria left Theodora dozing under the tree, surrounded by the fertile landscape, lulled by the sound of the sea. Walking back to the hotel reception, she switched on her phone. A call from Isla arrived. Had she put it on recall mode? Telepathic timing? She saw Isla in the first picture she had ever found of her in a magazine, Martìn with the twins in his arms, Antonia not more than three or four years old. She had thought – I love Martìn and I'm a bad person.

'You have to come back,' Isla said. She sounded in a panic. 'I need you here.'

'How's Martìn?' Valeria asked. Was this question too familiar and intimate? Who cares. If he's dead nothing matters any more.

'I can't finish this without you,' Isla said.

Did she mean the portrait or letting her husband die? Or letting their common love die?

'He's going,' Isla said.

'Tell her to come back,' said Antonia in the background. 'And stop saying he's going, Mum. I can't deal with that fucking sentence.'

Then suddenly Antonia was on the phone and it was her voice that found its way to Valeria's heart. 'OK, famous writer, Mum needs to finish the portrait because painting it helps her. She says you didn't tell her anything and just left. Is this how you do it? She might be a mess. Yes, you are, Mum, you are a mess. Anyway, Dad is getting worse, it's true, and you can't just charge into people's lives in times of disaster and disappear on them at your convenience. So, what I'm asking is, get the fuck back here, please? I beg you.' Antonia started crying.

'Antonia,' Valeria said, 'listen to me. My mother is sick. I'm with her in Rhodes.'

Antonia snorted. She repeated the sentence back to Isla.

'Is she in a worse or better condition than Martìn?' Isla asked from the background.

Valeria smiled. Who made hit-lists of such things? 'Hard to tell,' she whispered.

'Hard to tell,' Antonia repeated.

'As all things are,' Valeria said.

'As all things are,' Antonia repeated and she hung up the call.

'How is Theodora doing today?' a monk said.

They were standing behind her in the hall of the Calliope Hotel. Valeria turned around and saw near them the invented character from Julian's letter. It was the neighbour carpenter who wanted to build a family with them.

'She seems in better shape, today,' Valeria said. 'Does she often faint?'

317

'Fainting is just taking a small nap. Sometimes there are also nice dreams in there, very short but nice. Like you with your short stories. Did you give her the medicines?'

'I didn't know there were medicines to take.'

'Didn't you ever play doctors when you were a kid? In the doctors game, when you're sick, you take medicine, so then you get better.'

She wanted to kill them. 'What medicine?' she asked instead.

'She needs to smoke cannabis, that is common knowledge,' the monk said severely, 'and she needs to put tea tree oil on her forehead. She needs laughter. Also, she needs you to take her temperature from time to time. You can do it with a pen or tiny stick of wood, then make a fake injection after taking a fake temperature. In the morning, she needs meditation.'

'You mean she needs to meditate?' Valeria said. Who were these people?

'She needs you to meditate for her. To say it's OK to go,' the monk said. 'Now go rest with her under the tree. And rock 'n' roll.'

Valeria walked back to her mother – but not because the monks had told her to do so – and found Theodora asleep in her sun chair. She pushed hers as close as she could to her mother's, making a single seat for the two of them. She started to read more letters from Julian. Each one sounded like the last, a rather repetitive, dull mantra, that instead of becoming more powerful, was losing its intensity, just like when you repeat the same word hundreds of times, or you wear the same bridal dress, until it loses its meaning.

Valeria must have fallen asleep.

'What are you writing about now?' Theodora was asking.

Was Theodora going to read her again?

'Two women who have loved the same man for all of their lives. The man is now dying.'

'Who knows what?'

'Well, that question never has a straight answer, does it?' Valeria said.

'Who did he love more?'

'Who did you love more?' Valeria asked. 'Sorry,' she added.

'What are you always sorry about?'

'I'm not sure.' Valeria stood up, Theodora still lying there under the cover. 'It's getting cold, shall we go inside?'

As they were about to step inside, Valeria saw a couple of Julian's letters lying on the grass. She picked them up and placed them in her bag. Had Theodora read them?

That night, Valeria slept leaving the connecting door open. She woke up a few times and went to check on her mother's breathing. It was weak, distant. Unable to go back to sleep, Valeria sat in Theodora's room and waited for the sun to rise.

'What are you doing here?' her mother asked when she stirred. By then it was around seven. The Hotel Calliope had woken up, the coffee machines were warming on the stove, the steps of the first guests could be heard.

'I couldn't sleep,' Valeria said.

'I'm sorry I wasn't better,' Theodora said. 'And for my sadness. I did some horrible things. And I lied. It was wrong of me.'

'It's OK,' Valeria said. She said it with a strength that made it true. She rewrote life, and the past, so in any case, it was now OK. 'Shall we meditate? I'm not sure how it works but the monks seemed very keen.'

'Oh, yes. They told me that you really need to meditate.'

Theodora sat on the chair, fragile and minuscule, attempting to sit upright. Her nightdress revealed the lines on her chest, her whole story. She'd breastfed Sybilla and Valeria. She'd been young, in love and then lonely. She'd been abandoned many times. She was about to die. Valeria was overwhelmed by a wave of love so enormous she had to swim through it. She moved close to Theodora.

'I will guide you through it today,' Theodora said. 'You can do it tomorrow.'

Please let there be a tomorrow, Valeria thought. Tomorrow I will do my best to find the right words for my meditations and for life.

'Breathe in, and breathe out,' Theodora said. 'Deeply. Do not force your breathing. Do not force your thoughts.' Theodora was immediately out of breath. Valeria wanted her to stop, but the thought of her mother doing something with her and only with her was irresistible. So she moved closer, and in the twenty minutes that followed she enjoyed their closeness, the meditation lifting them to the moon and back.

'Done,' Theodora said abruptly after the last countdown brought them back to earth.

Valeria was feeling very good. She loved being taken to the moon. And alone, she never made it there. Then Theodora stood up and fainted.

'Help!' Valeria said, opening the door and shouting. 'Mum!' she said falling to her knees beside her mother. A trickle of blood ran down from Theodora's head.

FORTY

'So, it's as if I'm living for Rami too,' Martìn said. 'In the story you are writing the surviving twin has two loves, two homes, lives in two cities. He even has two jobs!'

Martìn and Valeria were in Paris. Valeria had double-locked all doors, not wanting to be interrupted by the housekeeper, Pamela or anyone else. Martìn was due to leave in a couple of hours and she was already missing him as if he was already gone. She missed everybody in her life as if they were all already gone. Even the strangers.

'I wonder if in real life Rami would have loved you or Isla.'

'That's beside the point,' Valeria said, irritated. She peeled herself off the bed, got in the shower and stayed there longer than necessary.

'My limp,' Martìn said, when Valeria was back in their room. 'He used to beat me up.'

'Who?' She sat on the bed. One towel on her head, another towel around her body.

'Rami. He would beat the shit out of me. Once, it got too bad.'

Valeria felt a rush of nausea.

'It was his pain, his sadness that would set him off. But that one time, it went beyond that. He punched me, I fell, my leg was twisted. He trod on it,' Martin said without showing any emotion.

Valeria's hand went to her mouth. She wanted to vomit.

'I passed out. I woke up at the hospital. Then nothing, doctors, me inventing a lie, the terrible pain. I remember knowing that something had been broken for ever. In my body and between Rami and me. I think my mother had always known, when she listened to our made-up excuses, she didn't buy them, I could tell, but she said nothing. After the leg incident, she had to face the truth. She was too scared something really bad might happen to me. I begged her not to say anything to him, not to put herself between me and my brother. She didn't listen.'

'Any mother would have done the same,' Valeria said.

'I don't care. It was his life or mine. She should have known better.'

'If she hadn't said something you would resent it to this day.'

'Rami had already come to me. Even in his silence, I knew he was asking to be forgiven. I have never seen him with such a horrified face. I was completely aware that it was better to be me than to be him – I just got lucky – and having to live with a limp was nothing compared to the hell Rami lived in.'

'What did your mother tell him?'

'He was forced to say that he was sorry and that he would never do it again. She made him promise me something untruthful. He knew he was going to suffer for ever and that he would have made me suffer for ever. Rami tried to kill himself for the first time that same night, as soon as she left the house, throwing himself out of a window. So the morning after, Helena had both her twins with broken legs. It would have been hilarious if it wasn't so sad.'

Martìn stood up, naked, and Valeria looked at his leg, at his body she loved so much. He was getting heavier, he was getting older. Watching it happening was sweet, even beautiful. Why didn't she have similar caring eyes for herself?

'I'm so sorry, Martìn,' Valeria said.

'I'm glad he is always with me. I love my limp. It's him.'

Martìn went into the shower, and he too, stayed in there longer than necessary.

It was a silent breakfast. Valeria couldn't stop imagining the young Martìn beaten up by Rami and Rami trying to kill himself. In her imagination, Rami had Martìn's face but longer hair, darker skin. Knowing about the violence changed all she felt for the lost twin and changed so much of what she felt for Martìn. Because he had been more in pain than she had imagined? Because in all their life together he hadn't looked for help or compassion? Because there was so much she still didn't know about him and she wanted to be near enough to somehow finish the story.

'Stop thinking about it,' Martìn said. He grabbed a cup and poured himself some coffee.

'I can't,' Valeria said.

He looked at her as if she were a lazy student not making the right amount of effort.

'What if it were the opposite?' he said. 'What if it were me beating the shit out of Rami? What if I just invented that version of the story? What if he was the beaten-up one and I broke his leg before trying to kill myself?'

'Why are you doing this?' Valeria asked. 'Why are you playing this game?'

She thought, He's his double, just like in my story, and that's why Isla and she could coexist for an entire life.

'I'm telling you how deeply we were united, how our bodies were one shared body, how at the end it doesn't matter at all which arm was punching which body, which mind was built in darkness. The pain – both in giving and receiving – was equal. Even if there could be such a measure for such guilt – if there is this guilt – it was fused, inseparable. So was the agony and the love. He was my twin brother, I loved him.'

'Did you beat him up?' she asked.

'I have to go,' Martìn said.

'Don't be angry with me. I'm just trying to understand.'

'I'm not angry with you, why would you say that?' Martìn hugged her.

She stood up and hugged him back.

Martìn put his jacket on, grabbed his suitcase. His

breakfast remained untouched. Valeria left it on the kitchen table through the whole weekend. The bread turned hard and the eggs became smellier by the hour.

At the Calliope Hotel, the doctor was called and Theodora and Valeria lay in bed waiting. Valeria had put a plaster on her mother's head, where the skin had opened. Theodora now seemed better, if a bit sleepy. Valeria didn't feel better at all and, to try and calm herself down, she'd been counting her mother's every breath for the last hour.

'Tell me more about you,' Theodora said. 'Your life, your days.'

'Can we not do this?' Valeria begged. Considering her mother's character, it was a conversation too similar to one she might want to have before dying. Not on her watch.

'But let's make it a choice,' Theodora said.

'Let's not make it a big thing either, like a choice.'

There was a knock on the door. There stood a woman wearing a ski jacket, a helmet. Her gym shoes were golden.

'Good morning,' the woman said with a very strong Greek accent. 'My name is Rosa.' Valeria shook hands with Rosa and said, 'I'm Valeria, and she's my mother Theodora.'

She let the alien doctor in, then sat at the desk, near the window, listening to the soothing flow of Greek words. As Theodora explained what had happened, for every word Valeria willed herself to memorize her voice, this moment. She closed her eyes while the doctor went through Theodora's medical reports. Maybe instead of memorizing everything she should let it all go. She could see herself aged twelve, sitting in a chair at the Rhodes hospital, and Theodora back then, talking with the doctor. She could see Sybilla, sleeping in the hospital, the dry lips, the distant breathing. She needed to let that go too. Like with erosion, like with the YouTube trainer. Change shape. Morph.

'Are you all right?' the doctor asked Valeria.

She was tapping her fingers on Valeria's shoulder. She felt guilty, both in the past and in the present, for attracting attention when it was the others around her who were sick. She was the lucky one, right?

'What were you thinking about?' Theodora asked from the bed.

'Sybilla,' Valeria said. 'I was remembering one day at the hospital, the three of us. You had on that blue dress, with the big pockets.'

'I still wear it,' Theodora said, 'those pockets are very handy. I would always have a few pebbles in there. You and your sister used to bring so many home. We must have had half of Rhodes under our beds.'

It was the first time Theodora had spoken of a memory of Sybilla. *I love you girls.* Valeria saw a stone by Sybilla's bed, in the hospital. That same stone in Paris, in her house, today.

Valeria stood up. Getting closer to the doctor she could smell her sweat. Why would you go around with a ski jacket to end up drowning in your own sweat? She acknowledged the list of things she was being told to buy. The alkaline water, the energizers.

'If you come downstairs with me, I have some painkillers. Just in case,' the doctor said.

'I hate painkillers. I'd rather do pain,' Theodora said.

Under the sunshine and in front of her motorbike, the doctor opened her jacket. Was it only there as a protection against sickness? Valeria looked at the olive tree and the almond tree, hoping that they would be the one talking with her about cancer and pain: talking about the fear of death with a tree was for sure easier and more pleasant than with a fearsome golden-shoed doctor.

'Your mother is dying,' she said.

'I know that.' In her mind, Valeria added, 'bitch'.

'It's going to be soon.'

'What's the definition of soon, given the speed of it all?' Valeria said. What was she, seven?

'I don't have painkillers with me. I just thought you might want to exchange a few words alone.'

Why would Valeria want to exchange a few words alone with someone so scared of life she used a ski jacket as armour?

'Today and the next few days will be like this. Your mother will faint. She might be stronger sometimes, but in general she will get weaker. She says she has no pain. That's impossible.'

'I don't think she is a liar, if that is what you are implying,' Valeria said.

'Oh,' the doctor replied. 'That's not what I meant. Sorry.'

'You should be more careful with your words.' Then, 'Is that all?'

'If you need nothing more from me, yes it is. That'll be forty euros.'

'That's cheap,' Valeria said. 'You're cheap.'

Maybe she could punch the doctor, to let some of her fear go.

'Forty euros for twenty-five minutes is enough. Here's my card, should you need me. I hope you enjoy your last days with your mother.' She climbed onto her bike.

'See, you did it again. Why did you just say, "last days"?' Valeria asked and then walked away, back to Theodora's room.

The monks were sitting at the end of the bed, her mother was asleep. She was snoring.

'The doctor is a bitch,' Valeria murmured.

'Soon you can go to London,' the monks said. 'We can talk disapprovingly about the doctor for you. You can also suggest which bad words you'd prefer us to use.'

'What? You've been obsessed me with coming here!' Valeria said. 'Where do you all want me?'

'No crying now, OK? Or cry but don't be sad. You two needed to hug, and it's done. She wanted to open again your door to Rhodes and it's done. And you opened it for her too.'

'I don't want to go away,' she complained. 'What if she dies when I'm not here?'

'Theodora is not afraid of dying, you have to know this. She likes the idea of a good, long rest. And the remote – very remote – possibility of being closer to Sybilla. It's a pleasant thought, right? Remote, but still pleasant.'

'Yes, still pleasant,' Valeria said.

'You are pleasant too,' the monks told her.

'Thank you,' she cried.

As the fear of Theodora dying became more concrete, Valeria realized she hadn't stopped worrying about when it might happen since their hug the other day. Or maybe since she was seventeen and their lives had taken different directions. Seven? Every day since she was born.

'She is fine,' the monks said.

Valeria saw them as if from a satellite far away. They were very tiny, sitting on a very tiny bed, in a very tiny hotel, in their very tiny lives. She took a picture of the scene. She framed the picture.

'I'm so hungry,' Theodora said, waking up. 'I could eat an entire cow. Or even a tomato if it was as big and fat as a cow.' Then she fell asleep again.

Valeria was left there sitting on the bed with the biggest tomato ever.

FORTY-ONE

'Do you have any music?' Theodora asked Dimitri. He had said yes to driving them around Rhodes within minutes. He pushed the CD into the player and immersed in the Greek music and in the beauty of the island the quintet made their way to the village of Lindos. It was very windy but Theodora wanted the windows open. With every turn Theodora would slide closer to her daughter, and with this new closeness, Valeria thought she could do a lot. At the very least knit a blanket for the colder months.

'The island hasn't changed too much around here,' Theodora said. 'What do you think, Dimitri?'

'The air is the same. So is the sea,' he said.

The first flat they were shown was fine but it had no views. They then drove to the second one and were shown around by the owner's daughter. She had very long hair and looked like an Egyptian goddess. She was more striking when in profile, which would work perfectly for Egyptian portraits.

The flat was cosy and in a sleepy road that led to the Acropolis. From one of the bedrooms you could see the sea. The kitchen had a little terrace, with two chairs and a table.

'My assistant mentioned the little terrace,' Valeria said. 'She thought we'd like it.'

'Thank your assistant for such a delicate thought,' Theodora said. 'Shall we give her a name?'

'One we choose for her?' Valeria smiled.

'Let me hear the real one first.'

'Pamela.'

'Thank Pamela for the terrace. If you give me her number I'll thank her personally.'

Valeria welcomed more peace. She welcomed the sea she could see from the bedroom.

The Egyptian beauty showed them where they could see the sun rise – in the tiny room – and where they could see it ending its daily journey – on the terrace and in the kitchen. Valeria imagined a short story filled with characters from around the world, each describing where the sun rose and where the sun ended its daily journey. 'So it starts here,' someone was saying in Mumbai, 'and it ends here,' someone else was saying in Boston. 'The New Life' could be a good title.

'It's a nice flat,' Dimitri said.

'Nice flat, yes,' both Valeria and Theodora confirmed.

The monks nodded and smiled.

'The sofa looks very comfortable,' Dimitri said.

'Try it,' the Egyptian beauty suggested and they all sat there, on the very comfortable sofa.

From where Valeria was sitting she could see the bed in the bigger bedroom. She imagined herself, watching Theodora sleep. She saw the monks making a vegetarian meal in the kitchen. She smelled the cumin and the coriander. The lemongrass.

'It's one hundred and twenty a week,' the girl said. 'But if you take it for more than three months we can cut you a good deal. Is July a good plan?'

'I don't think we'll still be here in July,' Theodora said.

A part of Valeria collapsed and died. She saw herself swimming with Theodora in the clear waters of the Plimiri beach. Then herself, alone, swimming somewhere darker. The place where she was swimming alone didn't have a beach to go back to.

'July,' Theodora added, 'seems far off.'

'It's not,' Valeria said. 'It's just around the corner.'

'June seems a better idea,' Theodora said to the girl. She turned around to Valeria and whispered to the monks, 'Even if I die beforehand, I'm sure you'll enjoy Rhodes, right?'

Her smile was so free of fear that Valeria almost saw the beauty of the monks being here, in this flat, after Theodora had gone. She saw them sitting where the sun rose, and life for a few seconds wasn't frightening or mysterious at all, but very, very simple. She looked again at the empty bed in front of her. She imagined Theodora's weight had left an impression. The impression was a hole. The hole was full of light.

Valeria spent that night checking that Theodora was still breathing. Unable to sleep, she lay near her mother, browsing the internet on her phone. She wore her headphones and listened to her messages.

'Hope you and your mother are doing well and that the little terrace of the flat was as lovely as it looked in the pictures. I just wanted to let you know I'm thinking of you,' Pamela was saying. Was she tipsy? 'I guess I just wanted you to know. And perhaps I'd really like to be invited to Rhodes now.' Then nervously: 'Oh, one last thing: a large box was delivered to your place from Argentina. Want me to send it there? Let me know. Bye, I miss you.'

A box from Argentina. What did it mean? Why now? Valeria switched to a Bach playlist. She pictured both portraits, hers and Martìn's, hanging in her bedroom in Paris and they didn't fit well together. I should take Martìn's back to Holland Park, anonymously, she thought. She then looked online for the happy trainer who had promised to change her. She was still asking for the same things, in her eternal present. How can you transform in an eternal present?

Valeria stepped down from the bed and lethargically did some squats.

'What are you doing?' her mother asked.

'Training for a marathon?' Valeria tried.

'Which marathon?'

Valeria opened the curtains and sunlight flooded the room.

'Our marathon?' Valeria said with a smile.

'Who is the man you love?'

Valeria paused before replying. She looked at her mother. How could she know?

'What do you mean, "who is he"?' she said, relieved that she had found a sentence that could be read in at least two or three safe ways.

'If you don't want to talk about it, it's fine.'

'He is dying,' Valeria said, and as soon as she said it she couldn't help but cry.

Theodora tried to get out of bed but she had to lie down again.

'Come here,' she said instead and Valeria sat beside her. Theodora sat still, looking at her daughter. Valeria knew that she was totally unfamiliar with this intimacy. 'You should go to him. He's dying.'

So are you, Valeria thought. So am I.

'Don't worry,' Valeria tried. 'I'm exactly where I want to be.'

'That's never the case. Probably for anybody,' Theodora said. 'And there's not a single thing in this world that worries me, Valeria. I wanted to bring Rhodes back to you. And to me too. Simple is very beautiful.'

While crying Valeria thought of telling Theodora everything, but when she managed to pull herself together to do so, she saw her mother had fallen back to sleep. She was seated upright, but asleep. Like a horse.

'More!' Sybilla shouted. 'More!'

In the hospital, Valeria and Sybilla were hiding

on the top terrace, Rhodes at their feet, the doctors and the nurses panicking downstairs.

'Hide me,' Sybilla had begged Valeria. 'I can't be touched one more time.'

Valeria had said, 'Yes, let's go.'

She had checked the hallway and covered her sister with her own jacket.

'Now,' she whispered.

A very weak Sybilla held Valeria's hand. Though unsure on her legs, her sister was very sure in her will. They reached the back stairs in less than thirty seconds, crossing paths with an old man dragging his IV drip-stand with him. Safe, behind the stair doors, the girls climbed up to the terrace.

'I'm slow like the old man we just saw,' Sybilla said. 'I'm an old man.'

'You are a turtle,' Valeria said. In her mind she transformed her sister into a turtle – she would scrub her shell with a toothbrush, it would shine. Turtle she could do. Old sick man she couldn't.

Under the sun and out in the open air, Sybilla smiled. They lay together on the tiles, resting. As soon as Sybilla had caught her breath, she asked Valeria to help her settle on the edge of the building. They sat beside each other, their legs dangling in the void.

Valeria grabbed her sister's hand.

'I wouldn't mind jumping,' Sybilla said. 'The only thing that stops me is that you would freak out. Is that why you're holding my hand?'

'Shut up,' Valeria said. Yes, that was why she was holding her hand.

Sybilla looked at her sister and Valeria knew she was asking her permission. 'Better to die with a jump than in that bed,' Sybilla said. She freed her hand from Valeria's grip. 'You know it, I know it. We are way funnier than that fucking first floor.'

Sybilla had a firm stare. Valeria's heart broke. She felt her happiness leaving her – for ever. She wanted to bring her sister back to the fucking first floor, then back home and, possibly, to the past. She had to protect Sybilla, not put her in danger. She had to help her live for as long as possible, not to die sooner.

'Stop!' Sybilla said, reading her thoughts. 'Don't be so scared.'

'You stop!' Valeria said, staring at her sister.

Sybilla's eyes closed in pain. And reopened in pain.

'If you jump, I will jump,' Valeria told her.

'I would never jump if you were the one that was actually going to die.'

'You would.'

'Fuck no!' Sybilla said. Then whispered, 'Let me. Tell me you'll be fine.' She looked away and Valeria saw a tear roll down her cheek. Then Sybilla started shouting. She was putting so much effort into it that Valeria couldn't believe it was really happening. Sybilla was shouting the letter 'A'. Constant. Long. Like an animal. Overcoming her own terror, Valeria joined in with Sybilla's scream. Two 'A's, desperate and full, enormous and heavy, were sent out flying and fighting, into the Rhodes sky.

'More!' Sybilla told her. 'Scream more! Break the sky!'

Valeria shouted more and tried to break the sky.

When they were both exhausted, a gaggle of terrified doctors and nurses arrived panting on the terrace. Sybilla saw them, then turned around and started coughing up blood. The medics picked her up, and helped her into a wheelchair. Valeria walked alongside her sister as she was wheeled downstairs, pushed by a nurse. She felt guilty for not having liberated her sister. She hadn't let her choose.

'Last time I scream,' Sybilla said that night into Valeria's ear. She even attempted a smile. She had a temperature. She was in pain. Her eyes were closed, her lips so dry they looked like broken clay.

Theodora ran a wet napkin across her daughter's forehead and Valeria felt it on her own forehead, as if her mother was passing it across her skin too. She made a promise that it was the last time she would ever scream. Three days later, Sybilla was dead.

FORTY-TWO

After sunset, they all sat on Theodora's bed. The monks were back from their daily walk, Valeria was done with her daily writing.

'Did you like the sunset?' Theodora said to the monks. 'I've asked Pamela the assistant to help us with that too.'

Valeria smiled. Theodora laughed.

'Magic,' the monks said. 'Same colour as the one we saw when walking down the Omhida mountain.'

They touched Theodora's hands, they hugged her. Valeria felt a jealousy that was painful, but also ridiculous. She didn't even know if the Omhida mountain existed. How many names of mountains did she remember? Ten? Thirty? Acanagua, Cervino, Kilimanjaro. Olympus.

'Your mother loves walking,' the monks said.

'Sybilla and Valeria used to walk every day, for hours,' Theodora said. She was proud. 'The girls would take me to the most incredible valleys, where the lake waters were warm. We would come back smelling of sulphur, our fingers cooked by the water.'

'We could go to a warm lake tomorrow,' Monk Two said, then to Valeria, 'And you can leave afterwards.'

Theodora was still smiling.

'Wait, what?' Valeria said. 'Stop this! I don't want to leave tomorrow.'

'Let's see how all this sounds after you are well scrubbed and washed,' Theodora said, 'then we'll ask Pamela the assistant to organize it for you to go.'

'I'm not going anywhere,' Valeria said. She missed Martìn and the Aclàs' house, yes. Desperately. But leaving was wrong. Now that she felt pushed away by Theodora and the monks, it seemed even more wrong.

'I'm hungry,' Monk One said.

'Me too,' said Theodora and Monk Two.

'Is this a tactic to avoid conflict?' Valeria stood up. 'Pretend to be hungry when we are talking about something important? You do it when we are on the phone too, Mum.'

'We're just hungry, Vale,' Theodora said. 'It's way past dinner time.'

'You did it again!'

Theodora slowly stood up and dressed before them, not caring at all about showing her fragile body. She took off her nightgown, exposing an unhealed wound on one shoulder, and another on her chest. If she were to cover herself up who would she be protecting and from what? She put on her trousers, a thick jumper, socks and boots.

'You're very beautiful,' the monks said.

It was true. With the open wounds and with the signs of life, she was like the olive and the almond tree out there, with whom she could talk, maybe without fear, about the fear of death.

One after the other, adjusting to Theodora's slowness, they walked to the hotel restaurant. The fireplace was lit, dry octopuses hung from the ceiling. They ordered the chickpea soup and the salad. The red wine. During dinner Valeria kept looking at her mother's eyes, which kept closing. She was clearly in pain. Whenever they opened, it was only out of effort. Theodora was trying not to scare her daughter.

'Don't worry,' she whispered to Valeria.

The monks drank more wine, ate more soup. Then the three of them finished Theodora's meal. Valeria helped her mother walk upstairs, while the monks went to their room. She sat on her mother's bed, undressed her, cleaned the wound and helped her into a clean nightdress.

'Can you tell Julian I'm dying?' Theodora said while lying down. 'He needs to know. And you two might need each other.'

'I'm fifty-five years old,' Valeria said. 'I don't need him for sure.'

'He might need you.'

'That might also be true.'

'He should have known,' Theodora said. 'I should have told him about your sister.'

Valeria saw herself leaving Hampstead Heath after having re-enacted Sybilla's last cry for help. She had lied to Julian. She had told him Sybilla wanted to see him. She hadn't. Or at least, she hadn't mentioned it.

Valeria saw Theodora crying when the girls were three, four, ten.

'He's your father.' Theodora was so tired she could barely talk. 'He was Sybilla's father too.'

Valeria covered Theodora with a blanket.

'It's time to sleep,' she said.

'I'm your mother. I'll be the one to say when it's time to sleep,' Theodora replied. She switched her bedside light back on. After ten seconds she switched it off again and said, 'And now it's time to sleep.'

In her room Valeria opened the *P/The Portrait* document on her laptop. She began to write, trying to describe Antonia's pain now that her father was in a coma, and that probably was coming from knowing that her mother had lied too. The fear of loving girls, Oksana who had left. Valeria went way back with her memory, writing about Julia who had told Antonia she was disgusting when they were nine, and she went even further back. She could honestly state she'd known Antonia since she was born and before that. She grabbed her phone.

'Antonia,' Valeria said. She could see the timer counting the seconds. 'Are you there?'

The call connected but there was no answer so Valeria hung up then tried again. Again, Antonia picked up but wouldn't speak.

'I'm sorry, Antonia,' Valeria said. 'My mother needs me.'

'It's not because of your mother. It's because of what Luc said. You are all a bunch of liars.'

Valeria's heart missed a beat. Her mouth dried up. The entire universe was dry too. 'I heard what he said to you,' Antonia said. 'I always hear you guys.'

'It's not what you think,' Valeria tried, and immediately hated the sentence. She begged for a good story to come to mind. Luc had sent her away because he had loved her too? He hated her novels and couldn't stand the writer she was? Kind of fun, but no.

'Don't even bother,' Antonia said. 'If you can't tell me the truth, don't tell me anything. I'm morally and politically against lies.'

'Except when you disappear on everyone.'

'I disappear. I don't lie.'

'I miss you,' Valeria said. Because it was true and she knew it. Valeria also knew that she and Antonia were connected in a way that was going to survive everything. This present, the lies, the pain.

'Right now I don't care if you do,' Antonia said. 'Anything else?'

'I think about you all the time.' Valeria listened to Antonia breathing, then lighting something up. Puffing. She wished Antonia was hers. But she was, in a way.

'You know that story you wrote, where the woman spends the summer alone on Shelter Island? You know when she says she can love because of the pain, not despite it?'

'Yes,' Valeria said. She wrote it during the summer when Martin had to be with Antonia. Valeria hadn't read it since.

'I don't mind the pain either,' Antonia said.

'You do,' Valeria said, 'because you should and because you have to. I will be there for you, Antonia. I know it's hard to believe me. Especially today, when you think I have left you at the toughest time. There are things that we cannot discuss yet, but you have to trust me. I will keep you safe. I will always take care of you.' Could she take care of her always? She hadn't even taken care of a damn dog in her life.

Antonia puffed more.

Why was it that every sentence spoken to a teenager felt acted out? Is it a matter of translation between ages, just like with languages? Love/love, life/life, good/good.

From London there came a noise, of breaking glass. 'What's going on?' Valeria said. A rap song started in the UK.

'The twins are doing this horrible music thing. It's the closing beat for their piece. That's another reason for you to come back: they won't have the studio to themselves any more.'

Valeria smiled. 'Now that's a reason.'

'Oksana writes to me every day, you know? But I'm not sure I can be with her. Maybe you could write a story about this for me. Something about a person who can't do love?'

Valeria had the whole story in front of her in a beat. It was set in Canada. The protagonist was very tall. Valeria bought her a gigantic coat.

'I'll write it. Is there anything else I can do for you?'

'You can come back,' Antonia said. 'Stop making me ask for it.'

'I'm not sure how I'll feel if my mother dies when I'm not with her,' Valeria said.

'That's what we all do, have you forgotten? We're never there when someone dies.'

'It may sound genius while smoking Bea's grass, but I'm not sure it works for me right now. I'm suddenly into holding hands,' Valeria said. 'And you are too. You don't even want to go to school not to be too far from your dad.'

'How is it to be back there?' Antonia said.

'To holding hands?'

'And to Rhodes.'

Valeria remembered the many interviews she had given about never going back to Greece. Antonia had been able to create a picture of Valeria from this coverage and from reading her work too. But she also knew more.

'Easier than I thought,' Valeria said. 'Almost as if I never left.'

'Maybe you never did. Maybe you've always been there and the life you think you've lived is pure invention. Are you sure you exist?'

'You've definitely read me too much. Stop. It's bad for you.'

But Valeria saw it all. Never leaving Rhodes, never going to Italy or New York, never meeting Patrick Toyle or Martìn. Maybe working in a shop in Rhodes, having a family, living her life beside Theodora. Growing old together, having weekly lunches. She saw two Valerias, one with one life and one with another. She placed them in a sleepy, sunny street in Lindos – dressed identically – and made them embrace.

'Pamela texts me, you know?' Antonia said. 'She's fun.' Then, 'OK, gotta go to bed now. Tomorrow I have my first GCSE mocks.'

'Good luck,' Valeria said. 'You'll do well.'

In her mind she prepared a packed lunch for Antonia: an apple, a BLT spicy sandwich with no crusts. She squeezed an orange. She left a handwritten note in the lunchbox. It said, *I love you*.

FORTY-THREE

Valeria was sleeping when she heard the movements in her mother's room. She jumped out of bed to find the monks near Theodora. Valeria got down on her knees beside her mother. She looked at her face and saw a mask of pain.

'Mum,' she whispered.

Theodora wasn't getting enough air in and at the same time she was in too much pain to even want air. Every breath was a stab. Valeria remained on her knees, her gaze transfixed by Theodora's face. She breathed more gently, counting, to help herself feel better and to help Theodora feel better. The monks counted too, as if through their whispers they could put life in order. Theodora started breathing better and shut her eyes. Valeria crawled into bed beside her.

'Sleep in your own room,' the monks said. 'She'll rest better, and so will you.'

'I don't want to be too far,' Valeria protested. She spooned uncomfortably around Theodora. Her body was so tiny and fragile Valeria felt she could break it.

'But she might need you to be far,' they said.

'Let me go,' Sybilla had asked her.

They were spooning too. She had no hair, she had no colour, she had a little, little life left.

'I will go even if you don't let me, goose,' Sybilla had said.

Her temperature was high. She hadn't spoken for the rest of the night, falling in and out of a profound sleep. In the morning, Valeria had woken up beside her sister's dead body.

Valeria woke up in her own bed. She imagined the monks had enabled her to levitate her way to her own room, so she chose this option for the memories she would use of these days in Rhodes.

She went to Theodora's room. Her mother wasn't there so Valeria dressed quickly in her jeans and a jumper. She picked up the phone, already walking towards the breakfast room. She called Pamela.

'Listen, I need a favour,' she told her.

'Illegal or legal? Really hoping for illegal,' Pamela said.

'You have to open the box I received from Argentina. I need to know what's in there. And promise me that you won't tell anyone what's in the box.'

'I'd never tell your secrets,' Pamela said. 'Not that I know any of them, of course.'

'Not funny,' Valeria said.

Walking downstairs she spotted the trio sitting at the table for breakfast. Maybe she could live with them in

Sunville. She could morph into Theodora. Or even into the Omhida mountain.

'Still there?' Pamela asked.

'I need to go now,' she told her, then, after she closed the call and, mostly to try the sound of it, she said, 'I love you.'

The second short story Valeria had written about Pamela had to be sent out without Pamela reading it. It was called 'PA' and Valeria had been inspired by something Pamela told her about a friend who was organizing the life of both a husband and a wife. Restaurants, flights, medical insurance, all of it. Valeria had thought of how the assistant must have come to know most of their tastes, preferences and fears, and had then imagined her using the information to be adopted by the couple. She had started going through the wife's expenses with new eyes, studied the books they bought, went to the exhibitions they saw. She learned by heart what they ordered in restaurants and took up running because they both ran. She learned Spanish, because he was from Argentina and joined a yoga class because the wife did yoga. After the plot build-up, Valeria had made the assistant, the wife and the husband have one dinner together, to celebrate the assistant's birthday: she had pretended to be in need of cheering up. Once at the restaurant, every choice from the menu was a disappointment for the girl. She knew them too well not to notice that they were trying to save time

349

by not ordering a bottle of red to go with their supper, as they usually did.

'We are moving to Singapore for a year or two,' they told her on the way home.

It was the husband who had spoken. The wife added, 'They have asked me to curate the launch of the new collection at the Laze Museum.'

How was it possible she hadn't seen it coming? But she could do Singapore. She'd even heard of the Singapore University. She would enrol in a cooking class. Asian food was yummy. And the whole Singapore life would have led to a complete new existence and who knows, moving there with them would not only secure the bond with her possible future parents, it would also bring new people into her life, new friends, a man. Maybe a new language to learn. Was it Chinese?

'It's not going to be before next September, but this will give you time to find out what you want to do next,' the wife said. 'Our references will be so positive that you will have a queue outside your door.'

There was a silence in which the assistant saw them both dead.

'This is for you,' the husband said. 'Happy birthday.'

He handed her a small black box. It represented all that she was going to lose. Them, a different life, this effortless elegance. She was going to miss their emails, the music they listened to, their fridge stocked with pink coconut water. But they didn't love her. Even though she now knew a lot more about Yves Klein, Calder and Sufi music. Even though, through their donations to Darfur, Syria and

Afghanistan, she had convinced herself that she did care about less fortunate people.

She went closer to the wife, smelled her perfume. It was now her perfume too. She hugged the wife and kissed her on the lips.

'What are you doing?' the wife said. She wiped her mouth.

The assistant gave the black box back. It could have contained a pen, a bracelet, something technological like a mini mp3 reader. It could have also been an infinite series of black boxes one inside the other. She didn't want to know. Once the box was open, everything else would disappear.

The four of them had breakfast. Theodora drank hot water and lemon. Valeria chewed the bread, ate two eggs, ordered more coffee and more bread. She had a croissant, the biscuits. It was going to be tough getting into the sitter clothes again. Were the purple panties still under Martìn's bed?

'We are moving to the flat in an hour,' Theodora said. Her voice was low, her energy even lower. She took her daughter's hand. 'You should pack your things. Get on a flight.'

Valeria looked Theodora in the eyes. There was something comforting in being pushed back to Martìn, but it was also painful. Her mother wanted her to be away, even now, when for the first time she could hold her hand.

Two opposite emotions arrived at the same time: inside, the house, outside, the world. Here, Theodora. In London, Martín, Antonia. Isla. Stay, disappear.

But all of this – the territory, the ownership, the past – was mattering less with each passing moment so Valeria welcomed a family beyond them. It had no home, no shape and no boundaries and could include the monks, Antonia, Joe, Pamela, the living and the dead, the never-born sons and other people's daughters. It was a family with many more stories and threads than a single narrator could handle.

'The journey back is long, you might need more bread,' the monks said.

'They don't mean it. They just think you are bingeing,' Theodora said.

'Yes, joke,' the monks said. 'You need detox soon.'

FORTY-FOUR

The monks packed Theodora's clothes while she
rested. Valeria packed her own bag, and before
closing it, she stole the Calliope Hotel's soap.

When her mother woke up, they all left for the flat in
Dimitri's car. It was a crispy day, the wind was strong but
the sun was bright.

They spent the morning filling the house with food,
water. They opened the windows, prepared Theodora's
bed and the monks' room. In the afternoon they sat on the
balcony, enjoying the sunshine, Valeria still not knowing
if she would be able to leave or not, still not knowing if
this was the last time she would spend with Theodora, or
whether she should not think about it at all and just be
with her, very simply. Like cats, like cherries. She felt torn.
She had received a boarding card from Pamela.

When had Theodora called her? Valeria wondered.

'I love you,' she told Theodora many times. Then she
grabbed the letters from Julian and while Theodora lay
resting she read a few of them aloud to her.

'It seems like another life, I don't feel anything any more about it,' Theodora said.

Valeria wondered if Theodora was trying to free Valeria from the anger she was holding on to. If the new plan was for Theodora to bring Julian back into their lives – into Valeria's life – Theodora had to forgive him so Valeria could forgive him too. Theodora wanted to hear more letters, so Valeria read aloud until the sun set and the sky turned to a darker blue.

'He did call,' Theodora said.

'Who did?' Valeria's mind went to Martìn. It always did.

'Your father. He called when Sybilla was already very sick.'

Valeria felt shame for her thoughts about Martìn, and a tiny, remote pain. Like a jellyfish sting in the guts.

'He did?' Valeria couldn't tell any more what was a lie, a fake memory, truth. She imagined the call, Theodora telling Julian that Sybilla was sick. Him deciding not to come. So why did Theodora want Valeria to meet him now?

'I didn't tell him,' Theodora said.

Valeria saw the other possible lie Theodora was delivering – freeing Julian of his guilt, cleaning at least some of the dirt to make him better in Valeria's eyes. In this other possible truth, Theodora had been vindictive, worse than Valeria could ever have imagined. Way more than what Theodora had planned while rehearsing the sentence. She had let the girls down so badly. She couldn't keep the secret forever.

'You didn't tell him what?' Valeria asked.

'That Sybilla was sick.'

'Is this a lie?'

'I lied back then. This is the truth.'

'Why didn't you?' Valeria said. She felt sorry for all of them, and for humanity. She felt sorry for the bees that were disappearing, and for the dying people. Those with sad, unlucky lives, those fleeing war-torn countries, the oppressed children, the mothers and the fathers, choking under the dust of their drone-targeted homes. She pictured all the people who commit suicide in a year, in ten years, thirty, killing themselves in the same moment, hanging, jumping. Shooting. The outcasts and the oppressed and the tortured. She felt sorry for the dinosaurs that had gone for ever. And for every mistake that mankind had ever made, would always make.

'I'm not sure,' Theodora said. 'I thought I was back then, but now I'm not.'

'So what did you say?'

'Not much. Just hello. Then complete silence. Then bye,' Theodora said. 'I'm sorry.'

'I imagine you are,' Valeria said.

The story in the letters was different. Or would it change once again if she kept on reading?

'It was wrong of me.'

It was. It wasn't. Valeria cared and she didn't care at all, two opposite emotions at the same time. The past and the present. My lies, theirs. Valeria felt compassion. And it was compassion for herself, for Theodora. Everyone being everyone.

'I don't really know how to explain what I did,' Theodora said.

'Maybe because it's not possible,' Valeria said. 'Maybe you can't explain it.'

'I was very sad and I was exhausted. It was selfish. Forgive me.'

'OK, now stop,' Valeria said.

'Sybilla didn't get to see him.'

'She didn't think much about him.' They thought about him all the time. His absence was a presence: it would walk with them, go to sleep with them and never leave. That absence had a shape and that shape was their father, his words came from there, so did his teachings, and his hugs. That absence too was an imaginary coat. A hat.

'She did. But that's the only time he called and I lied,' Theodora said. 'I don't want you to think he called other times and I didn't tell you.'

'I won't,' Valeria said.

'I'm sorry.'

'Don't be sorry any more, please,' Valeria said and she hoped with every pore of her being that Theodora didn't feel sorry any more. She must have carried the guilt all her life. But now Theodora had opened to Valeria the door to Rhodes. Was this the one to Julian?

'I'll go for a walk,' Valeria said.

Valeria took the bus near the church, getting off near the Northern Cove, and began her descent along the signed path and along her past, stumbling upon the sloping trail that she and Sybilla had discovered together.

356

As she followed its path down to the sea, she quickened her pace, the trail becoming steeper. As soon as the trail was wider again, Valeria started running until she arrived at the small bay with its soft sand. She undressed. She closed her eyes.

'Shall we?' Sybilla smiled beside her.

Valeria stretched her arms and spread her right arm wide, trying again to feel Sybilla's fingers interlaced with hers. She grabbed some of Julian's letters.

The two sisters walked to the water, and it was cold.

'It's fucking cold!' Valeria laughed and she began to swim, releasing Julian's letters and letting them sink. It was always the same story in the letters, so some versions of this story should just sink here, unread.

In the swim that followed, for every stroke, Valeria called her people to join her. Theodora pregnant with a child she didn't want, Olympia, the bra-seller, the fishermen. Joe when she had enveloped him in a hug after that festival in Normandy and he had whispered, 'I'm free and I still can't say it out loud.' She called Pamela, still waiting for Valeria to open a door through which to come closer. Antonia, alone in the bathrooms at her high school, sobbing then being able to stop and swim towards Valeria, in the water, lighter than ever. Her father Julian on a ferry, aged twenty-five, smoking a cigarette, diving towards her. Helena, Bernardo, Rami beside Martìn – lying down under the stars in a field of corn, cigarettes in their hands – joined her in the sea too. The monks, Dimitri, her ex-husband Patrick. She called Isla giving birth to the twins, sweaty and red-faced. Cosmo, Nico. Then she saw her own reflection in the seawater. She chose for that shadow to be Sybilla and when everybody else disappeared, Sybilla and Valeria swam together, skirting the coast, for the longest swim ever.

'When your shadow disappears I will let you go,' Valeria said.

So Valeria swam, in the freezing cold, until her own shadow, Sybilla, was ready to go. And when the sun set, Sybilla was gone.

Am I ready to let you disappear because I'm closer to disappearing? Am I ready to let you disappear because I'm ready to stay? Valeria swam back to the bay where she had started her crawl, her teeth chattering, her fingers turning blue.

I will be cold for ever, she thought.

But she wasn't cold for ever. She quickly dried herself off and walked back up the mountain, alone for the first time in her life.

'She needs you to go,' Monk One said as soon as Valeria was back at the flat.

Theodora was snoring, the monks were still cooking.

'Do we have salt?' Monk One asked Monk Two.

They had salt. They added a bit to the soup.

'Go,' Monk Two said to Valeria. Then, 'Add the turmeric.'

'Now?' Valeria said. She added the turmeric, speaking through her tears. 'So I'm right when I say that you guys always speak about food during emotional moments?'

'Now. Not that the *now* really exists. Or that *you* really exist. This is common knowledge,' the monks said. 'She just needs the empty space to be free.'

Lucy from the Scheherazade Bliss would have given the same advice.

'We'll not swim in the warm waters again?' Valeria asked.

'You will,' they smiled. 'You'll take Theodora everywhere.'

Valeria looked again at Theodora sleeping. She breathed her in. She counted. Then she stopped counting and called Dimitri to ask him to come pick her up.

Pamela had booked Valeria a seat on the last evening flight to London and texted her: *I'll see you Friday, in London, usual schedule. Px.*

Before getting out of his car, Valeria asked Dimitri to take care of Theodora and the monks, to go there every morning and every evening, and let Valeria know what was happening with her mother.

'We had already agreed the same among us,' he told her. 'Don't worry.'

He dropped Valeria at the entrance of the airport, just as he had dropped her off in front of the Eurostar entrance a few weeks back. Who had queued with her in Paris? She could only remember the man in the leather suit. Everyone else from that day and from that queue was lost. They would all be soon too.

'I'm sorry,' Valeria told Dimitri. She was a daughter leaving her dying mother alone. It wasn't straightforward to understand. Valeria hugged him too tight.

'Take care, madam,' Dimitri said.

Valeria turned away from him and from Greece. She walked to Gate 3, to seat number 1B, and to Martin.

FORTY-FIVE

Valeria's plane landed at Stansted late, due to the strong winds and violent thunderstorms. The turbulence that preceded the landing awoke the passengers, who made faint sounds of fear, holding on to their seats. Every bump seemed to Valeria like a giant step. For every step of the giant staircase, there was another giant step a little further down. There was lightning. There was torrential rain. Valeria smiled at the girl on her left, who was very young and in major discomfort. The girl didn't smile back.

Once landed, a single sigh of relief echoed through the cabin. The adrenalin kicked in and they were all in a good mood, even if it was three in the morning and the weather in England was crap. They were still alive. Most passengers thought that this was a good thing.

After thirty minutes at passport control, walking through the airport, fifty minutes on the train and twenty minutes in a taxi, in the gushing rain and now at the beginning of a new day, Valeria was finally back in Holland Park.

Her flat was freezing. She took in the sight of the box with Julian's other letters, the books about portraits and artists, her clothes. She turned the heater on, had a shower and dressed in her jeans. Then, unsure, she changed into her portrait-sitting clothes, still hanging near the heater. Both the pencil skirt and the silk shirt were way tighter than before. Damn. She put a little make-up on.

I'm back, Martìn.

It was raining so hard that Valeria had to shelter at the bus stop. From under the awning she saw the deli open up and stared at Bea, wrapped in her shiny raincoat, dealing with the roller-shutter. She saw the neon sign *Wait and See* light up too. Valeria wanted a coffee. She wanted biscuits. She took another glimpse in the direction of the Aclàs' house and saw Antonia. Walking behind her were Nico and Cosmo.

'Come here,' she whispered.

Antonia was walking towards her, with her hood up, and still hadn't seen her.

Valeria waited for her to be closer and then stepped forwards. When Antonia saw her, her eyes opened wide, her mouth curled into a smile. She hugged her. Valeria could hear the music she was listening to: Leonard Cohen. She felt a longing for the hamburger they had shared the day the books were bought. It was like missing something that had happened forty years ago. Fifty. In another era. To someone else.

'Welcome back,' Antonia said.

The twins watched with a subtle sarcasm in their eyes. Valeria loved the subtle sarcasm in their eyes too. Hugging them featured another soundtrack, with a loud beat, some screamed swear words.

'I don't want to go to school,' Antonia whispered.

'I'll see you later,' Valeria said.

Antonia rolled her eyes. I'll protect you, Valeria thought. The bus arrived and splashed them with puddle water.

Valeria walked back towards the Aclàs' house. She sent a text to Dimitri and the monks. *How is Theodora doing? Please send news. Thank you, Valeria.*

She paused at the front steps, scrolling through her phone contacts until she reached Julian's number. She stared at it, playing with the letters. Ianluj. Lijuan. Valeria pressed call and then stopped the call. She walked up the stairs to the Aclàs' front door. She inhaled the air and all of her life. Then she exhaled.

She rang the bell. She looked up to the sky, through the branches of the magnolia tree. The door opened and Isla was standing before her. As soon as she saw Valeria she put her hand on her mouth. Valeria stepped inside, Isla hugged her.

'I'm sorry I left,' Valeria said.

She walked back inside, under Martìn Aclà's roof.

'Do you want to take them off?' Isla said, pointing at Valeria's sodden shoes.

Valeria took off her shoes, put them near the fireplace and moved to stand in its warmth.

'Has is it been raining since I left?' Valeria asked Isla, as thunder rolled in reply.

Isla smiled as if the reason for which it hadn't stopped raining was very clear. With all that is happening in our lives? Come on!

Isla was thinner and more tired than when Valeria had left.

'Red?' Mirela asked. And without waiting for the answer a red juice was given to Valeria.

'Thank you,' Valeria said. She drank her juice while looking at Isla. She was in her denim jumpsuit. Had she been painting? 'How are things going?' Valeria asked.

'Well, my sitter left me in the middle of our job. My husband's condition is deteriorating. Antonia hasn't stopped shouting at me when she's not giving me the silent treatment and I had to go out and look for her again the other night. To give a twist to my days, the twins' music – noise – has become their new survival mode. Apparently their online followers are dropping, though. I'm not sure if as a mother I should prepare them for the apocalypse. Or if I should let them be free and just see what happens. As a non-mother, as Isla, I wish I could kneel down and scream until I disintegrate,' Isla said.

'Sounds like you're doing fantastic,' Valeria said.

During her researches online, Valeria had read an article about a man who fell into a coma and woke up with amnesia. He couldn't remember his wife of twenty-six years and ended up falling in love with her all over again. Had it been worse losing all the good memories, of the times when they had been happy, or had it been better erasing all the mistakes and the lies? Valeria remembered the story of another man, a songwriter who had written a song describing being in a coma as stupid. Soon, after writing the lyrics, he fell into a coma himself. After he awoke, when asked how it felt to be in a coma, he said, 'It was just as fucking stupid as I wrote in my song.'

'So where was Antonia?'

'Turns out,' Isla said, 'she had been drawing those circles everywhere around town. So that night she was taking pictures of them.' She sighed. 'I'm not sure I can keep my pain and her pain in all at once,' Isla said. 'I'm on the verge of crashing. It's the burn-out phase.'

Valeria remembered when Martìn said that Isla had told him that she was on the verge of a 'burn-out'. They had had to reschedule a trip to San Francisco.

'She is pretending to be someone else,' Martìn had told Valeria.

'How do you mean?' Valeria asked.

'Like with her performances, you know? She pretends, for a week or two. She goes away, changes her name and picks up new habits. It's spookier to explain than to see it happening.'

365

'I wasn't thinking it was spooky,' Valeria said. 'It sounds quite cool, actually.'

'Makes you laugh?'

'Not at all,' Valeria said. But it did make her laugh. Even if she then stole the idea of disappearing in a character for her short story 'La Promenade', where the woman changes city, language, job.

'If you need to be away for a week or so I can stay here with your family,' Valeria said to Isla. As soon as she said it, she was ashamed. She was now going to take Isla's place and cuddle Martìn in their marital bed? Use her shampoo and her pyjamas? She knew details of Isla's life, her habits, that she shouldn't have known.

'Thank you,' Isla said. 'Even though I'd love to have some space for myself, I can't leave them or Martìn with you. Anyway, I still can't get out of the house for even an hour. I could never deal with a week.'

Valeria heard 'I can't leave them with you' as full of resentment. She wanted to write a short story about a hated woman. She would call it 'You Deserve It'.

'Do you mind if we start working? I can't do much more talking right now,' Isla said.

'Sure,' Valeria replied.

The two women walked down the stairs and into the studio where Isla lit a fire. Valeria went over to the stool, which hadn't been moved since her last sitting – the twins must have respected their space even in their creative storm – and checked if it was aligned with the chalk marks. She took off her jacket slowly, trying to go back into sitter mode. Then she thought it was wrong to try and mimic intensity and that these thoughts too were becoming a habit, a routine. So she shook her shoulders, stretched her neck and sat. She was very tired.

'I'm very tired,' she told Isla.

'Me too,' Isla said. She smiled. 'Or maybe this is just how we will feel until life is over.'

She unveiled the portrait and began to mix her paints, brown, ochre, her movements slow, gentle. She looked back and forth, between Valeria and the painting, the rhythm that of a rediscovery more than a wave of creation.

Was she readjusting her interpretation of Valeria? There was a version of this story in which a huge confession was part of the redemption, the prelude to an epiphany. Were they both in this room for that reason? Was Valeria the bad person and Isla the good person, the good wife, the betrayed one, the one who had remained solid whatever the storm? Because if Isla knew the part in her husband's life that Valeria had played, it also meant that she had chosen to stay. Or perhaps Martìn had forced her to stay? What version of the story would it be? Martìn a commander, Isla a victim. In a third, better version, Isla had decided to stay because she knew more about life than all of them.

'Are you falling asleep?' Isla said.

'I didn't get much sleep last night.'

'Coffee?'

'Thanks, yes,' Valeria said.

'Let me ask Mirela,' Isla said, then, 'Oh, you know what happened yesterday? Mirela found a pair of silk panties under Martin's bed. I mean, under *our* bed.' She was smiling. 'They weren't mine. As a writer, Valeria, what's the story of these panties?'

Valeria's mouth dried up. Was this a test? She was sad that the panties were no longer under the mattress. They were hers, for him, and they were purple, to recognize Valeria if she disappeared.

'I don't even know how to begin finding an explanation,' Isla said. 'I mean, *really!*'

'What did you do with them?' Valeria asked. Could a great confession start from a pair of purple panties?

'I'm kind of superstitious nowadays and wondered if they were there for good luck,' Isla said. 'So I've put them back.'

Valeria felt a relief that was not normal considering the topic. Yet, the panties were still there. Isla had done the right thing.

'I think you should just ask him when he wakes up,' Valeria said, blinking away the tears.

'Ha!' Isla smiled. 'He was never very good at answering my questions about other women, but the coma might have changed that.'

Mirela arrived with coffee. Valeria drank it with a clenched stomach. She needed to know what was in the box that she had received from Argentina.

'I like painting you,' Isla said. 'I like how you look at me.'

Valeria imagined herself saying, 'I like how you look at me too.' But she wasn't able to pronounce the words out loud.

'Do I look sad in the portrait?' Valeria asked.

'Why do you ask that?' Isla said. 'Are you?'

'Do I look happy?' Valeria tried.

Isla stepped away from the painting as if to decide whether such categories could fit the portrait.

'I wouldn't say you look happy,' she said. Then she turned back to Valeria and confirmed with her eyes that Valeria didn't look happy in reality either. 'The portrait, just like you – us – has several voices. It can be measured by waves, temperature. The portrait tries to reveal more than your face, your traits: it's what lovers try to do. Get in. Know more. Stay. Words like happy, or sad, tend not to explain much about it.'

Isla went back to painting. Valeria stretched her neck.

'You're impatient today. Tired and impatient,' Isla said, cleaning her brush and turning around. 'I think it's best if we call it a day.'

Valeria felt relieved and rejected at the same time. They left the studio and walked up to the ground floor. Valeria tried to focus on the noises coming from upstairs. Perhaps a beep from Martìn's breathing machine? Nothing.

'Shall we say tomorrow at ten?' Isla asked.

'Yes, see you tomorrow,' Valeria said. She opened the door and walked away, her face straight into the storm.

FORTY-SIX

Back home, even though it was still afternoon, Valeria crashed out in a sleep so deep she felt like she was sinking. She woke to the sound of the doorbell and found Antonia standing outside, carrying two pizza boxes and two beer cans.

'Welcome,' she said. Valeria took the pizzas and the beers and walked to the kitchen, Antonia behind her.

'I'm so hungry I could eat a cow,' Antonia said. 'Or a tomato if it was as big as a cow.'

'What did you just say?'

'Do you mind if I start?' Antonia asked. She moved to the living room with the food while Valeria rinsed her face, checking in the mirror that she was entirely present after her dream. Nose? Past?

'Do you have a lot of sex?' Antonia asked from the living room.

'How do you mean a lot?' Valeria laughed, going into the living room and sitting near her.

Antonia smiled and took what was already the last slice of pizza from one of the boxes. Valeria wondered if she should give Antonia some of hers.

'When I was your age I wasn't that into it. Why do you ask?'

'I don't fancy it,' Antonia said. 'I tried with a dude at school. Horrible. Like I had to run away kind of horrible. I tried with girls, but didn't like that much either. You look surprised. I'm not sure I'm gay, sorry.'

'What are you sorry about?' Valeria said. She sipped her beer. It was warm. And too bitter.

'Not fitting into a category that would sum me up,' Antonia said. 'A title. Can I have some of your pizza? You're so slow.'

'And Oksana?' Valeria gave her the pizza. She kept the beer.

'That's different. We don't even get close to touching. Or kissing.'

'Do you love her?'

'I think I do,' Antonia said, 'which makes it worse.'

When both pizzas were polished off and the beers finished too, Antonia scrolled down the screen on her phone, showing Valeria the pictures of the circles she had drawn around town. A glowing one in fluorescent yellow paint, a tiny black one on a stone in Hyde Park.

'Dad is already dead,' Antonia muttered.

'Don't say that,' Valeria replied. 'Don't you dare.' Her eyes filled with tears.

'How long have you known my father for?' Antonia asked. Her eyes wide open, no uncertainty anywhere.

'It's been for ever,' Valeria heard herself say.

'He told me he knew you,' Antonia replied. 'But whatever happens, don't ever tell Mum that.' She paused. 'It's our secret,' she said. 'And now I'll go.'

Antonia stood up, put the empty boxes and the beers in the plastic bag.

'Wait,' Valeria said. 'Don't you want to talk a little more?'

'It was just a quick welcome back,' Antonia said. 'So, welcome back.'

Her words were now so cold that Valeria felt physically cold. As if the temperature had actually dropped. What had Martìn told his daughter? Surely not about their love.

'I'm glad you didn't lie about him,' Antonia said.

Valeria hugged Antonia.

'I don't like hugs,' she added, not moving out of it. 'Or lies.'

'Me neither,' Valeria said, not moving either.

Once Valeria and Martìn had to cancel a trip together to Shanghai. Martìn, at the last minute, had decided to take Antonia with him instead. She was not attending school at the time because of the last episode in which they'd found her in the bathroom after having broken a mirror with her fist. Because Valeria had already bought her ticket to Shanghai, she didn't cancel it. She told Martìn that she understood his needs and that they'd see each other once he was back. Without telling him, she booked herself a new hotel and once there she wrote and she ran in the nearby park. Whenever her phone rang and she saw Martìn's number appear, she would immediately pick up so as not to let the overseas dial tone give her location away. Martìn would tell her about Antonia, and if he mentioned the weather in China Valeria would look up at the same sky. If Martìn told her what they had eaten for dinner, the following evening she would go to the same restaurant and order the same food. She wrote a short story about it and called it 'Same Sky'.

'She's calm when she is with me,' Martìn had told her on the phone. Antonia was sleeping in the second room. 'She eats, she's funny, kind. She even talks about the future.'

'I wish I could help more,' Valeria said.

'You will help, eventually,' Martìn had said. 'You two would be a good match.'

The following morning Valeria entered the Aclàs' living room to find another guest there. She was about her age. She was smiling. And she was soaking wet from the rain.

'This is my friend Sasha Liebski,' Isla said. 'She's a writer too.'

The art critic Sasha Liebski! 'The Making of Eyes'! Valeria still remembered big chunks of it. It was a critical biographical piece about Isla. *The artist Isla Lawndale has been part of the feminist avant-garde for more than a decade, pushing her approach to performance to the extreme limits – induced illness and the experience of*

severe self-poisoning shocked not only the viewers but the
general public: the artist was also questioned by the police.
Much of Lawndale's work has been about boundaries
and the exploration of what is admissible and achievable.
The artist is also known for her figurative painting.
Lawndale's classical style, which has received a positive
response from the art community, as she says, 'has to do
only with endurance. Painting is a performance. It is my
most uncompromising and oppressive journey. I'm not a
painter, I'm impersonating one.'

Back then, one word only had come to Valeria's mind: bullshit.

Sasha Liebski was petite, with the steely-eyed glare of someone fearful. Or perhaps someone hungry. She wore a sharply tailored black dress, flat sandals, a sculptural necklace and a single silver earring that dangled to her shoulder. Her handshake was weak. Just like her writing.

'I'm very excited to meet you,' Sasha said.

'Thank you, Ms Liebski,' Valeria replied. 'Lovely to meet you too.'

Isla nodded towards Sasha Liebski to let her know she could talk again.

'I will get right to the point, Ms Costas. Can I watch you two work today?' she asked. 'I'm in town for the art fair. Isla told me about her being back to painting and you being the sitter. She already said I could stay and watch you work but it is, of course, completely up to you. I just couldn't let the opportunity go.'

'Oh,' Valeria paused. Fuck. She didn't want her there. 'Well, if it's OK for Isla, it is for me too,' she said instead.

'Thank you,' Sasha Liebski said. 'It means the world to me.'

Valeria didn't add anything, thinking that a good punishment would be leaving this sentence floating in the air, declaring its own mediocrity.

The three of them finished their healthy juices and walked downstairs. The studio was warm, the music already on. During the sitting Sasha took notes and scarcely moved. Then suddenly she walked over to Isla. Isla didn't even flinch. She must have sensed Sasha walking towards her, Valeria thought.

Looking over Isla's shoulder, Sasha could see the portrait.

Valeria hated the idea of Isla letting someone else look at her interpretation of Valeria's face before she had even shown it to her. She felt betrayed, ridiculed.

'Pamela is arriving today,' Valeria said in her discomfort. Hey, I have a posse too. I have my own gang. Valeria saw the four of them, two against two, in a hip-hop street-dance contest.

'Can we invite her over for lunch?' Isla said.

Sasha Liebski was writing something down. Maybe she could help her with the edit, Valeria thought. Sasha did need help.

'Oh thanks, that could be great. I'll make a couple of calls and let you know.' Valeria rose up off the stool and walked upstairs to make the fake calls in fake privacy. Reaching the ground floor, she heard the women's talk from the studio downstairs.

'How long has it been?' she heard Sasha ask.

'A little more than eleven years,' Isla replied.

What had been 'a little more than eleven years'? Even if she wanted to keep on listening, Valeria kept walking and went straight to the first floor, where after running up the stairs, she gently opened the door to Martìn's bedroom. She ran towards him and knelt down, getting as close to his face as possible. He was now almost wrinkleless, as though ageing backwards, getting younger, his face chubbier than ever before.

She kissed him and she kissed him again. The feel of his skin was the same as she had always known it to be.

'We are still here,' she told him.

In her compulsive search online about comas Valeria had read of people waking up to explain that they had known everything that was happening around them but couldn't move. She had read about a machine that would trace the reaction of the brain to questions. 'Are you happy?' it was asked. Apparently, lights mapping the brain replied with a 'yes' and a possible explanation was that prolonged comas brought people to sensations similar to those experienced in meditation. Floating. Peace.

Valeria kissed Martìn again then left the room as quietly as possible, touching Antonia's portrait as she passed it. She walked down the stairs and into the living room.

I love you, Martìn. Don't disappear. Stay.

Breathless, she sat by the fireplace and called Pamela. The clouds outside were growing darker. The wind was rising. Stop judging me, wind!

'I'm almost at your flat,' Pamela said.

'We've been invited here for lunch,' Valeria said, 'but I'm not sure what I want to do.'

'Quick lunch there so we don't have to organize anything and then we go home to work?'

'Can you buy a bottle of red on your way here?'

'Sure thing,' Pamela said. 'I love you,' she added.

'I'm sorry?' Valeria said.

'What? Oh sorry,' Pamela laughed. 'Sorry! I'm so used to saying it at the end of my calls with Benoit. See you in fifteen!'

The wood in the fireplace was crackling. Valeria stared around the room, taking in the book covers, the art pieces and pictures, a flower drawn by Antonia. *PRETTY!* someone had written on the flower with a green pencil. It was *PRETTY!* Then Valeria stared at the voodoo face. She stood up and approached the mask. It smelled of old wood, humidity, time.

'Where do you come from?' she asked the face. 'Are you good?' She caressed it, it was smooth, earthy. She touched the jaw, its contours and suddenly noticed something white, peeking out from behind. A price tag?

A certificate of authenticity? She started pulling it off, trying not to rip it.

Her heart began beating faster, scared that Isla and Sasha would appear. She managed to remove the piece of paper and unfold it. And as soon as she had it in her hand, she realized what it was: the receipt for room service from a hotel in Istanbul. The signature was Martìn's. The breakfast was one that they had taken together. No doubt. *Libération*, the *FT* and the *Guardian* to read. Pomegranate juice. Black coffee. Greek yoghurt with nuts for Martìn. Her hot water with lemon. Toast and jam. She remembered that day very well. She had spilt the entire breakfast over the bed. How could she ever forget that pomegranate juice on the white linen?

I stanbul was a favourite destination for both Martìn and Valeria. It was a relatively short flight – doable, even when only free for one night. That evening they had met in Turkey, and Valeria had spent the afternoon writing. When Martìn returned from his meeting, she joined him in his room. For dinner they ordered room service.

They spoke about Luc, how Martìn was not sure if he was going to stick to his decision to separate some of their ventures and leave their biggest fund, and he told Valeria about a bank in Argentina that he was looking into.

'Looking into?' Valeria asked.

'Whether to become a shareholder,' Martìn answered.

They ended up speaking about wealth, and Martìn had

told Valeria that his success made him feel guilty. He was guilty.

'Most times I can't even remember who I was before Rami died, before the pain, when I still believed I could understand very clearly what in the world was wrong and horrific.'

'Are you going to give it all away, when you die?' Valeria asked, with her mouth full of French fries, ketchup, cheese.

'Should I?' Martìn asked her, and passed her a napkin.

'Are you telling me that this is the first time you've thought about what to do with your wealth?'

'I'm asking your opinion,' Martìn smiled. 'I already know mine.'

'I think that great wealth should go back to the people,' Valeria had stated. 'In an organized way, but back - to the world, to help, to try and make a change after having been on this planet and then being gone. We need equality, chances, fairness.' Valeria took more fries. Both her naive speech and that meal made her feel sixteen again.

Martìn poured her more wine, and lit a cigarette for himself.

'Should I leave something for you too?' Martìn said. 'Are you "the people" too?'

'You should choose something for me, yes. Something very romantic. Or very secret, that only I will know is for me and why.'

'How will I leave it to you? I mean, I can't put you in my official will, right?'

'Well, I can write that story. The one where I appear in the lawyer's room, with your family. Being dead, you will not have to worry anyway, I'll just take it from there,' Valeria smiled.

The following morning, Valeria woke up in Martìn's bed. What was the point of having two rooms if they then made such basic mistakes? When the waiter came in, with breakfast and the papers, she hid under the duvet. As soon as she heard the door click behind him, she uncovered herself, spilling the entire breakfast everywhere.

'You should lick it,' Martìn smiled. 'It's your fault and it's your turn.'

So she licked it.

FORTY-SEVEN

Hearing Isla and Sasha coming up to the ground floor, Valeria slipped the room-service receipt into her pocket. She grabbed her phone and pretended to be finishing her call. How did that bill end up there? Was it proof that Isla had found or a memory Martìn wanted to keep forever?

'Perfect,' Valeria said, ending the fake call. She turned around, scared she might look hysterical. Was her heart visible from under her shirt, like in the cartoons? 'Pamela and I will eat with you, thank you,' Valeria said. 'She'll be here in no time.'

'That's great,' Isla said, without looking at all delighted.

Sasha Liebski's face lit up. She was so keen it was hard to watch: she looked deliberately curious, she just wanted to stare, to know, to be part of this day, part of Valeria and Isla's bond. Did they have a bond?

Sitting near the fireplace, Valeria tried to focus on Sasha's shoes, the details of her dress, a tattoo she had on her wrist that from this distance looked like a doodle. It also looked like one of Antonia's circles.

'I have read most of your books,' Sasha Liebski said.

Which one hadn't she read? Was it because of the wrong titles?

'Thank you,' Valeria said.

'I've also read many of your columns and essays,' Sasha said. 'As Isla knows, I've been a huge fan of yours since the very beginning. I think I read *Black Bread* the week it was out. I still remember a review that called it "*a mellow stardust debut*".'

Valeria feigned a humble smile. She remembered the 'mellow stardust debut' and she remembered the exact font, the exact page, the magazine cover. She didn't keep those things, the articles, the reviews, the memories. Joe did. And now Pamela did the same. Who were they keeping it all for exactly?

'What a good memory,' Valeria said. 'Wow.'

'So, are you currently writing, Ms Costas?' Sasha asked.

'I'm always writing.'

'Always' sounded ostentatious, but it was true. Writing was like a marathon, and Valeria's approach was repetitive and austere – the only way through it. Nearly every single person she had met in her life had told her they wished they could be a writer or that she was so lucky she could write and that writing must be amazing. But it wasn't amazing. It was lonely. Very often boring. Oppressive and scary. It was an exercise of endurance, and willpower. An obsession. It was almost always about narcissism and that was sad. And complete fragility.

'So what's your routine?' Sasha asked. 'It's a banal question, but I really want to know.'

'I write. Every day,' Valeria said. Now she sounded rude. But this too was the truth. She wrote, every day. The following question was always where, in a studio? Or in the kitchen? So she added the answer, 'I write wherever I find myself to be, every afternoon. I try to work for three hours minimum. I never manage more than five in a day. After that I usually go for a run. But for the first time since becoming a writer, I've been slack with my whole routine.'

It was true, she realized with a start. She had been bad with it all. But Theodora. But Martìn. But Antonia. But Sybilla, starting to fade as never before.

'It's always short stories, right?' Sasha asked.

'Yes, it is.'

Sometimes she felt she had to explain why, in her opinion, it was always short stories. All theories were fake, pointless, fabricated. Once she had read that Alice Munro said that being a mother she only had so much time and short stories were all she could manage. Valeria had all the time she needed, all the freedom possible. So for her it was short stories just *because*.

Isla excused herself and went upstairs. Valeria imagined being her shadow, able to follow her without a reason.

'Have you and Isla been friends for a long time?' Valeria asked.

'We met in college and we've been friends ever since. We are very different, Isla and I,' Sasha observed.

You don't say, Valeria thought.

'But she inspires me. Isla's art, well, that's my personal obsession. I guess you must appreciate her work too. Isla tells me you asked her to do your portrait.'

'She said no, at the beginning,' Valeria pointed out.

'I'm sure that was part of the plan,' Sasha smiled. She touched her earring.

Did she have a recorder in there? Was she some kind of spy? Come on, Valeria. The bill on the statue, the camera in Martin's room, now the microphone in the art critic's earring! Just stop it, will you?

'The plan?' Valeria asked. Why did she say to Pamela that having lunch here was okay? Either it wasn't going to go anywhere or it was going to go to frightening places. Both options: bad.

'I'm sure receiving an email from you was something Isla was interested in. In terms of her work, I mean. The project is way more important than anything else.'

'Oh, so she's also told you about my email?' Valeria was annoyed. She was the excluded girl in the classroom. The two girls had been friends since college. The project?

'I'm sorry, I didn't want to intrude,' Sasha said. 'She knows I admire your art and hers. It must have felt natural to tell me how it all came to life. She knows I'm a sucker for stories. I'm sure you are too. Anyway, I think Isla is an incredible woman and artist, with an extraordinary talent. The depth of which – and how philosophical it is – is not yet revealed. Yours was a phenomenal choice.'

Was she for real? Or was she deluded?

'Why do you think she stopped drawing?' Valeria asked, to test Sasha's knowledge.

'She never stopped,' Sasha said, looking thrilled. 'Listen, how much do you know about Isla's performative works?'

'Not much,' Valeria said. 'But I've seen some clips

online, a while back. One was from a documentary on a collective exhibition. Isla was mentioned because she was working on a performance piece called *Everyone is Everyone.*' There was a pause. Could she see a tiny red microphone light near Sasha's earlobe? 'From what I recall she was pretending to be her mother in that one.'

'She wasn't just pretending to be her mother,' Sasha said, 'as the title suggests.'

The doorbell rang. Pamela, of course, had to arrive right then. Valeria wondered whether to stand up while Sasha didn't move. Maybe she was going through her vocabulary to choose what word to use after 'philosophical' and that would also rhyme with 'phenomenal'. Maybe 'ontological'? Before Valeria could stand up, Mirela went to the door.

Pamela appeared. She was gorgeous. She was safe territory and she was back.

In the documentary Valeria had watched, Isla said that honesty was the main purpose of her performance art, and truly experiencing the emotions involved was key. Isla not only wore her mother's clothes but went out with her mother's girlfriends, followed her same therapies, watched her mother's TV shows, so she could narrate – impersonate – her mother. She even wrote letters to her husband – Isla's father – and voted Conservative like her mother. She went to church, prayed and confessed. She took her antidepressants. She did physiotherapy for a knee that, since a fall while skiing, had been giving her mother problems.

Isla was part of an artistic movement and while she was re-enacting her mother, other women were going around naked spraying themselves with milk in kitchens, others were taking pictures of their body parts to then glue the bits together in massive collages. Others were self-harming as a rebellion against domestic abuse. Valeria was especially fascinated by a woman who had been on a six-month walk dressed like an angel. The photographs of her walk, hitchhiking from Seattle to New York, chronicled a metaphorical walk through prejudice towards women in America. It reminded Valeria of Olympia the bride.

Watching the conclusion of that documentary, which showed a long-haired and lady-like Isla, Valeria had cringed. She didn't know if it was because she felt embarrassed for Isla, or if it was because it reminded her of what it was like to write. It for sure reminded her of what it was like to steal other people's lives. She was also spying on the other woman in Martìn's life.

A few days later, she wrote a story called 'Of My Beautiful Body', managing to fit in some of the quotes from the documentary.

Valeria thought that yes, she was a thief, but that her writing, just like Isla's performance art, was also meta-something. She could be considered part of the same gang, part of the movement. She was a sister. Or at least she was impersonating one.

Valeria, Isla and Pamela ate everything that had been put on the table by Mirela. They drank red wine and poured coffee. Sasha barely ate, instead taking notes, asking Valeria and Isla questions about their craft, Pamela completely absorbed by the scene.

'You live alone, right?' Sasha asked Valeria.

'Right,' Valeria said.

'I do, too,' Sasha said.

'I might want to live alone too,' Pamela said and smiled at Valeria.

Why was she smiling? Because they were able to live alone? Because they preferred it to living with someone else? Were they a movement?

'Will I, too?' Isla asked them.

Valeria's smile broke.

'You've never lived alone,' Sasha said. 'Not even one day in your life.'

Sasha and Isla then told Valeria and Pamela about a night in college when a party gone wild led to their renting a flat in Mexico City two days later.

'Isla was working on her final thesis. It was called, wait, *Border* something, right?' Sasha said.

'*Border Lip*,' Isla smiled. 'How could you forget?'

'Of course!' Sasha shouted. '*Border Lip*! Well this took us to Guatemala and eventually Argentina. The very reasonable Ms Lawndale, Isla's mother, was diagnosed with post-traumatic stress disorder. And this was *during* the trauma!'

'What were you doing while Isla was working on her thesis?' Valeria asked Sasha.

The art critic's lipstick had now vanished. Her eyes were watery. All in all she was less tidy than she'd been three hours earlier. Did she go to AA meetings? Had she just broken her sobriety?

'I was following Isla,' Sasha smiled. 'Story of my life. But then Isla ended up falling in love with a tennis player and went with him to Miami, so I flew back home to New York.'

'Have you ever read any of Sasha's work?' Isla asked Valeria and Pamela.

She wanted to change the subject. Her discomfort was evident.

'I have!' Pamela said. 'I read your essay on body art at Oxford.'

'I'm afraid I haven't, sorry,' Valeria said. She hated the lie. Pamela might also know the truth: Valeria had kept several of Sasha's articles in which Isla had appeared.

'Share your thoughts about it,' Sasha said to Pamela. 'Don't be afraid, just go for it.'

'I like how your writing shows us how currents have nights, wild parties you dance at, or love stories to shape them. Every art choice comes to have a biography – names, lives and characters to sustain it,' Pamela said. 'Your words stay with the reader like a memory. As if it were your own past. Your own art.'

The smile on Sasha's face was one of satisfaction. Valeria's only wonder was if Pamela really liked Sasha's writing.

'Very nicely put. Now we should go,' Valeria said. She smiled, stood up. All too sudden not to appear suspicious. In the rush she tried to make her heart beat slower.

'Lunch was delicious,' Pamela said. She grabbed her jacket.

'Tomorrow?' Isla asked Valeria.

'Tomorrow,' Valeria confirmed. Yes, it was an abrupt exit. But she had to leave. Too much closeness. Too much danger. Too much Isla.

Valeria and Pamela went back to the flat and worked. They finished the book list for Marseille and drew up Valeria's favourite pieces of music for the radio show. 'Perfect Day' was going to be the last one. Leonard Cohen's 'Dance Me to the End of Love' was to be the first.

'Should I look for music that is more secret and unknown?' Valeria said.

'Why would it be better?' Pamela replied.

They went through Antonia's pictures of the circles taken around London and chose the one of the Aclàs' roof. The moonlight made it shiny enough to be visible, the night made it mysterious, the roof familiar.

'She texts me,' Pamela said.

'Who does?'

'Antonia,' Pamela said. 'She's a good kid.'

Pamela grabbed the box with Julian's letters.

'Is there anything I need to go through in here?'

'No, thanks,' Valeria said. 'What does she text you about?'

'About you, mostly,' Pamela answered. 'She says things like "Do you think Valeria would find x or y interesting for a story?" *X* or *y* being something that has just happened to her.' She paused, then, 'So, don't you want to know what's in the box from Argentina?'

'Yes, the box! Tell me everything!' How could she have forgotten?

'It's just a wooden box,' Pamela said. 'It's empty inside.'

Valeria saw it, immediately, as if it was right there in front of her. She saw it as she had always imagined it: Rami's wooden box. It wasn't empty, it had a double layer. She was going to find the pictures of naked women underneath the double layer. And possibly the letters Rami had written to his teacher. Why was it sent to her? Because Martìn had known that he was sick and hadn't told her? Had Martìn known he was going to die?

Valeria had to stand up, close herself in the bathroom and cry.

'Can I hug you?' Pamela asked her when she was back with her on the sofa.

Valeria shook her head.

She decided to go for a run and leave Pamela at home, busy fact-checking the new stories and making calls in Valeria's name, including to the journalist she had met in Paris. Why wasn't the piece out yet? Pamela also had to send the selected picture for Valeria's new book's cover to Joe, hoping that both he and the publishers would accept it.

'Leave it all with me,' Pamela said.

Valeria loved the sound of those words. She wished she could leave it all, *all*, with Pamela. The double-layered box. Her double-layered life. Sasha. Martìn's secrets. Her own.

'Go,' Pamela said. 'Run.'

When Valeria returned, she found Pamela holding one of the books on portraits she had bought at Rebecca's bookshop. She was in tears. Not you too, please, she thought. Valeria stared at her assistant, unsure what to do. She chose to stay still.

'Sorry,' Pamela said. She was sobbing.

'By leaving it all to you all I didn't mean that you should also cry for me,' Valeria said.

'I'm just a good assistant,' she smiled in her tears.

'What's wrong?' Valeria took two steps in Pamela's direction, even though that wasn't the direction she would have chosen. She wanted to take a shower. To feel calmer. She wanted, in general, to be happy. She wanted Theodora, Pamela, Isla, Antonia, herself, all of them to be happy. And to rest.

'Hey?' Valeria murmured.

'Don't worry,' Pamela said, trying to pull herself together. She put the book back. She wiped her face. She straightened up and adjusted her ponytail. 'Really.'

Did this mean Valeria should leave the room? The house? London?

Pamela started writing in her notebook.

'I'll go have a shower!' Valeria said.

'Sure,' Pamela said, trying to sound jolly, or at least to sound calm.

Valeria went to her bedroom and undressed, then stepped into the shower, under the stream of hot water.

She washed, began shampooing her hair but quickly had to wrap herself in a towel, walk back to the living room, and hug Pamela. When too much time had passed, she stepped back for a few seconds, before hugging Pamela again, with even more strength, and tighter.

'I love you', Valeria said loudly. 'I love you,' she repeated, trying to sound more at ease with the sentence. 'Also, sorry for the shampoo on your jumper.'

FORTY-EIGHT

Valeria woke up to a grey sky. And to her billion thoughts. She rolled over to the other side of the bed and reached for her phone. She called her mother.

'I'm feeling much better,' Theodora said. 'I probably just had to adjust to Greece.'

'I'm very relieved to hear that,' Valeria said. She saw the relief like a dirty child who had been sitting on her chest and had finally decided to leave her alone. He looked like the kid playing hide and seek between the rocks in Rhodes.

'I mean the sickness is still here,' Theodora said. 'Big time.'

'Well, I'm sure that is the case, yes,' Valeria said.

'It might also be the healing power of the island. Nothing beats Rhodes,' Theodora said. 'And the black olives.'

'Are you eating loads of black olives?' If Theodora wanted to speak about food rather than cancer, it was fine with her. That technique might even work.

'At least ten a day,' Theodora said, 'and I'm drinking plenty of water. What about you?'

'No black olives, not much water,' Valeria said. 'Not doing much writing either.'

'Tell me something you are doing. Not the things you are not doing.'

Well, she was hugging her assistant. And telling her 'I love you' too loudly. Could she start from there? As soon as she hugged her, Pamela had hugged her back, and said, 'Thank you' and 'I love you too.'

'I'm sitting for a portrait,' Valeria said.

'Who's the painter?'

'Her name is Isla Lawndale.'

'How is it going?' Theodora asked.

'She doesn't want to show it to me until it's finished.'

'I want to see it finished. Are we talking days, months, years?'

'Days,' Valeria said.

'Good timeframe.'

Valeria closed her eyes and returned to Pamela. 'That story, "PA", was about me, right?' she had asked. Valeria had nodded, and when that night Pamela went away, Valeria felt calm for the first time in weeks. She had let Pamela come closer. She had confessed at least one secret.

'The monks want me to go pray now,' Theodora said.

'Who do you guys pray to?' Valeria asked.

'Who are we praying to?' Theodora asked the monks.

'Today we are praying to ourselves,' Theodora said, 'to the gods that we are.'

'I like the sound of it,' Valeria said. 'I'll steal this one.'

After she hung up, Valeria tried to pray to the goddess that she was. She pictured herself as Valeria the goddess in ancient Greece, with Aphrodite and Athena her friends, living in the shadow of the Olympus mountain. She wore sandals. Somehow the words of her prayer seemed very much like the ones of the YouTube trainer. *You are the change!* So from the prayer she switched to doing abs, squats and push-ups. *You are the change!* And so was her story, and all stories within, that kept changing too – we're the change – just like the portrait kept changing, with every brush-stroke, like the strokes in a swim. Even if it seemed the representation of one single moment, it was so many of them, so many points of view and emotions, aims, causes, waves for one sea, seas for one ocean, pangea and panthalassa, tenderly but strongly wrapped together in one single stare, in one single picture.

Valeria walked towards the Aclà house, the grey clouds letting the sun come through for the first time in weeks. The sun reminded Valeria of something the director of Bodasha, her Japanese publisher, once told her, about how in Japan when ceramics break they mend them with gold, not only making them more beautiful, but treating their damage and repair as part of their history, rather than something to hide and forget. He had told her they called this the art of the Kintsukuroi. Valeria had heard what the technique was, and what gold in those cracks meant so many times already – they even sold a

DIY kit on Amazon – just like everybody already knew the tips on the writing on the walls at the organic deli, on all mugs and T-shirts of the world. And all of the songs of her list for Radio 4. But listening about the golden river that illuminated the fractures of life, through the voice of someone who was able to narrate it, had suddenly made it precious. The sun today seemed to be just like that and Valeria felt a good, golden rush. But she also sensed – far, near her feet, at the end of her fingers – fear. It was the fear of when you feel good and at risk for it. As though you may be punished for your luck. Could she dive into this sea? She felt alive and vibrant, the brighter sky like a prediction of something good to come, of hugs she was able to give. What writing was there today in the sky? She looked and nothing was written up there, there were just the planes crossing the London airspace with the white traces they left in their wake.

Valeria rang the bell. Her face this morning, for the portrait sitting and for life itself, was going to be very different from yesterday. Sasha Liebski could stare today. So could Isla.

When the door opened, it was Antonia's face that she met.

Valeria thought about telling Antonia what had just happened with Pamela. Maybe sharing something so simple, unknown and true could help them both. They were all going to be OK. Valeria wasn't scared. Nor should

Antonia be. Maybe Antonia might work with her one day. They could travel together and start their own journey. Oh yes, that would be very cool. Even if she was never going to be a mother, she could help bring up this girl. She would be good at it.

'Dad is dying,' Antonia said. And she started crying so loudly that it started to rain again.

Everything in Valeria went back to being broken. The cracks weren't filled with gold but with darkness. She felt faint, her knees bent.

FORTY-NINE

Antonia grabbed Valeria, pulling her inside. The twins were sitting on the couch, crying. The voodoo face was crying too. Valeria's tears dried up for ever. She was a desert and she was the drought itself.

'Hello,' Valeria said to Nico and Cosmo. Her hello sounded like sorry.

'Hello, Ms Costas,' they said and stood up as they had been trained to do, kissing Valeria on both cheeks. The boys' tears were like water in the drought.

'Where's your mother?' she asked them, while Antonia squeezed her hand very hard.

'You need to come up,' Antonia said.

Maybe she wanted to let Valeria be close to her lover one last time? Or if she didn't know about their love, maybe she wanted to have Valeria by her side, to let it all go with less fear? Or maybe she wanted the best for her father. Well, that's a stretch.

Valeria left her coat on the chair and followed Antonia upstairs, the twins behind them. Were they all waiting for her to be able to stay in that room?

It's not only your story, Valeria. Move away.

Valeria continued up the stairs followed by the kids.

'Don't worry,' Valeria said. She secretly caressed Antonia's portrait with her right hand, and in her heart she said *I'm sorry* to that kid too.

When they arrived on the first floor, Martìn's door was open. Isla was sitting on the bed beside him and the nurse was checking the breathing machine. Mirela was perched on a chair, crying. Martìn was breathing badly, from a very distant place and in that place it was all unsure.

Was it pneumonia? His weak heart? Life?

Isla turned to Valeria.

'Oh,' she whispered, 'you're here. We need to finish the portrait.'

'Now?' Valeria said.

'Now,' Isla replied. 'Immediately.'

Valeria didn't want to leave the room. She wanted to stay right there, until the very last second – and beyond. She wanted to be here for the first second of the new world without him. She wanted to touch Martìn's hand. Could she say that she was trained as a doctor?

'You kids stay with Dad,' Isla said, without taking her eyes off Valeria.

Don't do this to me, Isla. Please. And don't do it to yourself either, willed Valeria.

She saw her entire story with Martìn so far – and she

saw it ending here, in this room, in the next few hours. Or would it be a matter of minutes?

'Can you do this for me, Valeria?' Isla said.

Valeria looked at Martìn. His eyes closed, his hands with almost no life left in them. She closed her own eyes and synchronized her breathing with that of the machine.

'Are you ready?' Isla repeated.

Valeria wasn't. Or was she? 'Yes,' she said.

'Do you want to say goodbye to my husband?' Isla asked.

'Mum?' Antonia murmured through her tears.

She was crying so much it broke all the hearts in the world. There was not one entire heart left intact, anywhere. Not even in Shibuya, Tokyo.

'I think we should acknowledge it all,' Isla said. 'It's the right thing to do.'

Please choose the right words, Valeria prayed.

'Martìn is here with us, in this room, in our home, so is Valeria. It's compassionate, tender and correct for us all to say goodbye properly,' Isla continued. 'He is leaving us, he's leaving everything.'

Valeria paused. Then she nodded. She went over to Martìn's bed, making her steps robotic. She tried to count, but found she couldn't. She tried to breathe normally, but found she couldn't do that either. She knelt down, took Martìn's hand. It was very hot. It was his hand. It was hers.

'Goodbye Martìn,' she whispered. She couldn't let him go, ever. When you go, I will disappear, she thought. 'Don't worry,' she told him. 'We are here.'

She could hear Antonia, the twins and Mirela crying. She caressed Martìn's skin, her last connection to him.

Don't leave me. Don't leave us. But she also thought, Leave me, leave us. Because the truth was, she could let him go. She breathed him in. And out.

'Thank you,' Isla said.

She said it as if Valeria was a good person, doing something good for her husband, but Valeria knew she had to stand up and let it all go. And so she did, slowly and gently. She caught a glimpse of herself reflected in the respirator in London and she saw herself reflected in those sunglasses nearly thirty years ago in Paris. Nothing had changed and everything had.

'Let's go,' Valeria told Isla.

'Let's go,' Isla told Valeria, kissing Martìn on the lips before leaving the room.

Valeria and Isla went to the studio and worked for the next few hours. Antonia or Mirela would sometimes come downstairs, step in, and announce things like Luc was with Martìn and then that Luc had left. They'd come and ask if the two women needed anything or to report that Martìn's temperature had gone up. Finally, Len the doctor wanted to speak to Isla.

'Could you ask him to come down here?' Isla said.

'What the fuck, Mum?' Antonia said, but did as she was asked.

Valeria, sitting on her stool, thought of how abominable

this might seem from the outside: a husband dying upstairs and a wife painting downstairs. But she understood Isla profoundly and Isla's face didn't allow such thoughts. Her skin was covered in tears, her movements were unsure. She was clearly doing all she could to keep it together. So when Len came into the studio he was as kind and careful as possible. He said that Martin's heart would not hold out for much longer.

'I'll be back very soon,' Len said, 'and then you'll have to come up.'

'Thank you,' Isla said. She picked up her paintbrush once again with her shaky hands and Valeria kept looking at her, without changing position. Their chins held up, quavering, their stomachs clenched, their hearts beating fast. The golden river on broken clay, running down their faces.

'Are you afraid?' Isla asked Valeria after a while.

She was working slowly, every brushstroke separated by a long stare. With each one, Valeria imagined a swimming stroke, a river or a sea to cross. She saw herself and Isla being able not to drown, making it to the other side.

'No,' Valeria said. Because she wasn't.

They continued their work, the silence only interrupted by Isla blowing her nose or crying louder. Valeria cried too, in silence, the tears flowing. She wondered if from where she was standing, Isla could see them.

If you see my tears will you show them in the portrait?

Being forced to sit for so long, through this moment, this day, these weeks, felt like the challenges she'd had with Sybilla. Will you jump first? Will you swim longer? Who will survive this pain, me or you?

'It's going to be a triptych,' Isla said. 'This is the last one of your three portraits.'

'What do you mean three?' Valeria said.

'I have changed the canvas three times. This is the third piece,' Isla said, 'and today is when we finish.'

Valeria wondered if what Isla said was true. And if it was, how she had not realized it herself. Maybe Isla had painted the other two portraits without Valeria being there? The first before they had even met, another from memory in her absence, and the third only had been created during the sittings?

Today is when we finish, Isla had said. But did Valeria want this to be the day when they would finish? Could she cope with the end?

'For me, this portrait is a study of you,' Isla said, 'so the triptych turned out to be the best way to deal with a study.'

'And what is it for me? What am I doing here?'

'The book cover?' Isla said. 'Or maybe you just wanted to be sure you existed.'

Valeria pictured Francis Bacon's *Three Studies for Figures at the Base of a Crucifixion*. She saw herself depicted in a similar way, the details erased, the soul taking over the body. She was the colours, the cancellation of herself, the revelation of truth. She wasn't the Valeria she thought she knew and she wasn't this one either. She was the movement, the passing of time, the changes. She was the woman Isla could see. She was many and none. And in this form, which was also the form of disappearing, of the void and the most luminous distance, she was sure she existed.

That afternoon, Martìn died. Antonia had cried out like an animal, as if she were a tiger, a lion, a puma, a daughter losing her father for ever – and Isla had rushed up the steps, like a tiger, a lion, a puma, a woman losing her man for ever, her movements shaky, her eyes wide open. Valeria remained seated, alone, in the studio, the last ray of sun of the day, the first real ray of light in months, beaming right in front of her. The line of light looked like a crack through existence, a passage between dimensions and galaxies. It was a light that was coming from the depths of the planet and the crack – even if it hid the abyss – wasn't frightening at all. In fact, it was very, very beautiful. It was easy to cross. And it was all gold.

Slowly, Valeria climbed off her stool and walked across the ray, pushing through it as if it had a density. It also had a temperature and it was a warm one. She didn't look at the portrait. She put on her jacket, went to the door and left the studio. Upstairs, she heard quiet sobs coming from Martìn's room. No panic, no fury, just the natural letting go of things. A breeze, the anticyclonic winds bringing the next season in. She closed her eyes, listened more. The steps, the patter of Rock the dog, the turning off of all machines. The ventilator, Martìn Aclà's ventilator, that went off too.

'Now?' she heard someone saying.

'It doesn't really matter,' someone else said. Isla.

Whatever she was referring to, she was right. It didn't really matter.

Valeria grabbed her coat and her scarf, put them on and thought, Maybe someone will arrive and tell me to stay? Maybe yes, they would stop her, invite her upstairs. She could see Martin another time. Be there for Antonia, hug her and hold her tight. But she didn't want to go into that room and she didn't know how to write this scene of the story. She only knew how to walk. So she opened the door, turned to bow to the voodoo face, then looked up the stairs once again. Staring at her from the first floor was Isla. Their eyes locked, acknowledging one another. Then Valeria walked out of the house, descended the eight steps under the magnolia tree, onto the road, and walked away.

FIFTY

Valeria walked for a long time and by what felt like a complete accident she went all the way back to the Portobello Club. She bought a beer at the corner shop and drank it while staring at Ari-Leo from the glass-fronted entrance. She wished he would come out for a cigarette and she wished it so hard that he did.

'The man I love just died,' she told Ari.

'I'm very sorry,' Ari-Leo said.

'I know you are.' Valeria finished her beer and smoked a cigarette with him. They hugged.

'Are you a guest of ours tonight?' he asked her.

'Unfortunately, I'm not,' Valeria said. Looking up at the sky she imagined Martìn, then Sybilla. Hello and be careful not to crash against the British Airways flight to New York City. It will cross that spot soon. 'How is your family doing?' she asked Ari-Leo.

'The dead are doing OK with death and the alive are doing OK with life,' Ari-Leo said.

'D'you know how to swim?' Valeria asked him.

'I'm the best swimmer,' Ari-Leo said. 'See?' and he showed her how, in the middle of a road in London, he could float and not drown. He was the best swimmer ever.

'Are you coming?' he asked her.

Valeria put down the cigarette, copied him, and so they swam.

After saying goodbye and walking back to her flat, she received a text from Pamela, *I am sorry about Martìn Aclà. I'll be back tomorrow, Px* and one from Joe that didn't say anything about Martìn but said that he was going to be in London too. *See you tomorrow,* he wrote.

Valeria tried to write and stopped. She tried to read and stopped. At dawn, after having been awake for the whole night, there was another text from Pamela. It said: *Yes, true, the box at home has a double layer: it's full of old pictures of naked women. Letters. And a first-edition of Virginia Woolf's* To the Lighthouse. *Inside it says, 'for ever'. Pamela x.*

Hello to you too, Rami, and to you, Mina, favourite busty girl from the secret box.

The morning after Martìn Aclà died was a Sunday.

It was a sunny day and when she left the flat, Valeria wore sunglasses and went to the deli. She sat under a new neon-lit sign, crying. The writing said *#blessed*. She turned around and saw Bea, dressed in stripes from head to toe. She was having a coffee too. Her earrings today had a peaceful sparkle.

'It's not coffee. It's a matcha latte,' Bea said.

'Disgusting,' Valeria said. She wiped her tears, letting new ones flow down her face.

Bea sat near Valeria and they spoke about the death of Martìn Aclà. Bea showed Valeria his obituary:

The Argentinian entrepreneur Martìn Aclà died yesterday morning. Founder and shareholder of multiple listed companies, ranging from biotech to banks, he had recently suffered from a stroke, which led to a coma. Mr Aclà died peacefully in his bed, aged 67, in his eight-bedroom house in Holland Park, London. Mr Aclà was surrounded by his closest friends and his family. He is survived by his wife, the former painter Isla Aclà, née Lawndale, and their three children, Antonia, 15, Cosmo and Nico, 13.

The obituary went on, but Valeria closed the paper. Bea tidied up the vegetables for sale then made Valeria another coffee. They went into the backyard, and under the sun they shared a joint.

'I can't believe they wrote about the eight-bedroom mansion,' Bea said.

'I can't believe the "peaceful" bit. Why do they always do that?'

Valeria felt dizzy and to try to suppress her rising panic, she started explaining to Bea about the Society of Life's Mass. Bea had never heard of such a thing, so she wanted to go see it. They checked online and saw that there was going to be a Mass that same day, at four.

'My Sunday sucks anyway, so it can't hurt,' she said and, as if she had read Valeria's thoughts, she added, 'Let's ask Antonia to come with us.'

Telepathy? Valeria wondered. Or maybe that's just what people did. They understood, sometimes, each other.

'Antonia is in,' Bea said receiving an immediate reply to her text.

The sign *#blessed* went off. When Valeria looked back up, it went on again. After the third coffee, Valeria texted Pamela and Joe that at four she was going to go to the Society of Life's Mass. She asked them to join her. Bea's phone buzzed again.

'Antonia's family is in, too,' she said.

Valeria walked to the park and from the park she called her mother. Her mother didn't pick up and so Valeria, without any warning and with way too much caffeine in her body, called her father. Her father didn't pick up either so Valeria felt free enough not to have to call anyone else. She just walked and during the walk she counted and during the count she cried. Then, as soon as she could, during the walk she just walked.

At lunchtime she was back at the flat. She emptied the fridge, her drawers, tidied up the books and cleared the bathroom of her things. She put Julian's remaining letters back in the box. Before she knew it, she found herself cleaning the whole flat. Too bad that her friends,

Anna and George the owners, didn't really exist. Valeria scrubbed. Rinsed. She brushed and scrubbed more. When she answered the phone, she was on all fours, her knees stuck to the bathroom tiles. She looked at the screen. She looked back at her life. Then, forward.

'Julian,' Valeria said.

'I called you as soon as they told me you called. Sorry for not picking up before.'

'Who told you?' Valeria said.

'The helper.'

'What helper?' Valeria stood up. She looked at herself in the mirror. She heard her voice when she was five asking her mother, 'Do I look like Julian?' and Theodora replying, 'How could you look like him?' Implying that a non-present father could not pass on his features.

'I don't see very well,' Julian said. 'The helper helps me.'

'What do you see?'

'Everything,' he said. 'But I'm technically blind.'

Valeria closed her eyes and imagined being blind.

'I have been for years. I don't dislike it too much,' Julian said.

Valeria pictured Julian with sunglasses, a dog.

'Do you manage to write?' Valeria asked.

'I dictate. At the beginning it was hard. Everything felt too exaggerated. Now, I think it sounds better than before I lost my sight.'

'Makes sense.'

'Dictating overblown sentences out loud is embarrassing.'

Valeria walked to the living room. She sat on the sofa. She searched very hard and very deeply for a resentment she couldn't find. She reached for Sybilla, to help her out in hating this man that went by the name of Julian. No answer. She heard Martìn's words about his brother when he told her that he knew very well that having to live with a limp was nothing compared to the hell his brother lived in. Valeria changed plan and searched for a forgiveness she wasn't able to shape, or choose. She let go of that plan too.

'And you, are you writing?' Julian asked her.

'I am,' Valeria said. 'I always write.'

'I know some of your stories by heart.'

Who else had said that? Did all these people know she had stolen bits of their lives? Maybe they had all just relearned bits of themselves by heart.

'Which one do you know?' Valeria asked Julian. Maybe he was a liar.

'"To the Light",' Julian said. '"Brother and Sister". I know all of "Marriage" too.'

'That's just five lines.'

'Still, I know them. "When you wake I hear you standing up. You walk away from our room—"'

'Don't! I beg you,' Valeria interrupted him. Then she listened to Julian breathing and she tried to remember Sybilla's breathing, Theodora's breathing, and to mix the rhythms together. She wanted to hear her family's breathing. She wanted to hear all the people she had chosen in her life breathing. It was a symphony.

'Mum is sick,' Valeria said. 'That's why I was calling you.'

'I know,' he said. 'Sometimes your mother and I call each other.'

'Do you?'

'We do.'

And then Julian said that he was sorry, and Valeria said that she believed he was, and somehow they spoke a bit more about easier things. What was his favourite song? She searched again for a rancour that wasn't there any more and she took a good, direct look at that empty space rancour had left. It needed to be filled with something else. A bear? A story? Love?

'Yesterday I lost my favourite person on the planet,' Valeria said. 'Martìn Aclà, my lover, died.'

'I hope I will be able to help you with your pain. That's all I want to do.'

He said it so quickly that Valeria wondered if the sentence – clearly not edited to sound less overblown after he became blind – had been rehearsed for all these years and whether these were the words he had missed out on saying to her when she had just lost her sister. And he, his daughter. The words that he regretted all his life not having uttered, making him into the man he wished he hadn't been.

Let me be with you, she had thought for so many years.

Let me be with you, he had thought for way longer than her.

'I'm sorry,' he repeated.

'I know.'

She said goodbye. Her father said goodbye too, and Valeria sat on the sofa, staring at the sun outside. She tried hard to think if there was one single thing she could do to feel slightly better, less lonely. A bird passed near the window. A leaf moved. Valeria tried to imagine duties, activities, bets, anything that would fill the void. No characters from her stories replied to her call to action. But the pink flowers were back. And so she welcomed the void.

When Pamela arrived, they hugged and managed to stay in the hug. Just weeks before it would have been impossible – so too that in the epic collapse of all things, of this whole story, Valeria was still alive. And hadn't disappeared.

Valeria prepared tea and put out some biscuits.

'I'm sorry about Martìn Aclà,' Pamela said, chewing biscuit number ten and getting closer to Valeria.

When Valeria hugged her again, it was easier than the first time, and the one there had been immediately after. The door buzzed, she went to open it and seeing Joe, in his goofy yellow jacket, Valeria's heart melted. She smiled. She hugged him too and in the hug she saw all the stories they had taken around the world together.

'Thank you for being here,' Valeria said. Were they here because they knew she had lost the most important person of her life? Or was it synchronicity? The ending of the portrait, Valeria's going back to Paris, Joe's meeting UK publishers and clients before the London Book Fair. Or maybe this was love, and simple understanding between people who cared.

Later they walked all the way to the Sunday Mass, crossing Bayswater, Hyde Park, Mount Street. And at the Sunday Mass, in the back of a packed Brown's Café, one after the other – and together with a couple in their forties, three businessmen in suits, a chubby man dressed entirely in leather, a decrepit man with a very old briefcase, a young girl, a woman in a green hostess-uniform that showed her pantyline cutting her arse into four – they were joined by Isla, Antonia, the twins, Mirela, Bea, Dimitri, Calypso, the Uber drivers, the Greek bride Olympia, Sybilla, Martìn, Rami, Damien's mother and father, the four drowned sisters and all the protagonists from Valeria's written and unwritten stories. Fierce and smiling, they each took their place and stood tall, their backs straight like strong walls. And when the singer, in her buttoned-up shirt and rock-star jeans, walked to the stage and bowed to them all, they all bowed back. She made them sing Bob Dylan, Lou Reed, Leonard Cohen and Beyoncé and invented songs they had never heard before but all knew by heart. And together they sang as loud as thunder, as roaring as love.

EPILOGUE

On Monday, Valeria, Antonia, Pamela, Bea, Joe and Rock the dog walked around London for hours, looking at Antonia's circles. On Tuesday, there was the funeral and Antonia recited by heart the last paragraph of a story by Valeria called 'The End of Time'. It was about Antonia and she probably knew it. It included 'the letter of impossible goodbye' that Valeria had written for Sybilla the day she was buried.

Oksana was there too and after the funeral she held on tightly to Antonia's hand.

Isla didn't speak but with her eyes thanked everyone for being there, Luc always by her side. Valeria was standing far from the family, in the back rows. Julian was in the congregation too and when Valeria hugged him, it felt like the familiar body of a stranger.

After the ceremony, she didn't go near the Aclàs, nor to the burial that followed.

That same afternoon, together with Pamela, she left London.

A few weeks later, Valeria received the portrait from Isla. She unwrapped it while alone in her living room in Paris. She had to force herself to look at it but her fear was unjustified: the triptych was beautiful, kind. It had been created with compassion. She recognized both herself and Isla in each image. The time they had spent in the studio, the closeness, that light. Bach, Martìn. Each second, stroke, pause. Every secret.

In all three pictures, on the back, was written, 'This goes near Martìn's.'

Valeria brought out Martìn's portrait. She hung it in her studio. On the other side of the studio, she hung the triptych.

That same day Valeria flew to Rhodes where she spent the last few weeks beside her mother. Together with the monks she went to the heated ponds, and alone with her mother, she swam one more time in the Northern Cove. Theodora died a few days later, Valeria holding her hand. It was an imperceptible death and in that moment Valeria understood what it meant to 'die peacefully'.

Valeria and Antonia remained close friends.

Both of them missed Martìn for the rest of their lives, but with the passing of time they stopped thinking about him every minute. Once, they travelled together to Argentina. In the grounds of Bernardo Aclà's house, during the most glorious thunderstorm, they went searching for the oak tree, and for the box with the diary Martìn had buried.

They didn't find it.

When she was twenty-five, Antonia organized the first retrospective of the works of her mother, Isla Lawndale.

It was called *Everyone is Everyone*. It was Antonia's graduation project but the exhibition was very well reviewed so it toured the world for a couple of years. The rumour was that Isla Lawndale never saw the show but didn't hold back in giving all the materials needed.

Valeria did visit the exhibition.

It was morning and the gallery – an abandoned warehouse – was almost empty.

In the main space, her triptych, which Antonia had asked to borrow, hung alongside Martìn's portrait. The room, its walls painted black, was called *The Portrait*.

On the first floor were displayed tens of sketches of Valeria aged from around thirty to her mid-fifties, together with Isla's self-portraits. Lawndale, the accompanying description explained, 'had been studying her husband's lover for the better part of their marriage'. It had been a therapy, 'a performance of resistance, devotion and love'. It was now a tangible, epic work of art.

The selection on view was only part of Lawndale's study that had led to the final portrait. All the works had been created as a form of 'healing and narration'. The drawings of Valeria and Isla had been kept locked in boxes for decades, and these too were now at the gallery, as was the email from Valeria Costas to Isla Lawndale in which she asked to be painted by Isla. There was a shot of Isla's text message to Sasha Liebski, the only friend who knew about the ongoing, spectacular project.

A few letters between husband and wife were displayed too, revealing how Martìn Aclà had been made to accept the project from the very beginning and how he had eventually fallen in love with it – along with loving his wife and lifelong lover, writer Valeria Costas, profoundly.

It seems to me a work, as you say, about love, he wrote in one of his letters to his wife, *but mostly, about mortality.*

Isla had made her husband share his receipts from restaurants, hotels and trips with Valeria Costas. The artist also possessed three private letters written to her husband by his lover. The fact that the letters Martìn had given to Isla were exactly three, it was explained, was the outcome of a very long negotiation between them.

In the gallery, near one of the receipts, hung a giant picture of Martìn's phone screen, showing an incoming call from Charlie Brown. There was a montage of videos in which Isla Aclà was studying Valeria's interviews, her short story collections, and the audio download of Martìn's answering machine was played on a loop. There were a pair of Valeria's purple panties, framed, and the only picture in which Martìn and Valeria appeared together.

It was the same as the one Valeria kept in her studio, but it wasn't her copy.

'Being a painter,' Sasha Liebski wrote in the catalogue of the exhibition, 'was just a portion of Isla Lawndale's performance, the tip of the iceberg. Within the stunning triptych of the writer Valeria Costas, the message, in its intimacy, carries the whole plot. Looking at it – thirty-five years after everything started – I was brought back to when Lawndale first mentioned her idea to me.'

Once again, Valeria hadn't particularly enjoyed Sasha Liebski's writing but still, she had highlighted one of

Sasha's sentences: 'To be desired makes you the closest that you can ever be to feeling immortal.'

In the show, Antonia had used some of Valeria's short stories too, printed on acetate film sheets. They were there to fill in the narrative voids and to change perspective. There was also a copy of the *Sunday Meta* with the short story in which Valeria and Martin had thought they were going to die on a plane over the ocean. It was on the third floor, printed on a bigger piece of paper, above the Japanese translation of that same piece.

Valeria walked through the exhibition shaking, and even though by then she knew everything about it, and thought it was fair for it to exist, for Isla and Antonia to show their side of the story, and even if Antonia had talked Valeria through all of it many times ('Did Isla sell your father's portrait as part of a plan?' 'No, but you did do your best to add a twist for it to become one. My father was bidding against you. Coincidence?') after visiting it she felt sick and hid in the restroom for nearly an hour, before being able to walk back to the Portobello Club.

But she did walk back, and once at the hotel she had a cold beer with Ari-Leo.

Valeria's first and only novel, *The Portrait*, was published the following September.

It was September the twenty-second, which just like every year since years were invented, was the last day of summer in the northern hemisphere. It was a warm, bright day all over Europe and it was particularly pleasant in London. In all editions of the novel worldwide, on the cover of the book, there was Valeria Costas' face in the form of Isla Lawndale's triptych.

The UK book launch was held that same Tuesday, at six o' clock, at Rebecca's bookshop in Holland Park Road. Then, even after that Tuesday, life went on and many other things happened. To them all and to the other human beings. To all the animals too. Even to the bees. To the spiders. And to the ice. Eventually, one after the other and one way or the other, they all died. And they all disappeared.